Remember Wynn

me Soro!!

Sinila

Remember Wynn

Tommy L. Crelia

2007

Remember Wynn

Dedicated to my wife Linda Lee
and my daughters, Melissa Anne,
April Lea, Janie Marie and Jana Lee

PROLOGUE

It's such a pretty world today
Look at the sunshine, look at the sunshine

These words were running through Henry's mind as he boarded the bus in Boston. The lines were from a song by Henry's favorite singer, Wynn Stewart, and they fitted his mood perfectly. He was leaving the Navy for good. An invading army would have to be crossing the Red River before Henry would ever volunteer for the military again.

Henry wore his blue, bell-bottomed, thirteen button, gabardine dress uniform. His small, white, cotton hat was tilted back on his head, a violation of the Navy's Uniform Dress Code. The cuffs on his jumper were turned up revealing colorful, embroidered screaming eagles, another violation of the Uniform Dress Code. He wore black, highly shined, round toed Wellington boots, another violation of the Uniform Dress Code.

The uniform had no pockets, so like all enlisted sailors Henry carried his money and his smokes in his boots. In his right boot he carried his wallet; in his left boot he carried a Camel cigarette package containing four, high grade, Columbian marijuana cigarettes, also known as reefers or joints.

Smoking was allowed in the back of the bus and Henry took a seat in the last row across from the restroom. He stared out the window at the changing countryside until he grew bored and fell asleep. When he awoke the bus was dark and after a few minutes he drifted back to sleep.

The bus stopped the next morning in Baltimore and the passengers were allowed thirty minutes to eat and stretch their legs. An hour after sunset the bus pulled into Memphis where Henry had a two hour layover to change buses. He walked to a liquor store near the bus terminal and purchased a bottle of Jim Beam whiskey. By the time the bus arrived in Oklahoma City, where Henry had to change buses again, the bottle was empty. An hour later, Henry boarded the bus for Grainsley, Texas. Another two hours and he'd be home.

Near Pauls Valley, Oklahoma, just before entering the Arbuckle Mountains, Henry felt a bowel movement. He entered the small restroom and unbuttoned the thirteen buttons on his pants. At that moment the bus took a sharp right curve throwing Henry against the door, his pants still around his ankles. Henry steadied himself and reached down again. The bus took a sharp left curve throwing Henry against the door again and the door flew open. Another curve threw Henry out into the aisle. He looked up at an elderly couple and rolled over trying to crawl back to the restroom. The bus started down a long grade and he felt himself sliding toward the front, his pants still below his knees. After what seemed an eternity he managed to reach the restroom and crawl back inside. When he checked his left boot the Camel package was gone.

Henry didn't come out of the restroom until the bus reached Grainsley.

CHAPTER ONE

Henry Lee McCarthy Ridge entered the world kicking and screaming August 30, 1946 at four a.m. in his grandmother's house in Joneston, Oklahoma, population less than three hundred. His mother was a local Cherokee whore named Erica Ridge and his daddy was listed as unknown although most believed him to be Charles McCarthy, a character doing time in a Texas prison for writing a bad check. With her long, black hair and delicate facial features Erica Ridge was considered one of the prettiest women in the county. She was also considered one of the easiest.

Henry weighed slightly over six pounds and since no doctor had been present to assist with the birthing was left uncircumcised. The only other peculiarity was the congenital lip deformity associated with the cleft palate where Henry's upper lip failed to form completely, leaving a vertical indentation above the mouth that split the lip perfectly and gave him enough of a Leporidae look for his great aunt Patricia to ask, "What the hell did you do Erica, screw Bugs Bunny?" In other words, Henry Lee McCarthy Ridge had a hare-lip.

Erica Madeline Ridge could trace her family back to the seventeenth century. Her grandmother, eight times removed, was Sehoya, also called Susanna Ridge, wife of the great Cherokee warrior Ridge. Her ancestors made the Long Walk on the Trail of Tears from Tennessee and settled in the eastern part of Indian Territory, now Oklahoma, near Honey Creek, a tributary of the Neosho River. Her grandparents, Otis and Rowena

Ridge, moved farther south in 1887, two years before the government opened up most of the territory to homesteaders. They settled on land that was mostly swamp and planted cotton and corn, gradually draining the land. Fiercely independent they refused any assistance from the government and raised two sons, Thomas and Benjamin, and a daughter named Leta.

In 1908, fourteen year old Thomas was sent to the Chilocco Indian Seminary to learn a trade. Here he met a pretty Cherokee girl four years his junior, Lahoma Watie. Lahoma and her younger brother, Levi and her sister Patricia were sent to the Seminary after the death of their parents from influenza. In 1912 Thomas left the Seminary and took a job as a carpenter. He returned to the Seminary a year later in a rented buggy and talked Lahoma into eloping with him. They moved to Joneston and a few months later Levi and Patricia joined them. Thomas helped Levi obtain a job working with a construction crew and Levi soon moved into his own home. Patricia stayed for several months until marrying a local mechanic, Bryon Friedman.

October 13, 1914, Lahoma Ridge gave birth to a son, Robert Thomas Ridge.

Infants and toddlers were a familiar sight in the cotton fields and Robert was no exception. Infants rode their mother's twelve foot sacks as the women pulled cotton two rows at a time. The toddlers played in the shade around the wagon where the cotton was carried to be weighed and emptied as the field boss, usually the owner of the field or his son, wrote the weight down in a spiral notebook. Parents watching their own toddlers kept an eye on all toddlers. At five years of age Robert, like all farm brats, was given his first sack, a burlap feed bag with a strap sewn across the top to hook around the neck and under the armpit.

He was expected to earn his keep, pulling cotton paid two cents a pound, and was given the grand sum of a quarter a week to spend any way he wanted. By the end of summer he was averaging a hundred pounds of cotton a day.

The holidays were special. The families would gather at Thomas' parents, Otis and Rowena. In addition to Thomas, Lahoma and Robert there would be Benjamin and his wife Marge and their son Michael; Leta and her husband David Cole and Lahoma's siblings; Levi and his wife Mahoya and Patricia and her husband Bryon.

The twelve foot dining table would be covered with food. Ham, turkey, yams, mashed potatoes and gravy, peas, corn, beans, deviled eggs, cornbread, hot dinner rolls and sliced onions, cucumbers and tomatoes. A smaller table held pumpkin and pecan pies, homemade brownies and cakes. The kids ate on the porch or if the weather was nice in the back yard. The adults ate at the large dining table. Just before dusk everyone would start hugging and saying their goodbyes.

Erica Madeline Ridge was born May 5th, 1928 and like Robert was introduced to the fields as an infant. At the age of five she was given her own sack. The cotton field hadn't seemed all that bad when she was playing in the shade of the wagon and watching others work but she hated the work immediately. On her second day of pulling cotton she drank too much water and got sick to her stomach. Her father told her to lay in the shade until she felt better. She stayed the rest of the day. The next day she threw up again. Then the next day and the next. Erica learned to throw up at will knowing her parents wouldn't force her to work if she was sick. After a week they began to leave her in the care of Lucy Grayson, a seventy year old widow that lived near the fields. Lucy babysat for several other parents and usually had between four and twelve children in her care ranging in age from a few months to a few years. She sat in her rocking chair the first part of the morning and read scriptures from the Bible. At noon she fixed sandwiches for the older children and bottles for the infants. After lunch blankets were spread on the floor and everyone was expected to lay down and take a nap. The afternoon was spent with more Bible reading. A dried "bull nettle" was used to maintain discipline. Late afternoon parents would start arriving to collect their children. Erica hated Lucy's almost as much as she hated the fields.

April Ist, 1941, Otis Ridge dropped dead of a heart attack. Rowena Ridge died a week later.

Robert hated the fields and he hated school. He ran away from home when he was eight years old and his father whipped him with a belt. He ran away again a few days later and his father whipped him harder. He tried again at age twelve and again at fourteen. The last time he ran away, at sixteen, Thomas Ridge decided to let him stay gone. Erica was a toddler when he left and she remembered him from his occasional visits as a good looking man that always wore a gray fedora and a smile and smoked cigars. A drifter, who preferred freight trains, he tried to return home at least once a year, usually with gifts and a pocket full of money. He'd stay a few days until he grew bored and restless.

In the spring of 1942, a few weeks before Erica's fourteenth birthday, Robert and a companion robbed the First National Bank of Mayetta, Oklahoma. The sheriff and two deputies were waiting when they came out and the two robbers split up trying to escape. Robert's companion got away but Robert was trapped in a cellar, his eyes shot out by a scattergun. He died a few hours later refusing to name his accomplice. The money was never recovered.

The first week of November Thomas Ridge kept an appointment with a doctor in Grainsley, Texas. He'd been feeling fatigued and thinking he might be anemic had gone in for tests a few days earlier. He was told he had cancer. He drove home, went into his bedroom and came out a few minutes later and walked out to the back porch. He walked back inside to the kitchen where Lahoma was making lunch and told her how much he loved her. When she asked what the occasion was he told her he just wanted her to know how much she meant to him. He returned to the back porch and wrote a note. He folded the note, placed it in his pocket, pulled a thirty-eight revolver from under his shirt, placed the barrel under his chin and pulled the trigger.

Erica cried for days. Lahoma sold the house and moved her and Erica to a smaller one closer to Joneston.

Joneston, Oklahoma sits on state highway 44, four miles north of the Red River. The town consisted of fifty or so houses, a red brick, two-story school, Luther Carlson's General Store, the Highway Diner, a combination Post Office, barber shop and Justice of the Peace and three churches: Methodist, Baptist and Church of Christ. A dirt road ran south from the highway in front of the Post Office for a half mile. Lahoma and Erica moved into a small, brown, two bedroom house at the end of the road. The house came with five acres of land that included a dozen peach trees and a small pond at the south end of the property. The house had a large front porch covered on the east side with honeysuckle vines. In addition to the two bedrooms, bathroom, kitchen and living room the home had a large storage room. Lahoma converted this area into a work room and put her

Singer sewing machine in a corner near the window that looked out over the back yard. She moved her RCA phonograph and her set of 78 r.p.m. records to the right of her Singer and set up her ironing board in a far corner. Soon she was taking in sewing and ironing. She began work immediately after washing the breakfast dishes and often worked until midnight listening to her records as she made alterations or ironed. She enjoyed a diverse range of music from Hank Williams and Jimmy Dickens and the stars of the Grand Ole Opry to Frank Sinatra and Billie Holiday.

Erica loved the change. Any time her mother needed anything Erica was all too happy to make the short walk into town. At first she'd complete the errand fairly quick but soon began taking more and more time but Lahoma wasn't particularly worried. She remembered how it felt to be young and to her knowledge no child had ever been harmed in Joneston.

A few months after moving to Joneston a local man twice Erica's age persuaded her to join him and a bottle of wine in a deserted barn near the edge of town. She discovered two things that day; she liked wine and she liked sex. Erica spent the next two years skipping school and having sex with any man who got her high. At fifteen she met Charlie McCarthy and at sixteen she was pregnant. Her mother, who once held Erica on her lap and told her how a hundred years earlier she'd have been a princess in the Cherokee tribe, now started scolding her and telling her how a hundred years earlier the tribe would have cut off her nose.

Charlie Samuel McCarthy was born April 2nd, 1920 to Layton and Mary McCarthy, sharecroppers living on the southern end of the Dust Bowl. Another son, born the previous year, had died after less than four months. The family shared a three room, tar paper shack heated by a wood burning, pot-bellied stove. Wood was as scarce as money and the stove was used sparingly for cooking or extreme cold. A one-hole outhouse sat fifty yards from the back door.

Mary McCarthy was a devout Christian and totally submissive to her husband. She never talked back or argued, did as she was told and when she wasn't cleaning, cooking or serving, sat in her rocking chair reading her Bible. Layton McCarthy believed in discipline and often used a razor strap he kept hanging on a nail near the bedroom door. When Charlie upset him he'd make the boy bring the strap to him then make him hang it back on the nail after the beating. He was a large man with large appetites at both the dinner table and the bedroom. Countless nights Charlie lay awake on his pallet and listened to the sound of bedsprings and his mother's grunting coming from the bedroom. Everyone rose before daylight and the elder McCarthy would leave for the fields before the sun was up and not return home until dusk. After supper he'd sit down in his rocking chair then remove his boots and prop his feet on the wood box. A few minutes later he'd be asleep, his head back and his mouth open, snoring like a hog in heat. Mary McCarthy would sit in her rocker on the other side of the stove and read her scriptures until nine o'clock. Then she'd tell Charlie it was time for bed, lay her Bible down, blow out the kerosene lamp and lead her husband to the bedroom. Charlie would lay down on his pallet and soon the creaking and grunting would start.

When Charlie was four a log exploded while his mother stoked the fire to prepare for breakfast. The explosion burned her eyes and the doctor in Denison, Texas that treated her told her to leave the bandages on for at least a week. Layton McCarthy couldn't afford to stay home and tend his wife while her eyes healed and he had no one to look after Charlie. The following morning he ran a line of baling wire from the back porch rafter to the top of the outhouse. He tied a twenty foot rope around Charlie's waist then he tied the other end to the wire line. The 'dog run' assured the boy wouldn't wander off and still allowed him freedom to come inside. Layton hooked his son to the wire every morning for a week before daylight, releasing him when he came back home at dusk.

Charlie hated the hard life. The older he became the more he was expected to do. He joined his daddy in the fields a year before he started school. After school he drew water and chopped wood. During summer he worked with his father in the fields. Layton was as strict in the fields as he was at home often beating the boy with a cotton stalk when he made too many trips to the water can or took too long returning to his row.

Charlie ran away when he was fourteen and got as far as Durant, Texas before the police picked him up and threw him in jail. Charlie's parents had no telephone and it took Layton two days to find his son. On the trip home Layton stopped his pickup on a dirt road and beat Charlie with his fists. A few weeks later Charlie ran away again. This time the police caught him burglarizing a home and he was sent to the Boy's Reformatory in Pauls Valley, Oklahoma until his eighteenth birthday. After his release he found work at a Texaco station in Grainsley. He soon quit and took an easier job as a night watchman at a factory that made airplane parts. He was laid off a few weeks after the end of World War Two and went to work as a janitor at a shoe factory. After work he frequented the bars along Red River. One night he met a pretty fifteen year old Cherokee girl and after a few drinks she left with him. A few weeks later she was pregnant.

Erica moved into the small, one bedroom house Charlie was renting in Grainsley. She didn't let the pregnancy interfere with her drinking and she and Charlie drove to the river every night.

In her seventh month of pregnancy Charlie hatched a scheme he was sure would bring them some easy money. A farmer Charlie met was willing to sell a few head of cattle below market price to avoid going to the trouble of hauling them to the auction barn. Charlie's plan was to borrow a livestock trailer and drive to the farmer's Wednesday morning, pick up half a dozen or so steers, drive across the river and sell the animals at the weekly cattle auction in Mayetta, Oklahoma. Not having any money he figured to write a bad check, sell the steers, then deposit the money before the check reached the bank. But Charlie had misjudged the farmer. The man had a bad feeling about Charlie and had driven straight to the bank with the check. After being told the check was no good the farmer drove to the sheriff's office. The farmer, the Texas sheriff and the local sheriff showed up at the Mayetta auction barn and Charlie was arrested. He was tried and sentenced to five years in the Texas State Prison at Huntsville, Texas.

Lahoma Ridge was forty-eight when her grandson Henry was born. She was still a pretty woman, slightly plump with waist length salt and pepper hair she kept tied in a bun at the base of her neck. In the three years since her husband's suicide she'd cultivated a small clientele that depended on her for their sewing and ironing. She was friendly, dependable and considerably cheaper than the dry cleaners in Grainsley. If a senior high boy needed a suit or a girl needed a gown for the prom they came to Lahoma. If she said she'd have it ready at a certain time on a certain date she would have it ready, even if she had to work all night. Still she found time for Henry.

Erica stayed home for a week after Henry's birth then returned to the bars. A few days later she took Henry and moved in with a man from White Rose, Oklahoma. Two weeks later she moved back in with her mother. Less than a month later she moved in with another man. A few weeks later she returned to Lahoma's. The third time she wanted to move in with a man Lahoma begged her to leave Henry with her. Erica refused. A few weeks later they were back. Once, Lahoma refused to babysit while Erica went to the bars. She thought this might force her daughter to stay home with Henry but Erica grabbed Henry and stormed out. Two days later a friend called Lahoma and told her Henry had been sleeping in the back of a car parked at a river bar. After Erica returned several days later Lahoma never again refused to look after Henry. Erica learned how to use her son to get anything she wanted from his grandmother. If she wanted money and Lahoma refused Erica would grab the boy and storm out of the house screaming, "You'll never see me or Henry again". Lahoma would chase after her begging her to bring the boy back. Then she would give Erica the money she wanted.

Henry loved his grandmother. At night he'd watch her untie her bun and comb her hair until it shone. Then she'd sit Henry on her lap and tell him stories from the Bible about Samson, David, Moses and Solomon. She read scriptures about the pure at heart and the evils of the flesh. Some nights she'd tell him stories of his ancestors, the warrior Ridge and the great Cherokee General Stand Watie, the last Confederate officer to surrender. She tried to teach him self-respect and respect for others believing the two went hand-in-hand.

The first Monday in March, 1951 Charlie walked out of prison and boarded a Greyhound bus for Grainsley. The next day he showed up at Lahoma's driving a ten year old Ford pick-up. That evening Erica told her mother she needed a hundred dollars to rent a house for Charlie, Henry and her. When Lahoma told her she didn't have a hundred dollars to give her Erica threatened to take Henry away forever and Lahoma believed her daughter was selfish enough to do it. She borrowed the money from her brother Levi and gave it to Erica. Erica rented a house three miles west and two miles south of Joneston.

The house was a wooden, run-down, bug and mice infested house with a large front porch, living room, kitchen and two bedrooms. An old 'smokehouse', originally built for curing meat and now was used for storage sat thirty feet to the right of the house and a 'two-holer' outhouse sat thirty feet from the back door. A hundred foot well was located in the center of the front yard about forty feet from the front porch. A mailbox stood near the road and a propane tank sat in back and to the left of the house. On the front porch was an old sofa, a wringer style washing machine and a pair of wooden kitchen chairs all left behind by the previous tenants.

The house came with two acres of land and sat two hundred yards off a dirt road. A large sprawling oak tree stood a few feet to the right and shaded most of the front porch. Two scrub oaks stood in back a few yards from the propane tank. Wood ticks infested the trees and stripping and being inspected for ticks became routine. Erica would sit with a lit cigarette to touch to any tick that had attached itself to Henry's body. The heat from the cigarette made the tick loosen easier, reducing the chance of leaving the head of the tick still attached after the body of the parasite had been removed. Often, especially after a few beers, Erica would confuse a freckle or a mole for a tick.

The property was owned by Winston Hunnicut and rented for forty dollars a month, utilities not included. A barbed wire fence at the back of the property separated the rental land from the fields. Winston's new brick home was located on the other side of the field. Separating the landlord and the tenants were two hundred acres of cotton, a hundred acres of peanuts and a hundred acres of hay.

During the summer the outhouse smelled and the flies were everywhere. In the winter the small building was freezing. An old Montgomery Ward catalog was used to clean oneself. During spring yellow jacket wasps built nests in the corners. At night an old Folgers coffee can was placed inside the house near the back door to serve as a 'slop jar'. This 'slop jar' was used for any late night calls of nature.

Charlie 'laid down the law' to five year old Henry as soon as they finished moving. He would have certain chores to do and he would be expected to do them every day without being told. He was to never argue or talk back and to say 'yes sir' or 'no sir' and 'yes ma'am' or 'no ma'am' when asked a question. Charlie asked if he understood and Henry nodded. Charlie slapped him hard enough to stagger him.

"Let's go through this again you ignorant hare-lip! When you answer me you say 'sir'! Do you understand?"

"Yes sir" Henry mumbled. Charlie slapped him again.

"Don't mumble when you talk to me you stupid shit! Do you understand?"

"Yes sir".

"You're going to learn to respect me if I have to beat it in you!"

"Can I go?" Henry asked. Charlie hit him again.

"What did I do?"

Charlie popped him on the skull with his index finger like one would do to check the ripeness of a melon.

"Think goddamn it! You do know how to think don't you? When you talk to me you say SIR! Do you understand?"

"Yes sir. Can I go sir?"

"Get your ugly ass out of my sight."

Erica sat in the kitchen staring toward the back door with her head lowered. Henry's head hurt.

One of Henry's chores was to dump the Folgers can every morning over the barbed wire fence behind the outhouse. He was also expected to carry out the trash to an old fifty gallon oil drum at the far right hand corner of the back yard. When the drum was full Charlie would light a fire in the drum and Henry would stand on an old pail and poke the fire with a stick to make sure all the trash burned. Holes were poked in the side of the drum near the bottom so any rain water would drain out. In spite of the holes water often accumulated at the bottom providing a breeding ground for mosquitoes. After a good rain and a few hours of sun the drum would begin to stink. Henry was expected to do any yard work that was needed. The yard was mostly dirt with a few islands of grass scattered here and there. Besides pushing the hand powered lawn mower he was told to get on his knees and pull any grass the mower didn't reach. What grass they had was filled with 'grass burrs', a weed with small thorns that would break off in a finger and cause the finger to fester until the thorn was removed. Charlie had Henry try to draw water but he only managed to draw the bucket up a few feet before the rope slipped and the bucket dropped. Charlie cursed Henry and told him to get his worthless ass back to the house. The next day Charlie nailed a five foot piece of two-by-four to the center of the well. He then showed Henry how to draw water up as far as he could and wrap the line around the two-by-four until he was rested enough to pull it up a few more feet. He was to pull and rest, pull and rest until he had the bucket high enough to reach over and pull it to the side of the well and balance it. Reaching up with both hands he could take the bucket and lower it to the ground where he would transfer the water to another bucket. Henry lost more water than he managed to carry to the house.

Charlie 'laid down the law' at the kitchen table too. Mealtimes had always been pleasant at his grandmother's but Charlie made each meal an ordeal. Henry was told to sit straight with his elbows at his side. He was told to keep an eye on Charlie's plate and make sure he always had a biscuit on it. He was to eat everything on his plate and ask permission to be excused before leaving. Any infraction brought a hard slap from Charlie, often hard enough to upset Henry's chair dumping him on the floor. After the meal he was to get on the floor and pick up any crumbs he might have dropped. He noticed most of the crumbs were around Charlie's chair.

Three days after moving into the house Charlie drove to Grainsley and returned a few hours later with a roll of chicken wire, a dozen ten foot poles and a fifty pound sack of dog feed. He unloaded the feed and carried it to the 'smoke house' then he built an eighteen foot by twenty foot fence around the building leaving a small door in the fence facing the house. He left the next morning after breakfast and returned that afternoon drunk. On the back of the pick-up was a wood and wire mesh cage with eight fox hounds, six males and two females. He backed the truck up to the fence and unloaded the dogs one at a time grabbing them by their thick heavy leather collars and dragging them through the door in the fence. Charlie had decided he wanted to be a fox and wolf hunter.

Wolves, foxes and bobcats were a nuisance to the farmers and ranchers of the 1950's, particularly around the Red River.

When the problem became too great, bounties were placed on the animals. Over a period of years these animals were hunted to near extinction, first for the bounty, then for the sport. Charlie knew more than a dozen men who owned hunting dogs and these men gathered three or four nights a week to turn their dogs loose while they sat around a campfire and passed the bottle. While they drank they listened to the dogs barking and chasing some unfortunate critter. When they thought the dogs were nearing a kill they would load up in their pick-ups and drive as close as they could get to the pack to be there when the dogs tore the animal apart. Around daylight the group would break up and go home. The dogs were trained to return to the place where they had been released and each man would return later to pick up any dogs that wandered back. A few dogs might not return till the following day and often they wouldn't return at all. The dog's owner would receive a collar in the mail or a call that their dog had been found dead near a highway or poisoned by the wolf traps the rancher's set out. The dogs were the principle reason Charlie had a telephone installed. He sent Erica to her mother's to borrow the money for the deposit.

One afternoon Charlie called Henry over to the dog pen and handed him a shovel and a bucket. Then he told Henry to get inside the pen and shovel the dog shit into the bucket. When Henry started to open the door he heard growling noises. He threw the shovel down and backed away. Charlie hit him and knocked him down.

"You stupid little coward! Those dogs know you're scared of 'em! Now pick up that shovel and get in there."

Henry picked up the shovel and started for the pen. He heard growling again and threw the shovel down. Charlie hit him again.

"You can beat me all you want to," Henry told him. "but I ain't going in there."

"You hare-lipped little coward! Maybe they think you're a rabbit!" Charlie grabbed his arm and pulled him toward the pen. "Maybe I oughta feed you to 'em!"

Henry broke free and ran toward the house while Charlie laughed. Then Charlie told him to get out of his sight. He watched Charlie shovel the waste from the pen into the bucket. He hoped the dogs would turn on Charlie and take turns biting him.

Saturday morning Charlie ordered Henry to draw water for his bath. The galvanized bathtub needed several buckets to fill it halfway. Erica helped him while Charlie sat on the porch and drank beer. Later he ordered Henry to draw water for the laundry. Erica helped him carry the water and she heated it in a small round galvanized tub. Charlie helped her carry the tub from the stove to the wringer washer then returned to his chair and his beer. After the wash was done Henry helped his mother hang it on the line. He then drew water for his mother's bath. Then he bathed using the same water his mother used. The water was nearly cold by then and Erica drew another bucket and heated it, pouring it in the used water.

CHAPTER TWO

Charlie found jobs that spring for him and Erica hoeing cotton. Hoeing paid by the hour and a worker was expected to keep up with the other hands. Henry was too small to keep up and was taken to Lahoma's every weekday morning. Erica told her mother they would pick Henry up every afternoon after work and they did on the days Charlie wanted to go hunting that night. Other days they'd stop at the bars and wouldn't pick him up until late. Some nights Henry would sleep in his grandmother's bed and Lahoma would beg them not to disturb him but Charlie always insisted on taking him home only to return him a few hours later.

Henry loved staying with his grandmother. He'd ride the pedal of her Singer sewing machine and listen to records. She let him outside to play near the pond, catching tadpoles and crawfish while she watched through the window in the sewing room. Often she'd take a break and go outside and join him.

And Henry hated going home. Charlie and Erica were always fighting and on the way home Charlie would find an excuse to backhand her in the mouth. At home the fighting would continue and the thin wall separating the bedrooms allowed Henry to hear everything. The cursing, the screaming, the loud moans and then his mother begging, "Please don't hit me again. Please. I'll do anything you want. Just please don't hit me." And then the bedsprings, squeaking louder and louder, then silence.

When cotton harvest started Charlie hired the family out to pull cotton. Henry was given his first cotton sack, the traditional burlap feed bag with a strap sewn across the top to hook around the neck and under the arm. Next year he'd be given a store bought eight footer, a year later a ten footer, then a year or so later a twelve footer. Henry worked the fields until school started, averaging fifty to eighty pounds a day his first year.

On the second Monday of September Erica drove Henry to the Joneston school for enrollment. Less than two hundred students, grades one through twelve, attended the school and the whole procedure took less than two hours. Regular school classes would begin the following morning and a school bus would pick Henry up in front of his home between seven and seven- thirty.

Henry was waiting by the mail box Tuesday morning when the school bus stopped and he climbed aboard. Four other students were already seated at the rear of the bus and Henry recognized them from the fields as the Slidels; Luke, Harry, Willie and their sister Luann. Luke was ten, Harry was eight, Willie was seven and Luann was six. Henry thought the dark haired Luann was the prettiest thing he'd ever seen. The bus followed the same route every trip. The driver drove west three miles then turned left on a dirt road. One mile later he picked up the Slidels, then Henry, then Tony Mitchell, Jim Reed, David and Linda Scottle, Eddy and Doug Carter, Bruce and Wally Allen, Lucinda and Martin Pierce and Leon, Jacob and Joshua Holton. The bus would then turn north and meet the highway again six miles west of school. It made three stops on Highway 44 for James Springer, Marci and Brian McDaniel and Luther Cordell. A few minutes after eight the bus would arrive back at the school and unload its passengers. While Henry's bus was picking up its load three more buses were driving different routes picking up other students in the district.

Henry's first grade class consisted of fourteen students; six girls and eight boys. The teacher, Irma Eubanks, was a heavyset redhead in her late thirties. At ten a.m. all students from the sixth grade down were allowed outside for a twenty minute recess. The teasing began at once and soon Henry found himself in the middle of a circle with several kids throwing dirt on him and calling him names like 'dirty rabbit' and 'rabbit face'. A second grader, Sammy Laughlin, a boy ten pounds heavier and four inches taller than Henry stepped into the circle and shoved him down.

"My daddy says you don't know who your daddy is," he taunted. "He says that makes you a bastard."

Henry stood up and swung at the bigger boy. Sammy laughed and hit him knocking him to the ground. Mrs. Eubanks saw the scuffle and ordered the students back inside. She scolded Sammy calling him a coward for fighting someone smaller. When she asked Henry if he was hurt Henry shook his head 'no'.

At noon the students were given a thirty minute lunch break. Some students were given money each day to buy lunch and ate at Luther's or the diner. Most, like Henry, carried their meal in a tin lunch box or a paper sack. Henry carried his sack around the corner of the school hoping to avoid Sammy Laughlin and some of the others but Sammy and his two friends, Randy Dietz and Kevin Moran, saw him duck around the building and followed. They took his lunch then pulled his pants off leaving Henry and his trousers in the dirt. At two p.m. the students were given another twenty minute break. Sammy went straight for Henry, saw Mrs. Eubanks watching and changed direction. When the bell rang at three thirty, signaling the end of the school day Mrs. Eubanks called Henry to her desk.

"Are you all right, Henry?"

"Yes ma'am."

"Are some of the other students treating you badly?"

"No ma'am."

"I know your grandmother. She's a good friend of mine. If you ever want to talk to me about anything I hope you feel free to do so."

Henry didn't ride the bus home. Instead he walked to his grandmother's where Charlie and Erica would pick him up later.

When the cotton season ended Charlie and Erica found jobs across the river in Grainsley, Texas. Erica went to work as a 'cutter' in a shoe factory while Charlie found employment pumping gas at a Standard service station a few blocks away. Erica worked from seven a.m. till four p.m. After work Erica would walk the few blocks to the station and wait for Charlie to get off then they drove straight to the bars. Charlie worked two weeks then quit, complaining he was working like a dog for someone who didn't appreciate him.

The teasing continued at school but after several weeks it didn't seem as bad. Most of the kids left him alone and called him names only when they felt they were impressing someone. Because of his small size and dark hair and skin some of the older boys called him 'Little Runty Rabbit' or 'Chief Rabbit Head'. Later they shortened it to 'Rabbit' and the name stuck. One afternoon he complained to his grandmother.

"So what's so bad about being called a rabbit? Rabbits are smart and cute. Look at Bugs Bunny. The Cherokees have a saying, 'the moon is not shamed by barking dogs'. Be like the moon and ignore those hounds."

Lahoma also kept Henry in decent clothes. She often drove to Grainsley to shop for bargains at 'second-hand stores'. She purchased used clothes that were slightly large and altered them to fit Henry then let them out as Henry grew.

Lahoma was scared of tornadoes and the first dark cloud would send her and Henry to the small cellar near the center of her back yard. There they'd sit among the pickled okra, pickled carrots, pickled onions, pickled cauliflower and peach preserves until she was sure the storm had passed. The place was cool, musty and full of spiders. If the storm was bad enough Charlie would usually decide not to make the drive to pick him up and Henry would spend most of the night on a cot in the cellar with his grandmother.

Henry hated the weekends. The other students looked forward to Saturday but Saturday for Henry meant drawing water and working most of the day. Worse than that it meant being around Charlie all day and watching him sit on the porch barking orders and drinking. Charlie seldom called Henry or Erica by their proper names. It was 'bitch get me a beer' or 'hare shit draw some more water'.

The dogs changed Erica's social life. Charlie preferred hunting with his friends to bar hopping with Erica. He would load his dogs shortly before sundown and meet the others for a night of passing the bottle and listening to the so-called 'music' of a pack of dogs barking. Henry spent Saturdays silently praying for good weather so Charlie would go hunting. After he drove away Erica would make Henry's supper then open a beer and turn on the radio. On Saturday night, weather permitting, she could listen to the Grand Ole Opry broadcasting live from the Ryman in Nashville. After a few beers she'd pull Henry up on her lap and tell him over and over how much she loved him. A few more beers and she'd start singing along with the radio. Later she'd start to doze and Henry would try to lead her to bed. Sometimes she'd stagger to her room but most often she'd tell Henry to leave her the hell alone and go to bed. Around daylight he'd awaken to the sound of bedsprings.

And the abuse grew worse.

The first few days of November had been cold but during the week of Thanksgiving the temperature had risen to the high sixties. On Thanksgiving Day Charlie drove Erica and Henry to Lahoma's for dinner. Since Thomas' suicide Lahoma had little contact with her brother-in- law Ben or her sister-in-law Leta. She'd invited them and their families to share the holiday with her, her brother Levi, her sister Patricia and her daughter Erica and their families. The ten foot mahogany dining table was covered with meats, casseroles, vegetables (raw and cooked) and pies.

Charlie ruined the day.

Charlie made himself comfortable in a stuffed chair where he could see everything that was happening in the dining room or kitchen. There he sat staring at Erica and sulking. Every adult in the house tried to be cordial but Charlie answered questions with grunts and continued staring at Erica and pouting. Immediately after dinner he announced that they had to leave. He told Levi he had a sick dog that needed tending and couldn't be left alone too long. Lahoma asked Henry if he'd like to stay and she'd take him home later and Henry answered yes but Charlie wouldn't allow it and shoved Henry toward the door. At the truck he turned, bent over and grabbed Henry by the shoulders with both hands. He made Henry look him in the eye while he stared hard at the boy and told him in a voice that was hardly louder than a whisper, "goddamn you, you ignorant piece of shit, when I tell you it's time to leave I mean it's time to leave. Do you understand me?" Charlie thumped Henry hard on the top of his head with his middle finger and it hurt.

"Yes sir."

Charlie looked up and saw Lahoma and Levi watching from the front porch. He told Henry to get in the truck.

Charlie started cursing Erica before they were out of the driveway. Henry sat in the middle between the couple while Charlie accused Erica of flirting with her uncles and cousins. He called her a 'lying whore' and a 'filthy bitch' then struck her hard in the mouth with the back of his hand. A moment later he pulled the pick-up over to the side of the road and jumped out. He ran around to the passenger side and jerked the door open then grabbed Erica by the hair and pulled her from the truck. Erica fell on her knees with Charlie straddling her and still holding her by her hair. She started begging Charlie not to beat her in front of Henry. She told him he could beat her all he wanted if he'd wait until they were home. Charlie swung with his right catching her with his fist high on her cheekbone. Erica fell over on her side. Charlie pulled her up and twisted her arm behind her until she could touch her neck with the back of her hand then he swung again hitting her near the top of her head. Erica fell to her knees again.

"Get in the truck whore and if I hear one fucking whimper out of your mouth I'll stop the truck again!"

Erica crawled in the truck and sat with her hands covering her swollen mouth. At home Erica went to her bedroom and Charlie followed her shutting the door behind him. Henry heard a loud moan then the bedsprings started squeaking. He walked outside wanting to avoid Charlie as much as possible. Finally at sunset Charlie loaded his dogs and left. Henry walked back into the house and saw his mother sitting at the kitchen table holding an ice pack to her right cheek.

Charlie returned at daylight and Henry woke up to the sound of springs.

Before Charlie re-entered her life Erica had always left most of the grocery shopping to her mother. Lahoma preferred to shop at a large open air market in Grainsley and on Sunday afternoon she'd load Henry in her car and drive across the river to do her shopping. Erica was always invited to go but never accepted. She found grocery shopping boring. Now Charlie insisted she go shopping and Charlie insisted on going along. But Charlie didn't like the market. Too expensive buying fresh fruits and vegetables. Damaged goods were considerably cheaper and Freight Salvage had any canned goods the market had even if the cans were bent and impossible to stack. Freight Salvage also sold meal, flour, cereal and powdered milk. More often than not the flour, meal and cereal had weevils, tiny beetles that live in grain. If the weevils were too many, the meal, flour and cereal would be thrown in the dogs' 'feed bucket' to be mixed with the table scraps and dry dog feed. The powdered milk never had weevils. Even beetles wouldn't eat it.

Charlie also bought a twelve pack of Twinkies each week and placed them on top of the refrigerator. At first Henry assumed the Twinkies were for everyone and climbed on a chair one day and took one. The next day Charlie called Henry inside.

"Did you take one of those Twinkies?"

"Yes sir."

Charlie hit him hard on top of his head. Henry grabbed his head and bit his lip to keep from crying.

"Don't you ever touch anything up there!" Charlie yelled, pointing to the top of the refrigerator. "Do you understand me?"

"Yes sir."

"I need them when I work! Someone has to work to feed your sorry ass!"

Henry wanted to tell him those Twinkies wouldn't be fit to eat if he waited till he got a job to eat them.

The next Saturday, coming home from Freight Salvage, Charlie stopped the truck again. Erica had smiled at a clerk and Charlie beat her for it.

Four inches of snow fell the third week of December. The temperature stayed near freezing and snow covered most of southern Oklahoma on Christmas day. Driving was difficult and hazardous in many areas and Lahoma's siblings and in-laws decided to stay close to home. There would only be four of them at Lahoma's for the holiday dinner.

Charlie spent the morning pouting and Henry spent it in a chair. As soon as they entered Lahoma's house Charlie told Henry to sit in a chair and stay there. Charlie watched Erica help set the table and Charlie watched Erica eat and Charlie watched Erica help clear the table. As soon as the dishes were done Charlie announced they were leaving. Before they were out of sight of Lahoma's Charlie accused Erica of talking about him behind his back. A few minutes later he stopped the truck and drug Erica out into the snow and beat her. At home he shoved her into the bedroom slamming the door behind him. Henry listened to his mother's begging and moaning and then the bedsprings started.

Charlie skipped the hoeing season and insisted Erica keep her job at the shoe factory. When the cotton season started he bought Henry a new eight foot cotton sack and hired the two of them out to pull cotton.

Even in the fields other children found moments they could enjoy. They talked and joked while pulling the long rows of cotton but Henry wasn't allowed to talk or joke. Charlie spent little time working, preferring to stand around the wagon and talk while watching Henry like a hawk. Once another boy had thrown a green cotton boll at Henry. Henry looked to see if Charlie was watching, saw that he didn't appear to be, then threw a boll at the boy. When he looked up again Charlie was coming at him with a cotton stalk. He stripped the stalk until it resembled a buggy whip then grabbed Henry by the shirt collar and beat him from the shoulders to the knees, leaving welts on Henry's back and legs.

"You lazy hare-lipped bastard," he yelled. "I'd better not see you stop or look up again! Do you hear me?"

"Yes sir."

The whole field had witnessed the beating and Henry was embarrassed. He spent the rest of the day pulling cotton and wishing God would hit Charlie in the back of the head with a green cotton boll the size of a watermelon.

Henry was happy to see school start again. He was hoping second grade would be easier and the other kids wouldn't pick on him. The first day Sammy, Randy and Kevin drug him around a corner at recess and pulled his pants off. Sammy took his pants and dropped them near the main entrance. When recess ended Henry stayed in the yard near the corner of the building. He had no idea where his pants were. A moment later Mrs. Lomax, his second grade teacher, came around the corner carrying Henry's pants. She handed him his pants then turned her head while he put them on in an attempt not to embarrass him any further.

"Thank you ma'am."

"You're welcome Henry. Now if you'll tell me who did this I'll put a stop to it."

Henry kept silent.

"Henry you have to understand that this will keep happening unless we put a stop to it. I can't do anything unless you tell me their names. Don't you want it to stop?"

"Yes ma'am."

"Then tell me their names."

Henry kept silent.

"Very well. If that's the way you want it."

During the lunch break Henry sat in front of the school near the main entrance. Sammy and the others wouldn't take his lunch or his pants with so many people in sight. All they could do was throw dirt clods and call him names.

After school Henry walked to his grandmother's. She decided Henry needed a haircut and instead of trimming it herself as she normally did she chose to walk him the half mile to the Post Office/barber shop. Key Larson was postmaster, barber and Justice of the Peace. Often while one of the customers was 'getting his ears lowered' a state trooper would bring in a speeder. Key would hold court and fine the man while he cut the customer's hair.

Benches sat in front of the white wood building and two metal rods used for pitching horseshoes were driven into the ground about forty feet apart. During the warm weather the benches were filled with as many as a dozen men at a time, most retired farmers or ranchers, chewing tobacco, rolling cigarettes or smoking 'ready rolls' and pitching horseshoes. During the colder weather the men would occupy the two benches inside or stand and lean against the wall. A large wood burning, pot-bellied stove stood near the center of the room. The barber chair stood to the right and the postal area and rental boxes were behind the chair. The same group of men would spend a good portion of the day filling spittoons and telling stories while Key worked. Lahoma called them 'wishers'. Always wishing they'd done this or done that. Henry was still too young to know what he wanted to be but he knew one thing even then. He didn't want to be a 'wisher'.

Most of the 'wishers' were gone when Lahoma and Henry walked in. Key was sitting in his barber chair talking with two other men. He smiled and stood up when he saw Lahoma. "Well hi there young lady. I haven't seen you out and about lately."

"I stay pretty close to home Key. I just brought my grandson Henry in for a haircut." Key lowered the chair several inches and told Henry to climb up. When Henry was seated Key raised the chair to its former height. He reached around Henry with a towel, snapped it once so it would lay flat against Henry's chest and stomach then pulled the towel up and fastened it around his neck. Henry wanted to run and Key sensed it.

"I don't recall ever having you in this chair before. I promise it won't hurt a bit but I need you to sit real still for me. Can you do that?"

"Yes sir."

Henry sat as still as possible expecting to see one of his ears fall on the floor at any time. Five minutes later the ordeal was over. Lahoma paid Key his quarter, thanked him, then walked Henry to the diner and bought them both a coke.

By the fourth grade most of the students had stopped teasing Henry. He could still expect to hear a remark occasionally, particularly in a crowd, but most of the time it was said in fun. Everyone called him Rabbit, even his teachers, and only his mother and grandmother called him Henry.

Since the third grade Henry had been spending his lunch and recess with Bernard 'Bucky' Stevens. Bucky had moved here with his family a year earlier and the quiet, overweight boy had been singled out from day one. A few weeks after moving to Clovis County four older boys had seen Bucky walking and offered him a ride. Once they got him in the car they took him to a secluded area near the river and threatened to beat him if he didn't perform oral sex on each of them. The next day they made sure every student in school knew what they had made Bucky do. It made little difference to the other students that Bucky had been threatened and they teased him the way they'd teased Henry by throwing dirt on him and calling him names like 'peter eater' and 'fat queer'. Henry liked Bucky and felt sorry for him.

Sammy still singled Henry out anytime he was bored and having Henry and Bucky together gave him two people he could torment. Near the end of the morning recess Sammy and Randy walked over and stood in front of the two friends.

"Rabbit head and peter eater. I wonder whose pants I'll take first," Sammy said.

Henry stood up and Sammy hit him in the chest knocking him down.

"I'll take hare-lip's first. You just stay where you are peter eater and I'll get to you next."

Sammy dropped down on Henry's stomach with his right knee pinning him to the ground.

Henry felt Sammy undoing his pants and tried to shove him off. He fell back and felt a rock near his right hand. He picked up the rock and swung catching Sammy on the left side of his head. Blood appeared immediately and Sammy screamed, falling over on his side and holding the left side of his head. When Sammy tried to sit up the ear flopped over like a Cocker Spaniel's. Blood covered the left side of his face and ran down his neck and under his shirt. Before Henry could rise, Mr. Rice, the seventh grade science teacher, pulled him up by his shirt collar and half-walked, half-dragged Henry to the principal's office. Sammy was taken to a doctor in Mayetta, Oklahoma and Henry learned later it took a dozen stitches to sew Sammy's ear back on.

Henry knew he'd get a whipping. Principal Nickles loved to show troublesome students his two foot, polished wood paddle and brag about the countless backsides he'd paddled in his twenty-five years as a teacher, but Henry didn't expect to be given a lecture on 'fighting fair'. He called Henry a coward for using a rock and warned him there was a place in Pauls Valley for boys like him. He told him his parents would be informed of the incident and they would also be responsible for Sammy's doctor bill. He then told Henry to bend over and grab his ankles. Principal Nickles swung his pride and joy against Henry's backside fifteen times then ordered him back to class.

Henry took longer than usual walking from school to his grandmother's house. He knew he had to tell her and he was sure she'd understand why it happened but he knew Charlie wouldn't.

Henry told Lahoma about the fight and the paddling. She asked Henry to drop his pants and turn around. When he pulled his pants up and turned to face her again he could see she was angry.

"I'm sorry grandmother. Please don't be mad at me."

Lahoma pulled him close and hugged him for several seconds. "Dear boy I'm not mad at you. Don't think that for a minute."

Lahoma had seen several bruises on Henry's legs caused by the paddling. She planned to call Principal Nickles when she had her temper under control.

"Charlie will beat me."

"Maybe not." Lahoma decided not to wait to call Principal Nickles. She called and offered to pay Sammy's doctor bill and asked Nickles not to call Henry's parents. Nickles agreed to let her pay the bill and assured her he wouldn't call Charlie. An hour later Charlie and Erica arrived at Lahoma's to pick up Henry. Nickles had lied to Lahoma and called Charlie as soon as they'd finished talking. Charlie came through the front door like a bull and Lahoma met him in the center of the living room. Henry hid in the kitchen.

"You'd better get out here now!" Charlie bellowed.

Henry stepped through the doorway and started for the front door. Lahoma stopped him and glared at Charlie while Charlie glared at Henry.

"You better get your ass in that truck!"

"What are you going to do to him?"

"I'm going to have a long heart-to-heart talk with the little bastard!"

"Talk hell! I know you Charlie! You can't utter a word to a woman or child without using your fists!"

"Do you know what he did?"

"He told me. He also told me why he did it and I'm not sure I wouldn't have done the same thing!"

"Forty dollars I'll have to pay to have that kid's ear sewed back on!"

"If it's the money that upsets you I'll pay the bill!"

"The little bastard needs to learn he can't go around hittin' people with a rock!"

"And you think a good beating will do that?"

"Who says I beat him?"

"No one has to say it Charlie, I've got eyes. I know you beat Henry and Erica both. You're a damn coward Charlie!"

Charlie's face turned beet red. He clenched his fists and took a step toward Lahoma.

Lahoma stood her ground.

"It's none of your business old woman. You remember that."

"I'll remember it Charlie. You can bet I'll remember it. I'll damn well remember it the next time you need money!"

Henry climbed in the cab and slid over close to his mother. Erica put her arm around him and Henry smelled stale beer. She asked Henry why he'd hit Sammy but before he could answer Charlie climbed in behind the wheel and slammed the door hard. He hit the gas and spun his wheels throwing dirt and gravel on Lahoma's porch. Erica stared out the window and chewed her lip. Charlie backhanded Henry hard in the mouth. He tasted blood and his lip started to swell. He put his hand to his mouth and moaned.

"Whimper one more goddamn time and I'll stop the truck!" Charlie screamed. "When we get home and I get through with you you'll run backward every time you see a rock!" Charlie parked his truck near the dog pen then dragged Henry out by his shirt collar. Henry heard his top button pop and the collar tear. He turned Henry around to face him then swung catching Henry above the left temple and knocking him down.

"Forty goddamn dollars you cost me! Forty goddamn dollars!"

"Please Charlie," Erica whined. "Don't hit him again! If you have to beat someone beat me but don't beat Henry."

"Get in the house bitch!"

"Please Charlie."

"Get your fat ass in the house and I mean now!"

Erica lowered her head and walked slowly to the house. Charlie turned his attention back to Henry.

"Get up rabbit shit for brains! You ain't hurt...yet!"

Henry stood up and Charlie hit him on top of the head staggering him. Henry grabbed his head and turned away and Charlie hit him high on the back of his shoulder knocking him face down. Henry rolled over on his left side and curled in the fetal position.

"Forty goddamn dollars! You ain't worth forty goddamn dollars!"

Charlie kicked Henry high on the tail bone. The needle-toed cowboy boot sent a jolt of pain up Henry's back and down his legs.

"You plan on hittin' anybody else with a rock rabbit shit?"

Henry didn't answer and Charlie kicked him again.

"You better answer me hare-lip!"

"No sir," Henry mumbled.

"You do and we'll have this talk again." Charlie squatted down near Henry's face. "Won't be no Santa Claus for you rabbit shit for brains. That forty dollar doctor bill is all the Christmas you're getting."

Henry wasn't thinking about Christmas. Christmas was two months away and Henry's head, mouth, shoulder and tail bone hurt.

Henry was embarrassed to go to school. He'd looked in the mirror before catching the bus and saw that his left eye and the left side of his head was purple. His tail bone hurt also and he knew he'd have trouble sitting all day. During the first recess Mrs. Eubanks brought Principal Nickles outside and called Henry over. Nickles grinned and said something to Mrs. Eubanks that Henry didn't hear and Mrs. Eubanks walked away. Henry was also ordered to come home on the bus instead of going to his grandmother's. Charlie would look after him from now on.

Christmas day was cloudy and in the low forties. Charlie, Erica and Henry arrived late in the morning. Levi and his wife and four year old daughter and Patricia and her husband were already there. Benjamin and Leta wouldn't be coming.

Two hours later Charlie was ready to go. Lahoma wanted Henry to stay.

"He has chores to do," Charlie told her.

"For God's sake Charlie it's Christmas. Can't he do them tomorrow?"

"He'll do them today!"

Henry had been standing halfway between the porch and the truck hoping Lahoma might get her way. Charlie turned and saw him.

"You better get in that truck now!"

Henry climbed in the truck and slid next to his mother. On the way home Charlie stopped the truck and beat Erica. Henry didn't know what reason he was using to justify it but he supposed his mother had enjoyed herself too much. That seemed to be the only reason Charlie needed. At home Charlie dragged Erica into the bedroom and slammed the door. Henry went outside.

The last week of April a car load of older boys grabbed Bucky while he was walking and drove him to the river. That evening Bucky walked out to the storage shed behind his home, threw a nylon cord over a rafter, climbed on a chair and hanged himself. No one bragged this time about picking Bucky up. Henry missed him and Lahoma couldn't find answers to her grandson's questions.

Lahoma bought a television and invited her daughter and family over. After watching Gene Autry, Red Skelton and Dragnet Charlie knew he had to have one. A few days later Erica 'borrowed' a hundred dollars from her mother and the following Saturday, while Henry and Erica worked, Charlie watched the delivery men from Kelly's Appliances raise the antenna and secure it with guy wires. He spent the rest of the day inside drinking beer and marveling at modern science. That evening he went hunting and Erica and Henry watched The Jackie Gleason Show and Your Show of Shows.

Erica's social life had been trimmed to two or three nights a week of bar hopping. Now with a television in the house Charlie quit taking Erica to the bars altogether. He chose the shows they watched when he was home preferring Treasury Men In Action to Four Star Playhouse or Shower Of Stars. He hated the comedies and chose westerns or cop shows whenever possible.

Charlie decided to stay home for the cotton harvest but told Henry he was expected to go to the fields. The fields were close enough to walk to and Charlie told him he was expecting him to pull at least two hundred and fifty pounds a day. Henry seldom pulled more than two hundred pounds and Charlie cursed him daily for being a lazy ungrateful bastard then ended the scolding by popping him hard on the top of the head.

CHAPTER THREE

Henry was at Luther's trying to decide whether he wanted
to spend his nickel on a candy bar or a coke. He chose a Milky
Way and was standing at the counter waiting to pay when he
saw Leon and Jacob Holton shoving cigars down the front of
their shirts while Joshua Holton kept an eye on Luther. Henry
paid for his candy and walked across the street to school. A few
minutes after class resumed Principal Nickles called Henry and
Leon out of their English Class and told them to go to his office
and wait. Jacob and Joshua were already seated in the waiting
area outside the office when Leon and Henry entered. A few
minutes later Nickles entered the room followed by Luther.

"Are these the ones?" Nickles asked. Luther nodded yes.

"Okay boys Luther wants his cigars back. He saw the four
of you take them."

No one spoke.

"I want to know where those cigars are and I want to know
now!"

No one spoke.

"All we want are those cigars. You boys are in enough trouble without making it worse. Just return Luther's property and
take your punishment and we'll forget this little incident ever
happened."

No one spoke.

Nickles let out a sigh, "Thank you for calling this to my attention Luther. I'll search their lockers and desks and anywhere
else they might have hidden them. I also intend on calling their
parents."

Luther left and Nickles called the boys in one at a time and gave each one fifteen hard licks with the heavy paddle. Back in class Leon told Henry that he'd told Principal Nickles that Henry wasn't with them at Luther's. Nickles searched each boy's locker and desk and didn't find a single cigar.

Charlie wasn't home when Henry climbed out of the bus. The phone rang when he entered the house and Henry ignored it. He walked into the kitchen, cut a slab of bologna, grabbed a handful of crackers and a raw turnip and left the house through the back door. He climbed the fence and made the twenty minute walk across the fields to the river eating bologna and crackers on the way. At the river he sat on an embankment and ate the turnip then spent the next hour following the river downstream. When the sun touched the tree tops he turned back, arriving home shortly before dark. Charlie was waiting for him.

"You thieving bastard!" Charlie hit Henry on the left side of his face just under the eye. Henry fell back against the back screen door and he heard the screen tear.

"I'll teach you to steal! I can't even go to town and face Luther because of a piece of shit like you!"

Henry climbed to his feet and tried to back away. Charlie grabbed the front of Henry's shirt and pulled him closer.

"I hear you like cigars rabbit shit. When I get done with you the last thing you'll want is a cigar!"

Charlie grabbed Henry's mouth and squeezed forcing his mouth open and his head up. He took a cigar from his shirt pocket and shoved it in Henry's mouth. Henry couldn't breathe and he grabbed Charlie's hand trying to force it away. He heard his mother screaming. "You're killing him Charlie! For God's sake he can't breathe!" Charlie turned loose of Henry's face long enough to hit him again. The blow split Henry's lip and slammed him into the corner. Henry spit the cigar out and

Charlie pulled him up and held him by the jaw forcing him to look into his eyes.

"Someone's going to pay for those cigars and it goddamn sure won't be me! I'll call Luther and find out what you owe and you'll pay him every goddamn penny! I don't care how or where you get the money but you will get it! Do you fuckin' understand?"

"Yes sir."

"You get your ugly ass in that bedroom and don't let me see your face again before morning!"

Henry awoke a few hours later to smell eggs frying. He dressed then carried the 'slop' bucket outside and dumped it, stopping at the outhouse before returning to the house. He stood at the kitchen basin and washed his face. The left side was swollen and his left eye was black. His bottom lip was swollen enough to where Henry could turn his eyes downward and see the lip protruding. He sat down at the table and looked around the room for Charlie. Erica set a plate of eggs, bacon and biscuit down in front of Henry and he asked where Charlie was.

"He's looking after one of his dogs."

"I hope the dog kills him."

"He's your father Henry. Show him some respect."

"He ain't my father and he never will be. I hate him."

Erica sat down next to Henry and sipped a cup of coffee. "Mr. Holton called last night and told us his boys said you had nothing to do with stealing those cigars."

"Did you tell Mr. Holton I got a beating for it?"

"That's none of Mr. Holton's business Henry."

"Everybody in school will take one look at me and know."

Erica chewed her lip and looked away.

"Don't worry," Henry said sarcastically. "I'll just tell 'em I fell off the porch."

Henry could feel the other kids staring at him. The left side of his face looked like a purple melon and his lower lip stuck out like an extra thumb. Mrs. Eubanks asked Henry what happened to him and Henry told her he'd fallen off a porch.

"That must have been a high porch," she replied.

During lunch Henry found a place near the pump house a few feet from the school entrance and sat down. Halfway through his sandwich the Holton brothers joined him.

Although Henry rode the bus with the Holtons every day he'd never spoken to any of them. The brothers always sat together at the back of the bus. Henry had never seen any of the three involved in a fight but he'd heard stories that they were all 'scrappers'. He'd also heard that their daddy, Orville, was one of the toughest men in the county and that their mother, Mona, was the toughest of the lot.

"Can we sit with you Rabbit?" Leon asked after all three of the brothers had already sat down.

"Sit where you want to," Henry answered.

Leon was Henry's age but a good two inches taller and ten pounds heavier. Jacob was close to Henry's height but stockier and a year older. Joshua was thin and tall and two years older than Henry.

"Thanks for not telling on us," Joshua said.

"Yeah, thanks," Leon added.

Jacob smiled then asked, "Did your daddy give you that beating?"

"I don't have a daddy."

"Sure you do. Everybody knows Charlie is your daddy even if he ain't married to your mama."

Henry turned red. "I told you I ain't got no daddy."

Jacob grinned. "Sure you do. You may not claim him but he's your daddy."

"Leave him alone Jake," Leon told him. "If he says Charlie ain't his daddy then he ain't his daddy. I wouldn't claim him for my daddy either."

"What are you doing after school?" Joshua asked.

"Going home I reckon."

"Why don't you ride the bus home with us? I promise I won't let Jake tease you about Charlie no more."

"I got chores to do first but I can meet you after that. You're not that far down the river from our house."

"We'll meet you on the river then."

During the afternoon recess the four sat together and talked. Joshua knew all the schoolyard gossip about which girl would show her tits or pull down her panties for a nickel or which would 'put out'. Henry was ignorant about most of what he heard but tried to act well-informed.

"I'd like to pluck Luann," Henry told them. The others started laughing and Henry blushed.

"It's fuck not pluck," Jacob told him. "Pluck is something you do to a dead chicken."

"I know that," Henry lied.

Charlie wasn't home when Henry arrived. He carried out the trash and checked the water bucket in the kitchen then climbed the fence and started across the field to the river. He followed the river downstream and had gone nearly two miles when he met the Holtons walking toward him.

"We thought we'd walk up river and meet you," Leon explained. The old man wants us to bring you to our house. He says he'll drive you home when you're ready."

"What does he want with me?"

"He just said he wanted to meet you."

Henry followed the brothers another two miles down river then up an embankment and another quarter mile to a white farmhouse with a hand-lettered plywood sign that read 'hay for sale 50 cents a bale' nailed to a fence post in front of the house. He followed the trio past the front porch and around to the back. At the back of the house the boys entered the house through the back porch and then into the kitchen. Henry saw a small woman pouring coffee into a coffee cup held by the biggest hands he'd ever seen. The man stood up from the table and extended a ham-sized hand to Henry. He was well over six feet and muscular. The woman wasn't much bigger than Henry.

"You must be Rabbit. I've heard the boys talk about you. I'm Orville Holton and this is my wife Mrs. Holton."

Henry shook his hand and the man returned to his chair.

"The boys say you got a whipping for something they did." Orville Holton was studying Henry's face. "Boy's would you mind stepping outside for a minute while I have a man-to-man talk with Rabbit? You don't mind do you Rabbit?"

Henry stayed in the kitchen while the others walked outside.

"What happened to your face Rabbit?"

"I fell off the porch."

"I didn't know we had porches that high around here. Listen...I don't condone what my boys did. I want you to understand that. When Luther called and then that damned Nickles called I was waiting with a strap when they got home and I took the strap to all three of 'em. They told me you took a whippin' when you could have told on 'em. You know why they told me Rabbit? It's because I've taught my boys there's nothin' lower than a snitch. Like I said, I don't condone stealing but I can tolerate a thief easier than I can tolerate a snitch. I called Charlie last night and told him what the boys told me. I reckin I called too late and I'm sorry about that Rabbit."

Henry started easing toward the front door. The conversation was making him uncomfortable. He felt Charlie would have beat him regardless of any phone call.

"You got a lot of your uncle Robert in you. Some of your grandmother too I suspect."

"You knew my uncle?"

"We grew up together. He was my best friend. And he was one of a kind Rabbit. They don't make 'em like your uncle anymore. You'd be the spittin' image of him if it weren't for that hare-lip."

Orville drained his cup and Mona Holton asked if he wanted a refill. Orville declined. "You're welcome here anytime Rabbit. You remember that. Why don't you go outside now and get the boys to show you their 'canyon'?"

Henry found the brothers sitting on the butane tank waiting.

"What did the old man tell you?" Leon asked.

"He said for you to show me your canyon."

"Then we'll go to the canyon," Joshua said.

Henry followed the brothers past a chicken coop to a fenced pasture two hundred yards or so from the house. A flat-bed trailer sat in front of the barn, its tongue resting on a cinder block. Henry counted three dogs laying in the shade of the trailer. They climbed the fence and walked across a pasture populated by several cattle until they reached a growth of small trees and shrubs. They climbed another fence and a moment later arrived at the 'canyon', a large ravine a dozen or so feet at one end to nearly forty feet in the middle. Several small gullies ran out in all directions from the main body of the ravine. The four climbed down an embankment and walked to the center. As they sat in a circle in the soft sand Joshua pulled six cigars from inside his shirt.

"Daddy didn't find these. He found the others and took 'em back to Luther but I had these hid under the butane tank."

Joshua gave everyone a cigar and put the other two back in his shirt. He pulled a small box of Diamond safety matches from his pants pocket and lit his and Leon's cigars then blew the match out. He struck another match and held it to Henry's cigar, then Jacob's.

"Bad luck to light three on a match Rabbit."

Henry had never smoked but he'd seen others smoke. He took a deep draw, sucking the smoke into his lungs and immediately went into a coughing spasm. The three brothers laughed.

"Here's how you do it Rabbit," Jacob said. He took a deep draw from his cigar and held it a second then exhaled, blowing smoke from his mouth and nostrils. Henry stared at his cigar. His head was starting to swim and his stomach was queasy.

"You'll get used to it," Leon assured him. "I nearly got sick my first time."

"I'd rather have a cigarette anytime," Joshua said. "But the old man won't leave his Camels laying around anymore."

"Not since he caught you stealing them," Leon said.

"Let's play slap," Jacob suggested.

"Rabbit can't play," Joshua told him.

"I forgot about his face," Jacob mumbled. "We can still play though. Our old man didn't beat us."

Henry was embarrassed and Joshua sensed it.

"Shut up Jake," he said.

"Why don't ya'll play and I'll watch," Henry told them.

"I don't wanna play slap with Jake," Leon said. "He slaps too hard."

"I'll play," Joshua said climbing to his feet.

Jacob stood up and the two brothers faced each other. Both boys held their hands together in front of their faces like they were praying. Jacob's right hand shot out and Joshua slapped it away. Jacob feinted with his left hand then swung with his right hand slapping Joshua hard on his left cheek. Joshua staggered back a step and grinned.

"I quit," Jacob said.

"We just started," Joshua reminded him.

"I saw you grin and I know you're going to try to hurt me."

Before Jacob could drop his hands Joshua's right hand shot out catching Jacob hard and staggering him. His left hand followed catching Jacob on the right cheek and staggering him again. He slapped Jacob three more times before Jacob could get away from him.

"Come on," Joshua yelled. "Let's play slap!"

"No! You hit too hard when you're mad!"

"The old man's calling us," Leon told them. Henry hadn't heard a thing but the three brothers started up the embankment at once. Orville was waiting by the back porch when they walked up.

"I better take Rabbit home," he told them. "Crawl in the back if you want to go with me."

"I can follow the river home sir," Henry told him.

"You'd never make it before dark and you don't need to be falling off no more porches."

The four friends rode in the back of the truck to Henry's. Charlie was in the dog pen with a shovel and a bucket. He left the pen, dropped the bucket and shovel near the gate and walked toward the truck.

"Where the hell have you been?" Charlie asked, ignoring the Holtons.

"It's my fault Charlie. I invited him to the house. If you have to get mad then get mad at me."

"I don't tell you how to raise your kids Holton and I damn well don't want you telling me how to raise mine!"

Charlie glared at Henry "Get in the house now!" he ordered.

Henry jumped down from the back of the pick-up and started walking toward the house with Charlie behind him. Orville Holton stepped out of the cab and hollered at Charlie to wait a minute. Charlie stopped and turned toward Orville.

"I don't have a goddamn thing to say to you Holton!"

Orville waited until Henry was in the house. Henry stopped inside the house and stood to one side of the door. No one could see him but he could hear everything the two men said.

"You think you're a big man beatin' a boy like that, Charlie?"

"Did he tell you that?"

"He didn't tell me nothin' except some bull shit story about falling off the porch. You could have come up with something better than that Charlie!"

"It's none of your business Holton! Now get the hell off my property! You're not welcome here!"

Orville took a step closer to Charlie and Charlie had to look up to face him. Henry, peeking around the door, could see the sweat on the back of Charlie's neck.

"I know where you hunt Charlie and I know the men you hunt with. If that boy falls off any more porches I'm going to show up at the next hunt and we're going to continue this discussion. Am I making myself clear enough?"

Henry didn't hear Charlie answer. Orville walked back to his truck and backed out of the driveway. Charlie walked into the house and slapped Henry down.

"I don't want you around those white trash Holtons! Do you hear me?" Charlie thumped Henry's head with his middle finger.

"Yes sir."

Henry left the house Sunday morning shortly after daylight. Charlie had come home an hour or so earlier and the bedsprings had awakened Henry. He walked to the river and started down stream toward the Holton farm. Two hours later he stood on an embankment and watched the Holton's house for any movement. After several minutes he saw three figures leave the house and walk towards the barn. Henry started across the field and arrived at the barn as Joshua was coming out carrying a bucket of milk.

"Hi Rabbit. Did you walk over here? Leon and Jake are in the barn. I have to take this inside and I'll be right back."

Henry walked into the barn and saw Jake and Leon engaged in a milk fight. Both boys sat in front of a cow with a pail under the animal's udders and a teat in their hands. They were turning the teats toward each other and squeezing, shooting a long stream of milk in each other's face. They stopped when they heard Henry.

"Did you walk over here?" Jake asked. Leon turned a teat toward Henry squirting him in the face. Henry took several steps backward until he was sure he was out of range of the teat.

"It's not that far using the river."

Joshua entered the barn and walked over to Henry.

"Can you stay awhile? We're going crow hunting."

"I don't have a gun."

"Maybe the old man will loan you one."

The boys finished milking and walked to the house to ask their dad if Henry could go crow hunting. Orville Holton had reservations about loaning Henry a gun especially after learning Henry had never held a gun before much less fired one. He agreed to loan him an old twelve gauge single shot shotgun providing Henry would let him show him the proper way to handle and fire a gun.

Orville sat several cans along an embankment in the ravine then handed Henry the shotgun and told him to pick a can and try to hit it. Henry raised the gun to his shoulder and Orville stood behind him and pulled the gun tight against Henry's shoulder and told him to hold it as tight as he could when he fired. Henry pointed the barrel and fired. The recoil threw the gun's barrel up and Henry back several feet. His shoulder felt like Charlie had kicked it. The can lay in the sand several feet from where it had sat.

"Well you hit the can and stayed on your feet. I guess that's something. How's your shoulder?"

"It's all right sir."

"You remember to keep that gun pointed up Rabbit. You boys keep an eye on him. Don't let him shoot any of our cows."

The boys walked away from the river toward a tree line at the east end of the pasture. Henry saw several crows circling the tree tops. Joshua cupped his hands to his mouth and began imitating the crow's cawing. In a couple of minutes the crows began to land in the tree tops. An hour later everyone but Henry had killed at least one crow. Henry had killed a couple of tree tops.

"Guess we oughta start back," Joshua told the others. "We told the old man we wouldn't be gone long."

Walking back Henry saw a crow flying low over the field. He raised the shotgun and fired. The crow flew off.

"Uh oh," Leon said. "Look at that."

Henry saw the cow a hundred feet or so away standing near the fence. The animal's legs were wobbling and blood spurted from a hole in her neck. She stood several more seconds before dropping to her knees and staying there, a pink foam coming from her mouth and nostrils. She snorted one last time.

"Holy shit!" Jacob cried. "You killed a cow." The three brothers started laughing.

"What a shot," Leon added. "When I get ready to go cow huntin' I'm calling you."

"I don't think the old man's gonna laugh about his cow getting shot," Joshua told them.

"He may not let us hunt no more," Jake said.

"Oh, he'll let us hunt but I'm not sure he'll let Rabbit hunt."

"Who's gonna tell him?" Leon asked.

"I think Rabbit ought to," Jake answered.

"We can all tell him," Joshua said.

"Why?" Jake asked. "We didn't kill his cow."

"Rabbit didn't take no cigars either, if you'll remember."

"I'll tell him," Henry said. "I'll have to face him anyway."

"I'll go with you," Joshua offered. "These chicken shits can wait in the barn."

"Hell fire," Leon said. "I guess I'll go too."

"If everybody else is going then I'll go," Jake offered.

The four boys walked to the back of the house and Joshua went in and asked his father to come outside. Henry told him he'd killed a cow and expected Orville Holton to hit him. Orville told the boys to show him the cow.

"Well he's dead all right." Orville squatted and examined the hole in the animal's neck.

"I'll pay for the cow sir," Henry told him. "I promise."

Orville started laughing. Henry wouldn't have been surprised if the man had wanted to beat him but he didn't expect him to laugh.

"I blame myself for this Henry, not you. Right now we need to do something with the cow. We can't leave it here. I'll get the tractor and drag it over to the gully. We'll get what we can to feed the dogs and you boys can spend the rest of the afternoon burying what's left. And you can forget about hunting for awhile."

The four friends didn't get the carcass buried until late afternoon. By that time Henry had decided to give up hunting. It was too much work.

The Holton brothers liked to smoke. After the cigars were gone they talked Henry into smoking grapevines with them. The vines burned Henry's tongue and mouth. From time to time Orville Holton would lay his pack of Camels down long enough for one of the brothers to steal a few but the opportunities were less and less. Today they were trying to roll their own from a sack of tobacco Joshua had bought. Over half the sack was gone and none of the four had rolled anything they could smoke. Henry had singed his eyebrow on the last 'cigarette' he'd tried to light. Finally Leon managed to roll one that didn't fall apart or burst into flame. Another hour and all four were smoking Bull Durham cigarettes that resembled the grape vines more than they did a Camel.

Orville Holton asked Henry if he'd like to work for him when school adjourned for the summer. Henry told him he would and when Charlie hired him out to pull cotton Henry didn't go to the field. Charlie was waiting when Henry came home that first day.

"Where you been you little bastard? Scott called and told me you never showed up!"

Charlie hit Henry hard nearly knocking him off the porch.

"I've been helping Mr. Holton with his hay."

"I told you to stay away from that white trash! Get inside! I'll teach you to mind me!"

Henry ran off the porch and around to the back of the house. He climbed the fence and took off toward the river. He could hear Charlie behind him threatening and cursing him. Henry didn't stop until he reached the riverbank. He sat down under an embankment trying to decide what to do and came to the decision that he'd live on the river until he was eighteen and free to leave home. A few minutes later he heard Charlie calling him from several yards away. He was hunting Henry. Henry hid in the embankment behind the exposed roots of a large cottonwood and watched Charlie pass. A few minutes later he watched Charlie pass in the other direction. He had given up on finding Henry and was going home. Henry waited until he was sure he was gone then took a kitchen match from his pocket and built a fire. He planned to spend the night behind the cottonwood roots then move further down river in the morning.

When Henry didn't return in two hours Erica called her mother thinking Henry might try to walk to Joneston to see her. When Erica hung up Lahoma called Orville Holton. Orville called Erica and told her he'd help locate Henry if she could promise him that Charlie wouldn't beat the boy. Charlie promised Erica he wouldn't. An hour later Orville found Henry's fire and talked the boy into going home assuring him that Charlie wouldn't beat him.

Charlie waited until Orville drove off then dragged Henry outside and hit him hard knocking him to the ground. When Henry tried to get up Charlie hit him hard again then kicked him in the ribs. When Henry refused to get up again Charlie kicked him in the tail bone then pulled him up. He hit him again breaking Henry's nose and blacking both eyes. Then he walked inside leaving Henry laying outside in the dirt. When Erica came outside to help Henry Charlie told her to leave Henry alone or she'd get the same treatment her son got. Erica helped him anyway. Charlie cursed her then got in his pick-up and left. He didn't return until midnight.

Lahoma drove up shortly before noon. Orville had called her the night before and told her Henry was home. She carried a large pot of pinto beans and a pan of cornbread. When she saw Henry's face she turned beet red, glared at Charlie and left. An hour later she was back with the sheriff. Sheriff Wesley examined Henry's face then asked Charlie to step outside.

A few minutes later the sheriff left and Charlie stormed into the house and ordered Lahoma out. He took the pot of beans and pan of cornbread and threw them in the yard behind her then climbed into his pick-up and left again. He returned a few hours later drunk and beat Erica for missing work that day to take care of her 'lazy, worthless, hare-lip son'.

The next morning Henry left the house before daylight and walked to the Holton's farm. Orville seemed surprised to see him and appeared angry when he saw Henry's face, but no one, including the brothers, said a word about Henry's condition.

Bringing in the hay was a Holton family affair. Mona Holton drove the tractor that pulled the flatbed while Orville Holton stood on the tractor and stacked the bales. The boys, working in pairs, carried the bales to the trailer. The work was hot and dirty but Orville made it as pleasant as possible stopping every hour for a fifteen minute break and reminding the boys often not to overdo it trying to keep up. While other farmers worked till dusk and sometimes later, Orville quit at five in the afternoon. This gave the boys time to play and swim in the cattle pond. Henry was paid a penny a bale for every bale they stacked in the barn. In six weeks the hay was gathered and Orville offered Henry another job at fifty cents an hour to help his sons mend fences.

Charlie hadn't said anymore about Henry working for the Holtons and he hadn't beat him since Lahoma brought the sheriff to the house. He still slapped him or thumped his head with his finger and he cursed him as much as ever but he hadn't used his fists on him.

One Sunday morning Henry awoke and found his mother in the kitchen smoking a cigarette and drinking a beer. Henry had never seen her drinking that early. He looked outside and saw Charlie's pick-up and asked his mother where Charlie was. He knew Charlie had been hunting the night before.

"He's in bed. He doesn't feel good."

"I hope the bastard dies."

Henry left and spent the day with the Holton brothers. When he returned shortly before dark Charlie was sitting in front of the television. His right eye was black and his lip and the left side of his face was swollen. When he shifted his weight in the chair he moaned and grabbed his right side. Henry had to go outside to keep from laughing in front of him.

Charlie hadn't asked Henry for the money he earned but he expected him to at any time. He hid his money in the bottom molding behind the bed using a spoon to pry the strip of wood out far enough to hide the bills then using the same spoon to tap the molding back. Charlie would have to tear the room apart to find it. A few days before the start of school Charlie demanded Henry's money. Henry refused to tell him where it was. Charlie hit him knocking him against a chest of drawers. Henry ran out of the room toward the back door. He remembered the warning he'd heard Orville Holton give Charlie that spring afternoon and he knew from Charlie's appearance that someone had given him an ass whipping a few days earlier.

"I'll tell Mr. Holton!" Henry threatened.

"You hare-lip piece of shit!" Charlie yelled as he started for Henry. "You ain't tellin' nobody shit!"

Henry ran out the back door and didn't stop until he reached the river. He hid under the cottonwood roots and waited expecting to hear Charlie hunting him. He heard no one calling and after nearly two hours he walked back to the house. Charlie's pick-up was gone. He entered the house and went to his bedroom. The room was a wreck. His mattress and bedding lay on the floor and his chest of drawers had been emptied and the contents scattered. Henry fixed his bed and wanted to crawl in it and go to sleep but he was afraid of what Charlie would do when he came home. He was planning to fix a bologna sandwich and return to the river when Charlie appeared at the bedroom door. Henry was trapped and expected to be beaten.

"You'll buy your own fuckin' clothes! You'll buy your own shit for school! You'll buy your own food! You keep your goddamn money but you pay your own goddamn way because I goddamn sure won't!"

"You never have! Mama does!"

Henry ran behind the bed. Charlie turned bright red and stood with his fist clenched then turned and left. Henry heard him start his pick-up and drive away a moment later. He crawled into bed and fell asleep at once. The bedsprings woke him later that night but he didn't lay awake like he normally did but fell back to sleep seconds after they stopped.

Henry kept up with his chores and avoided Charlie as much as possible. He did little yard work because the mower's blade was broken and Charlie had no desire to spend the time or money it would take to fix it. The sparse grass stood tall in the corners of the yard and in a few scattered islands. But Charlie preferred to drink and watch television. Henry tried to stay outside as much as possible returning home at dark or a little after and making a sandwich and taking it to his room. If Charlie was hunting he'd watch Ozark Jubilee and Lawrence Welk with his mother. If his mother got drunk and went to bed early he'd watch his favorite show, Gunsmoke. Erica cooked breakfast every morning and supper every night regardless of how much beer she consumed. On weekends or any time she wasn't working Charlie expected her to make lunch too. And Charlie liked grease. Eggs, bacon and potatoes were fried in grease and canned turnip greens and spinach were heated with a slab of hog jowl added. Lahoma often brought a large pot of beans or vegetable soup. Charlie hated his mother-in-law but he never refused to eat her beans. She also brought them fresh vegetables her customers gave her.

Henry seldom ate breakfast unless Charlie was gone. When he did eat he avoided the biscuits and gravy. He couldn't look at a biscuit without thinking about weevils and he wouldn't try to eat anything made from powdered milk.

Henry still spent his Saturdays drawing water and helping his mother with the laundry while Charlie watched television. He was big enough now to help his mother remove the water from the stove so Charlie had no reason to leave his chair except to go to the outhouse. Later, towards dark he'd load his dogs and go hunting.

Sunday morning Henry grabbed a raw turnip and a slab of bologna and slipped out of the house at daylight. Henry walked toward the Holton farm eating his breakfast as he went. He expected to be early and would have to kill some time alone waiting for the three brothers. But they were waiting for him when he reached the embankment near their farm.

"I figured I'd be early."

"We been waitin' an hour," Joshua said. "We've got a surprise for you."

"What is it?"

"We ain't tellin'," Jacob answered. "You'll have to wait and see."

"You're gonna like it," Leon added.

"Well where is it?"

"It's not far from here but we can't take you there yet. We have to make sure they've left for church."

"Make sure who's left for church?"

"We ain't tellin'," Jacob repeated.

"Let's tell him," Leon said. Leon didn't like keeping secretes. "We found some pussy Rabbit."

"Our folks made us go to Mrs. Lewis' last night for a table walking," Joshua explained. "She's mama's cousin."

"What's a table walking?"

"That's where some people sit around a table with their hands on top and ask questions and the table answers them."

"You're funnin' with me. A table can't talk and I'll bet ya'll don't know where no pussy is either."

"You have to ask the table questions you can answer with a number," Joshua continued. "Like how many cows someone has or how old someone is. It works too."

"I don't believe it. Someone kicks the table or somethin'."

"Nobody kicks the table," Jacob said. "You can see everybody's legs and nobody kicks nothin'."

"Anyways," Joshua continued, "Mrs. Lewis has a daughter named Josephine. While everyone else was walking the table she took us out to a shed and fucked all three of us."

"All three of you?"

"All three," Leon giggled.

"She lives with her mother and an older cousin," Joshua explained. "They go to church every Sunday but they don't make her go if she doesn't want to. Last night she said she wouldn't be wanting to go this morning and we could come by while they're at church."

"How much further is it?" Henry asked.

"Two or three miles I think," Joshua answered. "I hope her mama's already gone."

"What if she ain't?"

"We'll just hide and wait until they leave."

The Lewis home was located on a small hill less than an eighth of a mile from the river. Josephine sat on the back porch watching the boys approach the house. She left her chair and met them in the yard wearing a cotton dress that buttoned down the front. Her breasts were just large enough to make two small points. Jacob reached over and squeezed her left point. She made no effort to stop him as he unbuttoned the first three buttons on her dress and slipped his hand inside.

"Who's he?" she asked, pointing at Henry.

"This is Rabbit," Joshua answered.

"He's cute. And I like rabbits."

"Let's go out to the shed," Leon said.

Josephine led the way, the four friends following like pups in heat, to an old tool shed several yards to the right of the house. The shed was filled with old furniture and clothing and had a musty smell. Josephine lay down in a well cleared area, pulled her dress up and removed her panties. Joshua dropped his pants and mounted her. She lay still with her legs spread and her eyes closed, a low moaning sound coming from her throat, while Joshua unbuttoned her dress and exposed her breasts. Jacob mounted her next, then Leon, then Henry. The 'gang bang', from start to finish, had taken less than ten minutes and Josephine was begging the boys to stay a while longer. Jacob wanted to stay but couldn't convince the others. A few minutes later they were walking up river toward home.

Ticks were always a problem during the spring and summer months. Henry had long ago grown tired of being burned by his mother's cigarette and had checked himself regularly for any sign of the parasites. Fleas were usually a problem only to dog owners and could normally be controlled to some degree by dipping the animal in diesel fuel. This year, however, Charlie had neglected to dip his dogs early and the fleas were everywhere: In the dog pen, the house, the outhouse and the yard. Charlie purchased a white powder insecticide and sprinkled it all over the ground of the dog pen. It was too little, too late and Henry had to start school covered in flea bites. The other students knew the reason for Henry's constant scratching and teased him about it. The fleas remained a problem until the first hard frost of winter when the cold weather did what the insecticide had failed to do.

Lahoma had taken Henry shopping before school started and Henry had insisted on buying new clothes with the money he'd saved that summer working for Mr. Holton. He'd never had a new pair of Levi's and he bought four pairs. He also purchased a pair of Wellington boots with ten inch tops and a denim jacket with a wool liner. Lahoma convinced him to let her pick out the material for new shirts and told him she'd make him several for less than what two or three shirts would cost. Henry was proud of his new attire and changed out of the new clothes every day after school before walking to the river.

The four friends knew the river for several miles in either direction. They knew where every orchard, garden and watermelon patch along the river were located. They had also made several more trips to Josephine's house. Even the cold weather didn't stop her from pleasuring the boys.

Christmas dinner was spent at Lahoma's. Charlie, Erica, Henry, great-uncle Levi and great-aunt Patricia and her husband were the only visitors. Levi's wife had left him and the court had given her the house and what money they'd saved. Lahoma offered to let him stay with her and he'd accepted.

When Charlie announced they were leaving Henry told him he wanted to stay. To his surprise Charlie didn't object. That evening when Lahoma took him home Henry saw a new set of bruises on his mother. Charlie hadn't forgotten to give Erica her Christmas beating and Henry had felt guilty thinking Charlie may have used him as an excuse to abuse her.

The February Sunday felt like an April morning. The sun was bright and the temperature was in the low seventies. The four friends decided to visit Josephine and were hiding on the river waiting for Mrs. Lewis and her cousin to leave for church. Finally Josephine came out on the porch and sat down in a rocker scanning the area for company. The boys walked into the back yard and Josephine smiled when she saw them. A moment later they were in the shed. The 'gang bang' proceeded at once and Henry was the only one who hadn't taken his turn when they heard someone walking toward the shed. Josephine jumped to her feet and buttoned her dress. Joshua, Jacob and Leon found some loose boards at the back of the shed and made a hole big enough to get through. Henry had just enough time to pull his pants up and hide behind an old stove before Mrs. Lewis walked in. "What are you doing out here in this filthy shed?" she asked.

"Nothing mother, just looking around. Why didn't you go to church?"

"Anna forgot her purse."

Mrs. Lewis was suspicious. She didn't know what her daughter was doing in the shed but she was sure it wasn't to look around. She walked around inside the small building and came within a foot of where Henry was hiding. Henry held his breath and studied the small hole at the back of the stove wondering if he could crawl in it.

"Come inside and change your clothes. You're going to church with us."

"You're already late," Josephine said, looking for an excuse to stay home, "and you'll be later waiting for me to change."

"I'm sure the Lord won't mind if we're a little late," Mrs. Lewis said as she grabbed her daughter's arm and led her toward the house.

"I'll have to comb my hair too."

"You can comb it in the car."

"Why can't I wait and go next Sunday?"

"You're going next Sunday and every Sunday after that."

Henry stayed behind for several minutes then left the shed through the same hole the brothers had used. He found the brothers waiting on the river bank.

"You chicken shits left me."

"The only reason you didn't leave," Joshua told him, "is because you couldn't find a hole. Did old lady Lewis catch you?"

"No, I hid behind an old stove."

"Well don't be mad at us," Leon said. "You'd have run too if you'd had a chance."

"I'm not mad at ya'll. I'm just mad cause I didn't get my turn."

"We can come back next Sunday," Joshua said.

"But Josephine won't be there," Henry told them. "Her mama's gonna make her go to church."

CHAPTER FOUR

Henry had been looking forward to the start of eighth grade. School was easy for him. He learned enough to pass the tests from listening in class and could do all his homework in study hall. He seldom carried a book unless it was one he'd checked out of the school library and he expected this year to be no different.

Saturday morning Henry awoke and found Charlie gone and his mother sitting at the kitchen table in her bathrobe. He emptied the 'slop' bucket and walked back inside expecting to find her changing into work clothes to do laundry. She was still in her robe sipping coffee.

"I'm ready to start when you are," Henry told her. "The quicker we start, the quicker we get done."

"I'm doing the laundry at Aunt Pat's."

Henry couldn't help smiling. He had his first Saturday off and he planned to make the most of it.

"We're moving to Mayetta, Henry."

Henry lost his smile. "What do you mean we're moving to Mayetta? I don't wanna move. I like it here."

"You're thirteen years old Henry. You have no choice in the matter."

"I'll be fourteen in three weeks. Can't I stay with Grandmother? I don't know anybody in Mayetta."

"You'll make friends. And if you're smart you won't argue with Charlie about this."

"It's not fair. Why do we have to move anyways?"

"We got jobs with that new factory that opened up."

"You mean you got a job."

"Charlie got a job too, as a gate guard."

"He'll quit in a week."

"It doesn't matter whether he quits or not we're still moving. I'm tired of living like this with no running water and a stinkin' outhouse."

"It still ain't fair."

"Life ain't fair Henry. You need to learn that."

"But I have to enroll Monday."

"You can enroll in Mayetta. We're looking at some houses this afternoon and you can stay with Aunt Pat until we get moved."

"It still ain't fair."

"You've got today to say good-bye to the Holtons. Tomorrow morning you're going to Aunt Pat's."

Henry walked down river to the Holton farm. He knew the brothers would assume he'd be drawing water all day and wouldn't be expecting him. They were watching the Wild Bill Hickock show when Mrs. Holton answered the door.

"What are you doing here?" Joshua asked. "I thought you had work to do."

"I'll tell you later."

The Roy Rogers Show came on next and the four friends sat on the floor and watched the half-hour series. Henry had never seen either show and would normally have been excited to have the opportunity to watch them but the idea of moving depressed him. When the show ended Joshua suggested they go play on the river.

"What's wrong Henry?" He asked, as soon as they were away from the house.

"Mama says we're moving."

"Where?" Leon asked.

"To Mayetta. Her and Charlie's got jobs at that new factory."

"Mayetta's just twenty miles away," Joshua said.

"It might as well be a thousand," Henry replied.

"Won't they let you stay with your grandmother?" Leon wondered.

"I done asked. Mama says I have to move with them."

"We're gonna miss you Rabbit," Joshua told him. "It won't be the same without you."

"I'm even gonna miss you," Jacob said.

"Me too," Leon added.

Erica drove Henry to the Mayetta school Monday morning to enroll. They'd spent Sunday night with his Great Aunt Pat and would have to stay another day or two while they moved into the house they'd rented. The Mayetta school started a week earlier than Joneston and Henry was already behind in his studies the morning he enrolled.

Mayetta, Oklahoma, population near eleven hundred, was the county seat of Clovis County. Downtown was four blocks long and began at the courthouse and jail on the north end of Main Street and ended at the train depot on the south end. The high school sat four blocks south of the depot and nearly five hundred students attended. Across the street from the east side of the school was Duffy's Store, a small, white, wooden building with a covered porch that extended across the front and around the south side of the building. Inside, Mr. and Mrs. Duffy sold everything a student could want; beer, cigarettes and junk food. The students were ninety percent of the store's business and the place was packed every school day. Dropouts and students alike mingled in the store or outside on the porch eating Beanie Weanies and Hostess cupcakes and washing it down with soda. Mr. Duffy didn't sell beer to anyone underage but there was always someone around who would buy it for you if you had the money. Anyone who could reach the counter could buy cigarettes.

Charlie and Erica had rented a house on Third Street, three blocks west of the school. The house was thirty years old and sat on a half acre lot. A small oak tree stood on the south side of the house near an attic window. Inside the house was a large living room, a kitchen, bathroom and two bedrooms. To the right of the kitchen, near the backdoor, a flight of stairs led to the attic. The attic had been used previously for a bedroom and Henry decided this would be his room.

Charlie moved his dog pen and dogs before moving what furniture they had. Pat's husband Bryon helped and by the middle of the week Henry was out of Pat's house and dragging his bed from a bedroom on the bottom floor to the attic room. Henry told his mother he wanted the attic but Charlie had moved everything of Henry's into the other bedroom anyway. Henry had to move everything to the attic without any help but he considered the room worth the effort. He had a certain amount of privacy but the thing he liked most was the tree outside his window. He could use the window like a door and the tree like a ladder and he could come and go as he pleased.

The Joneston school had been all white and Henry had never seen a black person before except on trips to Grainsley. He'd noticed the 'colored' and 'white' drinking fountains and restrooms but he never had to interact with 'people of color'. The Mayetta school was integrated and black and white alike talked, played and studied together. There were no separate facilities and the mood was cordial although interracial dating was strongly condemned by both races. No white girl in town wanted to be called a 'nigger fucker' and no self-respecting black girl wanted to be accused of 'fucking whitey'.

Henry's classes consisted of English, Science and Mathematics in the morning and Agriculture, Shop and Study Hall in the afternoon. English was his best subject but he could pass all classes with minimum effort. He had to join the Future Farmers of America to enroll in Agriculture. The class usually consisted of castrating the teacher's hogs or vaccinating his cattle but Henry preferred that to sitting in a class room.

Henry liked his Study Hall hour. The school library was next to the room and after doing his homework He would visit the library and pick through the books. He read Thomas Thoreau, Poe and Twain and then discovered the works of Robert Service. The poet quickly became his favorite writer and he started writing himself. He wrote little eight and ten line poems about people and events in a spiral notebook he kept in a drawer at home and he had no intention of showing them to anyone, well aware of the teasing he'd receive from the other students if they knew.

Henry had been at the school for two weeks and he had kept mostly to himself. He'd had no teasing about his appearance but he missed the Holton brothers. He spent his free time at Duffy's Store sitting at the far end of the porch away from the other students. Today he was eating a can of pork 'n' beans when three boys and a buxom girl sat down a few feet away. The boys sat with their feet hanging over the edge of the porch. The girl leaned against a support pole and faced Henry. She crossed her legs and her dress rode up revealing her body from the waist down. Henry couldn't help but stare. The girl stared back and made no effort to pull her dress down. He tore his eyes away long enough to glance at her companions. One of the boys was staring at Henry and he didn't look happy. Henry looked away and took another bite of beans. "Hey you. What are you staring at?"

Henry ignored the boy. He appeared to be older, taller and heavier and Henry didn't want trouble.

"Hey hare-lip I asked you a question. What the fuck are you staring at?"

The girl made no effort to cover herself and Henry wanted to stare a little longer at the white panties and the small strands of pubic hair around the panty line. Instead he stared at his beans and took another bite. At that moment another boy walked over and sat down uninvited. Henry had seen him around school. He was huge, taller than most men in the county and built like a weight lifter with arms bigger than Henry's legs. Henry looked up at the stranger and saw him grinning from ear to ear like all this was some kind of joke.

"You're Henry Ridge right? They call you Rabbit?"

"Yeah. Why? Do I know you?"

"I used to live in Joneston. Me and Josh Holton had some classes together. I remember the day you hit the Laughlin jerk with a rock and nearly tore his ear off."

"How come I don't remember you?"

"We didn't live there long. Mama didn't like it there and when daddy got an offer to work for the highway department Mama made him take it and we moved here. She don't like it here either. By the way I'm Harvey Pike."

"Nice to know you Harvey."

"When's the last time you saw Josh?"

"It'll be three weeks Saturday."

"We oughta take a ride down and see him Saturday. I like Josh. He's a scrapper."

Henry had nearly forgotten about the girl until she stood up to leave and her boyfriend walked over.

"Harvey is this a friend of yours?"

"Lonnie this is Henry and he is a friend. Henry this asshole is Lonnie Dickerson."

"You oughta tell your friend to stop staring at what ain't his."

"Why don't you tell him yourself?"

Henry was getting irritated. He climbed to his feet and faced Lonnie holding the half eaten can of beans.

"You got something to say then say it to me."

"I'll do that." Lonnie poked Henry in the chest with his right index finger. "Keep your eyes to yourself hare-lip."

Henry stepped back a foot and threw the can of beans at him then stepped in and kicked him twice in the left kneecap. Lonnie grabbed his knee and started hopping around the porch yelling, "the bastard kicked me!" Henry could hear Harvey behind him laughing. Lonnie stopped hopping and leaned against the porch railing rubbing his knee. Pork 'n' beans dripped down the front of his shirt.

"You ruined my shirt! You owe me a new shirt!"

"You owe me a can of beans. Why don't we call it even?"

Henry had agreed to meet Harvey after school. He had no chores at home other than carrying the trash out occasionally. Charlie didn't have a working lawn mower and preferred paying someone else to cut grass as to buying another one. Henry had his afternoons to do as he pleased.

Harvey was waiting when Henry crossed the street to Duffy's, leaning against a lime green 1950 Dodge pick-up truck talking to another student Henry had seen in one of his classes.

"Henry this is Mike Bryce. Mike this is Henry. They call him Rabbit in Joneston."

"I never met a rabbit before," Mike grinned and Henry liked him immediately.

"I'd rather you call me Henry."

"Let's go for a ride," Harvey said. "Anyone have any gas money?"

"I'm broke," Mike answered. "What about you Henry?"

Henry had money in his pocket and more at home but he didn't have a job. He had to make his money last until he found an income but he liked these two. He reached in his pocket and took out the money he allotted himself for the week. He had a little over eight dollars.

"I've got enough for a couple of dollars worth of gas," he told them.

"What about beer?" Harvey asked.

Henry sighed and counted his money again. He gave Harvey five dollars. "I guess I'll be smoking Bull Durham this week."

Harvey drove to Loman's Texaco and bought two dollars worth of gas then drove to the Red Rock Tavern. He went inside and returned a moment later. A few minutes later a skinny gray-haired man came out carrying a sack and walked over to the truck window and handed the sack to Harvey. Harvey drove south past the school and turned onto the first dirt road to the right. Mike opened three beers and passed one to Harvey and one to Henry.

Henry hadn't done a lot of drinking although he could have anytime he wanted. He'd grown up in a house where there might not be milk or fresh bread but there was always beer. He took a drink of his mother's beer a few years earlier and the taste had nearly made him sick and he hated the sour smell of stale beer. He took a sip and tried not to make a face. Harvey turned his beer up and downed half the bottle in one drink.

Harvey turned left on another road and a mile further they passed a small oil refinery with the legend 'Dickerson's Oil' on the side of a large holding tank.

"Lonnie's old man owns that," Harvey told him. "He's that asshole you met on the porch."

"I heard about you baptizing Lonnie with your beans," Mike told him. "The first day I wasn't there and I missed it. Lonnie's a fuckin' loudmouth."

"Hell he can't help it," Harvey said. "He's a jock and all those fuckin' jocks are that way. Coach Killen's got 'em convinced their shit don't stink."

The three friends rode around the dirt roads drinking beer and talking. Henry learned that although Harvey was two years older than him and Mike he was only one grade ahead of them in school, having been held back in the fourth grade.. He also learned that Harvey liked to fight and would give any opponent the first punch. Mike told him that one time a man had hit Harvey with a tire tool and Harvey would have killed the man if they hadn't stopped him.

CHAPTER FIVE

Erica had taken a job at Wurless Manufacturing as a 'cutter', cutting back pockets for the pants they produced. Charlie took a job as a gate guard, work he was well suited for. Ninety percent of the time he sat in a chair and napped leaving his seat occasionally to check the paper work of incoming trucks. Henry knew he'd be broke soon if he didn't find employment and he knew he wouldn't be able to ask either one of them for money. Charlie controlled their money and even Erica had to beg for any part of her paycheck. He didn't think Harvey would know of any work but he asked him anyway.

"They always need help at the sale barn. It's just two days a week though."

"How many hours a day?"

"You can go to work at noon and work till two or three in the morning. I think they pay a dollar an hour."

Henry did some quick math in his head. "That's fourteen dollars a night."

"They pay at the end of the night too."

"Why don't you go to work with me?"

"I don't like gettin' kicked. You ever been kicked? I don't mean in a fight or nothin' like that. You ever been kicked by a horse or worse yet by a goddamn mule? Well I can tell you it hurts like hell and gettin' kicked is part of the job."

"I didn't think nothing could hurt you."

"A goddamn mule can. It's not too bad on Wednesdays. That's when they have the cattle auction. A cow will kick you but it won't go out of its way to. On Thursday they sell mules and horses and those ignorant sons-of-bitches like to kick. You ever been to a horse and mule sale?"

"No."

"So you don't know how they work?"

"Well I'm not totally ignorant. I know they run the animals into a ring and folks bid on 'em. It's just I never worked at nothin' but haulin' hay or pullin' cotton or mendin' fences."

"Well, the animals at a sale are given a number and that number is glued on their ass right above the tail. When someone pays for what they bought they're given a receipt with the number of the cow or horse or mule. Then when they're ready to load up they bring the receipt out to the holding pens and someone has to go in the pens and find that number and bring the animal out to it's new owner."

"That don't seem too hard."

Harvey laughed. "If you really want the job then I'll introduce you to Eddy Carpenter. Him and his brother own the sale barn."

Eddy Carpenter hired Henry on the spot and told him to report to work Wednesday at noon. The job was all Harvey said it would be. The majority of the day he worked opening and closing gates and penning the animals as they were sold. Later toward the end of the sale he was assigned to locating the animals and leading them out to their new owners. The cattle sale was easy enough. He had his feet stepped on a few times but he wasn't kicked. The horse and mule sale was different though. By the middle of the evening the pens became crowded with as many as twenty to thirty animals to a pen. Henry learned to climb to the top rail and locate the number before entering the pen. It seemed to him that every animal he wanted was always in the middle of the herd. He would ease into the pen with the cotton lead rope and try to work his way to the animal's neck while avoiding the rear end of the other mules and horses. Once he reached the neck he'd slip the lead rope on and work his way back to the gate watching for any cocked rear legs that might be in the way. Once outside he'd hand the animal over and after the new owner placed his own lead rope or halter on he'd remove his rope and search out another number. The first night he worked the horse and mule sale he was kicked in the hip. He was still limping at school the next morning when Principal Morgan called him into his office.

"Henry I'm concerned about your attendance. You've come to school a half day for the past two days. I've heard that you're working and I respect that. We have several students who work and their families need the income. But they have jobs that doesn't interfere with their education. I commend you for wanting to work but you're missing nearly half your Science, English and Math classes. I'm sure you could find another job that won't interfere with your schooling."

"I like my job and I'm keeping up with my homework."

"But you can't keep up if you're not here."

"If I start failing I'll quit the job."

"I can't make you quit but I wish you would. I've talked to your teachers and in the short time you've been here you've made an impression. Your English teacher, Mrs. Jenkins, tells me she's never seen you take a book home. You're a bright boy Henry, you may even be brilliant, but you'll never reach your potential if you're only here half the time."

"I need the work sir."

Principal Morgan leaned back in his chair and sighed. "If you like I'll ask around about another job for you. Maybe sack-ing groceries or working at a service station after school. Something that won't interfere with your attendance."

"Thank you sir but I like the job I've got."

Principal Morgan sighed again.

"May I leave now sir?" Henry asked.

"Go on."

When Henry wasn't working or in school he was with Harvey Pike. The girls liked Harvey and the boys respected him. But Harvey hated working and Henry paid for everything including beer, cigarettes, gas and an occasional hamburger. Still Henry considered Harvey's company worth it. He taught Henry how to drive his pick-up and showed him the parts (usually rigged with baling wire) to jiggle when the motor wouldn't start. After he was sure Henry could keep the truck on the road he would let Henry drive while he crawled in the back with a girl. Henry would adjust the rear view mirror and watch Harvey and the girl make out in the pick-up bed as he drove the dirt roads around Mayetta.

Henry was working the sale barn the night before Thanksgiving. This would be the only night he'd work that week since the horse and mule auction would be postponed until the following week due to the holiday. The night was bitterly cold and Henry was hunkered over a fire built in an old oil drum. He had the wool lined denim jacket pulled up over his neck trying to cover his ears and he didn't notice the cowboy until the man spoke.

"You look cold." The man wasn't much bigger than him and had the bluest eyes Henry had ever seen.

"I'm freezing my balls off sir." Henry assumed he was here to pick up some animals he'd purchased. "I'll need to see a receipt."

"I just came out for some air."

"You picked a good night. There's plenty of it. Did I mention I'm freezing my balls off?"

The cowboy grinned and pulled a pack of Lucky Strikes from his coat pocket. He lit a cigarette and offered it to Henry. Henry accepted the cigarette and thanked him.

The cowboy extended his hand. "I'm Billy Moore."

"I'm Henry Ridge. I've never seen you here before."

"I'm just visiting my folks for a few days."

Billy pulled a flask from his back pocket and untwisted the top. He took a drink and offered it to Henry. Henry took a drink and the liquid burned all the way to his stomach. His eyes watered and his nose ran and he felt warm all over.

"What the hell is that?" Henry gasped.

"Jim Beam whiskey. Ain't it sweet?'

A gray-haired overweight rancher left the auction barn and walked toward the pair. The man handed a receipt to Billy and said he'd be back in a few minutes. Billy handed the receipt to Henry and asked if he needed any help.

"No thanks. The cows are fairly easy. It's those goddamn horses and mules I have a problem with."

Henry found the four numbers on the receipt and a few minutes later turned the cattle over to their new owner then returned to the drum fire. Billy wasn't there and Henry assumed he'd went back inside. A moment later he saw him walking up with an extra hat in his hand.

"See if this will fit you," he said, handing the hat to Henry.

"I can't take your hat," Henry told him.

"Why? I can't wear but one at a time. You'd be doing me a favor. It'd be one less thing I'll have to tote. Besides that it'll keep your head warm."

Henry placed the hat on his head. It was too big. He removed the hat and offered it back to Billy.

"It's too big," Henry said, "but thanks anyway."

"It's not too big. It just needs a little sizing. I'll be right back. I got some sizing in my truck."

Henry placed the hat back on his head and hunkered over the fire. A few minutes later Billy returned with a strip of leather. He removed the hat from Henry's head and placed the strip inside the hat's sweat band and gave it back to him. Henry put the hat on and the hat fit perfectly.

"If you'll hang around till I get paid I'll pay you for it."

"Don't insult me. The hat's a gift. Just give me your word you'll take care of it. It's a sacrilege to mistreat a Stetson."

"Maybe I shouldn't work in it."

"That would be a sacrilege. Stetsons are made to work in. Just brush it now and then and never lay it on a bed. It's bad luck. I have to go now. My folks go to bed early and if I stay out too late I'll have to wake them up to get in. Good luck cowboy."

The gray, three inch brim Stetson had a pinched crown and was well worn. Brown sweat stains discolored the hat around the hat band but Henry thought it was the prettiest hat in the world. He wore the hat to school the next day. He liked the way it looked and couldn't understand why everybody wouldn't want to wear one. Most of the older men in the area wore a hat or a baseball cap but none of the students did. Henry expected to be teased but no one but Harvey seemed to notice.

Henry worked two days a week, from noon until early morning, Wednesday and Thursday and kept his school average at a high 'C'. What money he made he spent on gas, cigarettes and beer. At home he came and went as he pleased using the tree and the window more than he used the front door. He knew

he'd have to buy new clothes for the next school year in addition
to his school supplies. By the end of spring Henry was already
looking for a summer job.

Henry had met several local ranchers at the auction barn
and had given them the impression that he knew more about
horses than he actually knew. The first week in June a local
rancher offered Henry twenty-five dollars to ride a horse an hour
or so each day for a week. The following Thursday he wanted
Henry to ride the horse from the pasture on the southeast side
of town to the auction barn. He told Henry the horse had been
'green broke' and was ready to ride. Henry didn't know what
'green broke' meant but he assumed that broke was broke. He'd
never ridden a horse before but he'd seen others ride and it didn't
look too difficult. He accepted the job.

Henry waited until Saturday morning before walking to
the five acre lot where the horse was penned. The lot was less
than a block from Wurless Manufacturing and Henry could
see the guard shack where Charlie sat and napped five days a
week. He'd been given a key to a shed on the lot that contained
a saddle, blanket, bridle, halter, lead rope and a grooming box
containing a curry comb and a bristle brush. Henry planned
to catch the horse with the lead rope, lead it back to the shed,
saddle it and ride around the lot for thirty minutes or so then
unsaddle the horse and walk home.

After chasing the horse for nearly an hour Henry was ex-
hausted. He hadn't been able to get close enough to throw a rock
at the animal much less put a lead rope around it's neck. He
leaned against the fence post and lit a cigarette. He'd noticed a
small crowd of children gathered near the fence earlier. Now the
crowd was considerably larger. "Damn," Henry thought, "these
kids think I'm more entertaining than Saturday morning car-
toons."

Henry smoked his cigarette and stared at the horse across the lot. He had no idea how to catch the animal by himself and he hated the thought of being seen as a neighborhood clown. He was beginning to regret taking the job when a brown Chevrolet pick-up pulled to the side of the road several feet in front of the crowd and a man climbed out. Henry didn't recognize him but he knew he was too small to be the owner of the horse, Mr. Middlecalf. The man climbed through the fence and walked toward Henry. Henry recognized the man then as the cowboy who'd given him his hat last winter, Billy Moore.

"Hi cowboy remember me?"

"Every time I put my hat on Billy. What are you doing out here?"

"My folks live a few blocks over. I wanted to see what was drawing a crowd."

"I told Mr. Middlecalf I'd ride his horse a few minutes every day for a week. I'm beginning to think it might take that long just to catch him."

"You mind if I try?"

"Be my guest."

Billy took the lead rope and wrapped it around his shoulder and under his arm then started across the lot toward the horse. The horse watched and as Billy neared him he tried to run past him. The cowboy cut him off and the horse tried to bolt in the opposite direction. Billy cut him off and eased nearer talking in a low voice. Every time the animal tried to bolt Billy blocked his way. Soon he was rubbing the animal's nose and slipping the lead rope around his neck. He led the horse back to the shed and Henry met him with the bridle. Henry placed the bridle over the horse's head and tried to force him to accept the bit.

"You'll never get it on like that," Billy told him.

"Why?"

"You're putting it on upside down. Here let me show you."

Billy turned the bridle over and slipped the bit into the animal's mouth then slid the bridle over the head and buckled the small neck strap.

"You ever saddle a horse?" Billy asked.

"No, but how hard can it be?"

"Some people might say that about bridles."

Billy entered the small shed and came back out with the grooming box. He removed the bristle brush and started brushing the animal's back.

"Before you do anything else make sure you brush him good. A horse likes to roll around a lot and they pick up burrs or even small rocks. You put a saddle on a rock and you can rub a sore on him. You put a saddle on a burr and you won't stay in the saddle long. Always take the time to brush him first and brush him good."

Billy carried the grooming box into the shed and returned with the saddle blanket. He laid it upside down across the animals back and checked for any foreign objects. He then turned it over and adjusted it on the horse, pulling it forward slightly. Next he checked the saddle and placed it over the blanket. He tightened the front cinch securely then fastened the girth leaving it loose around the horse's flank.

"He looks kinda skittish," Billy told him. "I'll ride him first if you like."

"Thanks anyway but I took this job."

Billy held the horse by the bit as Henry climbed into the saddle. The horse jerked his head and did a nervous little 'dance'.

"Keep his head up. Grab those reins in your right hand and take up the slack. Not too much. If he drops his head he might try to buck. You want to keep his head up and still give him enough slack where you're not fightin' him. Pull your hand up to chest level and hold those reins tight."

Billy turned loose of the bridle and Henry nudged the horse in the flank with the heels of his boots. The horse took three steps and jerked his head down. Henry lost the reins and the horse lowered his head and began bucking throwing Henry several feet over his head. He landed on his back and felt every bone in his body rattle. Even with the loud buzzing in his ears he could hear the crowd at the fence laughing and he had a feeling that Billy was probably laughing too. He was right. Billy walked over grinning from ear to ear.

"A couple more shows like that and you'll be more popular with these kids than Elmer Fudd. You have to keep her head up cowboy."

Billy climbed on the horse and turned toward the center of the lot. The horse didn't fight or buck or so much as snort. "He makes it look so damn easy," Henry thought. After several turns around the lot he dismounted and handed the reins to Henry.

Henry mounted the horse again and held the reins tight near his chest. The horse walked a few feet and started jerking his head. Henry gripped the reins tighter and leaned in toward the animal's head. That was all he remembered. One moment he was in the saddle and the next minute he was flat on his back and his face hurt. He could hear the spectators laughing. Billy offered him a hand up.

"You oughta charge admission Henry. You'd make a lot more money than you would cowboying. This crowd loves you and I swear the crowd is gettin' bigger."

"What the hell happened?"

"You leaned in too close. He threw his head back and caught you in the face."

"I think he broke my nose."

Billy tilted Henry's head up and studied his nose.

"I think you're right. But it looks like you've broke this nose before. It kinda tilts to the right a little. Here let me help you up. We'll smoke a cigarette and study the situation."

"Ain't nothin' to study. I been here a damn hour and ain't rode nothin' yet. My nose hurts, my back aches, the folks are lined up laughin' at me and I got a feelin' I could turn out to be cheap labor."

"What made you take this job?"

"I needed the money and it sounded so simple. Just ride this knothead an hour or so a day then ride him to the sale barn Thursday."

"This horse can hurt you. Especially when you don't know what you're doing."

"I'll be the laughing stock of the neighborhood." Henry finished his cigarette and ground it out under his boot. "Ain't but one way to do this."

Henry took the reins and climbed back into the saddle again while Billy held the horse steady.

"Hold the reins tight and keep his head up cowboy."

The horse fought the reins humping its back several times. At one point he managed to lower his head enough to buck but Henry held on and soon was circling the lot at a slow trot. After a few minutes he dismounted near the shed.

"You did good cowboy," Billy told him.

"Piece of cake."

"You do know that you'll probably have to do this every time you ride him? It'll take time before all the buck is out of him."

"I don't guess you'd wanna hang around a few days and help me. I'd split the money with you."

"I'm leaving for Arizona. You'll do all right. Just remember what you learned this mornin'. Good luck cowboy."

"Thanks for helpin' me."

Henry sat on the ground near the shed and stared at the sleeve he was holding. A long scratch ran from the top of his shoulder to his elbow. He didn't notice Billy until he was only a few feet away. He hadn't noticed the crowd either. He'd gotten to the lot shortly after daylight and there hadn't been a soul in sight. Now nearly a dozen people lined the fence near the road.

"I didn't expect you," Henry told him.

"I thought I'd drive by on my way out of town. What happened?"

"The bastard throwed me into the fence and before you say anything I want you to know I kept his head up."

"He bucked you off?"

"Yes."

"And you kept his head up?"

"Yes."

"I'd like to have seen that. That's a pretty good scratch you got. That rusty barbed wire can give you an infection or worse. When's the last time you had a tetanus shot?"

"Never had one but I ain't worried about no shot. I just hate that I ruined a good shirt."

Henry stood up and brushed the dirt from his clothing. "I guess it's time to entertain the crowd."

He mounted the horse and turned toward the center of the lot. The animal made several attempts to buck but Henry didn't allow it. He trotted the horse around the field for several minutes then dismounted.

"I need to hit the road," Billy told him. "I just wanted to stop and tell you good-bye."

"Thanks for everything. I couldn't have done this without you. I hope I see you again sometime."

"I'm sure we'll meet again cowboy."

Henry rode the horse Monday and Tuesday both morning and evening. The crowd had grown smaller and only a handful of kids lined the fence. Mr. Middlecalf showed up at the lot Tuesday evening.

"I watched you ride for the past few minutes. I think we're ready for Thursday. Can you ride him to the sale barn?"

"I'm sure I can."

"He's never been rode around traffic so watch yourself on the highway."

"I'll take the back streets as much as I can."

"I'll see you Thursday at noon then."

Henry rode the horse Wednesday morning then worked the cattle sale from noon until two a.m. Thursday at noon he saddled the horse and started toward the auction barn. He hoped to avoid as much traffic as possible by staying on the residential streets until he was across the highway from the auction barn. The first car that passed Henry sent the horse into a fit. Henry dismounted and walked the animal to the highway then mounted and rode across the road when the traffic cleared. He tied the horse outside near the pens and sat on a fence railing to wait for Mr. Middlecalf. A few minutes later a smiling Mr. Middlecalf approached Henry.

"How'd he ride?"

"Gentle as a kitten."

"No trouble with traffic?"

"No trouble at all."

Mr. Middlecalf pulled a ten and a twenty from his wallet and gave them to Henry.

"I'll have to get change sir."

"You keep it. That five's a little extra for keeping your word. If you're interested I may have more work for you."

"Yes sir I'm interested."

"Good. We'll talk later."

The last trailer was loaded at three a.m. and the auction closed. Henry walked home with forty-five dollars in his pocket and climbed the tree to his bedroom. He woke up six hours later and ate a bowl of pinto beans for breakfast.

Harvey came by at noon and the two friends rode to the malt shop. Henry bought them both Dr. Peppers and a few minutes later Mike Bryce walked in and sat down by Harvey.

"We still keeping that date?" Mike asked Harvey.

"What date?" Henry wanted to know.

"The one we made last night while you were playing with the cows."

"Who in their right mind would be seen with you two?" Henry teased.

"Kate Willingham and Ricki Fox," Mike answered.

"You two must be hard up," Henry said, "or maybe your names just finally came up. I hear they've fucked everybody else."

"Pussy's pussy and I don't recall you gettin' any," Mike told him.

"We're gonna take them to the lake and fuck 'em and then see if they'll switch partners. Too bad you'd rather work than fuck. Might be able to talk them into fuckin' all three of us. I know Kate thinks you're cute especially since you started looking like Pecos Bill."

"You can tell me about it tomorrow. I've got to get to work."

"Loan me five dollars and we'll drive you," Harvey said.

"Why don't I just give you five dollars then I won't have to sit up at night wondering when you're going to pay me back?"

The horse and mule auction was over shortly after midnight and Henry was on his way home before one a.m. He met Harvey and Mike at noon the following day at the Malt Shop. He knew Harvey would expect him to ask about their dates the previous evening.

"Hi fellows, anyone want a Dr. Pepper?" Henry asked. Both accepted.

"How was work?" Harvey asked. "Meet any nice mares?"

"Easy night. Didn't get kicked once."

No one spoke for several seconds. Henry knew both friends were wanting to talk about their 'conquest' the night before. He deliberately avoided the subject. Finally Harvey couldn't contain himself any longer.

"Goddamn it Henry! Don't you want to know how it was?"

"How what was?"

"Kate and Ricki."

Henry started laughing. "I knew you'd have to tell me. I've been here less than five minutes and you're about to choke on it. Okay then, how was it?"

"Fuck you hare-lip," Harvey teased. "I'm not telling you now."

"I'll buy the beer after school."

Harvey and Mike started trying to talk at the same time.

"Kate's tits are real," Harvey said.

"So are Ricki's," Mike added.

"We took them both out to the lake," Harvey continued, "and fucked them."

"We switched partners," Mike giggled, "right there on the same blanket. They both got some good pussy."

"I never heard of any bad," Henry said. "Like they say 'even the worse is still good'."

"We're taking them out again Saturday," Mike told him.

"I guess I'd better hide my money," Henry thought to himself.

Henry woke to the sound of his mother calling him from the bottom of the stairs. He looked at the clock and saw it was barely eight a.m. He had stayed out the night before until three a.m. drinking and riding around with Harvey and he wanted to sleep this Saturday morning.

"Henry, Mr. Middlecalf wants to talk to you."

Henry dressed and went downstairs. Mr. Middlecalf stood just inside the door holding his hat in his hand.

"Are you free today Henry?"

"Yes sir." Henry was thinking he might have another horse he wanted rode.

"I've got some fence that needs a little fixin'. You can take your time with it and I'll pay you two dollars an hour. You still interested?"

"Yes sir."

"I've got my truck out here if you're ready to go."

"Just let me brush my teeth and get my hat."

Mr. Middlecalf drove Henry to a pasture a few miles out of town that Harvey and he passed almost daily. He unloaded six fence posts, a posthole digger, a hammer and a small bag of fencing nails. He'd told Henry to take his time but had also hinted that he expected the job to be done around noon. Digging six postholes and setting them in a four hour period meant he'd have little time to take any break. When Mr. Middlecalf returned Henry was setting the last post. The rancher sat in the cab of his pick-up and watched until Henry had finished then walked over and grabbed each post and tried to shake it. The posts held firm.

"You did a good job." Mr. Middlecalf pulled a ten dollar bill from his wallet and gave it to Henry then drove him home.

Henry had only five hours of sleep the night before and had planned to go back to bed. Before he could take his boots off he heard Harvey's pick-up pull up in front of the house. He walked back downstairs and met him at the door.

"Did ole man Middlecalf pay you?"

"How did you know I was working for Mr. Middlecalf?"

"I'm psychic."

"Then you know the answer."

"How much money we got?"

"We ain't got none and I don't have a whole lot. Why?"

"We need gas."

"You always need gas."

"This is different though. Kate wants to go riding with us."

"I thought you and Mike had dates with her and Ricki tonight."

"We do but her parents are gone and she wanted me to pick her up early."

"Well you don't need me. You just need gas money."

"I wanted you to drive."

"I don't feel like watching you fuck today."

"I thought you liked watching."

"Watching you fuck is a lot like going to the malt shop when you're hungry and watching somebody else eat."

"Maybe she'll fuck us both. She fucked me and Mike last night."

"Let me get my hat."

Kate was waiting on her porch when Harvey pulled into her driveway. She climbed in and straddled the gear shift, her right leg brushing against Henry's left and her left leg rubbing against Harvey's right. Her dress rode half way up her thighs and Henry tried hard not to stare. Harvey drove to the first dirt road and stopped the pick-up.

"I want you to drive," Harvey told Henry, "while Kate and I get in back."

Harvey climbed out and Kate followed swinging her legs over the gear shift and giving Henry a peek at her white panties. Harvey helped Kate into the back of the truck while Henry slid over behind the wheel and adjusted the mirror. Henry waited until he'd shifted into third gear before trying to watch the couple in the mirror. Kate lay with her head facing the cab of the truck and her dress pulled up above her waist. Harvey pulled her panties off and Kate turned around and saw Henry watching in the mirror. She pulled her dress down and Henry heard her yell. "I'm not fucking you with him watching." Harvey banged on the window and motioned Henry to pull over.

"She won't fuck with you watching."

"It didn't bother her last night with Mike watching."

"She says that was different, it was dark."

"I guess this means she's not planning on fucking me this afternoon?"

"Probably not."

"Tell her I'll close my eyes and we'll pretend it's dark. What do you want me to do, take a walk?"

"If you don't mind. I promise I'll hurry."

"I should have gone back to bed."

Henry walked several yards from the truck and sat down behind a small bush where he could watch the pick-up. A few minutes later he saw Harvey and Kate climb out of the back and into the cab. Harvey wanted the three of them to ride around together but Henry insisted on going home. Henry agreed to meet them later at the malt shop.

Henry arrived at the malt shop an hour before dark. Harvey and Mike sat in a booth with a tanned, stocky older boy Henry didn't know. Harvey introduced them.

"Henry this is Calvin. He's from Hardmor. Calvin this is Henry."

Calvin was staring at Henry and grinning. Henry had a feeling there was going to be trouble. He was right.

"Where's your dates?" Henry asked.

"We're not picking them up till dark," Mike answered.

"Hey hare-lip what happened?" Calvin sneered. "Your mama fuck a rabbit?"

Harvey stood up and hit Calvin hard on the shoulder with the palm of both hands shoving him onto the floor. "You fuck with Henry you fuck with me!"

Calvin stood up and raised both his hands palm out. "Hey man I don't want no trouble with you. We're friends."

Harvey sat down and Calvin half sat and half stood across the table from him. Henry sat down next to Harvey.

"Why are you pickin' a fight with me?" Henry asked. "I don't even know you."

"I don't have to know you to know I don't like you."

"Why don't you like me?"

"I just don't."

Harvey stood up and slapped Calvin hard on the left cheek staggering him. Calvin backed up and raised his hands.

"I don't want no trouble with you Harvey."

"Leave Henry alone!"

"You can't fight all his fights Harvey."

"No, but I can hurt you bad enough to make sure you'll never fight him. It might be hard to hit someone with both arms broke."

Henry had enough. He knew Calvin was right and sooner or later Harvey wouldn't be around but Calvin would.

"Fuck it Harvey I'll fight him. I'll have to sooner or later and I'd just as soon get it over with so I can start healin' up."

"I'm not fightin' you with Harvey around," Calvin said.

"Harvey won't interfere."

"I give you my word," Harvey told Calvin.

"Fuck your word! I'll just wait till you ain't around."

"You'll fight him now!" Harvey yelled. "You started this shit and if you don't fight now I swear I'll drag you outside and whip your ass on Main Street!"

"You promise you won't interfere?"

"I promise," Harvey answered.

"You ready to go out back?" Henry asked.

The four boys walked toward the back door and Henry noticed that everyone in the malt shop was following. On the way out he asked Harvey if he intended to keep his promise.

"Of course not."

"Good. Everything he does to me you do to him twice."

"You sound like you've already lost."

"I just got a feeling, Harvey, that Calvin does this a lot."

A dozen or so people formed a circle around the fighters. Henry studied his opponent. He was heavier and taller and had a longer reach. He figured the only chance he had was to get in close enough to kick his legs out from under him or if the chance presented itself maybe get him with a kick to the groin area.

Calvin fought like a pro. He danced to Henry's left stepping in every few seconds and hitting Henry on both sides of his head. Henry kicked and Calvin turned taking it in the hip. He hit him with ease and soon Henry lost count of the times he'd been knocked down. His nose, barely healed from the encounter with the horse's head, was swollen and bloody and one eye was nearly swollen shut. Henry stood up, looking for an opening while Harvey repeated, "Stay down Henry. You've already proven yourself." Henry wouldn't quit. Soon others were telling him to stay down but Henry climbed back to his feet. Calvin grinned and danced hitting Henry over and over knocking him down again and again. Finally Harvey yelled, "Goddamn it that's enough!" Calvin turned his head toward Harvey taking his eyes off Henry. That was all Henry needed. He stepped in and kicked twice catching Calvin hard in the groin. Calvin grabbed his crotch and sank to his knees holding one hand out. "Enough," he moaned. "I've had enough."

"Now you got him Henry," Harvey said. "Kick his fuckin' head off!"

Henry didn't want to kick anyone. The fight was over and he was happy to leave it at that. He didn't want to take a chance on getting hit again.

"Fuck it!" Harvey yelled. "If you won't I will!" He walked over and hit Calvin in the mouth. Calvin lay on his side, one hand holding his mouth and the other holding his testicles. Harvey tried to talk Henry into cleaning up in the bathroom and hanging around the malt shop while he and Mike went after the girls but Henry wanted to go home.

"But you're a winner," Harvey told him. "You have to celebrate."

"I don't feel like a winner. Besides you'll have a crowd in your pick-up with the four of ya'll. I'm going home."

"We'll drive you then."

"No thanks. I'll walk."

Henry woke up sore and stiff. His head and teeth hurt. He walked downstairs to the bathroom and studied his face in the mirror. His nose and lips were swollen and both eyes were purple. He rubbed his head and found several knots. When he came out of the bathroom Charlie was standing there grinning.

"Hey rabbit shit I heard you had a fight last night. I heard you won but I don't believe that shit. I think you got the piss beat out of you."

"Fuck you," Henry said, then climbed the stairs to his room. He heard Charlie laughing behind him and he intended to stay in his room until he healed some but a few minutes later he heard Harvey's pick-up pull into the driveway. Henry went downstairs and met him on the front porch. Harvey had another boy with him Henry didn't know.

"Henry this is Clyde, Calvin's younger brother."

Henry stepped back a couple of feet not knowing what to expect. Clyde threw up his hands and told Henry "I didn't come here to fight. I heard about those feet of yours."

"Clyde doesn't like his brother much," Harvey told him.

"I think he's chicken shit," Clyde said. "I'm glad you whipped his ass."

"If Harvey hadn't hit him you'd never know he'd been in a fight," Henry said.

"Harvey tore up his mouth alright but that ain't the reason he's walking funny," Clyde said. "He woke up the house screaming when he took a piss. He's pissin' blood."

Henry tried smiling but his face hurt too much. The idea that Calvin hurt more than he did made him feel better.

CHAPTER SIX

Henry worked three days clearing a five acre plot of land for Mr. Middlecalf for two dollars an hour. Summer was nearly over and he used the money to buy new clothes and a new pair of boots. Two weeks before school was to resume Harvey came by and told Henry he had a job for them. Henry didn't believe it. In the two years he'd known Harvey he'd never seen him work at anything but avoiding work.

"You mean you found a job for me," Henry told him, "and you want half the money."

"That hurt Henry." Harvey was trying to appear insulted and both were trying not to laugh. "It's easy money. Just unload a boxcar and we'll make fifty dollars. With the two of us working it won't take two hours to do it. I figure we could start early in the morning and be done before it gets too hot."

The August sun was hot. There was an old saying about southern Oklahoma and how it got so hot in August that the Red River would back up under a bridge to get in the shade. It was over a hundred degrees outside and at least ten degrees hotter in the boxcar. They'd been working half a day unloading hundred pound sacks of feed and they still had a half a boxcar to go. Harvey wasn't used to work and spent more time sitting and complaining than he did working. By noon he was ready to leave the job even though he knew they wouldn't be paid for the work they'd already done if the job wasn't finished. Henry looked at it differently. He wasn't working a half a day for nothing.

"You know, Harvey, Mike Bryce is a real nice fellow."

"Mike's all right."

"The next time you have a money making opportunity like this you oughta ask Mike if he wants in on it. You wouldn't hurt my feelings none."

"Why don't we just say fuck it and leave? We can always get money somewhere."

"I ain't working half a day for nothin'. I'm broke and won't have no money till the sale Wednesday. So why don't you get that large ass up and help?"

The two friends finished the job nearly eight hours after they started. Harvey was so tired he asked Henry to drive.

"Where to?"

"My house."

"What about getting paid?"

"The ole man has to call him. Him and Dad are friends. That's how I got offered the job."

"Why don't I just go home and clean up and come by when you get paid and we'll go out?"

"I'm not going out," Harvey said.

"Why not?"

"I'm too fuckin' tired."

Henry didn't see Harvey again for four days until he showed up at the sale barn Wednesday afternoon with his half of the money from the boxcar job. He told Henry he was tired of Kate and wanted to take Ricki out. He planned on asking his dad for the use of his car Saturday and wanted Henry and Kate to double date with him and Ricki.

"Kate may not want to date me," Henry told him.

"Kate will date anyone before she'll sit home on a Saturday night. Just let me handle it."

"Thanks a lot for the compliment."

They arrived at Kate's shortly before dark and she ran out

to the car and around to Henry's side. Henry opened the door and climbed out to let her in. Harvey's Dodge pick-up didn't have a radio but his dad's car did. Henry had been listening to WBAP, a country music station that broadcast from Fort Worth, Texas. Kate switched to KOMA, a rock station out of Oklahoma City.

"Ricki's already waiting for us," she told Harvey. A few minutes later they stopped in front of Ricki's and Kate nudged Henry in the side.

"Let's get in the back," she said.

Henry did as he was told. A few seconds later Ricki came out and climbed in beside Harvey.

"I'm hungry," Ricki said.

"Me too," Kate agreed.

"We'll get some burgers and go to the lake," Harvey offered. Henry instinctively reached for his money.

Harvey stopped at the bar and bought two six-packs of beer then took the long way around Lake Milor while they drank and ate their burgers. An hour after dark they pulled into an empty campsite and parked. Harvey and Ricki wasted no time. Ricki undid his pants while Harvey fumbled with her blouse. A moment later they sank out of sight onto the front seat of the car and the car started shaking. Henry had ran his hand under Kate's skirt and felt her legs part. He pulled her panties off while she unbuttoned her blouse. Then she pulled away, ducked her head and threw up in Henry's lap. Henry heard Harvey laughing and saw his head appear over the back seat long enough to see what had happened. He ducked back down and laughed harder. Then Ricki's head appeared over the seat for a few seconds before dropping back out of sight. Kate threw up again in the floorboard and Harvey and Ricki laughed like two hyenas while Kate lay her head on Henry's shoulder and apologized to him, telling him that had never happened to her before. Harvey and Ricki continued having sex while Henry sat in the back seat with a sick girl and a lap full of puke.

Henry's sophomore year had been the best. He was elected Vice President of the local chapter of the Future Farmers of America and had been nominated for the most popular boy in class although he lost. He continued working at the sale barn twice a week and helped Mr. Middlecalf on several weekends with branding, castrating and vaccinating his cattle. He let his hair grow over his ears and below his shirt collar and always wore a hat, boots, and during cooler weather, a leather vest. He seldom saw his mother and saw Charlie even less. If he came in early and the lights were on and Charlie's pick-up was parked in front he'd climb the tree and enter his bedroom through the window. If Charlie's pick-up was gone he'd use the front door and sit with his mother and watch television. The length of the visit was determined by how drunk she was. When he woke in the morning his mother and Charlie would already be at the Factory: Erica on the assembly line and Charlie napping in the guard shack.

The March morning was cool and Henry wore a denim jacket over his vest. Harvey and Mike were already at Duffy's when Henry arrived. Harvey saw the skunk first and pointed it out. The skunk was walking near the west entrance of the building. Harvey ran around to the back of Duffy's Store and returned a moment later with a cardboard box.

"Let's catch him!" Harvey said and started off at a trot toward the skunk.

"I'll head him off!" Henry volunteered.

"I'm not going," Mike said.

Henry got in front of the skunk and watched Harvey come up from behind with the box. Henry threw his hands up and shouted trying to turn the skunk toward Harvey. The skunk squatted and raised its tail. Both boys pedaled several feet backward to avoid the animal's spray. The skunk then lowered its tail and turned toward Harvey at a run. Harvey threw the box at the skunk and ran in the opposite direction. Then the skunk turned toward Duffy's store. Harvey picked up the box and the chase resumed. They kept the skunk in the middle of the school yard chasing him around in circles. The skunk stopped several more times to raise its tail. Finally Harvey managed to get the box over the skunk and trap him. He flipped the box over with the skunk inside and the skunk sprayed Harvey in the face. Harvey screamed and grabbed his eyes but the skunk was trapped. After a couple of minutes Harvey's eyesight returned.

"Okay, we got him. Now what do we do with him?" Henry asked.

"Let's turn it loose in the school."

Henry pointed to Duffy's. A crowd had gathered to watch the chase. "Half the school's seen us. We'll never get away with it."

"So what? The most they'll do is kick us out for three days."

"If we're gonna do it," Henry said, "we'd better do it quick. School'll be startin' in a few minutes."

Harvey grabbed a flap on the side of the box and Henry grabbed the opposite flap. They carried the skunk to the west entrance, opened the door and set the skunk free in the school hallway. They returned to Duffy's and the other students backed away from them. Henry thought he'd avoided the skunk's spray but several students told him otherwise. Everyone commented on how they'd enjoyed the show and promised they wouldn't be the ones to tell the teachers. 'They won't have to' Henry thought, 'the smell will give us away'.

The students started drifting across the street to the school.

"You ready to get this over with?" Harvey asked.

"I'm not going to school smelling like a skunk."

Henry heard the school bell ring and they watched the last of the students enter the building. A moment later students came running out the same door. Mike was laughing as he crossed the street and joined Henry and Harvey on the porch.

"What happened?" Henry asked.

Mike couldn't quit laughing. He'd get two or three words out then stop. The other students still kept their distance.

"That skunk ran into Mrs. Beaman's room," Mike finally told them. "When she sat down and slid her chair up she kicked the thing and it sprayed the shit out of her. She screamed and took off for the door and the skunk ran out behind her spraying everything in sight and took off down the hall."

Another student, Don Colder, walked over to Mike and told him school had been cancelled for the day. "That skunk ran into the auditorium and Principal Morgan sent the janitor in with a rifle to find it.

Henry walked into Duffy's and bought half a dozen large cans of tomato juice. Harvey was curious.

"I read where tomato juice is about the only thing that will take that smell out of clothes. I'm going home and take a shower and soak my clothes in it," Henry told him.

Henry woke early the next morning and lay in bed until he heard Charlie's pick-up leave. He could still smell the skunk on him so he doused himself liberally with Charlie's Aqua Velva after shave lotion. He walked out to the back porch where the clothes he'd worn yesterday lay soaking in tomato juice in a galvanized tub. He wrung the clothes out then placed them in the washer, added soap and set the washing temperature on cold. He smelled his hat and it stank so he sprinkled it with Aqua Velva, pulled it down on his head and walked to school. Harvey, Mike and several others were waiting on Duffy's porch.

"Goddamn!" Harvey said. "You smell like a whorehouse! I think that skunk smelled better!"

"Speaking of skunks," Henry said, "has anyone heard what happened to him?"

"The janitor found him hiding in a duct and shot him," Mike answered.

"Do they know who put him in the school?"

"They'd have to live on another planet not to know."

Henry and Harvey waited until nearly time for the bell before crossing the street to the school. Henry had barely sat down in his seat when the assistant principal called him out of class. Harvey was already sitting in the waiting area outside the principal's office. He looked up at Henry and tried to smile. Henry sat down in a chair next to him and waited. After several long minutes Principal Morgan opened the door to his office and called them inside. Less than five minutes later they were leaving the school. They'd been suspended for the rest of the school year and would have to repeat the year. Harvey would stay a junior and Henry would remain a sophomore.

"The ole man will kill me when he hears about this," Harvey said. "Shit will he be mad!"

"Maybe he won't find out for a while."

"Fuck, he knows everyone on the school board. He'll know before dinner. My ass is grass and daddy's the lawn mower." Harvey paused for a minute, then smiled and asked, "We got any money?"

"Some. Why?"

"Let's get some beer and go to the lake."

The friends stayed at the lake drinking beer and talking until late afternoon. Harvey drove Henry home and the two sat in the pick-up for over an hour. Harvey didn't want to go home and face his dad.

"What are you going to tell your folks?" Harvey asked.

"Nothin'."

"Won't they say something?"

"Are you kidding? Charlie doesn't give a rat's ass what I do as long as it don't cost him any money and Mama's always drunk. I use that tree more than I use the door and I could go a month without seeing either of them."

"I wish my parents were like that."

"No you don't."

Harvey showed up at the sale barn Wednesday, a few minutes after Henry started work. Henry asked him how it went at home.

"Just like I thought. The ole man threw a fit. He says I'm going to finish school if I have to stay there till I'm an old man. Wants me to work with him on that new interstate highway they're building. He thinks he can talk to the draft board and keep me out of the army until I graduate. Did your folks say anything to you?"

"I haven't seen them."

"What are you doing tomorrow?"

"What I do every Thursday, working."

"Why don't you take off? I got something I want us to do."

"I need the money. I'll go with you Friday."

A truck unloaded a cargo of cattle and Henry's help was needed to pen the animals. "I've got to go to work now. Why don't you come back after the sale starts?"

"I'll try. My ole man's got something he wants me to help him with. I don't know how long it'll take."

Henry didn't see Harvey until the following day. He showed up at the sale barn as Henry and another hand, Deb Malerra, were penning a load of mules. Henry hated the animals. They were old and ornery and would kick you or bite a chunk out of you if you gave them the chance. Representatives of the dog food companies would buy most if not all of the mules and soon they'd be turned into cans of ALPO. Henry had little sympathy for them.

"What are you up to?" Henry asked.

"Just came by to see you. You still going with me tomorrow?"

"Sure. Where are we going?"

"It's a surprise."

"I don't know why you won't tell me. I've already said I'd go."

"I want to surprise you. I'll pick you up about eight."

"No you won't. I plan on sleeping longer than that. I may not get out of here before two or three in the morning. Why don't you pick me up around noon?"

"Okay, noon it is. I'll see you around noon."

Henry heard the honking and opened his eyes. The clock read eight thirty-five and he hadn't had more than five hours sleep. He ignored the honking and after a couple of minutes the noise ceased. He'd almost drifted back to sleep when he heard the knocking at his window. Harvey had climbed the tree to Henry's bedroom and was sitting on a branch trying to open the locked window.

"Come on Henry! Open the window! I'm going to sit here till you do!"

Henry raised his head. "What if I open the window and shove your big ass out of that tree?"

"You better hope the fall kills me!"

Henry climbed out of bed and unlocked the window. Harvey raised it far enough to crawl into the room.

"Goddamn it Harvey! I said noon! Eight thirty ain't noon."

"It's noon somewhere in the world. Get your pants on and let's go."

"I smell like a horse. Give me time to take a spit bath and brush my teeth."

Fifteen minutes later they were on the highway headed south toward Texas.

"Okay Harvey, where are we going? I'm in the truck. I promise I won't jump, so tell me where we're going."

"Now hear me out before you say anything. I've put a lot of thought into this. You know I'll turn eighteen in a couple of months and I'll have to sign up for the draft. I can either go in the Army or work for my ole man on that fuckin' highway until school starts and hope he keeps me out of the Army while I repeat my junior year and after I graduate the Army will probably draft me anyways or..."

"Or what?"

"If we have to go in the military we oughta pick the one we want. In the Army you have to crawl around in a lot of mud and then they ship your ass to a jungle somewhere. In the Navy you stay clean, you sleep in a bed and you get to travel around the world."

"So you want to join the Navy?"

"I thought we'd check it out."

"I keep hearing a lot of 'wees'. Let me tell you again, I ain't joinin' nothin'. Besides that I couldn't join if I wanted to. I'm too young."

"You'll be seventeen in August and you could get your mother's permission and we could join together. I called two days ago and they told me we could join on the 'buddy system' and they guaranteed we'd stay together and have the time of our life."

"I won't be seventeen for four more months Harvey."

"I'll wait on you. I'll work with my ole man until you're ready."

"That one day unloading that boxcar nearly killed you. You tellin' me you're gonna work on that hot highway in the summer heat for four months?"

"Sure. I can do it if I know you'll enlist with me."

"I'm not joining the Navy. I'll go with you while you join and I'll be there waving a flag when you climb aboard the bus but I'm not ready for some silly looking uniform."

"The Navy's got the best looking uniforms of the lot."

"You must like bell bottoms and dinky little hats."

"The women like 'em too."

"Then let the women wear 'em!"

"Henry, listen to me. When you turn eighteen the Army will get you and ship your ass to Bumfuck, Asia or somewhere like that. This way we can see Rome and Spain and places like that together."

"How do you know we'll get to see Rome and Spain?"

"The recruiter told me we would. He said if we passed the test we could have our choice of where we're stationed. I told him we wanted a ship together and he said that'd be no problem."

"And you believe him?"

"Why would he lie?"

"Maybe to get you to enlist."

Harvey pulled up to a two story brown building at the north end of Main Street in Grainsley and parked. Henry saw a large sign above the door that read U.S. Navy Recruiter. A poster in the window showed a trim, young man in a tailored Navy uniform with the wind blowing the flap on his jumper and a ship in the background. Beneath the picture were the words 'Join the Navy and See the World'.

"It looks like a box of Cracker Jacks," Henry said. "I wonder if there's a toy surprise inside?"

Inside the building a Chief Petty Officer and a First Class Petty Officer sat at a desk drinking coffee.

"Can I help you men?" The older officer asked.

"We want to join the Navy," Harvey blurted out.

"Excuse me," Henry said, "But 'we' don't want to join nothin'. Harvey wants to join and I just came to keep him company."

"I'm the one that called a couple of days ago," Harvey said.

"I'm Chief Petty Officer Shula and this is First Class Gunner's Mate Jenkins. I'll need your full names and your date of birth."

"My name's Harvey Pike and this is Henry Ridge."

"I'm not here to join," Henry repeated.

"How old are you?" Jenkins asked.

"I'll be eighteen in June," Harvey answered.

"What about you?" Jenkins nodded toward Henry.

"It doesn't matter how old I am. I'm not here to join no Navy."

"He'll be seventeen in August," Harvey said.

"Well we can give you the tests now," Shula said, "and see how you do. You'll need your parent's permission to enlist since you're under eighteen. But if you pass the entrance exam we can hold your test until you have their permission or until you turn eighteen."

Shula pulled two entrance exams from the drawer in the desk and handed one to Harvey and one to Henry. Henry laid his down on the desk in front of Shula.

"I told you I just came to keep him company."

"This test will by no means obligate you in any way," Jenkins told him.

"Come on Henry take the test with me," Harvey pleaded.

Henry agreed to take the test and the two were led into a small room at the back of the building. The room contained several school desks and Harvey was told to sit in one on the far right side of the room and Henry was seated in a desk on the far left side of the room. The door was left open.

The test consisted of a hundred questions. Henry filled in his name, dropping the McCarthy, and date of birth. He thought the test was easy and finished in a few minutes. He looked across the room and saw Harvey still answering questions. He left the room and returned to the front. Two metal folding chairs had been set up in front of the desk while they were taking the test. He gave the test to the Gunner's Mate.

"Finished already?" Jenkins asked. "Have a seat while I grade this."

Jenkins placed another paper over the finished test and picked up a pencil. After several seconds he scribbled a number across the top and lay the paper down.

"You made a ninety-six Henry. That's one of the highest scores we've had since I've been here. I'll keep your test on file and if you decide to enlist at a later date we can process you immediately."

Harvey came out of the back room and gave his test to

Chief Shula who gave the test to First Class Jenkins. Jenkins graded the test, scribbled a score across the top and lay the test down.

"Henry would you mind stepping outside for a moment?" Jenkins asked.

Henry walked outside and lit a cigarette. A couple of minutes later Harvey came out. He appeared to be upset and went straight to the pick-up. Harvey didn't say a word until they were nearly half way home. Henry knew he was mad and didn't press him to talk.

"Chicken shit Navy!" Harvey said, then hit the steering wheel with the palm of his hand. Henry didn't say a word. "A bunch of fuckin' faggots wearing faggot uniforms!"

Henry couldn't keep quiet any longer. "Let me guess. You failed the test didn't you?"

"Fuck you Henry!"

Henry stayed quiet the rest of the trip home. Harvey dropped him off and left, squealing tires and throwing dirt and gravel everywhere. Henry climbed the tree to his room then wrote a poem about the Navy and Harvey Pike.

Henry didn't see Harvey again until the following morning. Mr. Middlecalf had called Friday evening and asked Henry to ride a green broke mare an hour or so each day then ride her to the auction Thursday. The horse was penned in the same lot as the horse he'd ridden over a year earlier. Again Henry drew a small crowd but now he was more comfortable with horses and could catch and ride the animal easily without the fear of being thrown. He enjoyed the work and had decided he wanted to be a cowboy. He'd been riding for several minutes when he saw Harvey pull up and park near the fence. Harvey climbed through the fence and walked toward the shed. Henry rode over, dismounted and waited.

"You still playing cowboy?" Harvey teased. Henry was glad he appeared to be in a good mood.

"You still mad?"

"Never was mad. Not at you anyways. When you gonna be done here?"

"Give me another half hour."

"Okay. I'll be back in half an hour."

Harvey was late. Henry had ridden the horse another half hour then unsaddled and rubbed the animal down. He'd been sitting by the shed for several minutes waiting and was ready to walk home when he saw Harvey pull up. Henry walked out to the truck and climbed in.

"I about gave up on you."

Harvey said nothing and Henry didn't push it. They drove to the bar and Harvey went to the back door. A moment later an older man came out carrying a six pack of beer and handed it to Harvey.

"Where'd you get money?" Henry asked.

"My ole man." Harvey drove toward Lake Milor while Henry pried the top off two bottles of beer and gave one to Harvey. "You know why my ole man gave me money?"

Henry didn't answer.

"Because the bastard threw me out of the house."

"Why? Because you got kicked out of school?"

"That's part of it but mostly because I don't want to work on that fuckin' highway all summer. We got in a fight about it last night and he jumped my ass again this morning. He threw some money at me and told me to get my sorry ass out!"

"How much?"

"Fifty dollars."

"Why don't we use some of that money and party this

weekend? Then Monday you can tell him you decided to take the job."

"I ain't working with my ole man! Goddamn it! I have to live with him and that's enough!"

"You got any idea of what you're gonna do?"

"I ain't gonna worry about it right now."

"You can stay with me if you don't mind climbin' a tree."

"I know I can but I don't know what I want to do. Right now I just want another beer."

Harvey dropped him off shortly after midnight. Henry invited him in again to spend the night but Harvey refused.

"Where you goin' then?"

"I guess I'll go home and tell my ole man I'll take that shitty job."

"Come by when you get up and around."

Henry didn't hear from Harvey the next day and he was hesitant to call not knowing the circumstances in the Pike home. When he still hadn't heard from Harvey by Monday he assumed he'd gone to work with his dad at the highway department. When he still hadn't heard from his friend Tuesday evening he decided to call Harvey at home. Harvey's mother answered.

"Harvey joined the Army, Henry. He left this morning for basic training. He wanted me to tell you good-bye for him and ask you if you'd drive his pick-up while he's gone to keep the battery built up."

"He didn't call me or nothin'," Henry told her.

Mrs. Pike was silent.

"Thank you ma'am. Tell Harvey when you talk to him that I'll come by a couple of times a week and start his truck."

"He wanted you to keep it and drive it while he's gone. He trusts you Henry."

"Then I'll come over and get it."

Henry walked to the Pike house and knocked on the door. Mrs. Pike answered and he could see her eyes were red and swollen from crying. She gave Henry the keys and he thanked her then started the truck and drove home.

TOMMY L. CRELIA

CHAPTER SEVEN

Six weeks later Henry had his driver's license and although he was no longer in school he decided to attend the graduation and the Sophomore prom. Mike wanted him to ask Kate out and double date with him and Ricki. The prom was held at the Lake Milor Resort and after attending for little more than an hour the four drove to a secluded campsite and had sex. Two hours later Mike dropped Henry and Kate at Henry's house and Henry drove Kate home in Harvey's pick-up. Later that evening he saw Mike and Ricki again and Mike told Henry he had to take his parent's car home but Ricki wasn't ready to go home. He asked Henry to take her off his hands and Henry agreed to. He drove Ricki to the same campsite they'd been at earlier and had sex with her and then drove her home. A few minutes later he was climbing the tree to his bedroom. A letter from Harvey was lying on the bed. In the letter Harvey told Henry he'd be finishing boot camp in a couple of weeks and wanted Henry to pick him up at the Grainsley bus station when he came home. He didn't know the exact date but would write or call as soon as he knew. He closed the letter by telling Henry he hated the Army.

Henry came home from the sale barn a week later and found a note on his bed from his mother telling him Harvey had called and would be arriving in Grainsley on the Monday afternoon bus. Henry was at the bus station before noon. He'd decided he'd rather be early as to chance being late. He passed the time smoking and sipping a Dr. Pepper until the bus arrived. Harvey was the last one off, stepping from the bus in his green uniform with his cap tilted slightly back on his head, his tie loose and the top button of his shirt undone. He smiled when he saw Henry and then did something Henry never expected; he hugged him. Henry was embarrassed but tried not to let it show.

"Damn it's good to see you!" Harvey said.

Henry looked down toward Harvey's belt. "What are you looking at?" Harvey asked.

"The way you hugged me I thought you might have a hard on."

Harvey laughed, then asked, "where's my pick-up?"

"Around the corner."

Harvey picked up his duffel bag and followed Henry. Henry climbed in behind the wheel and Harvey threw his duffel bag in back then walked around to the driver's side window.

"Do you mind if I drive my truck?"

"I don't know," Henry teased. "You sure you remember how to drive?"

Harvey opened the driver's side door and Henry slid over. They stopped at a river bar and Harvey bought a six pack of beer. Henry opened two bottles and passed him one.

"You look sharp in that uniform," Henry teased. "I think green's your color."

"Fuck you Henry."

"Is that anyway to talk to someone you were hugging just a few minutes ago?"

"Fuck you Henry."

"So tell me, you planning on making a career out of the Army?"

"Fuck you Henry."

Henry thought the first thing Harvey would want to do was change from his uniform into civilian clothes but Harvey drove straight through Mayetta and took the road to Lake Milor.

They finished the six pack and Harvey purchased another at a bait shop near the lake. He then drove east following the lake road as it circled the lake and turned north bringing them into Hardmor.

"I'm hungry," Harvey said. "How about you?"

Henry hadn't eaten since his usual bologna sandwich breakfast and it was now nearly six in the evening. "I could eat something."

Harvey pulled into a stall at the A&W Drive-in. They both ordered a burger basket and as they waited for their food Harvey struck up a conversation with two young, blonde females in a car in the stall on Harvey's left. Harvey left the pick-up and was leaning in the window on the passenger side of the car talking to the girls when Henry saw three men leave a car two stalls over. One man approached Harvey as his companions stood near the hood of the car and watched. The stranger took his wallet out and flashed a military I.D. at Harvey.

"I'm Lieutenant Stevens soldier. Straighten up that uniform!"

Harvey straightened up and grinned down at the Patton wannabe. "Why don't you go fuck yourself?"

"Soldier I'm giving you a direct order! Button that..." That's as far as the stranger got. Harvey hit him once knocking the man unconscious. He started toward the man's companions and both men threw up their hands and declared their neutrality. Henry was out of the truck trying to get Harvey back in before the police came. Harvey wanted to whip the other two and wait around for the man to come to so he could hit him again. Henry talked him back into the truck and they left without their meal. Henry was still hungry but Harvey said he'd lost his appetite. They followed the lake road to Mayetta and stopped at the malt shop. Ricki came in a few minutes later and

Harvey talked her into going to the lake. He wanted Henry to come but Henry declined and asked Harvey to drop him off at his house. Charlie's pick-up was gone and Henry entered the house through the front door. Erica lay on the couch passed out. Henry covered his mother with a blanket then made a bologna sandwich and carried it to his room. He didn't see Harvey again until Wednesday at the sale barn. He'd changed into jeans and a tee shirt and he had Ricki with him.

"I'm not going to be home but a few more days. I sure wish you'd take off and go with us. I've got money and what's mine is yours. Ricki wants to go skinny dippin' and we thought we'd ask Kate to go too."

"I've already started working."

"So what. Run your finger down your throat and puke. Tell 'em you got sick and have to leave. They won't know the difference. Just think about it Henry. Two naked bodies. Two young naked bodies. Two more than willing, horny, naked bodies."

Henry wanted to go. His heart, soul and loins wanted to go. But Henry knew he'd be leaving Mr. Carpenter in a bind if he did.

"I can't Harvey. You know that."

Henry didn't see Harvey again for two days. Friday morning he heard Harvey blowing his horn in front of his house shortly after eight a.m. Henry pulled on his pants and walked outside.

"You just hate to see me sleep don't you? I bet you get some perverted thrill out of waking me up."

"I don't have but eight more days of leave left. I just thought you might want to do something."

"I want to sleep."

"You can sleep on the way."

"Where we going?"

"Hell, I don't know."

The two friends spent the next few days drinking and riding around Lake Milor. Harvey insisted on paying for everything but soon ran low on money so Henry paid after that. They picked Kate and Ricki up on Monday and the four spent the day skinny dipping and having sex. After dropping the girls off they bought another six pack and rode around. Harvey would have to leave on Thursday for Fort Bragg and he made it clear to Henry he didn't want to go.

"I should have gone to Canada."

"You wouldn't like Canada."

"How do you know? You've never been there."

"No, but I know it gets cold and I know you don't like the cold."

"It gets cold here too."

"Not like Canada."

"I should have gone somewhere."

"It's nice to see you're adjusting to the Army life," Henry teased.

"I'll never get used to the Army."

The two friends were silent for several moments then out of the blue Harvey asked Henry if he liked Harvey's pick-up.

"Sure I like it. It's a good truck. Why?"

"Wanna buy it?"

"Harvey I'd love to buy your truck but I'm broke…or damn close to it."

"You can pay me ten dollars a week or ten dollars a month or whatever. I paid eighty dollars for it and I'll let you have it for the same price. Pay what you can when you can. Just take the money by the house and give it to my mama."

"You love this old truck Harvey. You sure you want to sell it? You won't be in the Army forever and you'll need something to drive when you're home."

"I know you'll take care of it. Besides this way when I'm home you'll have to chauffeur me."

Henry agreed to buy the truck and the next morning they took the title to a Notary Public. Henry now had ten days to come up with the money needed to pay for a title transfer and license plates.

Wednesday Henry worked the cattle auction and told Mr. Carpenter that he'd be late for the horse auction the following day. He explained that he'd be driving Harvey to the bus station in Grainsley where Harvey would catch a bus to Fort Bragg.

Henry drove and Harvey stared at the scenery all the way to Grainsley. "I never thought I'd miss this place," he said. "But damn it Henry, I do."

Standing at the bus waiting to board Henry had the feeling his big friend was close to crying. Finally Harvey climbed aboard the bus, taking a window seat and craning his neck around to watch Henry until the bus disappeared around the corner.

Henry needed more money than he was making at the auction barn. He'd already made up his mind not to return to school in September but he still needed new clothes and a new hat and he had a pick-up to pay for in addition to the cost of the title transfer and tags. With his own transportation he found work easily and took a job with a local rancher, Pat Barber, hauling hay. He continued working the auction barn Wednesday and Thursday evenings and soon had his truck tagged and paid for.

After the hay hauling job ended he took a job with another local rancher, Max Armstrong, helping with the fall round-up. The cattle were brought in from the pastures and held in an area where they could be branded and vaccinated and the bull calves could be castrated and de-horned. Henry's job was to keep the branding iron hot and help hold the animals down. The job paid a dollar an hour and Henry spent his seventeenth birthday holding the ass end of a cow.

Henry went shopping and bought new boots and a new Stetson and had the hat shaped exactly like the one Billy Moore had given him. He still wore the old hat for working and running around, saving the new hat for special occasions. He had money left but he was now working only at the auction barn. He was restless and he knew he'd never be allowed to continue living at home if he wasn't in school or working full time. The only reason he'd been able to live under the same roof with Charlie as long as he had was because they seldom saw one another. Henry was working the Thursday horse auction and still thinking about his future. Mr. Carpenter had assigned Henry temporarily to work the pen leading to the ring inside where the horses were bid on. Henry made up his mind to pursue the cowboy life and was trying to decide where he'd like to work. He knew employment would be easier to find in the west but he'd also heard Florida had a lot of ranches. He was standing on the fence railing herding a two year old gelding toward the front of the pen and daydreaming of riding a horse on the sandy beaches of Florida when the gelding kicked him between the eyes. When Henry came to a doctor was standing over him shining a flashlight in his eyes. He didn't know whose bed he was in or how he got the gown on he was wearing. All he knew was he had one hell of a headache.

The doctor held up three fingers and asked Henry how many he saw. Henry told him three and the doctor held up a pencil and asked Henry if he knew what it was. Henry told him and the doctor announced he'd be all right but he wanted to keep him a few days for observation. He told Henry he'd look in on him later and when Henry complained about having a headache the doctor told a nurse to bring him some aspirin. After the doctor left Erica came in and sat down near the bed. Henry saw Charlie standing near the door.

"You had us worried," Erica told him.

"I don't remember what happened."

"You got kicked in the head. Mr. Carpenter said they found you against the fence with your eyes rolled back in your head. How do you feel?"

"Like I got kicked in the head by a horse."

"Mr. Carpenter said not to worry about nothing. He is taking care of the doctoring bill and he said to tell you that you still have a job when you're ready to come back."

"Screw that job." Henry had decided he didn't want to be a cowboy.

Henry left the Mayetta Health Clinic Monday morning and walked to the auction barn. His pick-up was still parked in front and Henry started the truck and drove home. He suffered from severe headaches that came on suddenly and lasted anywhere from a few minutes to a couple of hours. After two weeks the headaches ceased.

Henry no longer dreamed of riding the range and he had no desire to return to the sale barn. Even if he did return to his old job he knew he'd need to work more than two nights a week to continue living at home. He got along with Charlie by simply avoiding him as much as possible and never asking for anything. Without attending school or working full time it would only be a matter of time until there was trouble. Neither Charlie nor Erica had ever mentioned Henry's expulsion.

Henry was sitting on the sofa with his mother drinking a beer and watching The Jimmy Dean Show. Charlie had gone hunting and Henry had come downstairs after he left. School had started a week earlier and Henry had been staying home until right before Charlie and Erica got off work then driving out to the lake and sitting until after dark. He faced the same dilemma Harvey had faced a few months earlier. He wasn't in school, had no steady job and would turn eighteen in less than a year. Even with a job he was sure to be drafted into the Army.

"Mama I want to ask you a question and I want you to think about it before you answer."

"What's the question?"

"If I decided to join the Navy would you sign the papers giving your permission?"

"Why would you want to join the Navy? You're still in school and you'll be a senior next year. Why not wait until after you graduate?"

Henry knew then that his mother knew nothing about his expulsion from school and he knew he had to tell her. "Harvey and I were kicked out of school."

Erica chewed her bottom lip and stared at the floor. "They didn't kick you out for good did they? You could talk to the principal and..."

"I don't wanna go back."

Erica started crying and Henry moved closer. He draped his arm around her shoulder and tried to hug her. She shrugged him off. "I just wanted you to have more than I've had Henry. I didn't finish school and I'll never have nothing. I wanted you to be able to have a nice house and all the things I'll never have. Please Henry...please go back to school. If you won't do it for me then do it for yourself."

"I'll think about it if you'll think about signing the papers."

Erica dropped her head and cried harder. "You've already made up your mind haven't you? You're just like your damn daddy! He never had nothing and you'll never have nothing!"

"I'm not like Charlie and he ain't my daddy!"

Erica wiped her eyes. "Just go away Henry. Go away. I don't want to talk about this right now."

The next morning Henry went downstairs before Charlie and his mother left for work. He couldn't remember the last time the three of them had been together. Charlie wore a crooked grin and Erica's eyes were red and puffy.

"So you want to be a swabby," Charlie sneered. "What makes you think they'd have you?"

"I've already taken the test."

"You're a sneaky bastard ain't you? Get your sorry ass kicked out of school and sneak around without telling anyone. Now we find out you snuck down to the Navy recruiter. Where else have you been sneaking off to?" Charlie quit talking and glared at Henry.

"Are you hungry?" Erica asked Henry.

"Let the Navy feed him!" Charlie yelled.

"I'm not hungry," Henry answered. "I'll eat later."

"He wants to wait until we're gone so he can sneak around and eat. Ain't that right rabbit shit?"

"Whatever you say," Henry answered. Charlie no longer scared him. He now looked at Charlie as an irritant.

"You got a smart mouth on you shit for brains. You still ain't too old to get your sorry ass whipped."

"I think I'll walk outside," Henry said.

"You don't go anywhere till I say so! Do you understand?"

Henry walked past him and into the living room. Charlie came out of his chair and grabbed Henry by the back of his hair, jerking him backward. Henry picked up an empty beer bottle sitting near a lamp and came around with it catching Charlie between the eyes. The blow cut the skin above the bridge of Charlie's nose and blood appeared. Charlie went to his knees and Henry drew his arm back intending to bring the bottle down on Charlie's head.

"No Henry don't!" Erica screamed. "You'll kill him!"

"I intend to!" Henry yelled.

"No Henry no! I'll sign the papers! I'll sign the papers!"

Charlie was struggling to get to his feet and mumbling, "I'll kill him. I'll kill him."

"Leave Henry," Erica begged. "Please leave."

Henry drove out to Lake Milor and sat until midmorning. He drove back home and saw that the house was empty. He went to his room and gathered his clothes and personal items and threw them on the bed. He gathered the four corners of the top blanket together, threw the load over his shoulder and walked outside to his truck. He dumped the load in the passenger side of the truck and drove toward Joneston.

Henry had intended to stop at his grandmother's but changed his mind and drove instead to the Navy recruiter in Grainsley and picked up the papers he needed his mother to sign. He drove by the Holton farm on the way back and found a pair of strangers living there. The couple told Henry they had no idea where the previous owners had moved to. He drove to Joneston and asked his grandmother if she knew.

"They've been gone a few months now Henry. I heard stories that the boys got in trouble in Texas and they had to leave to keep them from going to jail. That's all I know about it."

"Do you know where they moved to?"

"I heard they bought a place in eastern Oklahoma."

"I was hoping to see them before I left."

"Where are you going?"

Henry told her about getting expelled, taking the Navy entrance test with Harvey and the fight with Charlie.

"Why don't you stay with me and Levi and finish school in Joneston? You know everyone here."

"I'll think about it," Henry lied. "If I decide to join will you drive me into Grainsley? I'd like to leave my pick-up here. I don't trust Charlie with it. All you'll have to do is start it once a week to keep the battery up."

"You know you can leave your truck here but please Henry think about what you're doing. I don't think you're going to like the military."

"If I don't join I'll be drafted later. This way I'm going ahead and getting it over with. Besides the recruiter says I can get my high school diploma in the Navy."

Henry left Lahoma's shortly after three that afternoon. Charlie and Erica would be leaving work at four and Henry planned to be in front of the house when they arrived home. He hoped he could get his mother to sign the papers without any more trouble from Charlie. Sheriff Lydel Wesley pulled him over two blocks from the house. Henry climbed out of the pick-up and leaned against the door.

"Charlie came in this morning with a complaint about you Henry. He claims you tried to kill him with a beer bottle. He said you hit him when he wasn't looking."

"You wanna hear my side of it?"

"That's why I pulled you over."

Henry told the sheriff what happened. "I believe you Henry. I always knew you and Charlie would get into it some day. I hate to see you leave school but maybe the Navy wouldn't be such a bad idea. I'll follow you home and we'll see if we can't settle this mess."

Charlie's pick-up was parked in front and Charlie came out of the house and went straight for Henry as soon as he stepped out of the truck. The sheriff parked behind Henry and intercepted Charlie half way across the yard.

"I want that bastard arrested," Charlie screamed.

"Hold on Charlie," the sheriff said. "I'm not arresting anybody."

"That piece of shit tried to kill me!"

"From what I heard he had good reason. Now will you please ask Erica to come out here? I want to talk to her."

Charlie opened the front door and yelled, "Get out here!"

A moment later Erica came out the front door and walked over to where Henry and the sheriff stood. The sheriff removed his hat. "I'm sorry to bother you Erica but Henry told me what happened here this..."

"He's a lying piece of shit!" Charlie yelled.

"Shut up Charlie," the sheriff ordered. "Erica, Henry tells me you've agreed to let him join the Navy. Is that right?"

"I want that hare-lip bastard in jail!" Charlie demanded.

"Charlie if you open your mouth one more time I'll take you to jail. Do you understand me?"

Charlie didn't answer.

"There's no need in anyone going to jail," the sheriff continued. "Erica if you'll just sign these papers Henry's holding then we'll be on our way."

Erica signed the documents and walked back inside the house without saying a word. Henry thanked the sheriff and drove away leaving the sheriff and Charlie still standing in the yard.

Lahoma drove Henry to the recruiter's office the following morning. Henry signed his enlistment papers and an hour later was kissing a teary-eyed Lahoma good-bye and boarding a bus to Oklahoma City. Three hours later he was at an enlistment center standing in line in his underwear with several dozen recruits. He was given a physical then sworn in with a room full of other enlistees. By late afternoon he was on a shuttle bus to the airport where the group boarded a plane to Chicago. In Chicago they were loaded aboard a shuttle for the railroad station. From there they traveled by train to the Great Lakes Naval Recruiting Station. Riding another shuttle bus past the Naval Station's guard shack and under a sign that read YOU ARE NOW THE PROPERTY OF THE UNITED STATES NAVY Henry's heart sank to his knees. He knew he had made a mistake. Four years seemed like a lifetime and he had three years, eleven months and twenty-nine days to go.

Henry hated boot camp. From the time he arrived he was cursed and insulted constantly. He had to ask permission to eat, sit, stand, piss, shit or talk. Everything was done at double time and every question was answered with SIR, YES SIR. Any infraction brought demerits and demerits meant extra hours of standing and drilling with his 'piece', the military term for the dummy rifle they issued recruits. He lived with his piece. He memorized the identification number of his piece. He took it apart and put it back together so often he could do it in his sleep. He learned to answer to maggot or fuck-up or puke or scum or faggot. He learned how to drop on a dime and do fifty push-ups and he did a lot of push-ups. If he asked permission to piss he did push-ups and still didn't get to piss. If he complained about being cold after jumping in freezing water on a thirty degree day he did push-ups. During drills he learned to do push-ups while holding his piece with all his weight on his knuckles.

He endured classes that could put a wall painting to sleep. He fought to stay awake through hours of instruction on military rules and regulations. And they cut his hair so short he resembled a hare-lipped cue ball with ears.

Henry had been given three choices of duty when he enlisted. His first choice had been for sea duty, his second for journalism school and his third, made jokingly, for Officers Candidate School. During his eighth week of boot camp he was given his assignment. He was being sent to study radar. Henry had joined the Navy to see the world and all he'd be seeing was Georgia.

Ten weeks after arriving Henry graduated from boot camp. He was now a seaman apprentice with a heavy duffel bag he had to tote more than a mile to the train depot. He had sixty-four dollars, a ticket to Mayetta and two weeks to report to the Naval Air Station at Brunswick, Georgia.

Henry left Great Lakes on Monday afternoon and arrived in Mayetta Wednesday evening.

His grandmother met him at the depot and once Henry's duffel bag was in the trunk of her car she asked him if he'd like to stay with her and his Great-Uncle Levi during his leave. The question was asked out of courtesy. They both knew Charlie would not allow Henry to stay with him and Erica.

"How do you like the Navy?" Lahoma asked. They were on the highway heading toward Joneston.

"I don't like it. They're sending me to Georgia."

"Maybe it won't be so bad. I've heard that Georgia's a pretty state."

"I've talked to fellows that come from Georgia and even they don't want to be stationed there."

"You won't be there forever."

"I'll be there a year. A year in the military is like a dog year. One year equals seven."

"You should have thought of that before you joined."

Henry changed clothes while Lahoma cooked him a supper of bacon, eggs and biscuits with peach preserves. After he'd

125

eaten and washed his dishes he walked into her sewing room and sat down. "I haven't seen Uncle Levi, is he working late?"

"Levi doesn't work. He has emphysema and draws a government check. He leaves early and spends all his time in a domino parlor in Grainsley drinking and gambling and smoking three packs of cigarettes a day."

"Grandmother while I was at boot camp I met guys I envied. These guys had parents who really cared about them. Some of the parents even drove up to watch 'em graduate. And I met other guys who didn't have no one and I thought of you and Uncle Levi and how lucky I am. I just wanted you to know that."

"I love you too Henry." He saw her wipe a tear from the corner of her eye. "And Levi and your mother love you too. Now why don't you run along and let me work?"

The mid November day had been in the low sixties but Henry knew the temperature would drop to near freezing after dark. He decided to carry the warmest coat he had, his Navy peacoat. He placed his Stetson on his head and the hat fell down to his ears. With his hair cut off the hat was a half size too big. He found a strip of leather and lined the inside of the sweat band until the Stetson fit snug again.

Henry drove to the Mayetta auction barn and hung around nearly two hours visiting. He called Ricki's home from a payphone and her mother told him she was with friends. He called Kate's home and no one answered. He bought a six pack and drove out to Lake Milor, checking the 'make out' areas and looking for any car he might recognize. He drove by the boat loading ramp, a popular party spot, and was ready to give it up and return to his grandmother's when he noticed three males standing near the ramp. Driving closer he saw Mike Bryce's father's car. He parked his pick-up and walked over. He recognized one of the boys as a senior from Mayetta High, Harold Brady. The other boy he didn't know.

"Goddamn look who's here," Mike said. "I figured you'd be sailing the seas somewhere."

"Not hardly. What are you and Harold doing?"

"We've been having a gang bang. Ricki's in the back seat of the car drunk and buck naked. You know Harold and this other fellow's Kevin Pierce. Kevin's from Hardmor. You oughta go out to the car and get some. We've all had a turn."

Henry walked over to the car and looked in the back. Ricki lay naked, passed out and covered in her own waste. He walked back to the ramp.

"Damn Henry that was quick," Mike remarked.

"I decided I wasn't that horny."

"Why not? It's good pussy."

"She's covered in shit."

"You're kidding me!" Mike yelled.

Mike walked over to the car and Henry heard him a moment later. "It's all over the car! My daddy's car! Goddamn! The old man will kill me!"

Everyone laughed but Mike. "You have to help me clean up the car," He pleaded. "I think I'm gonna be sick."

Kevin decided it was time for him to go home. Mike cussed him as he drove away.

"I think it's about time for me to get back to Joneston," Henry teased. "Do you need a ride Harold?"

"Nobody's going nowhere," Mike said. "You got to help me get her out of the car. We'll throw her in the lake then clean up the back seat."

Mike pulled Ricki from the car and tried to steady her while doing his best not to look in her direction or get any of her waste on him. Henry and Harold helped walk her to the lake and Mike shoved her in. She screamed when she hit the water and crawled back to shore. Mike threw her in again. Ricki sobered up enough to cuss Mike and throw a rock at his head. She stood on the shore naked and shivering. Henry removed his peacoat and placed it over her shoulders.

"Bitch you shit in my car!" Mike yelled at her.

Ricki looked ready to cry. "I didn't mean to," she whimpered. Mike dug several empty beer bottles from a trash drum and began filling them with lake water to wash out the back seat of the car. Henry and Harold held Ricki upright and helped her dress. Harold was putting one of her legs in her panties when she passed gas.

"If you shit on me Ricki I swear I'll throw you in that lake and leave you till you drown," he warned. Ricki started crying. After she was dressed Henry placed her in his pick-up.

Henry drove Ricki home. Halfway to Mayetta she slid over and placed her hand on his thigh. "I don't have to be home for a while."

Henry knew he couldn't look at Ricki naked without having a mental image of her covered in shit. He wasn't sure he'd ever be able to look at any naked female again without having a mental image of Ricki covered in shit.

Henry woke early and found his grandmother already working. She quit sewing when he came into the room and asked if he was ready for breakfast.

"Do you have anything special planned for today?" She asked him.

"I thought I might ride into Grainsley and hunt Uncle Levi down. Why?"

"I think your mother's coming by later."

"That means Charlie's coming too. Grandmother I promise I won't start any trouble and if my being here will cause trouble then I'll leave."

"Don't be silly Henry. She's coming to see you. And don't worry about Charlie. Even that idiot knows a mother has the right to see her son. There won't be any trouble in my house. I promise you that."

Lahoma walked into the kitchen and turned a burner on under a black, cast iron skillet then dropped a half dozen slices of bacon in it. After turning on the oven and adjusting the temperature she sat down at the kitchen table and motioned for Henry to sit with her.

"You told me last night how you envied those boys at boot camp because their parents seemed to care about them. Well your mother cares about you."

"Grandmother I've heard stories all my life about how she'd leave me in the back seat of a car outside some damn bar while she shopped for a man. The only person my mother cares about is Charlie."

"Your mother is weak. She can't help it. It's just the way she is. But she's always loved you Henry. Don't judge your mother. You have no right to. And don't ever think for a minute that she doesn't love and worry about you."

"They'll have to take off work if they're coming before dark and Charlie won't like that."

"Go turn on the T.V. and find us a game show or something. I'll call you when breakfast is ready."

Henry found an old black and white western and was watching the posse ride past the same boulder for the fifth time when Lahoma came in and sat down on the sofa near him. "The biscuits will be done in a few minutes and then we'll eat."

Henry sipped a cup of coffee while they waited. Before the time came to check the biscuits again they heard the front door open and saw Erica enter. Henry heard Charlie's pick-up back out of the driveway and leave.

"Where's Charlie going?" Lahoma asked.

"To a bar I reckon. He said he'd be back later to pick me up."

Henry stood and hugged his mother. Lahoma went to the kitchen and the two were left alone on the sofa. He studied her face and thought she looked ten years older than she did when he left for boot camp. And she looked sad. A permanent sadness that no smile could hide.

"Breakfast is ready," Lahoma announced. The kitchen table was set with three plates but Erica said she wasn't hungry. "Do you have any beer?"

"I think Levi has some in the icebox," Lahoma answered.

Henry and his grandmother ate while Erica sipped a Pearl beer and asked Henry questions about boot camp. After breakfast they continued sitting at the kitchen table making small talk until they heard a horn blow in the driveway. Erica had been there less than an hour.

"That must be Charlie. I guess I'd better go before he gets mad."

CHAPTER EIGHT

Henry boarded a bus for Brunswick, Georgia the following Thursday morning. He arrived at Brunswick Friday evening and took a taxi to the Navel Air Station. He noticed the flag at half mast as they entered the main gate and he asked the driver if he knew who on base had died. The driver told him President Kennedy had been murdered that morning in Texas.

Henry reported to the duty officer and was shown to his barracks where he reported to the barracks officer. He was taken to a cubicle containing four beds and four lockers and told the bottom bunk and the bottom locker near the wall was his. After unpacking his duffel bag and placing the contents neatly in the locker he walked outside to the front of the barracks. He took a seat on a bench and was trying to decide what to do to kill some time when a short, stocky Puerto Rican sat down at the other end of the bench. After a few seconds he leaned toward Henry and extended his hand.

"Hi, I'm Thomas Bottita. My friends call me Tita."

"I'm Henry Ridge. I just got here."

"It looks like we're in the same barracks. Are you upper or lower?"

"I'm on the second floor if that's what you mean. Is there anything to do around here?"

"There's a cantina and a movie theater. There's also an enlisted men's club but you have to be twenty-one to drink anything but soda pop."

"Anything to do in town?"

"Brunswick? Brunswick sucks. The people hate us here. They have dances and things like that open to the public but they don't consider us public. Some of the bars even have signs saying 'no dogs, niggers or G.I.'s' allowed. One man from our barracks was jumped one night and got his jaw broken."

"Where do you go then when you want to leave base?"

"Jacksonville."

Henry liked the Puerto Rican. They talked over cokes and Henry learned Tita was from the Bronx, New York. Later Tita introduced him to the men in Henry's cubicle and any other man they encountered in the barracks. Many of the men were gone for the weekend.

The three men in Henry's cubicle were all New York Italians: Arthur Savetto, Anthony (Tony) Moriella and Robert Pastroni. Tony and Robert seemed friendly enough but Savetto appeared arrogant.

The next morning Tita came by Henry's cubicle and asked him if he wanted to go to breakfast. At the mess table, staring at the powdered eggs he knew he wouldn't be able to eat, he asked Tita the best way to get into town. Tita explained that the shuttle buses ran from the base into town several times a day from eight a.m. to midnight. After midnight you'd have to take a taxi or hitch hike.

"Why do you want to go into town?"

"Just to look around. I'm already tired of this place."

"If you're not going to make a day of it, I'll go with you."

"Just go in, look around and come back," Henry promised.

It didn't take Henry long to get tired of Brunswick. The town boasted a population of fifteen thousand but Henry couldn't figure out where they hid them. The downtown area consisted of an 'easy credit' clothing store next to a bar next to

an 'easy credit' jewelers next to a church next to a bar next to
another clothing store next to another jewelers next to a church
next to a bar etc. etc. They caught the shuttle bus back to the
base early that afternoon.

"When the weather's warmer I'll show you Jekyll Island.
You can lay in the sun and smoke and you don't have to worry
about anyone catching you."

"You mean they got laws here where you can't lay in the sun
and smoke? Now I know you're teasing me."

Tita squinted his eyes and looked at Henry then started
laughing. "You don't know what I'm talking about do you?"

"I thought I did."

The two men returned to the barracks and Tita asked
Henry to follow him to his cubicle. He unlocked his locker
and pulled out a small manila envelope. They then walked to
Henry's cubicle and found Robert lying on his bunk reading an
old copy of For Men Only. Tita invited him to take a walk with
them.

Henry followed the two for several minutes until they were
near the southwest corner of the base. From here you could see
anyone approaching from any direction. Tita ducked behind a
tree and rolled a marijuana cigarette then lit it and passed it to
Robert. Robert took a drag and held the smoke in his lungs
several seconds then passed the joint to Henry. Henry took a
long drag and started coughing. He passed the joint to Tita and
continued to cough.

"What is that shit?" Henry asked. "Johnson grass?"

"It's weed. Pot. Marijuana," Tita answered. "Don't you have
weed in Oklahoma?"

"We have all kinds of weed. I just never heard of anyone
smoking them."

Robert passed the joint to Henry and Henry took a smaller drag. His throat burned and he wanted to cough but he didn't. He passed the joint to Tita. His head was swimming and he couldn't feel his feet. For some reason he thought this was funny. Tita and Robert were watching him and both were grinning. Henry had never felt better in his life.

"Where can I get some of these cigarettes?" He asked.

"You don't call them cigarettes," Tita explained. "They're called joints or reefers."

"I don't care what it's called I want more." Henry started laughing. "I can't feel my feet. I'm walking on air and I'm hungry. Goddamn I could eat the ass end of a goat."

"You need to cool it when we go back," Robert warned. "They'll lock Tita up in a prison then throw him out of the Navy with a bad conduct discharge if they catch him with this shit. You can be high just don't act high."

After a few more passes Tita snubbed the joint out and placed the butt, or 'roach' as he called it, in the manila envelope then placed the envelope back in his sock.

Henry was getting hungrier by the minute. "Let's go eat something."

"You promise you won't act high?" Robert asked.

"I'll try not to."

Henry ate two hamburgers and tried to act straight. The food killed some of his high but he still felt like he was walking on air. They stayed at the table smoking cigarettes and talking. Henry learned that Tita and Robert had been smoking marijuana since before their teens. The marijuana Tita had came from New York and every time he went home he bought more to bring to the base. Henry asked Tita to pick him up some when he returned home and Tita said he would. Later that day the three men took another walk and smoked the 'roach' from the joint they'd started earlier. Henry was still high when they called it a night and turned in.

Tita, Robert and Tony spent the Thanksgiving holiday in New York. Everyone had Thursday, Friday, Saturday and Sunday off, unless you had duty, and everyone stood duty every fourth day. The ones who wanted to go home would find someone to take their duty for a fee, usually fifty dollars. This gave the men who wanted to go home a mini vacation from Wednesday evening to Monday morning. The bus depot in Brunswick ran buses to New York at a charge of ten dollars round trip. By taking the Wednesday night bus the men were able to have Thanksgiving dinner with their families and the men who couldn't go home made a few extra dollars. Henry took Tita's duty and told him to bring him fifty dollars worth of marijuana. Monday morning none of the three were back when Henry left the barracks to report for radar training.

The 'war' building was an easy ten minute walk from the barracks. Henry, not knowing where the building was, had left thirty minutes early. Once there he found a small break room and bought a cup of bad coffee from a vending machine and carried it to a table. Half way through his coffee a tall, lanky man carrying a Hostess cup cake and a small container of milk asked him if anyone was sitting in the chair across from Henry. Henry waited until he was seated then introduced himself.

"I'm Vernon Campbell," the stranger said, "but most folks call me Sippy; short for Mississippi. Where you from Henry?"

"Oklahoma."

"I bet Oklahoma's pretty country but it can't be as pretty as Mississippi."

Henry didn't get to say a half dozen words for the next twenty minutes while Sippy talked about his home state. He'd done the same thing Henry had. He'd joined the Navy to stay out of the Army and all he could think about was going home. He'd just got back that morning from the holiday and he was already counting the days until he could leave again. Finally at a couple of minutes before eight he asked Henry where he had been assigned.

"I'm supposed to report to a Third Class Radar man named Newton."

"I know where he is and if you'll follow me I'll show you. You ever been to Mississippi Henry? You'd like it. I bet you'd like it as much or more than Oklahoma."

They followed the hall until they came to a mock 'war room', Sippy talking all the way about the glories of Mississippi.

"Well, here it is. Newton's that redheaded fellow. If you ain't doin' nothin' later maybe we could get together and chew the fat or somethin'."

Henry lied and told him he'd like that. He liked the man well enough but he had no intention of spending the evening hearing about the wonders of good ole Mississippi.

In the 'war room' Henry was given a set of headphones and a piece of chalk. During the war games the radar operator called out the location of fictitious enemy planes (bogies) and allied planes (caps) every minute. Henry was taught to write their location on a large, clear plastic board that faced the 'war table'. This meant he had to learn to write backwards. He kept up easily at first but as the games continued more bogies and caps were added to the game until Henry was struggling to keep the board current. When they broke for dinner he expected to get a lecture but Newton surprised him and told him he was doing good for his first day.

"I thought I did piss poor," Henry said.

"It's your first day. Everyone does poor on his first day. By the end of the week you'll be writing backwards like a pro."

Henry decided to walk to the cantina and order a hamburger rather than stand in line at the mess hall. Sippy hollered at him as he was leaving the building. "Hold up Okie and I'll walk with you."

"You're welcome to walk with me. Just don't call me Okie. Call me Henry."

"You going to the mess hall Henry?"

"No. I'm on my way to the cantina. You're welcome to join me."

"I'm broke till the first."

"I'll buy you a burger."

"You ever been to Mississippi Henry?"

That afternoon when Henry returned to his cubicle he was relieved to see Robert lying on his bunk. "I was afraid ya'll didn't make it back."

"We just barely did make it in time."

"How was New York?"

"Still the greatest place in the world."

"I met a fellow from Mississippi that might argue that fact with you."

"I'll bet you met Sippy."

"You know him then."

"Everybody on base knows Sippy. That's why everyone avoids him. He's a nice guy but after thirty minutes or so you want to grab him by the throat and choke the Mississippi out of him."

"You must be talking about Sippy." The voice came from behind Henry. "Did you tell him about the time we took Sippy to Jacksonville?" Tita asked Robert

"I've tried to forget it," Robert answered.

"I think we need to take a walk," Tita said.

The three men returned to the same place they'd gone before to smoke. Tita pulled ten small manila envelopes from under his jumper and handed them to Henry.

"They're five dollars apiece and there's enough pot for five joints in each envelope. Now if you get caught with this you didn't get it from me. Understand?"

"I understand. Let's smoke one."

"Do you want me to roll it?" Tita asked.

"I can roll a cigarette," Henry answered. "I oughta be able to roll this."

Tita handed Henry a pack of Top rolling papers. Henry opened an envelope and started trying to pour the weed into a paper like he would with Bull Durham. Tita stopped him.

"You need to clean the seeds out first. If you don't a hot seed will fall out and burn a hole in your clothes." He shook the weed out in the palm of his hand and removed several small black seeds then carefully placed the weed in a paper and rolled it. He lit the joint and passed it to Henry. Henry took a long drag and held the smoke then passed it to Robert. Halfway through the joint Tita put it out and gave the 'roach' to Henry. Henry placed it in the envelope and they returned to the barracks.

"You need to find a good place to hide that," Tita warned.

"You got any ideas?" Henry asked.

Tita looked out in the hall to make sure no one was coming then asked Henry to unlock his locker. He took a pair of dungarees from the bottom shelf and told Henry to hand him the marijuana he wanted to hide. Henry gave him nine of the envelopes keeping the one with the 'roach' in his sock. Tita shoved the envelopes into the back pocket of the pants then refolded them and placed them back on the shelf. Then all three went back to the cantina and ordered hamburgers.

Henry was paid one hundred and sixty-four dollars a month as a seaman apprentice. He was paid twice a month on the first and the fifteenth and after taxes cleared sixty-eight dollars a check. After buying cigarettes, toiletries and other incidentals and paying for his dry cleaning he felt he couldn't afford a night out. He'd been at the base for nearly six weeks. He'd taken Tita's duty over the Christmas holiday and spent Christmas night standing watch in a freezing hangar. Now it was New Year's Eve and he'd been invited to go to Jacksonville with Tita and the others. Tony Moriella owned a ten year old Ford four-door sedan. The rust bucket barely ran but everyone assured Henry it would make the eighty mile trip to Jacksonville. Henry didn't care. He'd have walked if he had to, to get off the base for a while.

Henry was introduced to the world of 'tease'. They took him to a bar where beer was two dollars a bottle and young women danced topless on your table or in your lap as long as you shoved money down their G string. Henry was broke in half an hour and the young blond who had told Henry she was taking him home with her moved on to another table. An hour later they were all broke and on their way back to the base. Henry didn't even have money for cigarettes. Tita introduced him to a base 'loan shark'. He loaned money at fifty percent interest. If you borrowed ten dollars you paid back fifteen. If you borrowed twenty you paid back thirty. Henry borrowed twenty dollars and paid the shark back the next payday. He never borrowed money on the base again. A month later he was moved to a radar scope.

Tita was arrested the first week in May. He'd come by Henry's cubicle the previous evening and asked him to take a walk.

He'd rolled a joint earlier and left his manila envelope hidden in his locker. After snubbing the joint out he placed the 'roach' in the front pocket of his dungarees and they walked back to the barracks. He forgot about the 'roach' and when he took his pants off to go to bed the 'roach' fell out. The duty barracks officer, making his rounds after midnight, found the 'roach' lying on the floor near the corner of Tita's bunk where he hung his pants. A few minutes after seven a.m. two large men wearing suits and ties came into the barracks and led Tita out in handcuffs. They searched his locker and found four manila envelopes of marijuana. Henry never saw his friend again and he couldn't find anyone who knew what had happened to him. Several of the men in the barracks that smoked marijuana panicked and threw their supply away. Henry wrapped his in an old tee shirt and buried it under a rock near the western section of the fence. Everyone expected to have their lockers searched but it didn't happen. There were no lectures and no searches. After a few days Henry dug up his supply and brought it back to his cubicle but he didn't put it in his locker. Instead he placed it behind his locker between the locker and the wall.

Arthur and Tony were transferred out two weeks later. Arthur had never been particularly friendly toward him and he wouldn't be missed but Tony would. Two new men, Jerry Braumer and Mike Whitburn, took their bunks in the cubicle. They were likable enough but neither Henry nor Robert trusted either of the men to keep their mouths shut.

Robert was transferred in June. Henry had already lined up another source for his marijuana. There were a number of New Yorkers on the base and Henry knew several of them. He wasn't close to any like he'd been with Tita or Robert but he trusted them.

Henry had also learned to tolerate Sippy. The men drank coffee together every weekday morning and often had hamburgers at the cantina during their dinner hour. Sippy talked nonstop, always about his family or Mississippi, but Henry had learned how to tune him out when he wanted to. He liked the tall, thin man and was about the only one on base who could be around him for any length of time without him getting on their nerves.

Henry took his seaman's test in June and passed easily. He'd studied for the test while standing hangar watch on his duty nights. His pay would now be increased to two hundred and twelve dollars a month before taxes but like everything else in the military he would have to wait. His advancement in rank as well as his pay increase wouldn't go into effect for six weeks.

He applied for two weeks leave beginning the first week of August.

CHAPTER NINE

July was hot and sticky in Georgia. Henry didn't mind the heat and humidity so much, he thought it was worse in Oklahoma, but the gnats nearly drove him crazy. He couldn't walk outside without being swarmed by the pests. The mosquitoes were bad enough but the gnats got in his eyes, his ears and up his nose and they followed him whenever he left a building. Henry and Sippy were in the cantina playing a game of pool. Henry was fairly good at the game but Sippy was lucky if he hit the right ball. That coming Monday would be the fourth of July and that meant a three day weekend. Sippy wanted to go home and he wanted Henry to go with him. Sippy hated the military more than Henry did. Henry had accepted the fact that he was in Georgia and would have to be in Georgia until the Navy decided to move him. Sippy couldn't adjust to Georgia or any other place beyond walking distance of home.

"We can make it home and back on a three day weekend," he told Henry.

"You'd be taking a chance," Henry said, "trying to ride a bus and get back on time. Even if you could do it you wouldn't have any time to spend with your family. Just hi and bye."

"I'll bet we could do it if we hitchhike."

"You know Sippy, you remind me of a friend from back home. He uses the word 'we' a lot too. I haven't lost a thing in Mississippi and I don't intend to go to Mississippi. Besides that I'm nearly broke."

"I thought you passed your seaman's test."

"I did but I won't get my pay raise for a while."

"I'll fix you up with one of my sisters."

"Are they as pretty as you?"

"Sure are. Both of 'em."

"I may never go to Mississippi then."

Watching several of the men in his barracks preparing to leave base for the long weekend and faced with the prospect of being on base with nothing to do and no one to do it with, except the gnats and mosquitoes, Henry decided to hitchhike to Mississippi with Sippy. He didn't know if Sippy smoked marijuana or not but he knew he wouldn't feel right if he took something illegal to a friend's home so he left his stash where it was. He made Sippy promise that they'd note how long it took to make the trip and allow themselves more than enough time for the trip back. But Henry had a bad feeling about this trip.

Henry found a man to take his duty Sunday in exchange for Henry's promise that he would take his duty at a later date of the man's choosing. They left the base shortly after five Friday afternoon wearing their dress whites and carrying one small travel bag with their toothbrushes, four packs of Camels, two changes of underwear and one change of dungarees each. A few minutes later they were picked up by a salesman returning home to Waycross, Georgia. From there a trucker carried them to Columbus, Georgia, and another trucker took them to Meridian, Mississippi. Two drunks returning home from a night at a local bar dropped them off near Pulaski, Mississippi and a farmer carried them a few miles south until Sippy told him to stop and let them out. The sun had risen and Henry looked for a road or an exit of some kind but didn't see one. He thought Sippy might be lost until Sippy led Henry to the fence and pointed out a trail heading into the woods.

"We're almost home," he told Henry, then climbed over the fence and started following the trail. A few minutes later they came to a large clearing and a rundown house that reminded Henry of the house he'd spent the better part of his youth in. Four cheap, metal lounge chairs sat in the front yard near the door and Henry could see a faint light through the front window. An old dog laying near the southern corner of the house stood up briefly, yawned, then lay back down without so much as a whimper.

"That's a hell of a watch dog you got there Sippy," Henry teased. Sippy didn't answer which struck Henry as odd since he'd talked non-stop every inch of the way getting there.

The place appeared isolated until Sippy led Henry around the side of the house to the back door and he saw a dirt road that ran from the back yard down the mountain until it disappeared around a curve. A hundred feet or so to the right of the road stood an outhouse and beyond the outhouse was a small pasture. To the left of the road was a trough and water pump and chickens were everywhere. Sippy opened the back door and pushed Henry in ahead of him. He was in a kitchen a half dozen feet away from a thin, fairly pretty woman with gray hair pulled back and tied in a bun. Two girls in their late teens sat at a kitchen table sipping coffee doctored with milk while the woman prepared breakfast.

"Mama, this is Henry, the fellow I told you about. Henry this is mama and that's my sister Ellen and my other sister Hattie. Where's papa? I saw the truck was gone."

"Taking care of business," Mrs. Campbell answered. "How long you home for?"

"Til day after tomorrow. It took us just over thirteen hours to get here and we're giving ourselves seventeen or eighteen to get back on. We'll leave here noon Monday or there bouts."

Henry heard the girls giggle and saw Hattie, the youngest, blush. Both girls wore simple, pullover cotton dresses and both were thin and well-endowed. Ellen, the oldest, was rather plain and favored Sippy but Hattie looked more like her mother.

Mrs. Campbell placed two more plates on the table and told them to sit down. Henry ate eggs over easy, bacon and biscuits but passed on the grits. After eating, neither he nor Sippy could hardly keep their eyes open. Sippy asked his mother if they could lay down in her bedroom. The room was cooled by a ceiling fan and both men fell asleep as soon as their heads touched the pillows. Henry woke up several hours later alone on the bed. He changed into his dungarees then left the room.

The house consisted of four rooms; two bedrooms, kitchen and a large living room that held an old stuffed sofa, equally old or older Lazy-Boy lounge chair, a pot-bellied wood burning stove and a twenty-one inch television sitting on top of an old television console.

Mrs. Campbell sat on the sofa peeling turnips and watching a soap opera on the twenty-one inch television. "The kids are outside," she said, as though she'd read Henry's mind. "Did you get enough sleep?"

"Yes ma'am."

"Are you hungry?"

"No ma'am."

"Well if you change your mind there's some biscuits and bacon on the kitchen table. It'll be awhile 'fore supper."

Henry walked outside and found Hattie sitting on an old cane chair alone. She'd changed from the dress into a T-shirt and a pair of short denim cut-offs. "Where's the others?"

"They're down by the creek. I told them I'd wait here till

you woke up. I wanted to wake you when Vernon got up but mama wouldn't let me."

Hattie's nipples were outlined in the thin cotton T-shirt and Henry tried hard not to stare. Hattie looked up and smiled and Henry noticed several small strands of hair growing from her chin. The tuft of hair was light in color and barely noticeable but Hattie definitely had a goatee.

"You wanna walk down to the creek?" Hattie asked.

"Sure."

Hattie stood and took Henry's hand leading him over to a small trail that ran into the woods just south of the pasture. The trail led to a small creek and Henry saw Sippy and Ellen, both naked, laying in the sand near the creek bank. Neither made any effort to conceal themselves. He looked back at Hattie and saw her pulling her T-shirt over her head. Next she undid the top of her shorts, pulled the zipper down and let the shorts fall to her ankles. She wasn't wearing underwear.

"Well what are you waiting for?" Hattie teased. "You gonna take your clothes off or not?" She stepped out of her shorts and waded into the shallow creek. The water barely reached her hips.

"You didn't tell us he was bashful Vern," Ellen remarked.

Henry undressed and waded out to Hattie. She grabbed his genitalia and he got an instant erection.

"He don't look bashful to me sister," Hattie said. Henry looked over at Sippy and Ellen and saw both of them smiling. He lost his erection and Hattie laughed.

"Let's walk down the creek a ways," she suggested, still holding Henry by the penis and leading the way. A moment later she stopped and lay down in a small clearing pulling Henry down with her. "Make love to me...please." Henry couldn't turn a lady down, especially one who said please.

While having sex he heard giggling coming from the trees. After sex they returned to the area where they'd left Sippy and Ellen. Hattie reached for Henry's genitalia again and he gently removed her hand telling her she was wasting her time because it would be a while before he'd be able to have sex again. "I don't care if it's hard or soft," she whispered. "I just want to play with it. Let me play with it...please." Henry couldn't turn a lady down, especially one who was so damn polite.

The two sisters shared one bedroom and their parents occupied the other, the cooler one where Henry had napped earlier. After watching 77 Sunset Strip and Bob Hope Presents the Chrysler Theater Mrs. Campbell left the room and returned later with an armload of quilts. "You boys can make a pallet and sleep out here," she said, then went to her bedroom and shut the door. Thirty minutes later Sippy and Ellen slipped into the girls' bedroom and Hattie was busy preparing a pallet on the floor.

"What if your mother catches us or your daddy comes home?" Henry asked.

"Shoot, daddy might not be home for a week and mama never comes out 'fore mornin'."

Henry didn't know when Hattie left the pallet and slipped into her own bed. He woke with his arms around Sippy, nestled up close in the 'spoon' position. Mrs. Campbell was cooking breakfast and both sisters sat at the table smiling.

"Vernon told us you were friends," Ellen said, "but he didn't tell us you were that close." Both girls laughed.

Henry started to climb out of the pallet then remembered he was naked from the waist down. He could walk around in front of the girls naked but not the mother and he'd just as soon the mother not know he'd walked around naked in front of her daughters. "Would you girls turn your heads for a minute?"

"No," Hattie said. Ellen shook her head and mouthed 'no'.

"You girls turn your heads and quit teasing Henry," Mrs. Campbell ordered, "and Henry when you get your pants on you can wake Vernon up." The girls turned their heads slightly and Henry pulled his pants on then shook Sippy until he heard a loud groan. After a trip to the outhouse he helped Sippy fold the quilts and return them to the cedar chest in Mrs. Campbell's bedroom. After breakfast Henry helped Hattie and Ellen feed the chickens while Sippy pumped water and carried it inside to the kitchen. They sat in the backyard talking until the sun was high enough over the trees to reach the creek. The rest of the day was spent lying around naked near the creek and having sex. Henry didn't know what to think about Sippy having sex with his own sister and wanted to ask if he'd also had sex with Hattie but decided he didn't really want to know.

The four were lying in the sun talking. Henry and Sippy planned to leave before noon the following day and Sippy was already dreading it. "I don't want to go back," he complained. "I know I have to but God knows I don't want to. I keep thinking that they'd never find me here if I didn't want 'em to."

"What are you gonna do?" Henry asked, as Hattie fondled his testicles. "Hide out on this mountain the rest of your life?"

"You could stay here too," Hattie whispered. "I could hide you and I'd be yours for the askin'. Anytime you wanted me you could have me."

'Lord, give me strength', Henry thought. The more he was around Hattie the less he noticed her chin whiskers and laying there spread eagle while she massaged and fondled everything of his from his belly button down he wouldn't have cared if she had a full beard.

"I love you Henry."

"I think you're special too," he said.

It was after one o'clock Monday afternoon before Henry and Sippy were ready to leave. They'd spent the morning at the creek and Hattie had nearly convinced Henry to desert the Navy and stay on the mountain. They'd changed into their dress whites and Ellen and Hattie had followed them to the highway. Before returning home Hattie made Henry promise her that he'd be back as soon as he could. A few minutes later the men caught a ride with a couple and their two young kids that took them to Meridian. Their luck was good and twelve hours later they crawled out of a truck onto highway eighty-two a few miles east of Waycross. If their luck held they'd be back at base in time to get a few hours of sleep. Henry saw the lights of a car approaching and stuck out his thumb. A county sheriff's patrol car pulled over on the shoulder a few yards ahead of the pair and a deputy got out. He opened the car's trunk then leaned against the car and waited. "Put your bags in the trunk," he ordered when they reached the car, "and get in the back seat."

"Are we being arrested?" Henry asked.

"Just get in the car!"

They climbed in the back seat and the deputy slammed the door. Henry was hoping the man might be giving them a ride but hope faded when the lawman made a U-turn on the highway and drove west toward Waycross. "Why are you doing this?" Sippy asked. "We're just trying to get back to our base."

"We have laws against hitchhiking."

"Good God," Sippy moaned. "Everybody hitchhikes."

"Not in Ware County."

"We're not bothering anybody," Henry said. "We're just trying to get back to our base. If we're not there by eight in the morning we're in trouble."

"Tell it to the sheriff."

Henry and Sippy were searched. Their wallets, cigarettes, money, shoes and bandanas were taken, then they were locked in a cell. An adjacent cell held a number of prisoners, mostly black, but they had this cell to themselves.

"What about my cigarettes?" Henry asked.

"If you got 'em, smoke 'em," the jailer said and walked away.

"You took my cigarettes!" Henry yelled.

A few minutes after seven a.m. the sheriff came to their cell and told them they were free to go. "Why were we arrested?" Henry asked.

"Because I don't want your kind beggin' rides in my county! And I'll tell you something else. If I catch you hitchhiking again I'll bring you back here and lock you in that other cell! You boys understand what I'm saying?"

"How are we supposed to get back to our base?" Sippy asked.

"Walk! Goddamn it!"

The pair walked from the sheriff's office to the highway. An hour later Sippy was ready to start hitchhiking again but Henry told him he wasn't sticking out his thumb until they reached the county line. He told Sippy they were already late and it would be better to be a little late than to go back to that Waycross jail. A pick-up pulled over and a man offered them a ride. Sippy climbed in at once but Henry checked the highway looking for a patrol car before climbing into the truck. The driver carried them into Brunswick and they caught a shuttle bus for the base arriving a few minutes before eleven a.m. They were placed on report and restricted to the base. The next afternoon they were brought before the base commander. They tried to explain about the sheriff in Waycross being the reason they were late and were given a lecture on personal responsibility. They were told they should have never made the trip to begin with then were given ten days in the brig, a reduction in rank and fined ten days pay. The men were issued used dungarees with a large POW stenciled across the back of the shirt. They were then escorted to a cell block and placed in separate cells on the same side of the block where they couldn't see one another. They were the only prisoners there. The next morning after a breakfast of cold coffee, cold grits and cold toast, the steel door to the cell block opened and Third Class Gunner's Mate Swanson yelled "Campbell, Ridge on your feet. Come to attention!" Swanson wore a white helmet with a matching arm band that bore the initials MP. He unlocked their cells then marched them single file from the cell block through the outer office to a small 'paddy wagon' and ordered them to climb inside. Swanson drove the wagon and prisoners to the southeast corner of the base where the old creosote fence was scheduled to be replaced with a new ten foot chain link fence. They were ordered out and at attention while Swanson unloaded a pick, shovel and two sledgehammers from the cab of the wagon. He then took two small cardboard boxes from the front seat and placed them on the hood. Then he gave a speech Henry felt he must've stood in front of a mirror the night before rehearsing. "You two are trash. This is where the Navy sends its trash. You're here to work and if I want to I can work you all day and night until you drop! You're here to learn how to follow rules and be part of a team. What one does, both does. If one breaks a rule both will suffer the consequences. Do you understand?"

"Yes sir!"

The creosote poles had been set in cement when the original fence was built. The prisoners' jobs were to dig up the poles and use the sledgehammers to 'clean' the poles of any cement then stack the pole neatly out of the way. The heat and humidity made the work nearly unbearable.

Swanson was unarmed except for a black baton and while the two men worked he sat in the shade twirling his baton and hurling insults. He called Henry 'harelip' and Sippy 'hillbilly' and constantly stayed on their backs. Talking was part of Sippy's nature and trying to keep him quiet was like trying to change the color of his eyes. He tried to whisper comments to Henry and the guard always caught him. He stayed in Slippy's face calling him names and cursing him then ordering both men to do fifty push-ups. Two hours after starting Henry felt like he'd collapse at any moment but he kept going, stopping only to do push-ups when Slippy was caught trying to whisper something to him. At noon a gray pick-up drove up and another MP handed Swanson a brown, grease-stained paper sack and a thermos then drove away. Swanson put the sack and the thermos on the hood of the wagon and called a break. He took one cardboard box and tossed it to Henry and the other to Sippy. "You've got fifteen minutes to eat."

Henry and Sippy sat down under a tree and opened their boxes. Each box contained a thin piece of bologna between two slices of bread and a small carton of milk. The boxes had sat in the sun four hours and the bologna was hot, the bread had started to harden and the milk was warm enough to bathe in. Swanson ate a hamburger and french fries washed down by a thermos of iced tea. Fifteen minutes later they were ordered back to work while the guard continued eating.

Sippy refused to keep his mouth shut and Henry spent the

next six hours doing push-ups, swinging a sledgehammer and repeating over and over in his mind 'I can make it. I can make it', even though he felt like he'd collapse at any time. At six Swanson ordered them to put the tools in the cab and climb back into the cage of the 'paddy wagon'. They were taken back to their cells and served the same meal as they had eaten at dinner except the bologna and milk were cool and the bread was fairly fresh. Thirty minutes later they were ordered out of their cells and handed a broom, mop and mop bucket and told to clean the entire cell block. An hour and a half later they were given a twenty minute break to talk and shine their work shoes then they were taken, one man at a time, to a shower and given five minutes to clean up. At nine the lights were turned off and the cell door locked. The two men were separated by four cells and if they kept their voices down to a whisper they could talk without the night guard hearing them.

"I can't take nine more days of this," Sippy complained. "I didn't think I'd make it today."

"I must have done a thousand push-ups because of you."

"I can't help it Henry. It ain't natural to tell a man he can't talk. If God didn't want us talking he wouldn't have given us a mouth."

"But I never hear what you're saying Sippy. Half the time I don't even know you said nothin' till the guard yells at us to hit the ground and give him fifty."

"I'm sorry Henry. I'll try to keep my mouth shut."

Henry felt bad about saying anything to Sippy about his talking. "Hell Sippy don't worry about it. At least while we're doing push-ups we're not holding a shovel or a damn sledge hammer. Besides, nine days ain't that long. We can do nine days standing on our heads."

"I don't know if I can."

"You got no choice Sippy. You're here."

"I'm sorry I got you into this."

"You didn't get me into nothin'. I knew what I was doing. Besides it was worth it for two days with your sister."

"Hattie likes you Henry. So does Ellen and Mama."

"I like them too Sippy."

The night guard, Radarman Second Class Jackson, was fairly decent to the prisoners but Swanson, the day guard, made it plain from the beginning that he disliked both prisoners and he seemed to dislike Sippy more than he did Henry. Sippy couldn't go more than a few minutes without muttering something and Swanson couldn't stop him. He called both men every derogatory name he could think of and while Henry ignored him Sippy seemed to take it personally. On the second day, while the two men were bent over a hole trying to pull a pole out Swanson made a remark about Sippy's family tree running straight up with no branches. Henry glanced over at his friend and saw Sippy's face turn blood red.

"I'd have killed that bastard," Sippy whispered that night, "if I could have picked that pole and that cement up high enough to hit him with it."

"Just eight more days to go. Maybe they won't make us work on Sunday."

"I'll bet my ass they do," Sippy said.

"Your ass ain't yours to bet. The Navy owns it."

"Eight more days. I don't think I can make it."

"You said that yesterday and you made it."

"He's got no right insulting my family. He don't know my family. He goddamn sure ain't got no right to bad mouth 'em."

"Eight more days Sippy. Just eight more days."

On the fourth day Henry was beating the cement from a pole and worrying about Sippy. His friend had quit talking and now was grinding his teeth constantly. Even above the noise of the work Henry could hear him. To make things worse the guard had commented all day about how ugly he thought Sippy's family must be. "Hey hillbilly, I'll bet you was so ugly the doctor slapped your mama or maybe your daddy slapped your mama for having someone as ugly as you. Ain't that right hare-lip?" Henry didn't answer.

"Hey hare-lip I asked you a question and you'd better answer me!"

"What's the question again sir?" Henry straightened up and arched his back.

"I didn't tell you to quit working!" Henry swung the hammer knocking a large section of cement from a pole. "Just answer the fuckin' question!"

"What was the question again?"

"I'm beginning to think you're as stupid as your hillbilly friend! Now I'm going to ask you just one more time don't you think ole hillbilly here's just about the ugliest bastard you ever seen?"

"I've seen uglier sir."

"You must be talking 'bout hillbilly's mama and sisters."

"He has a pretty mama, sir, and pretty sisters." Henry talked between swings. "I've met them…..mama's pretty……sisters pretty……I didn't meet the daddy……but I'll bet…..he's pretty too." Henry glanced over at Sippy and thought he saw a smile.

"You've got a smart mouth hare-lip," Swanson growled. "Somebody's gonna shut it someday." The guard turned his insults back to Sippy. "Hey hillbilly do you know what I heard was the hardest thing about growing up in Mississippi? It was whether to fuck the neighbor's cow or fuck your sister. Which one did you choose hillbilly?" The guard had walked over to within a few feet of where Sippy was digging. "Did you shove the sausage to your sister or crawl under the fence and poke it to old Bessie?"

Swanson turned his back and Sippy swung the shovel hitting him between the shoulder blades and knocking him down. Sippy pulled the helmet off the guard and started slamming the guard's head against the ground before Henry could pull him away. "Oh shit Sippy! Oh fucking shit Sippy! We done it this time!"

"You had nothing to do with it!"

"Do you think this bastard's gonna tell 'em that? They'll hang both of us by our balls!"

Swanson tried to crawl to his feet and Sippy kicked him in the mouth. "What do you think we ought to do?"

"I'm thinking about crawling in one of those holes and pulling the dirt in on top of me. We'll be old men before we get out of here."

"Not me. I'm going home. You can come with me if you want to."

"They'll find us Sippy. You can't hide on that mountain forever."

"Wanna bet? I'm going. You can stay here if you want to."

Sippy kicked the guard again then stepped through the corner of the fence. Henry followed. He didn't know where he was going but he wasn't staying here and he wasn't going to Mississippi. They were walking into a wooded area but the railroad track was only a half mile or so away. Before they reached the railroad track they were waist deep in mud. Neither man had known the Naval Air Station was near the northeast corner of Okefonokee swamp. It took half an hour to reach the tracks and another two hours to follow the tracks to the edge of Brunswick. Here they hid in the brush trying to decide what to do next.

They still wore the brig dungarees with the POW stenciled on back and both men were covered in mud.

"Wait here," Sippy told him.

"What are you gonna do?"

"Just wait here. You'll see."

Thirty minutes later Sippy returned with an armload of clothes and tossed them down in front of Henry. "Where'd you get those?"

"Stole 'em from a clothes line. I damn near got caught too."

Henry picked up a bra and a slip. "What'd you do? Just grab something and run?"

"I didn't know you'd be so particular."

"I ain't wearin' no bra."

Henry removed his dungarees and tried on a pair of Levis he found in the pile. He couldn't button the pants at the waist and the bottoms of the pant legs came up past his ankles. Sippy found a pair of overalls that fit him perfectly. Henry dug around in the remaining clothes looking for another pair of pants. There were none.

"Goddamn it Sippy these are boys pants." Henry found a boy's nylon shirt and put it on. The sleeves came up nearly to his elbows but he could button the front. He tore a six inch strip of cloth from the slip and ran it through the two belt loops in the front of the pants and pulled it tight then tied it. At least he wouldn't have to worry about the pants falling off and with the shirt worn outside the pants no one would notice his pants weren't buttoned. Sippy still wore his dungaree shirt. The back of the coveralls covered the POW. Henry thought Sippy looked like a Georgia farm hand and he looked like the village idiot.

"Oughta be a train come by sometime," Sippy said. "We'll catch the first one headed south."

"Not me," Henry told him. "I've decided I'm going north."

"But Mississippi's the other way."

"I'm not going to Mississippi. I'm going to Canada."

"But why? You seen where I live. They'll never find us in the mountains."

"I'm hoping they won't find me in Canada."

"Hattie's going to be disappointed."

"Why don't you come to Canada with me?"

"I'm going home and when I get home I'm never leaving again."

The two friends stayed in the brush until they heard the whistle of a north bound freight.

"I'm catching this train," Henry told him. "I wish you'd change your mind and come with me."

"I'm going home. I wish you'd come with me."

Henry shook Sippy's hand. "Good luck and tell your family hi for me. I'm going to miss you hillbilly."

"I'm going to miss you too hare-lip."

Henry ran along side the train until he found an open box car. He pulled himself inside and sat near the door until his eyes could adjust to the shadows in the car. Seeing nothing but a pile of paper in the corner he moved away from the door and out of sight.

The train picked up speed and soon was moving at better than eighty miles an hour. Henry crawled toward the corner of the boxcar and away from the door. He heard movement coming from the pile then saw something sit up in the middle of the rubbish. He screamed and scrambled back toward the door ready to take his chance on jumping. "Don't be scared kid. I'm not going to hurt you." Henry looked over his shoulder at a thin, gray-haired man leaning against the wall of the car.

"I was hiding till I seen who you was. Never know what might crawl on here. I didn't mean to scare you kid."

Henry leaned against the wall and tried to stop his heart from racing. He'd heard stories of hobos who robbed other hobos. He'd also heard stories of murder and rape but the man who sat across the boxcar from him now didn't look like he could hurt anyone if he wanted to. He was thin, ragged and looked old beyond his years. Henry felt he could trust him not to cut his throat or rape him.

"What's your name kid?" the hobo asked, extending his hand.

"Henry Ridge sir. What's yours?"

"Jim. Just call me Jim. You running away from home Henry?"

"No sir. Just the Navy."

"You're in the Navy? You look kinda young. Never was in the service myself."

"You're lucky."

"Lucky? Been a long time since anybody called me lucky."

"How long you been hoboing?"

"Left home when I was fourteen I think. Never been back. You plan on ever going home Henry?"

"Sure. Sometime. When the Navy forgets about me."

"The Navy won't forget."

"How do you know so much about it? You said yourself you never was in the service."

"The Navy's part of the government and the government has a long memory. It don't take no brains to know that."

"I reckon I'll just stay in Canada then."

"Is that where you're headed Henry? Canada?"

"Yes sir."

"You got folks Henry?"

"Yes sir."

"You plan on seeing them again?"

"Sometime."

"You going to sneak back home to.....where's home Henry?"

"Oklahoma."

"You going to sneak back home to Oklahoma to see your folks or maybe you think they'll just mosey up to Canada and visit you?"

"I haven't thought that far ahead."

"I bet your folks will miss you."

"Grandma will and Mama might."

"Your daddy's a real bastard I'll bet."

"He ain't my daddy. He's just some trash Mama picked up."

"Did he beat you Henry? I bet he liked to use his fists."

"You sound like you know him."

"Don't have to know him. Had a daddy just like him. My daddy used to hunt reasons to beat me until I ran away. That's been more than forty years ago. I'm from Kansas, Henry. Lord I hated Kansas. But my mother was a saint and ain't a day goes by I don't think about her. Wasn't always like that. When I first ran off I could shove her to the back of my mind but the older I get the more I think about her. You know the worse part is I'm having trouble remembering what she looked like. Used to I could pull her face up as clear as day. Now I wouldn't know her if she climbed in this car." Jim stared at the floor of the boxcar for a moment. "Lord knows I miss her."

"Why haven't you ever gone home?"

"No one wants to go home a loser. I always dreamed that

someday through some miracle I'd go home in a new blue Mercedes. I didn't want to climb off some boxcar and walk home saying 'look Mom it's me, your little boy, Jimmy the loser, could I bum a bologna sandwich?' After awhile you wake up one morning sleeping on your shoes to keep someone from stealing them and it's too late to go home. You know the funny thing about it kid? You know it's too late and you'll probably never see home again but you can't stop the dreams."

"If I go back they'll lock me up in that damn cage again and throw the key away. You don't know what it's like being locked up in a cage."

Jim laughed. "Lord kid I've lost count of the cages they've thrown me in. I think they got a unique law for hobos called 'suspicion of being alive'. They lock us up one day and let us go the next if we promise to get out of their fair city. Anything that happens hobos get blamed cause it's easier for the law. Believe it or not kid some of the jails ain't half bad 'specially when it's cold out and you ain't ate in so long you can feel your spine through your navel. You might even luck out and get a jailer who's half-ass decent. If you don't like cages then you might oughta give some thought to changing your direction. Otherwise you might see a lot of cages."

The hobo raked up a large pile of paper and made a pillow then lay down near the wall. "I'm going to take a nap Henry. Savannah's coming up and we'll have to leave this comfortable boxcar."

"Why will we have to leave?" Henry asked. "I thought the train would be going further north."

"It will but they'll be switching cars in Savannah and railroad bulls will be checking any open cars. If you want to ride this train further north you'll have to walk to the north side and catch it again on its way out."

Jim closed his eyes and was snoring in seconds. Henry raked up a pile of paper and made a pillow intending to take a nap also. He found it impossible. The boxcar rode like the tracks were made of gravel and every bump pounded his head into the floor. Henry sat up and leaned against the wall watching the hobo sleep like he was on a feather bed. 'Maybe after forty years', Henry thought, 'I'll be able to sleep in one of these damn boxcars'.

It was late afternoon when the train stopped in the Savannah rail yard. The hobo left the train immediately and disappeared into the bushes. Henry started looking for anyone who could give him directions to the nearest highway . He spotted a brakeman and walked over and asked him. The brakeman studied Henry a moment and asked him if he'd come off the train.

"No sir. My folks live a couple of miles down the track."

"Look kid I personally don't give a damn if you rode the train or not. I just want you to know it's dangerous. A lot of nut cases ride these rails. If you want directions to Interstate 95 you just go down to the first street at the end of the yard and turn left. Keep going until you come to a red light then take a right. That'll take you to the interstate."

It was after dark before Henry reached the highway. A few minutes later he was crawling into the cab of an eighteen wheeler. Within an hour he was asleep. The driver stopped shortly after midnight and woke Henry up. "I'm getting some breakfast. Want some?"

"I'd like a cup of coffee."

Inside the truck stop the driver ordered two 'trucker specials'. Henry lied and told the driver he had eaten only moments before the man picked him up. "Suit yourself kid. I ordered two meals and I'll pay for two meals. You can eat it or throw it away. I don't care which." Henry ate the breakfast.

On the way out of the restaurant the driver bought two packs of Winstons and gave one pack to Henry. He let Henry out shortly after daybreak on the south side of Baltimore. The truck wasn't yet out of sight when a state trooper pulled to the side of the road a few feet behind Henry. The trooper climbed out of his car and called Henry over. "What's your name son?"

"John," Henry lied, "John Jenkins."

"Do you have any identification Mr. Jenkins?"

"No sir I lost my billfold a couple of days ago. As soon as I get home I'll get another license."

"Where's home Mr. Jenkins?"

"Canada."

"You won't be getting into Canada without some form of identification. Are you running away from home?"

"No sir. I've been to Atlanta visiting my aunt. Now I'm just trying to get home to Canada."

"What town in Canada? My wife's from Halifax."

"It's a itty bitty place. I doubt if you've heard of it."

The trooper smiled then asked Henry to place both hands on the hood and spread his legs. After searching him the trooper opened the back door and asked Henry to climb inside. "I think we need to talk more downtown."

The trooper took Henry to the Baltimore police station where he was fingerprinted and placed in a cell. An hour later the deputy police chief came back to Henry's cell. "Henry Ridge we're sending you back to Georgia as soon as we can arrange it."

"You found out who I am?"

"We always do son. We always do."

Shortly before noon the jailor brought an MP back to Henry's cell. Henry was handcuffed and led from the station to a military paddy wagon and placed in the back. He was taken to the Baltimore airport and, still cuffed, escorted aboard a plane to Atlanta. At Atlanta he was led from the airport to another paddy wagon. Three hours later he was being led to his old cell at the Brunswick brig. The night guard, Jackson, smiled as he unlocked Henry's cell door. "Welcome back Henry. We've missed you."

"I guess they haven't caught Sippy yet."

"Not yet Henry but they will. You can count on it."

Henry had been gone a little more than thirty hours and he'd been free for less than eighteen.

CHAPTER TEN

The court martial took less than thirty minutes. Henry was sentenced to four months hard labor, reduction in rank to seaman recruit and forfeiture of three quarters of his pay for the length of incarceration. He was led to a gray station wagon and placed in the back seat. An MP sat in the back with him while another MP drove to the federal brig at the Jacksonville, Florida Naval Air Station.

The prison sat alone in a far corner of the Naval Air Station and reminded Henry of something out of a James Cagney movie. The high walls were made of brick and each corner supported a tower manned by armed Marines. Henry was led inside to a guard station and turned over to a large muscular Marine sergeant. The sergeant ordered Henry to attention then glared down at him for several seconds. He walked around to Henry's back and leaned over and whispered in his ear. "You're mine now. Even God can't help you here. You don't do anything without permission. You don't eat, you don't shit, you don't think, you don't do a fucking thing without permission. Do you understand me?"

"Yes sir."

"Get out of my sight maggot!"

A few feet ahead sat another guard at a desk in front of a steel door. He walked to the desk and stood at attention and waited. The guard, a corporal, ignored him.

"Excuse me sir."

The corporal shot to his feet and appeared very angry. "You fucking piece of shit! You maggot bastard! You got shit for brains or what?"

Henry didn't know if he was supposed to answer or not. He decided not to. "You don't talk unless you get permission to talk! Is that too fucking hard for a piece of shit like you to understand?" Henry didn't answer. "You better answer me you son-of-a-bitch!"

"Permission to speak sir."

The corporal grabbed Henry by the throat and threw him against the bars, "I don't know if you're a fucking idiot or a fucking comedian but I don't like either one!" He spun Henry back toward the desk and ordered him to come to attention. Then he sat down and ignored him.

"Permission to speak sir."

"What do you want maggot?"

"Permission to pass sir."

The corporal opened the steel door and Henry walked another few feet to yet another steel door and another Marine corporal. He asked permission to speak then asked permission to pass. The guard opened the door and instructed Henry to turn to his right. A prisoner behind a counter asked Henry his shirt, pants and shoe size. He was issued two sets of dungarees, three pairs of boxer shorts and three pairs of socks. At another counter he was handed a small plastic bag containing a toothbrush, toothpaste, a bar of Ivory soap and a can of black shoe polish. He would be charged for the toiletries and the polish and the money deducted from his pay. At another counter he was issued a pillow, pillow case, sheet and wool blanket.

Henry carried the pile through two more steel doors before reaching his cell block. The block reminded Henry of a zoo. Cages, sitting side by side, lined both sides of the passageway.

The sides of the cages were made of steel bars and each cage held four men. There was no privacy at all and the guards and the other prisoners could see you at all times. Caddy-cornered from Henry's cage he could see a toilet and a shower. 'A prisoner can't scratch,' Henry thought, 'without being seen by anyone who cared to look'.

Henry was ordered to make his bunk then handed a mop bucket and ordered to help mop the entire cell block. At six p.m. they were mustered in groups of twenty and double-timed to the mess hall. Speaking was not permitted and they had thirty minutes to eat. No one was forced to eat anything they didn't want but anything you took you had to eat.

After mess they were ordered to continue cleaning the cell block. At eight they were given a thirty minute break to shine their shoes and brass buckles then ordered back to cleaning. At nine- thirty they were told to line up for their shower and after showering were allowed to brush their teeth. Prisoners needing to shave had to 'check out' a safety razor and return it after shaving. At ten p.m. everyone was ordered to bed and the cell doors locked. If a prisoner needed to use the toilet later that night he had to stand at attention and shout 'permission to speak' until a guard answered, usually after several prisoners were awakened.

Reveille was at five a.m. At five-thirty the prisoners were expected to be dressed and ready for thirty minutes of hard exercise. From the exercise yard they double-timed to the mess hall for breakfast. The exercise made many new prisoners sick to their stomachs and they learned to throw up while running to breakfast.

After breakfast they double-timed back to the brig where they were split into groups of twelve and loaded into vans then driven to different work sites. Henry's work site was at another corner of the base where a number of old, unused barracks were being torn down. Henry and five others were given sledgehammers and ordered to start knocking the building down and breaking the rubbish into pieces small enough to be loaded onto a dump truck. The other six men in the crew were ordered to load the truck. Three armed Marines guarded the prisoners and the work was hard as the work he'd endured at the Brunswick brig but here no one cursed or insulted you. A prisoner could straighten up from time to time and relax his back without being subjected to any verbal abuse.

The prisoners were given a five minute water break twice in the morning and twice in the afternoon. At exactly noon they were given a fifteen minute break to eat and each man was given a cardboard box. Henry didn't have to look to know the box contained the same meal he'd eaten in Brunswick; a hot bologna sandwich and warm milk.

Everyday was the same except Sunday. Sunday morning the prisoners were given their choice of going to church or cleaning the cell block. Henry and several others decided to try church. They double-timed to the chapel and were seated in the balcony away from the rest of the congregation. The men who had been there the week before scrambled for the seats at the railing. Henry found out why a few minutes later when four teenage girls entered the chapel and took seats near the back and almost directly under the balcony. Soon the men at the railing were elbowing each other and grinning from ear to ear. Henry, sitting on the third row, craned his neck forward until he could see the girls. They had lifted their skirts, exposing their panties and were fondling themselves, looking up at the balcony every few minutes and smiling. The preacher preached, the congregation prayed and sang and no one but the prisoners knew what the girls were doing. When the service ended they waved at their audience in the balcony and left. Henry made up his mind to attend church every Sunday and next time he'd get a seat at the rail.

Sunday afternoon was for laundry. The laundry room was in the corner of the building near the exercise yard. It contained a circular trough located in the center of the room. The trough was waist high with a water faucet every three feet or so. Here the prisoners scrubbed their clothes then hung them on clothes lines at one end of the exercise yard. The day was an easy one for the men. The rules were relaxed enough to where the prisoners could talk among themselves as long as they weren't loud.

Henry's section had two guards at all times. These Marines treated the men fairly and one guard, Corporal Benton, made efforts to be friendly to the prisoners.

Henry spent his eighteenth birthday swinging a sledge hammer.

Summer passed and the weather turned cool. The prisoners were issued light work jackets. The second week of November Henry was told to strip his bunk and turn in his bedding. His duffel bag had been packed and sent down with him four months earlier then kept in storage until his release. He was taken to an empty room where they gave him his bag and told him to change into his dress blue uniform then turn in the clothes he'd been issued at the brig. An hour later he was in the brig commander's office standing at attention while the commander reminded him he was being given a second chance. After the lecture he was given a white business envelope and a large manila envelope. The white envelope contained his pay and the manila envelope contained his orders. He was told he had three days to report for duty. Henry opened the white envelope as soon as he left the building and counted his money, eighty-three dollars, then read his orders. He was being assigned to sea duty aboard the U.S.S. Nathan B. Forrest. Sea duty had been his first choice when he

ι and all he had to do to get it was to get thrown in a cage
ιr months.

Henry caught a cab for the bus station and bought a ticket
to Norfolk. He called his grandmother from a pay phone to tell
her he was going to sea and learned Harvey had been sent to Viet
Nam. He wanted a beer but decided to wait until he reached
Norfolk. He wasn't taking any chances on being late and being sent back to the brig. At Norfolk he drank three beers then
caught a cab for the Navel Ship yards and reported for duty two
days early. Norfolk reminded Henry of Brunswick.

The U.S.S. Nathan B. Forrest was a twenty-seven thousand
ton assault helicopter carrier. Commissioned after Word War
Two as an aircraft carrier she had been converted in 1959 to
carry helicopters and troops to 'trouble spots', particularly in
the Caribbean and had participated in the 1962 Cuban missile
crisis. The Forrest was four hundred and forty feet long and
one hundred and fourteen feet wide and carried over a thousand
sailors.

Henry was assigned to the Deck Department, Second Division. Second Division was responsible for the care of the ship
from the midship to the fantail. First Division cared for the ship
from the midship forward to the anchor. In addition to swab-
bing decks they also took care of the lines and cables used to
tie the ship at dock and they painted. The majority of the work
was scraping old paint off and putting new paint on. Cargo nets
and scaffolds were hung from overhead and over the sides of the
ship. Crews of men crawled around in the nets or sat on two-
by-ten boards scraping or painting. For areas where the cargo
nets were impractical 'boatswain's chairs' were utilized. These
'chairs' held one man and were raised and lowered by a pulley.
The work wasn't hard but it was tedious and boring. The men
talked and listened to the Armed Forces Radio being broadcast

over the ship's intercom and tried to look busy when someone came around to check on them. At five the crews quit work except the men who had duty that day. Men who had liberty and planned to go ashore scrambled for the showers. The first couple of hundred would have hot water, the rest would have to take cold showers.

Second Division mustered each morning at seven a.m. on the ship's fantail. The division consisted of two First Class Boatswain's Mates, one Third Class Boatswain's Mate, thirty-one seamen and one seaman recruit—Henry. Four of the seamen were 'leading seamen', men who had passed their Third Class Boatswain's test and now had to wait until an opening became available before advancing in rank. These leading seamen headed the work crews. There were four crews in the division and Henry was assigned to leading seaman Earl Hobbs' crew.

Henry was assigned to a compartment two floors below the main deck. Forty-six men, counting Henry, of Second Division shared the cramped living quarters while the three petty officers shared a compartment above the fantail. The bunks were set in rows, four bunks to a row, with the first bunk only a foot or so off the deck and the fourth bunk about neck level. Lockers, also four high, stood across a narrow passageway from the bunks.

Five days later the ship sailed to St. Thomas, Virgin Islands, then Colon, Panama, Kingston, Jamaica and finally Guantanamo, Cuba for Christmas. Each visit lasted four days with every other day a liberty day. Duty days were the same day as any day at sea or in port. Cargo nets and scaffolds were filled with men who gazed at the shore and pretended to work. After leaving Cuba they joined a ninety-four ship war exercise off the coast of Puerto Rico that included amphibious landings, mine warfare, anti-submarine warfare and an open multi-ship missile shoot.

Henry was still at the bottom of the pay scale and could do little more ashore than walk around and look. Still he spent as much time as possible off the ship. A few men in his division complained about every port and were ready to leave after the first day but Henry loved the Caribbean and often fell asleep dreaming about jumping ship and staying.

The ship returned to Norfolk in late January. A heavy snow covered the area and the wind coming off the water was bitterly cold but men still crawled into the cargo nets and pretended to work.

Two weeks later the Forrest sailed for Viet Nam carrying three thousand soldiers from the Second Mobile Calvary Division in addition to the thousand sailors and two hundred and fifty helicopters already aboard. They sailed around the Cape of Good Hope arriving in the South China Sea in the middle of March. The ship anchored off the coast near Da Nang and two, thirty by ninety foot pontoons called 'ammi-pontoons' were moored alongside the ship. These pontoons served as docks and embarkation sites for the LSTs (landing, supply and troop boats) that carried the troops and their equipment ashore. A supply boat would be used as a shuttle, carrying food, fuel and ammunition to the troops north and south of Da Nang. Henry, Billy Fuggit and Howie Copeland were assigned to temporary duty as part of the boat crew.

The supply boat left Da Nang the following morning accompanied by three PCFs (patrol, craft, fast) more commonly known as 'swift boats'. The PCFs carried six-man crews, five enlisted and one officer and two fifty caliber machine guns, one mounted in the gun tubs on top of the pilothouses and another mounted on the fantails. Two enlisted marines were assigned to the supply boat. Russell, a baby-faced nineteen year old Corporal from Ohio and Wallace, a tall, muscled black New Yorker

Henry first thought he wouldn't want to meet in an alley or any-where else late at night. The boat's commander was Navy Lieu-tenant Junior Grade Von Hoy, a tall, thin 'ninety day wonder' fresh out of Officer's Candidate School. They sailed north on the Gianh River toward Dong Ha with Officer Von Hoy at the wheel. Henry, Billy and Howie stood on the fantail with Russell and Wallace. Russell was talkative and outgoing and had been at Da Nang for ten months. Wallace was quiet and laid back and had arrived four months earlier.

Wallace pulled a joint from his shirt pocket and lit it, took a toke, then passed it to Russell.

"I don't suppose you want any of this," Russell said, hold-ing the joint out to Henry.

"If he don't I do," Billy said.

"What if the 'ninety day wonder' sees us?" Howie asked, filling his lungs with smoke.

"He said something about it the first time Wallace lit one up," Russell answered, "and Wallace threatened to squash him like a bug. He hasn't said nothing about it since."

The supply boat returned to the Forrest for supplies every week. Henry and the crew carried the supplies as far north as Vinh and as far south as Cam Ranh, through lush, green jungles and through places that had been 'de-foliaged' by dropping a chemical called Agent Orange. These places reminded Henry of a scene from a 1950's English horror movie. Not a leaf or blade of grass alive, naked trees silhouetted against a pink and orange haze.

Wallace and Russell introduced the sailors to a Vietnamese drug dealer and they soon had their own supplies of marijuana. A one dollar carton of cigarettes could be traded for a brown paper sack containing a half pound or more of black Vietnamese marijuana. Soon Henry was smoking more marijuana than tobacco.

The Forrest stayed anchored in the South China Sea for six weeks before Henry, Billy and Howie were ordered back to 2nd Division. They returned to the ship with the bottom of their duffel bags stuffed with marijuana. The following morning they were up before daylight, watching the pontoon boats being moved, then the anchor raised and the ship sailed toward the Indian Ocean. Here they entered the Red Sea and sailed toward Egypt and the Suez Canal. The trip through the Suez took nearly eighteen hours and the temperature stayed well above a hundred degrees. Many of the crew were miserable but Henry was fascinated by the desert. Naked children lined the banks of the Suez shouting 'hey Joe' with their middle finger extended not knowing the true meaning of a gesture the Arabic people living along the Canal had come to think of as an American greeting. Everyone along the Canal banks, men, women and children greeted the sailors with their middle finger extended.

Henry saw villages that could have come straight from the Bible, oxen pulling wooden plows, camel caravans and watering holes and Arab men in long flowing robes astride sleek horses. Near Port Said, Egypt, the last city before the Mediterranean Sea, the scenery changed from naked children and women covered from head to toe to high rise apartments and topless women sunning near private pools.

The Forrest sailed to Athens, Greece, Naples, Italy, Marseille, France, the island of Palma De Mallorca and finally to Liverpool, England before returning to Norfolk, Virginia in early July.

A few days before reaching Norfolk an officer came down to 2nd Division sleeping quarters with a bag filled with boxes resembling those a jeweler used for rings and bracelets. He threw a box on each bunk then climbed the ladder and moved on to another Division's sleeping quarters. The crew were being 'awarded' their Viet Nam Service Medals. A few days later, almost a year to the day of his court martial, Henry was reinstated to Seaman. He requested, and was granted, two weeks leave.

Things had changed at home. Mike had left for Texas after graduating from high school and Kate had moved to Hardmor. Ricki was pregnant and half a dozen men were nervous. Harvey had been home on leave a few days earlier and was now back at Fort Bragg. Great Uncle Levi was confined to home and an oxygen bottle due to advanced emphysema. Henry spent ten days at his grandmother's home drinking beer and playing dominoes with Uncle Levi and taking occasional walks to smoke a joint then he returned to Norfolk. He'd called his mother once from Lahoma's and Charlie had answered the telephone. He'd asked Charlie to tell Erica that he'd called but his mother never called back. Lahoma had called and left a message and still no return call. Henry was certain Charlie had never told his mother he was home on leave.

The Forrest returned to Viet Nam in September delivering two thousand Marines and anchored off the southern tip of the country near Van Tau. Henry, Billy and Howie were again assigned to a small supply boat carrying supplies to troops. Henry asked everyone he met about Russell and Wallace but couldn't find anyone who knew either marine. Six weeks later the three climbed the gang plank again, the bottom of their duffel bags stuffed with Vietnamese marijuana. The pontoon docks were moved, the anchor raised and the Forrest sailed for four days of liberty in Hong Kong.

The men had been given a list of places that were off limits to military personnel. The sailors used these lists like guide books. They'd been particularly warned to stay out of the opium dens. Henry and Billy Fuggit found an opium den in less than an hour. Several hours later they followed two pretty, young prostitutes back to an apartment. Henry had never been with a prostitute and he found the experience disappointing. The young woman talked during the entire sex act asking questions like "are you cherry?" or "are you from Chicago, Texas?". After leaving the prostitutes they located Howie at the Susie Wong Bar and the three decided to get tattoos. Howie had a heart with his girlfriend's name put on his right shoulder and Billy had a small devil giving the 'finger' on his right forearm. Henry in his opium induced wisdom had a small, blue ukulele tattooed on his left knee. He watched the tattoo artist draw the ukulele on his knee then tattoo it on permanently and wondered why he couldn't feel anything. The opium made the experience seem surreal and dreamlike. The tattoo cost five Hong Kong dollars, the equivalent of one U.S. dollar. With the opium den, the prostitute and the tattoo he'd spent eleven U.S. dollars. Henry loved Hong Kong.

The next morning Henry awoke in pain. The area where he'd been tattooed was swollen to nearly twice it's normal size and pus was draining from the ukulele. Billy's right forearm and Howie's shoulder were also swollen and infected. The three men went to sick bay, were given penicillin shots, placed on report for destruction of government property and restricted to the ship for ten days.

Henry thought all sailors got tattooed and the Navy didn't care. He was partially right. The Navy allowed tattooing stateside but after a number of infections occurring from tattoos received in foreign ports the Navy had forbid tattooing outside the United States. Henry, Billy nor Howie knew this, but as usual, especially in the Navy, ignorance is no excuse.

Yokosuka, Japan, their next liberty port had been visited a few days earlier by an American nuclear submarine. The locals, many who remembered Hiroshima and Nagasaki, rioted and took to the streets attacking anything American. The Forrest stayed in port two days, with the crew confined to the ship, waiting for the rioting to end. Henry couldn't think of a better time to be restricted. He wasn't missing a thing. The third day the rioting showed no sign of ceasing and the Forrest sailed for Athens, Greece. From Athens they sailed to Naples, Italy then Barcelona, Spain where Henry, Billy and Howie bought an ounce of hash then spent the rest of the day trying to find a pipe and somewhere to smoke the hash without being caught by a Spanish lawman. From Spain they sailed to Liverpool and discussed taking a tour of London but after smoking a joint of Vietnamese marijuana and topping it off with a couple bowls of Spanish hash they decided to tour Liverpool instead. They made it to the nearest bar. After leaving England Henry was 'awarded' his second Vietnam Service Medal.

The Forrest returned to Norfolk, Virginia the middle week of January then sailed for Panama two weeks later carrying a small group of Marines. The ship stayed moored for ten days while the marines attended the Jungle and Guerrilla Warfare School at Fort Sherman. From Panama they sailed to Montegro Bay, Jamaica where Henry got into a fight with a Jamaican pimp who wouldn't take 'no' for an answer. From Jamaica the Forrest traveled to Roosevelt Roads, Puerto Rico for the dedication of a new dock and the crew spent three days wishing the ship would hurry and set sail. The ship returned to Norfolk in late March and Henry requested two weeks leave.

Lahoma had kept Henry's truck battery up and the old Dodge started with the first try. He had made up his mind to go to Mayetta and see his mother regardless of Charlie.

"Lydel wants to see you," Lahoma told him.

"What does the sheriff want with me?"

"He just wants to see you Henry. See how you're getting along. Why don't you ask him to help you see your mother?"

"Why should I have to ask the sheriff to see my mother?"

"Cause that's the way it is Henry. You know how Charlie is and that's the way he'll be until they bury his sorry tail. You know if you go over there alone there will be trouble."

"Maybe I could see her at work."

"Have you forgotten that Charlie works the gate?"

"From what I hear he's always asleep. They say the truck drivers have to wake him up to get in and out."

"I'll call your mother when they get off work."

"You know who'll answer the phone unless he's huntin'. I thought somebody would have killed him by now. Guess I'll have to do it."

"Don't even talk that way! Go see the sheriff and talk to him!"

"I'll go see the sheriff but I won't make no other promises."

Henry drove into Mayetta to the sheriff's office. Sheriff Wesley was out so Henry left his name and told the dispatcher he'd call back later. He then drove to the Highway 44 Diner and ordered coffee and used the pay phone to call the Pike home. Thelma Pike told Henry that Harvey had been home for Christmas.

Sheriff Wesley entered the diner and took a seat across the booth from Henry. He reached across the table and shook Henry's hand. The waitress sat a cup of coffee down in front of the sheriff.

"You look good Henry. I think the Navy agrees with you."

"Thank you sir."

"Don't call me sir. We're friends. Call me Lydel or call me sheriff."

"Did my grandmother call you?"

"About an hour ago. I drove out to the factory and had a talk with Charlie. If you'll be in town when they get off work we'll go over there and you can visit your mother."

"Hell of a thing ain't it sheriff? Can't even see my own mother without the law being there. Don't get me wrong, I appreciate everything you do and I know you go out of your way a lot of times but I don't understand why Charlie has to be such a bastard. I don't give a rat's ass if I ever see him. I just want to see my mother."

"You'll see her this afternoon."

"I ought to be able to see her anytime I want."

"Let's take it one step at a time."

The waitress appeared with a pot of coffee offering refills. Both men declined. "I've got to get back to work. Meet me at my office at four and we'll go see your mother."

The visit was anything but enjoyable. The sheriff sat on the couch talking with Charlie and trying to keep his interest. Charlie glared at Henry and his mother and tried to hear everything they said while the two sat at the kitchen table drinking beer. The conversation was one-sided with Henry doing most of the talking. Erica's left cheek was swollen and her nose had a crook in the bridge. 'She's starting to look like a prize fighter', Henry thought. Her face wasn't the only thing that revealed abuse. She sat with her head lowered glancing often at Charlie. She was terrified of him and Henry wanted to kill the son-of-a-bitch for that. All at once he had to get away. He finished his beer then kissed his mother's cheek and told her he loved her. The visit lasted less than twenty minutes.

Great Uncle Levi died in his sleep two nights later. Charlie and Erica didn't attend the funeral and Lahoma was angry. "I called and talked to Charlie," she told Henry, "and he said he would take your mother to the funeral. I guess one of his dogs got sick or something."

"You should have told him they were having a dog show right after the services. He'd have probably showed up early."

Henry caught a bus the following Monday and arrived back at his ship a day early. He called his grandmother to tell her he'd made it back alright and learned his Great Aunt Patricia had died the previous night from a brain aneurysm. He requested emergency leave to attend the funeral and his request was denied.

The third week in May the ship sailed for Barbados and Trinidad then around Cape Horn and into the Pacific Ocean arriving in Honolulu, Hawaii for four days of liberty. Before the ship sailed Henry and Howie bought a portable lime green Sears 'Party Time' record player and several 'country albums' from the 'ninety-nine cent' record bin. They set the player up where anyone in the compartment could use it. Soon other men in the division were buying their own records and the compartment was filled nightly with a mixture of rock, soul and country music.

From Hawaii the Forrest sailed to San Diego. When they left California the three major networks, NBC, CBS and ABC were on board. The Forrest had orders to recover the Apollo I space capsule scheduled to splash down in the Pacific.

Having the networks aboard made life easier for the crew. The Navy, always wanting to make a good impression, had ordered all crew to dress as neatly as possible. The normal paint splattered set of dungarees were not to be worn and all clothes had to be ironed and wrinkle free. There were no scaffolds or cargo nets rigged over the sides and the crew were ordered to look busy or stay out of sight. The only thing that kept the trip from being a holiday was the drills. The ship carried a replica of the space capsule and recovery drills were called with no notice. These drills could be anytime of the day or night and usually took two to three hours to complete.

The Forrest was sailing in circles waiting for the splash down when the capsule landed several hundred miles away and another ship, the U.S.S. Boxer, made the recovery. The Forrest returned to San Diego for four days then sailed for the Caribbean and a month of war games.

Mid-October they sailed into hurricane Inez. The Captain ordered everything tied down and all work suspended. The heavy ship rode the hurricane easily and Henry and several others amused themselves by standing on the fantail and watching the waves crash into the ship. A few hours after clearing the hurricane they received orders to sail for the island of Hispaniola to assist Haiti and the Dominican Republic. Inez had hit the island head on and the Forrest was ordered to join the other ships of the Caribbean Readiness Force. The ship's helicopters flew night and day to and from the island. Both deck divisions were sent in by boat to help with the clean up. Henry saw poverty worse than he'd ever imagined. These people had almost nothing before Inez paid her visit. Now they had less than nothing.

Howie turned over a large piece of tin and plywood and found the twisted, broken body of a young girl. He became sick to his stomach and afterwards wouldn't turn anything over large enough to conceal a body. The Forrest stayed off the coast of the island for a week then returned to Norfolk.

The ship returned to Viet Nam in February carrying three thousand Marines and two hundred assault helicopters. They remained for a month then sailed for Hong Kong. Henry was happy to see the opium den still operating. From Hong Kong they sailed to Okinawa for four days then to Manila, Philippines. The Manila visit was cut short when they found the head of a Chief Petty Officer sitting on the dock at sunrise. From Manila they sailed for New York and anchored off the coast of Queens near the Statue of Liberty. From New York they returned to Norfolk arriving the first week of June. Two weeks later they sailed for dry dock at the Boston Naval Shipyard. Here sandblasting crews would strip the ship's hull down to the metal and new primer would be applied.

Henry loved Boston, especially one five block square in downtown Boston called the 'Combat Zone'. The powers to be in Boston had decided years earlier that if they had to tolerate naked women and sexually oriented businesses it would be better to restrict them to one area of the city. They designated the lower area of Charles Street for 'adult entertainment' and forbid any adult establishments from operating outside that area. Henry could stand on one side of Charles and be among the polite tea drinkers and cross the street and be in a district respectable Bostonians avoided. Anything was acceptable in the 'Combat Zone' and even the police avoided the area unless they were called. Near naked women stood in doors enticing customers in. A stroll past the bars and strip clubs and you might see a couple in an alley having intercourse or a woman (or a man) performing oral sex in a doorway. Henry loved the place.

Henry met a merchant seaman at the 'Naked i' strip club and the two struck up a conversation. Henry mentioned that he'd be leaving the Navy around Christmas time and the seaman told him he should apply for his Merchant Mariner's card. "You can wear what you want and pretty much do what you want as long as you do your job. And the pay's good."

Henry went by the Coast Guard station on his next day of liberty and asked to apply. He was told he'd have to wait until he was discharged from the Navy.

Henry was released from active duty a week before Thanksgiving, six weeks early. He returned to the Coast Guard station with his discharge papers and applied for his Merchant Mariner's card. He had no idea if he'd ever use it. He left the station and walked to the bus depot and bought a ticket for Grainsley. After checking his duffel bag he walked to the Boston Commons and smoked a joint. An hour later he climbed aboard a bus. He'd been with the Navy for nearly four years and two months. Now he was going home.

His Merchant Mariner's card arrived in the mail two weeks later.

CHAPTER ELEVEN

Henry had less than three hundred dollars when he stepped off the bus in Grainsley and nearly half was payment for unused leave. Though the morning was early Lahoma was waiting when he arrived. "Thanks for picking me up, I've missed you," he told Lahoma.

"Well you've got that behind you and your whole life ahead. Do you know what you want to do now? I talked to Velma Beasley the other day and she said her husband could use some help at the feed store. You might want to talk to him."

"Have you heard anything from Harvey?"

"I was hoping you wouldn't ask. I wish you'd stay away from him Henry. Harvey's crazy. He beat a man a while back so bad they had to take him to the hospital."

"He wouldn't hurt me."

"He might. Viet Nam changed him. They say he likes to hurt people and you don't need to be around someone like that. You've got other friends you can see."

"You ever hear from the Holtons?"

"I've heard that Leon was in town a few days ago on a motorcycle. They're living near Vinita I think. All I hear are bits and pieces. Someone told me Josh had been in trouble and had to go to prison for awhile but I'm not sure how true it is."

Henry decided that he wasn't going to stay in Oklahoma. He wanted to write a book of poetry in the style of Robert Service. Poems that told a story and often had a twist to the ending. He had a notebook full he'd written in the Navy and would have to move some place where they had publishing companies but he didn't want to live in Oklahoma City. He was moving to Texas but he wouldn't tell his grandmother until after the Thanksgiving holiday. There would only be the two of them at the mahogany table on Thursday. Levi and Patricia were dead and Lahoma hardly ever heard from her in-laws. Charlie wouldn't attend and he wouldn't allow Erica to either.

Lahoma cooked a ham and all the trimmings. After dinner Henry wanted to take his truck and go to Mayetta but he didn't want to leave his grandmother alone. Lahoma seemed to sense this. She wouldn't let Henry wash the dishes and told him she had work to do later and the best thing he could do was to go somewhere and get out of her hair. As he was leaving she asked if he needed any money. "I got money. I won't be long. Just long enough to look around and maybe have a beer."

Henry called the Pike home from a pay phone in Mayetta and Thelma Pike gave him Harvey's address and telephone number in Hardmor. He called several times but didn't get an answer. He thought briefly of driving to Hardmor but decided against it. Henry drove to the I-44 club instead and sipped a beer hoping to see someone he knew. After an hour he gave up and returned to his grandmother's.

"Why do you want to move to Fort Worth?" Lahoma asked. "You don't know anyone in Fort Worth."

"I don't want to spend the rest of my life in Mayetta."

"Then move to Hardmor or Grainsley. You don't have to move to Fort Worth."

"Hardmor's worse than Mayetta. Besides Fort Worth isn't that far away. Just a couple of hours."

"I guess you've already made up your mind. You're just like your grandfather and your uncle. There's no talking to you when you make up your mind. When are you leaving?"

"Monday."

"Why so soon? Why not take a few days and relax?"

"If I do I'll be too broke to leave. I need to get there and get a job."

The following Monday Henry tried to call Harvey again and still didn't get an answer. After promising his grandmother for the hundredth time he'd call regularly and visit when he could he loaded his clothes in the Dodge pick-up and left for Fort Worth.

Henry stopped at a Piggly Wiggly in Haltom City, a sub-urb on the east side of Fort Worth, and bought a newspaper. He studied the classified ads looking for an affordable apartment and found one less than two hundred yards from the phone booth.

The small, one bedroom, furnished apartment at the Haltom Square Apartments cost Henry one hundred and ten dollars a month plus an eighty dollar deposit. He had less than seventy dollars left. Lahoma had given him a set of sheets, a quilt, four towels and wash cloths, a coffee percolator and a small combination clock/radio. Anything else he needed would have to wait until he found a job.

That evening Henry read the classifieds again circling any type of work he thought he could do. The next morning he bought a map of Fort Worth at a Texaco station and used it to help locate the first business he'd circled in the paper, F & D Head Company on 28th Street. He drove to the company and applied for a job and was hired on the spot.

F & D Company was a machine shop that specialized in making heads. Heads are the tops and bottoms of transport trailers that haul everything from oil and chemicals to cheap wine and milk. The companies that made the trailers ordered the heads from companies such as F & D that specialized in building them.

The first day Henry did little work. He was given a tour of the business and each machine, and what it did, was explained to him. He was told to observe and assist the others as they worked the hundred ton and sixty ton presses that shaped the flat metal circles into bowls. The work was hard, dirty and exact. Each head had to have a certain depth and curvature.

Henry liked his bosses and his four co-workers. The two older men did any welding, cutting or sanding the heads needed and the two younger men worked the presses that shaped the heads. Henry was put to work on a sixty ton press.

Saturday morning Henry went shopping. He bought groceries, toiletries, kitchen ware, a used Smith-Corona typewriter, a case of Budweiser beer and a carton of Camel non-filtered cigarettes..

Henry had been in Texas for nearly two weeks. He'd spent his nights typing his poems, all one hundred and forty, and had them neatly bound in a plastic folder. The following Saturday he purchased a used fifteen inch television and a cheap portable record player. After watching television for less than two hours Saturday night he became restless and decided to check out the bars. He chose a blue denim shirt to wear with his gray vest, gray Stetson Fedora and gray Wellington boots. After drinking two cups of coffee he pulled on his Navy peacoat and left the apartment. He turned left on the Denton highway and followed the road to Belknap. He continued down Belknap until he saw a marquee that read 'Rustler's Rest'. Below the name of the club the marquee announced that Jerry Lane and Carl Vaughn would be performing 'live and in person'. The club's parking lot was full and Henry had to park a block away on a side street. He could hear the music a half block away as he walked toward the entrance. Inside the club a bar approximately twenty feet long sat to the left of the entrance. At the end of the bar a doorway led to the dance floor and to a stage at the far end of the floor. A booth sat to the right of the doorway and a heavyset woman sat inside the booth collecting money for a 'cover charge'. A band and a large blond-haired singer, singing a Dee Mullins song, 'Texas Tea', occupied the stage. The club was full and the dance floor crowded. Henry made his way to the bar and ordered a beer. He carried his beer to the doorway leading to the dance floor. Inside he saw a sea of wide brimmed hats and silver belt buckles.

"What's the charge to go inside?" Henry asked the lady in the booth.

"Five dollars."

Henry paid the money and started through the door. "Just a moment sir. I need to stamp your hand."

Henry held his hand out and the lady stamped the back. He looked but couldn't see a mark of any kind. "I don't think your stamper has any ink ma'am."

"It's ultra violet. Here hold your hand under this lamp," she said, pointing to a small desk lamp. Henry put his hand under the lamp and saw a red 'R' appear.

"If you want to leave and come back later we'll know not to charge you again. Just don't wash it off."

"Thank you ma'am."

"You're welcome. I hope you have a good time."

Henry stood at the edge of the dance floor and looked around. The club could easily hold three hundred people or more and all the seats were taken except for a table to the left of the stage and near the men's room. A heavyset man sat alone at the table. Henry walked over and stood near a chair across the table from the man. "Is this seat taken?"

"This is the band table. I guess you can sit here till the band takes a break."

Henry removed his peacoat and draped it across the back of the chair. After sitting down he extended his hand across the table. "I'm Henry Ridge."

The stranger ignored his offer to shake hands. A moment later a thin, pretty, dark-haired young woman took a seat next to the stranger and smiled at Henry. "Hi," she said, "I'm Pam."

"I'm Henry and it's always nice to meet such a pretty lady."

"Oh ain't you sweet. Are you a picker?"

"No ma'am."

"Are you friends with the band?"

"He's just sitting here till the band takes a break," the stranger growled, "then he can find another table."

"Maybe it'd be better if I found another table now."

"Don't pay any attention to Jimmy," Pam told him, "he's just being his usual obnoxious self."

A waitress came to the table and asked if they needed anything to drink. Henry gave her his empty beer bottle and ordered another beer. Pam ordered a Tom Collins and Jimmy ordered coffee. When the waitress returned Henry gave her a ten and said he'd pay for Pam and Jimmy also. "Coffee's free," she told him, then placed his change on the tray and held the tray in front of Henry. Henry took his change then gave her a two dollar tip.

The band ended the set with 'Cotton-eyed Joe' then took a break. The guitarist, drummer and bass player left the stage and came over to the table. Henry stood up to leave. "You don't have to leave," the bass player said, "there's plenty of seats."

Henry sat back down and extended his hand, "I'm Henry Ridge."

"I'm Clay Clayton," the bass player said, shaking Henry's hand, "and this is Perry Michaels and Dan Hartman."

Clay was a small man a few years older than Henry with blonde hair combed back in a duck tail. Perry, the guitarist, was thin, dark-haired and slightly taller than Henry. Dan, the drummer was short, overweight and appeared to be in his teens.

"I haven't seen you here before," Clay said. "Are you a musician?"

"No, I just like to listen."

"Does anyone have anything to smoke?" Perry asked.

"Belmon does," Dan answered.

"I've got enough for us," Jimmy said, "but not enough for the hare-lip."

"Do you have to act like an asshole?" Perry asked.

"Fuck you Perry. It's my pot. I got a right to say who smokes it. You ready to go outside?"

"You can go without me," Clay said.

"I don't want any either," Perry added.

"Why are you taking this hare-lip's side?" Jimmy asked. "He's not a picker!"

"Neither are you Belmon!" Clay answered.

"You folks go ahead," Henry told them, "maybe I better leave." Henry picked up his beer and carried it to the bar. A few minutes later he left the club and drove back to his apartment.

The following Saturday night Henry returned to Rustler's Rest. He sat at the bar drinking beer and listening to the band. He didn't dance and he saw no reason to pay a cover charge to enter the dance area.

"Hi. Remember me?" Henry turned and saw Pam standing behind him. "You're Henry right?"

"Yes ma'am and you're Pam."

"Oh how sweet. You remembered me."

"I never forget a pretty lady."

"Are you coming inside?"

"I hadn't planned on it."

"We've got plenty of room at the band table."

"Is your fat friend with you?"

"Jimmy? Don't pay any attention to Jimmy."

"I think I'll stay out here."

"I wanted you to dance with me."

"I don't dance ma'am."

"I'll teach you. And stop calling me ma'am! You make me feel old!"

"Yes ma'am."

"You're cute. You don't dress like the other cowboys."

"What cowboys? I doubt you could find a cowboy in here. Lots of pretty hats and buckles though."

"I really wish you'd come in and sit with us."

"Maybe later." Henry watched Pam walk back to the table then he ordered another beer. A few minutes later the band took a break and Clay and the blond-haired singer came out to the bar area. Clay saw Henry sitting at the bar and walked over leaving the singer at the booth talking to the lady inside.

"Hey you're back. Why didn't you come inside?"

"I can hear the band fine from here."

"I want you to meet someone."

Clay led Henry over to the booth. "This is Jerry Lane. Jerry this is Henry." The singer shook Henry's hand then asked, "Do you pick?"

"No, I just like good music."

Perry joined the small group and whispered something to Clay.

"Do you smoke anything other than cigarettes?" Clay asked Henry.

"I've been known to."

"Walk outside with me and Perry."

Henry followed the pair outside and around to the back of the building. Perry pulled a joint from his shirt pocket and lit it then passed it to Clay.

"Is this all we got?" Clay asked.

"That's it," Perry answered. "I know where we can get more but I won't have any money until Marie pays us."

After the joint made its way around a few times Henry felt his head swimming. He hadn't had any marijuana since Boston and he'd missed it. "I'll buy some if you can find it and they don't want an arm and a leg for it."

"It's ten dollars an ounce," Perry told him. Henry pulled a ten dollar bill from his wallet and gave the money to Perry.

"I won't be able to get it until the next break."

"I'll be here."

"Hi, I'm Jerry Lane." Henry heard the singer announce from the stage.

"We'd better go," Clay said.

The band scrambled onto the stage and Jerry kicked off the set with a song Henry had never heard called 'They Never Made Me Say I'm Sorry'. When the song finished Jerry called Clay to the microphone and Clay sang an old Al Dexter song, 'Too Late to Worry, Too Blue to Cry'. Jerry did two more songs then called Carl Vaughn up on stage. Carl sang three songs then gave the microphone back to Jerry. Jerry sang four more songs then closed the set with a Johnny Cash song, 'Cocaine Blues' then announcing the band was taking a fifteen minute 'pause for the cause'. The dance floor emptied as everyone returned to their tables and the juke box was turned on. Clay joined Henry at the bar.

"You sang your ass off," Henry told him. "What was that song Jerry did about never saying he was sorry? I never heard it before."

"Jerry wrote it."

"He's a hell of a writer."

Perry came out to the bar and asked if they were ready to go outside. Outside the bar he pulled a sandwich bag filled with pot out of his pocket and gave it to Henry. Henry rolled a joint and the three smoked it then returned to the bar. His head was buzzing. "This is some good shit, we'll do this again the next break."

Carl Vaughn kicked off the next set and fifteen minutes later called Jerry to the stage. Pam came out to the bar and asked Henry if he'd like to sit at the band table with her. "Is your friend with you?"

"You mean Jimmy? Don't pay any attention to him."

"I don't think he likes me."

"Jimmy doesn't like anyone unless they're on stage. He stays pissed off because he's not up there."

"I take it he's not a musician."

"He's an accountant who wants to be in music. He tries to write songs but none of them make any sense. He's been trying for a long time to get Jerry or Carl to do one of his songs but everything he writes is a piece of shit. I wish you'd ignore him and sit with me."

"I never could turn down a pretty lady." Henry paid the cover charge then followed her inside and took a seat across the table from Jimmy. Pam sat next to him and Jimmy glared at the two then left the table. The next break Henry walked outside with Clay, Perry and Dan and rolled two joints.

"One more set then we can get out of here," Perry said. "Are you going to Soul City with us Henry?"

"What's Soul City?"

"An 'after hours' club. Everyone goes there after the other bars close."

"I don't know if I can stay awake that long."

"Ask Clay to give you something."

"A few hours sleep is all I need. I'll tag along but I can't promise how long I'll stay."

Clay rode with Henry and they followed Perry and Pam to a small club off Beach Street. The place didn't look like it would hold fifty people. A young woman sat at a counter in front of the door collecting a dollar a head from 'civilians', people not involved in the music industry. Anyone working in a band or associated with music entered free. Henry paid his dollar and followed Clay inside. A bar ran from the entrance to a small stage and the only thing anyone could purchase to drink was coffee or soft drinks. The place was already crowded and all the seats were taken. Clay pointed toward a table where Perry and Pam were sitting with Jimmy Belmon and two young ladies. Pam tried to wave them over but Henry couldn't see any vacant seats. Clay walked over and said something to Perry and Henry ordered a cup of coffee. He was beginning to wish he'd gone home. It was nearly three in the morning and he was sleepy. Anyone that wanted to sing could take the stage at Soul City and do three songs. Most of the performers were mediocre at best, wannabe singers that couldn't find work in the clubs, but a few were worth staying up for. These were the entertainers that worked the other clubs around Fort Worth and came to Soul City to 'jam' and party. Clay introduced Henry to several that night; Larry Welborn, lead guitarist for Wynn Stewart; Ray Robbins, singer and bass player with Billy Dee at the Hitching Post; pianists Don Carson and Eddie Long and bassists Wayne Davenport, Bruce Whitaker and Sam Coleman.

Henry stayed at the bar and drank another cup of coffee. He could hardly keep his eyes open and he didn't feel like explaining to anyone why he was leaving. He waited until Clay had gone on stage then quietly snuck out, drove home and went to bed.

Henry slept until noon. He dressed and fixed the coffee pot, then left it to perk while he walked to Haltom Square and bought a Sunday newspaper. Back in his apartment Henry poured a cup of coffee and lit a joint. He planned on reading the paper from cover to cover but halfway through the local section he felt his stomach rumble. For a moment he considered having his usual bologna sandwich then decided he'd had enough bologna for awhile and instead drove to a Denny's he'd passed on the way to Rustler's Rest the night before.

Henry ordered a club sandwich and a cup of coffee and was wishing he'd brought his paper with him when Clay and Perry entered the restaurant. Both had on the same clothes they'd worn the night before and neither appeared to have had any sleep. They started to sit in a booth near the front until they noticed Henry and came back to the booth where he was sitting. The waitress brought Henry's sandwich to the booth and Clay and Perry ordered coffee. "This sandwich looks good," Henry told them. "If you're hungry I'll buy your dinner."

Clay rubbed his forehead and made a face. "I couldn't eat if you put a gun to my head."

"Food's the last thing I want," Perry said.

"It's none of my business but it looks like both of you need to go to bed."

"We can't," Perry said. "We have a matinee at two at Rustler's."

"We need a fucking joint," Clay said. "Do you have any pot on you?"

"I don't have any on me but if you'll follow me back to my apartment I'll roll a couple."

"Can't you eat any faster?" Clay asked.

Clay and Perry followed Henry back to his apartment in Perry's ten year old Ford. The car was six different colors and looked like something someone had abandoned on the side of the road.

The three men were seated at Henry's small kitchen table sharing a joint when Clay noticed the coffee pot and asked if he could make a fresh pot of coffee. While the coffee perked Clay turned on the radio and played with the knobs, hearing part of a song, then part of another, then part of another.

The two men liked to talk and while Clay played with the knobs and the coffee perked he learned a part of their background. Clay Clayton's real name was Clayton Grimstad and he'd moved with his parents from Los Angeles to Fort Worth when he was seventeen. At one time he'd dreamed of being a star with his own band and had taken Clay Clayton as a stage name. While still in school in California he'd formed a band that played at school events and local clubs. He found he wasn't comfortable being in the limelight forty-five minutes out of the hour and preferred to play bass and stay on the side. He was eight years older than Henry and still lived with his parents. His mother, a devout Christian, prayed every night that her son would give up music and leave the bars behind but Clay had no intention of changing.

Perry Michaels came from Canada and had traveled to Texas with a second rate band from Halifax, Nova Scotia. The band was cheated out of their money after working a week at a Dallas club and disbanded, leaving each member on their own. While the rest of the group called home for money to get back to Canada Perry found a gig with a local band and stayed. Since then he'd worked with most of the country bands in the Dallas/Fort Worth area and was considered one of the finest guitar players in Texas. Perry was ten years older than Henry.

Clay refilled his cup and continued playing with the radio knobs. "Where you from, Henry?" Perry asked.

"Oklahoma."

"What made you move here?"

"I thought it might be easier to find a publisher."

"Are you a writer?"

"I try."

"What kind of writing?" Clay asked.

"I guess you'd call it poetry. You ever read any Robert Service?"

"Never heard of him," Perry answered, "but I'd like to read some of your poems."

Henry went to his bedroom and pulled his folder of poems from the night stand drawer.

He laid the folder on the table in front of Perry. "The only thing I ask is that you give me an honest opinion."

"Why wouldn't we?" Clay asked.

"Some folks think they're doing someone a favor and sparing their feelings by telling them they like something when they don't."

"Well we won't." Clay assured him. "If we don't like it we'll tell you."

Perry read the poems and passed them to Clay as he finished. Henry rolled a half dozen more joints and sipped a cup of coffee. After a few minutes Perry handed Clay a poem and told him to read it next. "Funny New Sounds, I like the title," Clay told him.

"I think you could make a song out of it," Perry said.

"It looks like it's got about twenty verses. It'd take thirty minutes to sing it."

"What if we trimmed it to three? We ought to take it to Jerry and see what he thinks."

"Or Carl and Marie," Clay said. "Carl Vaughn's looking for material."

"I know who Carl Vaughn is," Henry said, "but who's Carl and Marie?"

"Carl and Marie Patton," Clay answered. "Marie's the woman that works the booth at Rustler's. Her and her husband Carl own the place. They're also producing Carl Vaughn."

"You'll need a tune for it," Perry said. "Jerry could do that if you don't mind splitting the writing."

Henry was feeling excited. He'd had dreams of being a writer but he'd never considered song writing and he liked the idea. "What would it take for the two of you to help me?" Henry asked. "What I know about music you could put in a thimble."

"Light another joint and I'll think about it," Clay said.

Henry lit another joint and passed it to Clay. Perry started laughing and passed another poem to Clay telling him, "Read this, it'll knock your dick in the dirt."

The poem was entitled 'Mary's In The Garden' and was about a man who killed his unfaithful wife and buried her in the garden among her roses then told her lover about it as he served him a cup of poisoned coffee.

"It's a shame you can't get this to Porter Waggoner," Clay said. "He could make a hell of a recitation out of it."

Perry handed Clay another poem about a lonely security guard having a conversation with his coffee cup and told him to read it. "You write like an old man," Perry commented, "and I mean that as a compliment. Can I have a copy of this?"

"You can have a copy of anything I've got."

Clay and Perry picked through the poems and chose a half dozen more. Clay poured another cup of coffee then took a black capsule from his shirt pocket and swallowed it. Perry asked Clay if he had any more and Clay pulled another from his pocket and gave it to him.

"It's nearly one-thirty," Perry said, "we'd better get to Rustler's and set up. Why don't you come with us Henry? You can show Jerry your lyrics and see what he thinks."

Henry promised to meet them at the club later. He waited an hour, smoked a joint, then drove to Rustler's Rest and took a seat at the bar. Marie waited until he got a beer then called him over to the booth. "Clay showed me your poems. You've got some strong words there. I'd like for you to talk to my husband later. Did they tell you we're looking for material for Carl Vaughn?"

"Yes ma'am."

"Do you pick or sing?"

"No ma'am."

"Too bad. You need some kind of tune with them and they'll have to be shortened. Do you mind if Jerry reads them?"

"No ma'am. I appreciate any help I can get."

Henry walked back to the bar and ordered a beer. Marie motioned the bartender over to the booth and whispered something to him. Henry saw the bartender nod his head.

At a quarter to four the band took their second break and Clay, Perry and Jerry Lane came over to where Henry sat. Jerry was carrying the copies of Henry's songs he'd given Clay and Perry earlier. "I'd like to see what tune I can come up with for the words to Funny New Sounds."

"Jerry's had songs recorded by Waylon Jennings and Charlie Pride," Clay remarked.

"You've got some good ideas," Jerry told him.

"You're welcome to anything I've got," Henry replied.

"Did you bring anything to smoke?" Clay asked.

"I brought four joints."

"Let's walk outside."

Jerry declined the invitation to join the three outside. Ten minutes later they were back at the bar. Clay and Perry ordered coffee and each took another black capsule before returning to the stage for their third set. Henry ordered another beer and threw two one dollar bills on the bar. The bartender shoved a dollar back at him and then added three quarters. Henry had been paying a dollar and a half for a beer and he told the bartender he'd made a mistake and given him back too much change. "Marie told me to charge you the house price."

Henry walked over to the booth and asked Marie why he was being charged so little.

"That's the price we charge people in music."

"But I've never had anything recorded."

"That doesn't matter. You're still a writer. You won't have to pay a cover charge either. All the clubs around here have the same policy. You make Clay and Perry introduce you as a songwriter at the other clubs."

The club had been half full when Henry arrived and now was almost packed. A number of local singers and musicians were in attendance and Marie introduced Henry to several. Many gave Henry the impression they were shaking his hand only out of respect for Marie but many were friendly and easy to like.

Jimmy Belmon arrived and Marie called Henry over to introduce them. Henry told her they'd already met and he couldn't help but notice that Jimmy seemed a lot nicer around Marie. "Jimmy's an accountant," she told him. "He knows Ray Price and Johnny Bush. If you wanted to get a song to one of them Jimmy could help."

Jimmy didn't comment and Henry had already made up his mind he'd die and go to hell in a bushel basket before he asked Jimmy Belmon for any favors. Henry returned to the bar and Jimmy walked inside and sat at the band table. During the next break Jimmy walked outside with Clay and Perry. Clay invited Henry to join them but he told them he'd rather stay at the bar. When they returned he told Clay and Perry that he'd be leaving soon. "Why don't you wait around?" Clay asked. "We'll be through here at six then we can roar."

"I have to work tomorrow. I think I'll just go home and purr."

"We can find something to help you at work."

"You got a wetback in your pocket?"

"No," Clay answered, "something better."

Henry agreed to wait until they were finished at six. He drank two double shots of Jim Beam and chased it with beer and was feeling the effects. He agreed to leave his truck and ride with Clay and Perry in Perry's car.

The December day had been in the high forties but when the sun went down the temperature dropped several degrees and Perry's car had no heater. Henry wore his peacoat but Clay and Perry wore light jackets. The cold air blew through the car from under the dash.

Why don't you get a heater for this car?" Henry asked.

"A heater would cost more than what I paid for the car," Perry answered.

Henry decided to light a joint and looked around for an ashtray. There was none. Everything under the dash that separated the motor from the front seat was missing.

"How much further?" Henry asked. He lit the joint and passed it to Clay. Clay was huddled over like a hunchback and Henry could hear his teeth chatter.

"Just a few minutes." Perry answered.

The Hitching Post was a large rambling building that reminded Henry of a converted car dealership. The club was bigger than Rustler's Rest and could easily seat four hundred people or more. A horseshoe shaped bar sat in the center. There were less than fifty people at the club when they arrived but more were entering every minute. Clay introduced Henry to the owner as a songwriter with Jerry Lane. At the bar the bartender put a cup of coffee down in front of Clay before anyone had a chance to order. "I know what Clay drinks. What are you drinking Perry?"

"Coffee."

"And your friend."

"Larry this is Henry," Perry said. "He's a songwriter from Oklahoma."

Henry reached over the bar and shook the bartender's hand. "Since I'm not driving I'll have a Jim Beam and Budweiser."

A tall, thin, dark-haired man entered the club carrying a guitar case followed by a shorter, stocky built younger man carrying a bass guitar and a duffel bag. They put their equipment on the stage then walked over to the bar. "Clay, Perry," the tall man smiled and shook their hands, "how was the matinee?"

"Packed as usual," Perry answered.

"Billy", Clay said, "this is Henry, a songwriter friend of ours. Henry this is Billy Dee."

"I'm glad to meet you Henry. Have you written anything I might have heard?"

"He's new in town," Clay answered. "Jerry's putting a tune to one of his songs for Carl Vaughn to record."

"And this," Clay said, reaching over to pat Billy's companion on the head, "is David Porterhouse."

"Where's rockin' Ray Robbins?" Perry asked. "I thought he was playing bass."

"You know Ray," Billy answered.

"Looks like you might have a full house tonight," Clay commented.

"God I hope so," David said. "It'll make the time go faster. Does anyone have any help on them?"

"Here." Clay reached into his shirt pocket and pulled out two black capsules offering one to Billy. He declined the offer.

"What about me?" David asked.

"I ain't giving you shit." Clay was smiling and it was obvious to Henry that he was having a little fun with his friend. After a moment he gave David a capsule.

Billy and David ordered coffee and returned to the stage and started setting up their equipment, pulling lines and cords from the duffel bag and plugging them into amplifiers. A few minutes later a short, overweight man came in carrying part of a drum set. Billy and David followed him out of the club and returned with the rest of the drums. A moment later a thin man with shoulder length hair and a Van Dyke entered the club carrying a guitar case and joined the others on stage.

Henry finished his whiskey and looked around. The club was nearly full and it wasn't yet eight o'clock. "When does the band start?"

"Eight on Sunday," Clay answered. "They pick till midnight then we'll go to Soul City."

"I can't tonight," Henry told him. "I have to be at work early tomorrow."

"We'll make sure you're home before then."

"I can't stay out all night. If I do I'll be falling asleep at my machine tomorrow."

"Don't worry about it. I'll give you something to keep you awake."

"I think I'd better go on home. This whiskey's hitting me kind of hard and I wouldn't be much fun if I'm passed out."

"Order a cup of coffee," Clay said, pulling another capsule from his pocket, "and I'll give you one of these."

"What is it?"

"It's speed. A 'west coast turn around'. Eat one of these and you can drive to the west coast and turn around and drive back without shuttin' an eye."

"I don't know about that shit. You sure it won't hurt me?"

"You've watched us eat 'em. It hasn't hurt us yet. The only time it hurts me is when I'm out of 'em."

Henry took the capsule and ordered another beer. "Don't drink any beer," Clay ordered. "It'll kill the speed and you'll be wasting it. Drink some coffee or if you don't want coffee order some whiskey. You'll be a wide awake drunk."

Clay had given Henry a diet pill containing amphetamine. The drug slowed the digestive muscles reducing the appetite while increasing the heart rate, pulse and respiration causing the brain to release dopamine, the substance the body uses to reward itself. Halfway through the coffee Henry felt his body start to tingle and heard a slight buzzing in his ears. His eyes felt too small for his head and he arched his eyebrows, trying to widen the eye sockets. He could hear better, see better and felt more alive than he'd ever felt in his life.

"How are you feeling?" Clay asked.

"Like I could run a foot race with anybody here....and win."

"Let's walk outside and smoke a joint. It'll take the edge off."

"I'm not sure I want the edge off."

The three walked outside and smoked a joint. Henry was still speeding and gritting his teeth when they returned but he wasn't wanting to challenge anyone to a foot race any longer. Billy and the band had already started and after a few moments Ray and Perry were called up to 'sit in' for three numbers and David and the guitar player left the stage and came to the bar.

"Henry this is Danny Conners. Danny this is Henry, Clay and Perry's friend." David lowered his voice and leaned toward Henry, "Clay says you have some smoke and you might take us out in the parking lot and get us high."

"Be happy to."

A few minutes later they were back in the club and David and Danny were back on stage.

"Still want to go home?" Clay asked.

"Fuck home."

Henry saw Pam and two other young, pretty women walking toward the bar and all at once he was hornier than he'd ever been in his life. Usually he could put sex in the back of his mind but now all he could think about was a naked female body. Any naked female body.

Pam and her companions walked over to the bar and Pam introduced the two women, Carla and Amy, to Henry then looked at Henry's eyes and began laughing, "Oh honey, you look like a scared rabbit."

"I'll bet I could outrun one," Henry replied.

Pam rubbed her body against Henry. "I hear those pills make you horny." Before Henry could answer she stepped back and all three women laughed. Henry was being teased. She knew he was ready to fuck a broom if he could find one with tits.

Carla, a small, perfectly shaped, long-haired brunette, smiled at Henry then told Pam, "He's cute as a rabbit, I wonder if he fucks like one." Henry could feel his face turning red as all three women laughed harder. Clay and Perry were laughing also.

"Let's get a table," Pam suggested.

"I don't think we'll be able to find one," Perry told her, "looks like they're all taken."

Pam and Carla walked away from the bar leaving Amy, another perfectly shaped brunette at the bar with the three men. A moment later Pam returned and told the others they'd found an empty table near the back of the club. Once they were at the table they could only find five chairs. Henry told them he'd return to the bar. "No, you stay here," Clay told him. "I'm waiting for someone anyways, then we'll get out of here."

Ten minutes later a heavyset man in a pair of bib overalls and a John Deere baseball cap entered the club and stood at the cover booth scanning the crowd. Clay saw the man and left his stool at the bar and walked over to him. They spoke briefly then left the club together. A few minutes later Clay returned alone. He came back to the table and asked Perry and Henry if they were ready to leave. He told the women they were going to the Stagecoach Inn and they'd meet them later at Soul City. Outside he pulled two small containers, originally meant to hold camera film, from his pants pocket and held them up. "All he had was fifty blacks."

"What'd he charge you?" Perry asked.

"A quarter each," Clay answered.

"I'll buy 'em all," Henry offered.

"Over my dead body," Perry remarked.

"David and Ted want some," Clay said.

"Who's Ted?" Henry asked.

"You haven't met him yet. He's Billy's drummer."

"So there's five of us," Perry said. "That's ten apiece. Ten times twenty-five is two fifty. I'll pay you when we get to the Stagecoach."

"I'll pay you now," Henry offered.

Clay counted out ten capsules and gave them to Henry. Henry transferred everything he had in his right pocket to his left and put the pills in the right pocket alone. He didn't want loose change to damage them.

From the Hitching Post they drove the short distance to the Stagecoach Inn on Sylvania Avenue. The temperature had dropped a few more degrees but Henry didn't seem to notice the cold as much. His whole body tingled, his ears were buzzing and he was gritting his teeth so loudly he could hear them grind.

The stagecoach Inn covered most of the block and could easily hold more than double the people Rustler's Rest could accommodate. Over a hundred people were in the club but because of its size the place appeared nearly empty. Clay introduced Henry to Ginger, the pretty young woman collecting the five dollar cover charge, as a songwriter and Henry followed Clay and Perry to the bar where a medium-built man with short, coal black hair sat alone.

"Henry this is John Maynard. John this is Henry." John nodded toward Henry and Henry could tell by the man's eyes that he was on something.

"Do you have any dope?" John asked.

"Judging by your eyes," Clay told him, "you've already found some."

"I'm talking about pot," John said.

"Henry does," Clay answered.

John looked over at Henry and said, "Well Henry, what are we waiting for...Christmas?" The four men walked outside and

Henry rolled a joint. Back inside the club John left the others and took a seat at the bar next to an extremely overweight young woman. "John likes them fat," Clay told him when they were seated at a table. "He knows a few doctors who will write prescriptions for diet pills and he picks up these fat girls and gets them to fall in love with him then he takes them to a doctor and gets them a prescription. He gives them a couple of pills then he keeps the rest for himself."

A waitress came to their table and all three ordered coffee. The joints they'd smoked earlier were beginning to kill Henry's speed and he yawned. He reached in his pants pocket and pulled out another capsule then washed it down with coffee. In a matter of minutes the tingling and the buzzing returned.

The band had been on break when they arrived and was now taking the stage. Henry looked over at the band table and saw Jimmy Belmon sitting there. He was hoping he'd stay where he was but as soon as the band started Jimmy walked over to their table and sat down. Henry finished his coffee and ordered whiskey. Jimmy watched him pay and saw the waitress bring his change. "Why is he paying band prices? I don't get my drinks at band prices."

"He's a songwriter," Perry answered.

"He's a fuckin' hare-lip for Christ's sake!"

Henry was fed up. The speed was making him short-tempered and Jimmy had been insulting and rude from the first moment they'd met. He leaned over the table until he was only a few inches from his face. "I'm tired of your mouth! If you've got a bone to pick with me we'll walk outside and settle it now! Otherwise keep your goddamn mouth shut!"

"Don't fight in here," Clay warned, "or you'll have to fight that man." He pointed to a police officer standing near the bar watching their table.

Henry sat back down and lowered his voice, "Belmon you listen to me. You keep riding my ass and someday I'll catch you when the law ain't around and when I get done you'll run backwards every time someone mentions hare-lip." Jimmy's face turned red and he stomped out of the club.

"What's his problem?" Henry asked.

"He's an asshole," Clay answered.

"He's a legend in his own mind," Perry said. "Don't let him get to you."

At a quarter to the hour the band took a break and the singer, an older man in a suit and white cowboy hat, walked over to their table. "Clay, Perry would you like to sit in for awhile?"

"Not tonight," Clay answered. "Ray this is Henry. Henry this is Ray Chaney. He owns the place. Henry's a songwriter."

"I'd like to hear some of your songs," Ray said, then excused himself and walked over to the band table and sat down with two other band members.

"Ray records some," Clay told him. "It's mostly on local labels but at least you could get some things heard."

During the next break Clay introduced Henry to Three Finger Cecil, the guitarist for Ray Chaney, and Charlie, the steel guitarist for the band. After the band returned to the stage Clay was ready to leave.

"Where we going?" Henry asked.

"To Dodge City," Clay answered.

Dodge City was a small club only a few blocks from the Stagecoach Inn. The club was in the middle of a small shopping center with a clothing store on one side and an office supply store on the other. The three ordered coffee and Clay introduced Henry to David Chamberlain, a singer/songwriter who performed songs ranging from George Jones to Tony Bennet. After one set the three left Dodge City and drove to Soul City.

Pam, Carla and Amy were at the club when they arrived. The crowd was small and after a few minutes Pam suggested they leave and go to the apartment she shared with Amy. At the apartment Clay and Pam went to Pam's bedroom. A few minutes later Amy led Perry to the other bedroom. Henry sat alone in the living room with Carla and his erection, too bashful to make a move. Carla went to the bathroom and returned a moment later naked except for her shirt. She took a pillow from the sofa and lay on the floor. Henry removed his clothes and joined her. He didn't make it back to his apartment until late afternoon. He chug-a-lugged three beers, went to bed and fell asleep. He'd completely forgotten about work.

Henry had been in Fort Worth for four months. He'd missed too much work at the machine shop and had been fired after less than a month. He was addicted to diet pills and was staying up for days at a time. He'd been back to Oklahoma once, Christmas Day, full of speed and restless to get back to the clubs. He'd lost weight and had started chewing his fingernails. He hardly ever had an appetite and had to force himself to eat at least once a week. But he loved his life and couldn't imagine staying home as long as a bar or club was open and a band was playing.

He was also gaining a reputation as a song lyricist. He knew all his material by heart and could write the words down to any of his songs anytime anyone requested them. The speed made him want to write and he wrote anytime he could, sometimes as many as ten songs a day, and on those rare moments when he was straight, he'd re-read them and throw ninety percent of them away.

He'd moved in with Carla for a brief period after being fired from the machine shop. Carla was an exhibitionist and a sex addict. She had long brunette hair, a smile to die for and a body that could have been a centerfold in Playboy. Henry thought he'd died and gone to heaven. The speed gave him stamina and during the first few weeks they had sex three or four times a day. If Henry went out without her she met him at the door naked when he returned. Henry loved watching her run around the apartment nude until the novelty wore off and he came home one morning and yelled, "for Christ sake put some fuckin' clothes on!" That night she refused to go to the club with him and when he returned two days later all his belongings were on the door steps.

Since being fired from F&D Head Company Henry had worked as a carpenter's helper, a dishwasher, a bus boy and a laborer. He'd moved into a room at the Park Plaza Motel on Lancaster Avenue. The rent was thirty dollars a week and included a phone and a color television. Several country musicians also had rooms at the Plaza including Wayne Davenport, Don Carson, Sam Coleman and Saul Carter, a part time bass player and full time marijuana dealer. The room came with maid service and mice and the motel had a small pool, a restaurant and twenty-four hour room service. A speed addict could order a fresh pot of coffee at any hour and, if the evening was early, and he was lonely, a female was nearly always available.

Henry had been accepted into the music community but he still hadn't had anything recorded.

Clay came by his room on a Wednesday morning in an eight year old Pontiac he was buying from a car dealer on Belknap for three hundred dollars, paying thirty dollars a week for ten weeks. The brakes were bad and the car barely ran. Henry was next door in bed with the motel's night clerk, Liz, a plump young blonde with a talent for performing fellatio, more popularly known as 'giving head'. Henry heard Clay knocking and looked out the window to see who it was. He opened the door and told Clay to come in.

"Why don't you come out here? I need to talk to you about something."

"I'm naked Clay."

"Well get your clothes on and let's go to your room."

"I'd rather stay here. Besides, if you're here to borrow money you're shit out of luck. I'm gettin' cold holding this door open. Are you comin' in or not?"

"Just five dollars. That's all I need."

"I don't have five dollars Clay. If I did I'd give it to you to go away."

"What about her?" Clay asked, pointing toward Liz, now wide awake, laying on the bed.

"She don't have it either. What do you need it for?"

"I can't tell you here. Can we go to your room? Maybe I can call someone."

Clay waited outside while Henry dressed. Inside his room he asked Clay again why he needed the money. "I can't tell you. It's too embarrassing." Clay sat on the edge of the bed and stared at the floor.

Henry had to know what it was. "Tell me what's bothering you and I'll try to borrow five dollars for you."

"I caught the crabs."

Henry couldn't help laughing and once he got started he couldn't stop.

"It's not funny!" Clay yelled.

Henry laughed harder.

"I've got 'em from my knees to the belly button! The bastards are eating me alive!" Clay was scratching his groin with both hands. Henry's sides were aching.

"You better hope they don't get in your duck tail. Might be like that boll weevil that found a home. You might never get 'em out."

"Just get me the money and I'll go buy some shit to kill 'em!"

Henry walked next door and asked Liz if he could borrow five dollars. The clerk had less than three dollars but she offered to loan it to Henry. Henry thanked her but refused to take her last three dollars.

"Did you get the money?" Clay asked.

"She didn't have it."

"You told me you'd get me the money if I told you why I needed it!"

"I lied. Would you mind sitting somewhere else, like maybe outside? You might be gettin' crabs all over my bed."

"You start fuckin' with me," Clay warned, "and I'll take my pants off and roll around on everything in this room."

"I just don't want the mice to catch 'em. I've gotten used to their scurrying around. I'm not sure I could get used to hearing them scratch all night."

"You think this shit is funny?"

"No, I think it's hilarious. What are you going to do now, wait until they gnaw their way to your arm pits?"

"These sons-of-bitches are chewing my balls off. I'm gonna call John. Maybe he'll have some money."

Clay called John Maynard and John told him he was broke. After Clay explained why he needed the money John told him to come by his house and he had something that would take care of his problem. Clay asked Henry to ride with him and Henry agreed to go providing Clay would tell him what girls Clay had been with in the past two weeks.

John had been sharing a house with Anne, a pretty-faced,

overweight, twenty-year old college student. When Henry and Clay arrived John was sitting in the kitchen floor with a magic marker drawing a life size sketch of a stove on the wall where a stove had once been. Henry wandered through the house and saw that every piece of furniture and all the appliances were gone. Except for John's clothes hanging in the bedroom closet and a few odds and ends in the pantry and cabinets the house was completely empty. John had drawn a queen size bed and dresser, complete with drawers and knobs, on the bedroom walls, a sofa, lounge chair and end table with lamp on the living room walls and a refrigerator and finally the stove on the kitchen walls.

"I'd offer you a cup of coffee but you'd have to wait until I drew a coffee pot."

"You said you had something for crabs," Clay reminded him.

John stood and walked over to the pantry and took a can of Raid Roach and Ant Killer from the shelf and handed it to Clay.

"I can't use this," Clay moaned.

"Why not? I don't need it."

"It's bug killer for Christ's sake! When you said you had something to kill crabs I thought you meant some ointment from the drugstore. This shit doesn't say nothin' about crabs. It's insecticide!"

"If it'll kill roaches and ants then it damn well oughta kill crabs. I'll even let you use my bathroom if you want."

Clay took the can of Raid to the bathroom and closed the door. A moment later they heard him scream. Henry heard later that folks as far away as Denton and Weatherford had heard Clay scream.

CHAPTER TWELVE

Henry needed to earn at least thirty dollars a week to pay his rent at the Park Plaza Motel. He needed double that much and more to buy marijuana, diet pills, gas, cigarettes, beer, whiskey and an occasional hamburger. He no longer took full time jobs because he knew he wouldn't work full time and being fired was always embarrassing. He worked three, sometimes four, days a week for Manpower, a private employment agency that provided men for menial labor. The only drawback was the winos he had to wait with in a small room until his name was called. Most were homeless and they all smelled like cheap, stale wine.

Clay was having trouble keeping a job. He'd been fired from Rustler's Rest for falling asleep on stage in the middle of a song and was now working with other local bands when they needed a bassist. Some of the bars Clay worked were as rough as the bars on the Red River.

Henry rode with Clay one night to a small bar on the Jacksboro Highway called the Saw Mill. The entire stage had a ten foot high chicken wire fence around it to keep any stray beer bottles from hitting the band members or their equipment if and when a fight broke out. Henry took a seat at the band table near the corner of the stage and sat with his back to the wall where he could watch the crowd. The crowd stayed friendly and at two a.m., Charles Dean, the band's vocalist, paid Clay fifty dollars and asked him to work the following night. Clay accepted and asked Henry to accompany him again but Henry refused.

"I'll meet you later at the Country Palace."

"Why won't you come back here with me?" Clay asked. "There wasn't any trouble tonight."

"There wasn't any women either. At least none that was unattached and I didn't like the way some of the men looked at me. You got that chicken wire between you and them and I gotta sit among 'em. One old drunk kept calling me sweet thing and asking me to dance."

"Maybe they think you're an ugly whore with that long ass hair of yours and that half ass hat." Henry had been out of the Navy more than two years and hadn't had a haircut in all that time. His long, black hair hung several inches below his shoulders.

"They can think what they want. I'll meet you at the Palace when you're done here."

Soul City had closed a few months earlier and the crowd had moved to another after hours club on the Jacksboro Highway near Lake Worth. The Country Palace was a fifteen minute drive from Rustler's Rest or the Stagecoach Inn and at two or three in the morning any patrol car that saw him was almost certain to pull him over. Henry and Clay were pulled over regularly. The patrol officer, or officers, would pull the front and back seats out of the car and onto the pavement, empty the contents of the glove compartment onto the floor of the car, search the trunk and empty its contents onto the pavement and then tell them they were free to go. Henry and Clay would then spend the next several minutes putting the seats back in and picking up the contents of the glove compartment and the trunk. They soon learned to take the side streets whenever possible and avoid any road that might have a patrol car on it.

Perry called Clay Wednesday and told him they needed a bassist for Thursday night at the Watering Hole in Grand Prairie. Clay accepted the job and asked Henry to go with him. On their way back, around three in the morning, a radiator hose in Clay's car burst. Clay pulled into a convenience store that appeared to be open hoping to buy some duct tape to repair the hose enough to get them back to Fort Worth. Although the store's interior lights were on the store was closed. After checking the door and finding it locked they returned to Clay's car to discuss what to do next. As they were trying to come up with a solution that didn't involve a lot of walking two patrol cars pulled up, one in back of Clay's car and one in front of Clay's car, boxing them in. They were ordered out of the car and face down on the ground. After checking under the hood and seeing that the hose had indeed burst a police sergeant explained that when they saw Henry and Clay checking the front door they thought they might be trying to break in. Another officer offered to give them a roll of duct tape he kept in the trunk of his patrol car so they could repair the hose enough to hold water and get them home. Everything was going exceptionally well considering the circumstances until Clay opened his mouth. "I'm tired of you bastards fuckin' with us! You got no right to treat us this way!"

The sergeant walked over to Clay and glared down at him. "What did you call me?"

"You heard me!" Clay replied. "I didn't stutter!"

"Cuff 'em," the sergeant ordered.

Henry and Clay were handcuffed and taken to the Hurst, Texas jail. A tow truck was called to take Clay's car to the impoundment yard. At the jail they were searched then locked in separate cells wearing only their pants, shirts and socks. Both cells were at the far end of the cell block and the only light in either cell was a small blue light above the toilet. The cell contained a metal bunk that extended from the wall but no pillow or blanket. Henry knew he had enough diet pills in him to make sleeping impossible but he wished he had a pillow or a blanket to make a pillow so he could lay down. Clay spent the rest of the night yelling that his rights were being violated and woke up every prisoner in the jail that was asleep. Soon other prisoners were hollering for him to shut up. Henry heard one prisoner yell "let me in there with him! I'll shut the bastard up!" Clay kept yelling and threatening to sue everyone from the janitor to the governor.

Shortly after eight a.m. Henry heard the jailor open Clay's cell. A few minutes later the jailor returned and led Henry to the office of the Chief of Police. The chief told him to sit down then asked him if he knew why he was there.

"My loud mouth friend," Henry answered.

"That's right. Your friend is waiting for you outside. I explained to him how we can pick him up anytime he's in the area and hold him for seventy-two hours without booking him then turn him loose and pick him up five minutes later and hold him another seventy-two and we can do that as long as we want to. Do you understand the point I'm trying to make Mr. Ridge?"

"You don't want us in your fair city."

"You're a smart man Mr. Ridge. Not like your friend out there. You're free to leave now Mr. Ridge. You can pick up your things and get out of Hurst, Texas."

Henry dressed and walked outside. Clay was waiting around the corner and he was still angry. "They had no right to arrest us," he complained, "and they damn sure had no right to impound my car."

"You couldn't drive it anyways with a busted hose."

"But I didn't need no goddamn tow charge."

"Have you called anyone?" Henry asked.

"I called Pam and woke her up. She sounded pissed. She probably had some cowboy in bed with her. Those fuckin' pigs had no right arresting us."

"They hear you calling them pigs and you'll be right back in that cell and I'm not keepin' you company. If you'd kept your mouth shut last night we wouldn't have had to spend the night in that piss hole! They were trying to be nice to us for Christ sake! When's the last time you met a nice cop?"

"Fuck you Henry! If you wasn't wearing that goddamn Al Capone looking hat they probably wouldn't have gave us a second look! With that silly hat and that goddamn long hair you look like a part of some fuckin' Indian Mafia! If you have to wear a hat get one that looks like everybody else's."

"So you think if I'd been wearing one of those four inch umbrellas like those goddamn drugstore cowboys wear they'd have left us alone?"

"You bet your ass I do."

"Well maybe it ain't my hat. And maybe it wasn't my hair. Maybe it's that cute little duck tail of yours! Those trashy looking duck tails went out of style ten years ago! The only ones that wear 'em anymore are convicts! Maybe they saw your greasy duck tail shinin' in the moonlight and thought you were an ex-con!"

"That's the silliest shit I've ever heard!"

"It's no sillier than that shit you've been spoutin'!"

"Fuck you hare-lip! From now on if you ride with me you have to take your hat off!"

"You ain't got a car no more Clay!"

Pam pulled up to the front of the building and Clay climbed in the front seat and Henry climbed in the back.

"What did you two do to get throwed in jail?" Pam asked.

"Nothin'," Clay mumbled. "Not a fuckin' thing."

Henry's pick-up was leaking oil and they'd been using Clay's car but now Clay's car was sitting in the Hurst, Texas Police impoundment lot with a busted water hose. The car dealer had made it clear to Clay that he still expected payments to be made on the car regardless of where the car was sitting or what condition it was in. Henry had to use his truck to drive Clay to any gigs he had so Clay could make payments on a car he didn't have and couldn't drive. The truck's oil leak grew worse and soon Henry was having to add at least a quart of oil every time he drove the truck anywhere and carry a quart to add later to drive home.

Friday night Henry drove Clay to a gig at the Safari Club. The band quit at one a.m. and Henry and Clay left the club as soon as Clay was paid. Both men wanted to get to Panther Hall before the two a.m. closing time to hear Wynn Stewart and his new band, We Three Country. Hap Arnold and Larry Weldon had quit Wynn's band and a new group had been formed. Darrell Smith had been hired to play bass and his brother Kenny had been hired to play drums. Jody Payne, lead guitarist and vocalist with a Detroit based, southern rock band called The Dalton Boys, had been hired to play guitar and act as front man.

Jody Payne was thirty-three years old and originally from Kentucky. Music had been a part of his life since he was a toddler. He sang and played mandolin at his older sister Imogene's first year graduation and at age ten sang with his father on a radio show on WHIR in Danville, Kentucky. At fifteen he was on the road with Charlie Monroe's bluegrass band before returning home and moving to Cincinnati, Ohio, with his family. He was drafted into the Army in 1958 and served his time honorably. In the spring of 1961 he moved to Detroit and began playing at a bar called the West Fort Tavern. In 1969 Hap drove to Detroit and brought Jody Payne and three thousand pills back to Fort Worth with him.

The pick-up's engine caught fire less than a mile from the Annex. Henry and Clay beat out the flames and Henry took a good look at the damage. The truck would probably need a new motor and Henry was a few dollars shy of being poor. He signed the title then returned the document to the glove compartment. They walked several blocks to a convenience store where Clay used the phone to call around until he located Pam. Forty minutes later Pam arrived at the store and fifteen minutes later they were pulling up to the Panther Hall Annex, across the street from Panther Hall.

Panther Hall was one of the largest dance halls in Texas. The place could hold two thousand patrons and booked the biggest stars in country music. It had its own television show that was seen in three states every Saturday from six p.m. to six-thirty p.m. Across the street at the Annex the stars and bands and road crews gathered to relax, drink and shoot pool before and after the show at Panther Hall. Wynn Stewart preferred the Annex over Panther Hall and performed at the small bar so often they'd erected a sign out front that read 'Home of Wynn Stewart'.

It was nearly closing time when they entered the club. Only a handful of people remained.

"There's John," Clay said, pointing to a table in the corner near the pool table.

John Maynard was sitting with a plump, red-haired woman in her early forties. "You just missed the band," John told them. "Man that Jody Payne picks his ass off."

"Henry's piece of shit pick-up caught on fire," Clay said, "or we'd have been here an hour ago."

"You still driving a taxi?" Henry asked.

"Hell yeah. You couldn't run me off my job. I'm gettin'

more pussy than I ever got in my life and I'm gettin' paid for it. I take the women out on a dirt road and leave the meter runnin'."

Pam turned away with a disgusted look on her face.

"Who's your lady friend?" Clay asked.

"This is Anita. She's one of my regulars."

Henry looked at the woman expecting to see her blush but she seemed indifferent to John's remark.

"Anita," John continued, "this is Pam, Clay and Henry the hare-lip." Anita gave Henry the same look he'd given her a moment earlier.

"You going to the Palace from here?" Clay asked.

"I can't. I have to have Anita at the doctor's at nine so she can get a prescription for diet pills."

Pam said she wanted to leave and the three said good-bye and walked out to her car.

"That John's a fuckin' pig," she said as she slid behind the wheel and slammed the door. "He shouldn't talk about that woman like she was a piece of meat with her sittin' there. Someone oughta slap his stupid face."

"Some women like that kind of treatment," Clay said. "Maybe she gets off on it."

"Then someone oughta slap her face."

The Country Palace was a horny man's dream. There were several young women there nightly who were willing to have sex with nearly anyone who asked and if you didn't ask them chances were good they'd ask you. A man could have sex in the parking lot or take it home with him. Henry loved the Country Palace but Pam's remark 'someone oughta slap her face' made him think of his mother being back handed by Charlie. That thought and the thought of being 'truckless' had ruined his mood.

"If you don't mind could you drop me off at my room?"

"Why?" Pam replied. "I thought we were all going to the Palace."

"I hate going anywhere without my truck."

"That piece of shit burned up," Clay reminded him.

"I like being able to leave when I want to."

"You've ridden with me a bunch of times," Clay replied.

"Please I'd just rather skip the Palace tonight."

Pam dropped Henry off near the door to his room. He'd taken enough speed to keep him awake several more hours and for a moment he thought about knocking on the day clerk's door. He walked to the motel's restaurant intending to order a large glass of milk and take it back to his room. The milk and half a quaalude would kill the speed enough to allow him to fall asleep. He saw Saul Carter sitting alone in a corner booth sipping coffee. Saul motioned him over and asked him to sit down.

Saul lived five doors down from Henry but the two men ran in different crowds. Tall, muscular, with a full beard and hair that hung below his shoulders, Saul reminded Henry of a mountain man. Saul played bass occasionally with some of the local bands and often 'sit in' when he wasn't working. Everyone knew Saul had done time in a Texas prison and they also knew he was a good source for drugs, especially marijuana. He'd also heard that Saul dealt with some dangerous people.

"I figured you'd be at the Palace," Saul said, "chasin' pussy."

"My truck caught fire. I'm on foot. I couldn't do nothin' but sign the title and walk off."

"That's too bad. I liked that truck. It had character. What you planning on doing now? You can't get no pussy on foot. Like the song says 'when you walk you walk alone'."

"It could be worse. At least I'm walkin' distance from

Manpower and there's everything I need at this motel includin' pussy."

"If you're talking about the day clerk I saw her leave with some man a couple hours ago."

The waitress came over and Henry ordered a large glass of milk. "I wish you'd order coffee," Saul said. "I need to talk to you." Henry changed his order to coffee.

They finished their coffee and Saul ordered a pot to take back to his room. Henry had been to Saul's room several times attending some of the parties Saul liked to throw. Saul would serve 'electric screwdrivers', a combination of vodka, orange juice and a hundred hits of microdot acid mixed in a five gallon water cooler and served in small Dixie cups. Half the people at the party would end up in the parking lot holding hands and staring into space.

Henry carried the coffee and followed Saul inside. Saul sat down near a coffee table and rolled a joint the size of Henry's index finger. "Anything we say here doesn't leave this room, understand?"

"I understand," Henry answered.

"I like you Henry but this is the way it is. I did time for manslaughter and I can get a lot of jail time if I'm caught with this shit. If I go back to prison because you ran your mouth I'll have your fuckin' throat cut. Nothin' personal you understand."

Henry knew the warning was nothing personal but he still felt insulted. "You either trust me or you don't. I don't give a rat's ass either way."

"If I didn't trust you we wouldn't be having this conversation. Now here's the deal. I've got a hundred pounds of pot coming in tonight and I need someone to bag it up into one pound bags. I'll pay you a dollar for every pound you bag. There's usually a little extra and anything over a hundred pounds you can keep. You can do it here or take it to your room."

"I'd rather use your room."

Saul offered Henry a diet pill and Henry took it washing it down with coffee.

Two joints later the coffee pot was empty. Saul didn't want room service while he was waiting for a delivery so Henry offered to walk to the restaurant to have the coffee pot refilled. Halfway there he saw a car pull into the parking lot and stop at Saul's door. He thought about turning around and walking back to the room then decided the less he knew and the fewer people he met the better off he'd be. When he returned with the coffee the car was gone and Saul was examining the contents of two large, plastic lawn bags. Satisfied with the bags' contents Saul opened a closet door and took a set of triple scales and a paper bag containing several boxes of one pound freezer storage bags from the top shelf. He placed the scales and the paper sack on the coffee table in front of Henry. "I'll be back later. Just shove the pot in the closet when you're done and make sure you lock the door when you leave. I'll see you later at your room. I've got a friend that owns a car lot off Belknap and one day next week, maybe Monday or Tuesday, I'll run you over there and we'll get you something to drive."

"I just got some fresh coffee. You sure you don't wanna help me drink it?"

"Hell no," Saul answered. "I've got some pussy waitin' for me."

It was mid-morning before Henry finished bagging and weighing the marijuana. He had nearly half a pound left and he took this to his room and hid it in the top of his closet. He didn't see Saul again until that evening.

Tuesday morning Saul drove Henry to a used car dealer

where Henry purchased a 1958 Studebaker for eighty-five dollars. It wasn't a pick-up but it was better than walking.

Henry had met Wynn Stewart briefly, not much more than a handshake and a few words and he'd seen him perform several times at the Annex. He knew Hap Arnold, Wynn's former bassist, and Ralph Mooney, Wynn's steel guitarist, well enough to call them friends. He also liked the members of Wynn's new band, We Three Country.

One night Henry watched a tall, skinny songwriter with a load of lyrics under one arm and a load of reel-to-reel tapes under the other back Wynn into a corner and insist that Wynn take a tape of one of his songs. Wynn put the tape in his shirt pocket, thanked the songwriter and shook the man's hand. The following week Wynn was shooting pool when he saw the same skinny songwriter enter the bar with a load of lyrics under one arm and a load of reel-to-reel tapes under the other. Wynn dropped his cue stick and disappeared out the back door.

Hap Arnold told Henry he needed to be more aggressive if he wanted his songs recorded. "Hap if you put a skirt on a lot of these songwriters you'd think they were groupies," Henry told him. "I'd rather not have a song recorded if I have to act like a 'star fucker' to get it done."

Ralph Mooney quit Wynn and took a job playing steel guitar for Waylon Jennings. Carl Vaughn decided not to record Henry's song 'Funny New Sounds' and recorded the Marty Robbins song 'You Gave Me a Mountain' instead.

Henry had a reputation as one of the best lyricist in the area. His biggest problem was that his songs weren't on tape. Most recording artists can't envision the way a song would sound by reading lyrics. They needed some idea of a tune and Henry couldn't even whistle good. Many of his musician friends, including Clay, Perry and David had agreed to help him get his songs on tape. Henry had even purchased a second hand reel-to-reel tape recorder at a pawn shop. But speed addicts are not dependable and getting them to sit down long enough to do anything was nearly impossible. They agreed to meet at Henry's room at a certain time but were always late or didn't show up at all. When they did show up they wanted to party, promising they'd 'get to those fuckin' songs' later.

Henry was lying in bed with a young lady named Sherry. He'd had Clay drop him off earlier so Clay could use Henry's car to circle Pam's house every hour or so. Pam and Clay had an open relationship and both dated other people although Clay would have preferred that Pam not date anyone but him and he date anyone he wanted to. Earlier Clay had Henry drive him by her apartment and a red Ford pick-up was parked in her driveway. An hour later Henry drove Clay by Pam's apartment again. The red Ford was gone and a blue Chevy pick-up occupied the driveway. Henry told Clay he could borrow the Studebaker and had Clay drop him off at Sherry's apartment.

Sherry was blonde, buxom and slightly plump and Henry liked her attitude. "I don't wanna make love," she told him their first time together, "I wanna fuck. You make love when you're ready to get serious, you fuck when you're having fun. I like having fun." She'd had her bedroom wallpapered with pornographic drawings of the Zodiac. Each sign depicted large breasted women and well endowed men in various sexual positions. Some of the signs would have required a contortionist to accomplish and Sherry liked to brag that she'd tried every position but Taurus. She also kept a fresh cucumber in a night stand near her bed. "A few of these cowboys I bring back on occasion have trouble drinking and getting it up too. I keep this near just in case."

They had sex until nearly noon and both were getting

sleepy when they heard someone knocking at the front door. Sherry pulled on her robe and left the room to answer the door. She returned a moment later with Clay following behind her. Henry was getting irritated.

"What the fuck's wrong Clay? Pam's company didn't leave? I said you could keep the car and pick me up tonight."

"No Pam's company didn't leave but that's not why I'm here and if you keep talking to me like an asshole I won't fuckin' tell you why I'm here. I just thought you might like to know Bobby's in town."

"Bobby who?"

"Bobby Wayne."

"You talking about Haggard's front man?"

"The one and only. Now if you'll get your sorry ass out of bed we'll go to his room and I'll introduce you."

Henry wasn't turning down a chance to meet Bobby Wayne. "I need some speed and some coffee." Sherry sat on the edge of the bed still wearing her robe. "You wanna go with us lady?"

"No, I just want you to get out of my bedroom so I can get some sleep."

Clay gave Henry two diet pills and Henry swallowed them dry. They stopped at a Denny's on the way to the motel and bought two cups of coffee to go. When they arrived at the motel Pam, Carla and Perry were already there. Clay gave Pam his best 'I've been hurt look' and Pam ignored him. Carla gave Henry her best 'I hope you wither away and die' look and Henry ignored her.

"Bobby," Clay said, "this is Henry. He's a songwriter."

"Henry, huh?" Bobby said as they shook hands. "Does anyone ever call you Hank? Hank's as country as you can get. Harelip Hank. Now there's a stage name. I could go on stage with a name like that and make a million dollars." Henry liked Bobby but he wasn't sure if he was teasing or not.

"You ever think about recording Henry?"

"I can honestly say I haven't. Being on stage never interested me."

"Then you're different from most songwriters. Most are frustrated singers who would love to be on stage. Listen guys I hate to break up a good party but I need to take a shower and rest a little before tonight."

"We'll leave and let you clean up," Clay said. "Where you gonna be later?"

"We'll probably go to Rustler's Rest and see Jerry Lane."

"Then we'll meet you there."

Henry dropped Clay at his parents' home then drove to his room and showered and changed clothes. He took two pink and white tablets of speed called 'speckled birds' he had hidden in a pair of socks then walked to the motel restaurant and drank several cups of coffee. He'd told Clay that he'd pick him up at eight that evening but he knew from past experience that Clay wouldn't be ready on time. Clay was never ready when he said he'd be and Henry had no intention of sitting with Clay's parents and watching television, surrounded by religious artifacts and paintings, while he was high on speed and waiting on Clay to comb and recomb his duck tail. He finished his coffee then walked to Saul's room to ask if Saul would have anymore work for him anytime soon. Saul assured him there'd be another shipment in a few days and asked Henry to smoke a joint with him.

An hour later Henry returned to his room and rolled half a dozen joints of his own pot and hid them in his boot. Shortly after nine he left the motel and picked up Clay. They arrived at Rustler's Rest a few minutes before ten p.m. Bobby Wayne was on stage with Jerry Lane singing harmony on the Righteous

Brothers' classic 'You've Lost That Loving Feeling'. Hap Arnold was sitting in on bass and Ray Robbins, Jerry Lane's bassist, was sitting at a table with Pam and Carla.. Pam asked them to sit down and join them. Henry wondered where Amy was but didn't ask. Jerry left the stage when the song ended and Bobby sang 'The Pleasure of You' before ending the set with an old George Jones song 'She Thinks I Still Care'.

Bobby Wayne was stocky, curly haired and extremely talented. During the next set he went from one song to another like he knew every country song ever written. The next day the marquee at Rustler's Rest read 'Live in Person, Jerry Lane and Bobby Wayne'. Bobby had two weeks off before going back on the road with Haggard and Carl and Marie knew first hand that he drew a crowd at any club he worked. Bobby and Jerry played four nights a week and Henry was there every night.

Dan Conners introduced Henry to Toni Stockton, a flight attendant with American Airlines. Toni and Dan had dated and Toni had become addicted to the night life and the drugs. Like Henry she hated leaving a good time to go to work and soon was calling in sick regularly. She used her sick days and vacation time and was finally fired. That didn't stop her from having a party at her apartment nearly every night after the bars closed. Several drugs were available at her parties including marijuana, cocaine, speed and amyl nitrate, a drug used to revive heart attack victims.

Henry met his first gay friend at Toni's apartment. He'd been around gays but they'd always been trying to get in his pants. Daniel, Toni's hairdresser, was different and Henry felt comfortable around him. He wore make-up and women's clothing but no amount of rouge could hide his 'five o'clock shadow'. He told Henry he preferred to be called Danielle and he was saving his money for a trip to Europe for a 'sex change' operation. Henry liked Daniel but Clay didn't and one morning on their way to Toni's apartment Clay offered his opinion. "I don't like smoking after him," Clay said. "How do I know he didn't suck a dick before he came to the party?"

"What business is it of yours if he did?" Henry asked. "I've seen you smoke after a Palace snuff queen knowing she'd just taken some man out to a dark corner and sucked him dry."

"That's different! Goddamn it! And you know it's different!"

"The only difference is you know that gal's been suckin' somebody's pecker and you just suspect Daniel has."

"He's a fuckin' pervert!"

"I've heard a couple of gals say the same thing about you. Daniel doesn't try to tell anyone what they can or can't do in their own bedroom. What makes you think that you or anyone else has the right to tell him what he can and can't do?"

"The Bible says it's wrong! The Bible says a man don't fuck another man!"

"When's the last time you picked up a Bible Clay? My grandmother taught me a lot about the Bible and one of her favorite verses was 'judge not, lest ye be judged' or something like that."

"I can't talk to you! You're as sick as that fuckin' queer! I wouldn't be surprised if you went to Europe with him and had your dick cut off too!"

Henry had copies of his lyrics spread all over Fort Worth and half of Dallas. He gave a copy of anything he'd written to anyone who asked for it and he'd heard rumors that someone had been claiming they'd written one of Henry's songs but as far as he knew they were only rumors.

Clay paid off his car but never bothered to get it out of the Hurst Police Impoundment. Instead he arranged to buy another 'junker', an eleven year old Cadillac, for eight hundred dollars payable in payments of forty dollars a week. The car used oil, the brakes were bad and the price was too high but Clay didn't care. The car was a 'Caddy' and Clay had wanted a Cadillac for a long time.

Two weeks later they were on their way to the Plaza to pick up a few joints then drive to Pam and Amy's apartment. Two miles from the Plaza the Cadillac's brakes went out at a stop light and Clay rear ended a new BMW. The Cadillac suffered minor damage but the BMW looked like a beer can someone had squeezed then threw out a window. Clay asked Henry to wait with the car while he walked to a nearby telephone booth and called the police. Henry walked over to the driver of the BMW and told him Clay was calling the law and would be back in a moment. When he turned back toward the phone booth he saw Clay a block away running like his pants were on fire. It took Henry ten minutes to catch him. "What the hell are you doing?" Henry was doubled over trying to catch his wind. "You were going to leave me there.....to wait for the cops......you little chicken shit."

"So what?" Clay was sitting on the curve holding his stomach. "They wouldn't take you to jail. All you have to do is tell them it's not yours."

"What makes you think anyone would go to jail?"

"Did you see the other car? I don't have insurance. Do you think they'd just let me go home?"

"Well you'll surely go to jail now unless you think you can get back to that car before the law arrives. You seem to forget that the car is registered to you and they'll find you sooner or later."

"Not if I don't go home."

"Where you plan on going?" Henry asked.

"I thought I could stay with you."

"I don't have but one bed Clay. You stay with me and they'll be calling one of us 'Danielle' before too long."

By the time Henry and Clay walked to the Plaza Clay had accepted the fact that he would have to go home and face the music. Henry drove him to his parent's house and let him out. As he was driving away he saw a police car pull up in the drive way. Clay was arrested and taken to the Tarrant County jail. The next morning he was taken before a judge and fined five hundred dollars for leaving the scene of an accident and another fifty-eight dollars for court cost. His parents 'loaned' him the money. Clay's Cadillac had been towed to the Fort Worth Police impoundment lot the day of the accident and once again Clay was paying for a car he didn't have and couldn't drive.

Perry Michaels was working Saturday night at the Stage-coach Inn playing lead guitar for Ray Chaney. Ray, who owned the club, had once recorded for Columbia Records and still recorded occasionally on one of the local labels. He booked many of the top country stars at his club including Charlie Rich, Mel Tillis and Jack Greene and, like Rustler's Rest and the other country dance halls, any professional singer or musician could go on stage and 'sit in'.

Henry dropped Clay off at the Sawmill and told him he'd be back at two a.m. to pick him up. He drove to Rustler's Rest and drank two cups of coffee while talking to Marie Patton then drove to the Stagecoach Inn to listen to Perry play guitar. The band was on break and he spotted Perry sitting at a table with Sam Coleman, Ray Chaney's bassist, and a pretty young blonde named Lorena. Perry asked Henry to sit at the table and keep Lorena company after the break was over and he and Sam had to go back on stage.

The break ended and Ray Chaney kicked off the set with a Ray Price song 'Heartaches By The Number'. After the third song he asked the crowd to 'put your hands together and welcome Wynn Stewart'. Wynn took the stage and sang his first chart hit 'Wishful Thinkin'. Henry turned his chair until he was facing the stage. Halfway through the song he heard someone say '"hare-lip come over here a minute." Henry turned and saw Jimmy Belmon sitting a couple of tables over with two young ladies and a stocky built 'cowboy'. Henry ignored Jimmy and turned back to watch Wynn. A moment later Jimmy came over to the table and told Henry someone wanted to meet him. Henry told Lorena he'd be right back then followed Jimmy to his table. Jimmy asked him to sit down for a minute. "Doug, this is the hare-lip I told you about, Henry Ridge."

Henry reached across the table to shake Doug's hand. Doug leaned back in his chair, smiled then folded his arms across his chest. "I hear you're a hare-lipped thief."

Henry had no idea why a stranger would call him a thief but watching Jimmy grin made him think that Jimmy was behind it. He scooted his chair back and was starting to stand when Doug stood up and swung at him. Henry saw it coming and pulled his head back several inches. Doug hit nothing but air. Henry swung catching Doug with an uppercut and knocking him back into his chair. He felt two strong arms grab him from behind and he looked over his shoulder and saw a police officer. Another officer had his hand on Doug's shoulder holding him down in the chair. Doug's bottom lip was split and a thin line of blood ran down his chin and dripped on his shirt. "You two are going to jail," the officer holding Henry told them.

The band quit playing and Sam and Perry left the stage and walked over to where Henry and the officer stood. "Doug swung first," Sam said. "Henry was just defending himself."

"That's right officer." Henry turned toward the voice and saw Wynn Stewart standing to his left. "I was watching from the stage and this man swung first," he said, pointing at Doug.

The officer released Henry and the other officer handcuffed Doug and led him off to jail. Jimmy demanded that his friend be released or Henry be arrested and taken to jail with him. Ray Chaney walked over and after a few words with Wynn and Sam he told Jimmy to leave and not come back. Sam took Henry's arm and pulled him over to the side. "Wynn, this is the man you've been looking for, Henry Ridge. He's the one that wrote that song you like."

Henry shook Wynn's hand and told him they'd met at the Annex. "I remember seeing you at the Annex but I didn't know you were a songwriter. I think I've got one of your songs and I'd like to record it."

"You're welcome to any song I have," Henry told him.

"There's just one problem, someone else claims they wrote it."

"What song is it?" Henry asked.

"What Might Have Been."

"Who put their name on it?"

"Jimmy Belmon," Wynn answered.

"I don't know why that bastard thinks he can get away with it. Half the county knows I wrote that song."

"I believe you. Listen, I'd like to talk about this later on. Can you wait around until closing?"

"I can hang around as long as you want me to."

Henry asked Perry to pick Clay up at the Sawmill and Perry said he would. Henry didn't talk to Wynn again until after the final set when Wynn walked over to the table where Henry was waiting. He invited Henry to take a ride with him and Henry followed him outside and climbed into the passenger side of Wynn's gold Cadillac. Wynn drove to an old house off 28th Street that had a small sign in the front yard that read 'Hearns' Publishing and Recording'. Wynn unlocked the front door and turned on a light revealing an old sofa sitting against the wall, two chairs and a coffee table. He opened another door and turned on a light and Henry saw the control room of the recording studio. A glass partition ran the length of the instrument panel and another light revealed the microphones and stools behind the partition. Empty egg cartons covered the walls and ceiling. Wynn led Henry to a table with a Sony reel-to-reel tape recorder sitting at one end and asked Henry to sit down. He left the room and returned a moment later with a flat top guitar and several bottles of burgundy table wine. He pulled two pieces of paper from his back pocket and unfolded them, smoothing them out until they lay flat on the table. Then he sat down and picked up the guitar. Henry reached over and picked up the papers and studied them. "This is my song but it's not my writing."

"That's Jimmy's scribble."

"How did you know he didn't write it?"

"Jimmy's been bringing me lyrics for years and they've all been garbage. When he brought me this song I knew as soon as I read it that he didn't write it. He says he did but a person doesn't consistently write trash then come up one day with a song like this. I wanted to record it but I wanted the right name on it. I asked Sam and the others to help me find whoever Jimmy had stolen the song from. I remember seeing you at the Annex several times but I didn't know you were a writer." Wynn opened the bottle of wine, took a long drink, then passed the bottle to

Henry. "There's just one problem," Wynn said. "If I record the song with your name on it we could wind up in court. I believe you wrote the song and I'm sure there's a lot of people who know you wrote the song but Jimmy has friends who believe he wrote it. You met one tonight. They may be willing to go to court and swear Jimmy wrote the song years ago and it would be your word against theirs."

Henry kept hoping the wine would improve in taste but after several drinks the first bottle was nearly empty and the burgundy still tasted like vinegar. "Got any suggestions?" He asked.

"We may have to put both your names on it."

Henry felt his stomach churn, not from the wine, but from the idea of having Jimmy Belmon's name on one of his songs.

"We'll talk about that later," Wynn said. "Right now we need to put a tune to this. You feel like singing?"

Henry nearly choked on a drink of wine. He could feel the burgundy dripping from his nose. "I'm not a singer. I can't carry a tune in a bucket as my grandmother used to say."

"Sure you can. I just need you to sing a couple of lines so I can get an idea of the tune you had in mind."

Henry drank the last of the first bottle and opened the second one. After a couple of drinks he started singing the first line of 'What Might Have Been'. Wynn started laughing and Henry quit singing. Wynn took a long drink of wine then said, "I'm sorry. Try it again and I promise I won't laugh."

"I told you I couldn't sing."

"Sure you can," Wynn reassured him. "You just need a little practice. Hang with me and I'll have you on stage. Now let's try it again and I promise I won't laugh."

Henry started singing again and Wynn started laughing. Henry threw the lyrics on the table and reached for the wine.

"I'm sorry," Wynn said. "I'm trying not to laugh."

Two hours and four bottles of wine later and they had a tune for "What Might Have Been" and a 'working' tune for another one of Henry's songs. Before they left the studio Henry was singing harmony with Wynn on every old country song they could come up with. It was close to noon when Wynn drove Henry back to the Stagecoach Inn. "It's been an honor meeting you Henry. I'd like to get together again and see what else you have."

Henry felt like he was walking on air. He'd drank wine and written a song with a man he'd admired for years and now this man was telling Henry he was honored to meet him. Henry pulled several pages of typewritten lyrics from the Studebaker's glove box and handed them to Wynn. "Take these and see if there's anything else you like. I'm staying at the Park Plaza if you ever want to get hold of me." Henry extended his hand and Wynn shook it. "Thank you for a night I'll never forget." Henry drove back to his room, took half a Quaalude and went to bed.

Winford Lindsey Stewart, the architect and originator of the west coast country sound, was born in Missouri and moved to California with his family when he was a young boy. They settled in the Florence area and at age eight Wynn got his first guitar. He recorded his first record at thirteen and was working the beer joints before he was twenty-one. He signed his first contract with Intro Records in 1953 and recorded the song 'I've Waited A Lifetime'. His big break came when he met Capitol Recording artist Skeets McDonald on the set of a local television show and Skeets arranged a meeting with Wynn and Capital Records' A&R man Ken Nelson. Skeets introduced Wynn to a fork lift operator named Harlan Howard. Harlan would go on to write such country hits as 'Pick Me Up On Your Way Down', 'Heartaches By The Number', 'Streets of Baltimore', "The Choking Kind' and hundreds more. Wynn recorded Harlan's first song

"You Took Her Off My Hands' and followed it with such classics as 'Waltz Of The Angels', 'Keeper Of The Keys' and 'Hold Back Tomorrow'. A then unknown singer named Buck Owens sang harmony with Wynn on "Hold Back Tomorrow'.

His first steady 'gig' was at Sherry's Red Barn in Paramount, California. He moved from there to George's Roundup Club in North Long Beach and was a regular on Channel 13 in Los Angeles. Capitol Records dropped him in 1957 when he refused to switch from country to rock and roll. In 1958 he signed with Jackpot Records and recorded another Harlan Howard song 'Above and Beyond'. A year later he recorded a song he'd written with his sister Beverly called 'Wishful Thinking'. The song spent twenty-two weeks on the charts, peaking at #5. Later he recorded 'Playboy', a chart failure that soon became an 'underground classic'. He moved to Las Vegas in 1961 and started performing at the Nashville-Nevada Club. A few weeks later he recorded his last chart song for Jackpot Records, 'Another Day, Another Dollar'.

Wynn returned to Capitol Records and in 1962 hired a young ex-convict named Merle Haggard to play bass with his band in Las Vegas. A year later Merle Haggard recorded his first hit, 'Sing a Sad Song', a song Wynn Stewart had written.

Wynn returned to the studio using musicians like Bobby Wayne, Ralph Mooney, Tommy Collins, Glen Campbell, Dave Allen and Dennis Hromek. During this period he recorded several chart songs including 'Half Of This And Half Of That', 'Sing A Sad Song' and one of Henry's favorites, 'I'll Never Forget Ole What's Her Name'. In October, 1966 he recorded a song written by Dale Noe. 'It's Such a Pretty World Today' went to #1 on the country charts and stayed for twenty-three weeks.

In 1968 he moved his family to a twenty acre ranch he'd bought near Mansfield, Texas, a few miles south of Fort Worth.

Henry loved watching the five foot five inch singer perform. Wynn would cup his right hand over his right ear, holding the microphone in his left, working it back and forth, holding it at arm's length one moment then bringing it in close enough to kiss the next. Ralph Mooney told Henry he considered Wynn to be the greatest singer that ever lived and Henry agreed.

Monday afternoon Wynn called Henry and invited him out to his Pretty World Ranch. Henry followed Wynn's directions and thirty minutes later was turning through the gate leading to the ranch house. Wynn introduced Henry to his wife Dolores and their two young daughters, Wren and Tatia, then led him into the living room and told him to make himself at home.

"Have you heard about Belmon gettin' killed?" Wynn asked. Henry told him he hadn't heard a thing. "He got hopped up on coke and picked up some woman on the Jacksboro Highway and took her home with him then for some reason he decided to beat her. He beat her bad from what I heard. She waited till he passed out then stuck a thirty-eight in his ear and pulled the trigger. The police took her to the hospital and they took a few pictures and released her. They're not filing any charges." Wynn lit a cigarette and stared at the floor for a moment then asked, "Did you know Belmon had two sons from his first marriage?'

"No I didn't. He made it clear from day one that he didn't like me. I didn't know nothin' about him, other than the fact that he was a thief, and I didn't want to know anything about him."

"I've got a proposition for you. You offered me half writer on 'What Might Have Been', right?"

"You wrote the tune Wynn. We both know you didn't get it from my singing. You're entitled to half."

"Would you mind if I put Belmon's name on my half?"

"You can do anything with your half. Put the devil's name on there if you want to."

"It'll give his kids something to remember him by and it may keep us out of court. I got another song of yours I'd like to work up while you're here. You feel like singing?"

"How much wine you got?"

"I don't have any wine but I've got some good gin."

Henry became a regular visitor to the Pretty World Ranch, usually driving out in the early afternoon and leaving after a couple of hours. Other country artists who were booked in the area and had time off would drop by. Henry met Mel Tillis and Bobby Bare at the ranch and one spring day he met the legendary Bob Wills. Bob had suffered a stroke a few weeks earlier and was staying at a nursing home. Wynn knew Bob loved to fish and he drove to the nursing home and signed Bob out then took him back to the ranch where he pushed Bob out in his wheelchair to a shady spot near the pond and handed him a fishing pole.

He noticed that every time he visited the ranch Dolores and the girls would be gone or would leave shortly after his arrival. He hoped he wasn't the reason they left.

Wynn was a night person and when he wasn't booked out of town he was usually singing for free at the Green Acres Club on Highway 287 or the Panther Hall Annex. On occasion Ray Chaney would book him at the Stagecoach Inn or Dewey Groom would book him at his dance hall in Dallas, the Longhorn Ballroom.

Henry and Wynn had different priorities that kept Henry from spending more time with him. Wynn was faithful to Dolores and had no interest in party girls. Henry couldn't be true to any woman for more than a week and wanted a woman at least every other night or so. After the bars closed Wynn wanted to find a studio and create music. Studios had started boring Henry and after he heard a song a few dozen times, over and over, even one of his own, he was ready to scream. He still met Clay at the Palace three or four nights a week. Wynn had never been to the Palace and had made it clear he had no desire to go.

Henry was doing too many drugs and he knew it. He was taking speed and staying up days at a time then taking downers when he finally felt he had to sleep. He was five feet eight inches tall and weighed less than a hundred and twenty pounds. His clothes appeared baggy on him and his face was shallow and drawn.

The drugs were affecting his sex life also. Where once the diet pills had given him stamina in bed they now had the opposite affect and often left him unable to perform. He found himself apologizing to the ladies for taking them to bed and being unable to maintain an erection. A few nights earlier he'd had to watch Sherry use her cucumber while he lay next to her and as he was leaving she sarcastically said, "Thanks for nothin' cowboy."

Driving back to his room one night he stopped at a stop sign and sat several minutes waiting for it to turn green until a car pulled up behind him and the driver blew his horn. And he was seeing things. He thought he saw a cow crossing East Berry Street early one morning and nearly ran a car off the road avoiding it. Back in his room a few days later he swore he saw a rat the size of a small hound run across his room. He spent several hours moving furniture and crawling around on his hands and knees and found nothing larger than a small frightened mouse. He made enough money bagging marijuana to pay his expenses and cover his vices. He loved the night life and being accepted as a part of an industry he loved and most times he wouldn't have traded places with Jesus Himself. But he hadn't made a nickel from anything he'd written.

Wynn was in Nashville recording his new album and Henry and Clay were at the Hitching Post with Toni Stockton and her latest boyfriend, Tim Inohe. The four had been at Toni's apartment earlier where Henry and Tim consumed the better part of a quart of scotch and all four had used cocaine and amyl nitrate while smoking high grade marijuana and listening to Johnny Darrell and Mickey Newberry albums. They'd grown tired of sitting around the apartment and someone suggested they go to the Hitching Post.

It was early in the evening, a good two hours before the band would start and only a handful of people were in the club. Henry noticed four men, casually dressed and hatless, sitting at a table watching them. Henry turned his attention back to the bar and ordered a cup of coffee then struck up a conversation with Millie, the short, well built waitress. A moment later he heard a chair overturn and Toni yelling "stop them! They're killing him!" Henry turned and saw Tim on the floor and the four men from the table beating and kicking him. Henry instinctively started pulling the men away from Tim. One man turned and called Henry a long haired, hare-lipped hippie and the next thing Henry knew he was backed up to the bar fighting two of the men. Bob Williams, the club's owner, entered the club, took one look at what was happening and ordered everyone to quit fighting. One of the men pulled a badge and told Bob that Henry and Tim were under arrest. The two men were handcuffed and taken to the Tarrant County jail where they were separated and Henry was placed in the 'drunk tank'. A dozen or so men lay on the floor passed out and that many more were standing up. Puke or piss covered sections of the floor and a man who sat or lay down on the floor was taking a chance of being puked or pissed on or both. Henry decided he'd stand up. A few hours later a jailor came after him and he was released. Toni and Tim were waiting outside.

"Where did they take you Tim?" Henry asked. "I hope it was better than that toilet they put me in."

"They released me last night. I wasn't here fifteen minutes."

Henry couldn't believe what he was hearing. "They what? You mean they kept me and let you go home? Tell me why that don't make no fuckin' sense to me. It was your fight and I'm the one they threw in jail!"

"They were off duty cops. They didn't want to push it. It looks bad on Fort Worth's finest to have their cops involved in a barroom brawl. I've had trouble with a couple of 'em before."

"Then why the fuck did they keep me?"

"You made 'em mad. You butted in."

"I made 'em mad! They throwed me in that filthy ass drunk tank cause I made 'em mad! I kinda got the idea they were mad at you when they had your ass down on that floor whippin' the shit out of you!"

Toni and Tim were smiling but Henry didn't see the humor in it. "I appreciate your helping me." Tim reached over the back seat and offered Henry his hand. "That took guts. Not too many people would have done it."

"I can understand why. The next time I see a small herd of cops whippin' your ass I'm looking the other way."

Wynn had fallen behind on a few bills and was booking more shows out of town. Henry had two songs on Wynn's new album and a handshake agreement that Wynn would try to include two of Henry's songs on any future album Wynn recorded. The new album was released in April. Wynn was on the road and Henry was in jail.

Henry was driving, Clay was on the passenger's side and John and David were in the back seat. They were on their way to an all night drive-in theater. The admission price was a dollar a carload and the theater showed four movies, usually all the same genre: four kung fu or four westerns or four monsters or four horror movies. Henry had an ounce of marijuana hidden in the seat and they'd stopped earlier at a pizza parlor in North Richland Hills where all four had pitched in their money and bought two large pizzas. Less than two blocks from the Fort Worth city limits a North Richland Hills patrolman pulled them over. The officer took everyone's driver's license and carried them back to his patrol car. Everyone considered the stop a minor nuisance as long as the patrolman didn't search the car. After a few minutes talking to the dispatcher he walked back to the Studebaker and gave Clay, John and David their licenses back. Then he told Henry he was under arrest and asked him to step out of the car.

"What the hell did I do?" Henry demanded to know.

"It's what you didn't do," the officer answered. "You didn't pay a ticket."

"What ticket? Nobody's pulled me over and given me a ticket."

"It's a parking ticket. Now lean against the car and spread 'em. I'm sure you know the routine."

The patrolman told the others they were free to go. Clay climbed behind the wheel of the Studebaker while Henry was handcuffed and placed in the back of the patrol car.

Henry spent the trip to the North Richland Hills Police station wondering why he couldn't remember getting a parking ticket. Even if he'd thrown it away he'd have remembered getting it. He didn't even know of any places in North Richland Hills where parking wasn't allowed.

At the jail Henry was searched again and everything but his shirt, pants and socks were taken. He was locked in a cell with a metal bunk, no pillow, no blanket and a bright ceiling light that they kept on all night. He was angry, hungry and wanting a cigarette. He kept telling himself he'd be released in the morning as soon as Clay or one of the others came to the jail with the money to get him out.

The next morning they brought Henry a lukewarm cup of stale coffee and an egg sandwich. He didn't see anyone the rest of the day and he had no idea what time it was. He finally yelled "does anyone know the time?" The jailor came in long enough to tell him it was four thirty. He asked the jailor if anyone had been trying to visit him or have him released. The jailor told him no. Henry was madder than a wet hen. His 'so called friends' had left him there.

Henry slept in spurts the second night. Even if he'd had a pillow the ceiling light made sleeping nearly impossible. Midmorning he was given another cup of stale lukewarm coffee and a chicken salad sandwich. An hour or so later the jailor came for him and led him to the property room. He was given back his personal possessions and told he was being released. He walked toward the front entrance and saw Wynn Stewart standing near the entrance.

"Goddamn what are you doing here?" Henry asked, grinning from ear to ear. He couldn't ever remember being happier to see anyone. "I heard you were on the road."

"I got back yesterday," Wynn said. "I didn't find out you was in jail until this morning."

"What did it cost to get me out?" Henry asked. "I'll pay you back as soon as I can."

"Don't worry about it. It wasn't that much. Just fifteen dollars."

"It was enough to keep a few of my so called friends from carrying their sorry asses down here."

"I'll take you to your room," Wynn said, "then I have a few things I have to do. Why don't you come out to the ranch later?"

"I've got a few things to do myself and as soon as I find my car and a good baseball bat I intend to do 'em."

"Why don't you let it go? It's not worth it."

Henry had cooled off by the time Wynn pulled into the Park Plaza. He was surprised to see his car parked in front of his room with a note under the windshield wiper. Henry thanked Wynn again for bailing him out of jail and asked him where he'd be that night just in case he didn't make it to the ranch.

"I'll be at the Annex or the Green Acres. Oh, I almost forgot." Wynn stepped out of the Cadillac and opened the trunk. "This is yours," he said, handing Henry a record album. Henry studied the front cover. "Turn it over," Wynn said. Henry looked at the back of the album cover and found two songs with his name on both as co-writer. Henry thanked him again as Wynn drove away.

The note on the windshield informed Henry that his car keys had been left with the desk clerk. He checked under the seat of the Studebaker looking for his marijuana. He wasn't surprised to find it gone. He took a long hot shower and was trying his best to sleep when the phone rang. It was Clay.

"Hey, you're out of jail."

"No fuckin' thanks to you."

"You sound pissed off."

"I don't think pissed off is the right word. I passed the pissed off stage the first night."

"You 're not mad at me are you?" Clay asked.

"What do you think? You left me in that goddamn jail! Don't you think I have a right to be fuckin' pissed? On top of that my pot's gone!"

"We couldn't do nothin'!"

"You telling me ya'll couldn't rake up fifteen dollars between you?"

"We couldn't rake up five dollars. We barely had enough to get in the drive-in."

"You bastards went to the drive-in and smoked my pot and it didn't bother you a bit that I was in jail. Was the pizza good Clay?"

"We didn't get that ticket! You got the fuckin' thing! We couldn't get you out of jail! What the fuck did you think we were going to do? Sit around and whine about the poor harelipped Indian? If it had been one of us you'd have done the same thing!"

Henry was doing his best to remain angry but he couldn't argue with what Clay was saying. If Clay or one of the others had been locked up instead of him he'd have gone to the drive-in and ate pizza and smoked pot too.

"I just don't understand how I got a ticket and don't remember it."

"It was a parking ticket," Clay reminded him. "Maybe the wind blew it off."

"I'm sure gettin' tired of this state," Henry said. "I've been in three Texas jails and I'm beginning to think Texas doesn't like me."

Two weeks later Henry was standing with Sam Coleman watching Wynn ride his horse around the corral area. Something spooked the animal and the horse bucked Wynn off. Sam doubled over laughing but Henry didn't see the humor in it. Wynn was slow getting up. Wynn dusted the dirt from his pants, limped over to where the two men were standing and ordered Sam off his ranch. Henry asked Wynn if he wanted him to leave also. Wynn asked Henry to stay.

"You look like you have a lot on your mind," Henry told him.

"I'll be alright."

"I still feel like I'm imposing. Why don't I just meet you later tonight at the Annex?"

"I'll be on the road for a while. I have a show tomorrow night in Omaha then I think fifteen or sixteen more after that."

Wynn hated the road. He hated leaving home.

Henry hadn't seen Wynn in over a month. He'd driven by the ranch three times in the past week but Wynn's Cadillac wasn't there so Henry hadn't bothered to stop. And Wynn hadn't been to the Green Acres, the Annex or Hearns' Recording Studio.

Henry returned to his room shortly before noon. He was tired from a night of eating diet pills and chasing women and disgusted with himself because he couldn't maintain an erection when he finally talked a young lady into bed. He barely had his boots off when he heard a knocking on his door. Henry opened the door and Saul Carter dragged two garbage bags filled with marijuana into the room.

"This came last night. I would have bagged it myself but you have my scales. Besides I figure you need the money."

"I do need the money. I'm also going to need some coffee. I was planning on trying to sleep."

Saul gave Henry a black capsule and two fifty dollar bills. Henry took the diet pill then called the restaurant and ordered coffee. Saul stayed long enough to drink a cup of coffee and smoke a joint then left to meet a woman. Henry started breaking the marijuana down and bagging it in the one gallon freezer bags. After bagging one hundred of these he weighed each one, removing or adding marijuana until each bag weighed one pound. When he was finished he placed the freezer bags in the garbage sacks and sat them near the door. He had one hundred dollars and nearly a pound of pot for himself for less than two hours work.

Henry had more pot than he could smoke. Besides the marijuana he earned today he had another half pound or more in his closet. He knew he could bag it and sell it for ten dollars an ounce but he didn't want the 'traffic' at his door. 'Traffic' drew the law's attention and too much 'traffic' could get you busted.

"How much do you pay for a pound of pot Saul?"

"That's none of your business."

"I'm not trying to cut in on you. I've got a pound in my closet and I'd like to sell it."

"I pay sixty a pound when I buy a hundred pounds or more."

"I'll sell you mine for fifty."

"I'll give you forty." Saul pulled two twenty dollar bills from his wallet and offered them to Henry. Henry took the money and pulled the bag of marijuana from the top shelf of the closet and handed it to Saul. Henry still had nearly half a pound left for himself.

"Have you seen Wynn lately?" Henry asked.

"It's been a couple of weeks. Why?"

"I was just wondering if he was still on the road. I've driven by his ranch a few times but I didn't see his Cadillac."

"He's not living at the ranch."

"What do you mean he's not living at the ranch?"

"Doesn't anyone ever tell you anything? Wynn and Dolores separated. Wynn's living with his mother. I guess you haven't heard either that Capital dropped him and he doesn't have a label."

"No I haven't. But he'll have a new label soon."

"Maybe he will and maybe he won't," Saul replied. "What are you going to do if he doesn't get one?"

"Keep pitchin' songs I guess."

"Pitching to who? You can't make money off local labels. Wynn's the only one you know around here that had a major label."

"I'll do something."

"What you oughta do is move to Nashville."

"What the hell would I do in Nashville? I don't know anyone in Nashville."

"You know Pete Mitchell. He's working with Tubb now and I got his number in my billfold. You've had two songs recorded on a major label. That puts you one jump ahead of most of the songwriters already."

"I'll think about it," Henry lied. He had no intention of moving to Nashville or anywhere else. Nashville had too many songwriters already.

Three weeks later Henry returned to his room at the Park Plaza around four in the morning. He saw four police cars parked in front of Saul's room and a moment later he saw Saul, handcuffed, being led from his room to the back of a patrol car. As Saul was being placed in the back seat Henry saw an officer point toward Henry's room. Henry took the diet pills hidden in a sock in his dresser drawer and flushed all ten capsules down the commode. Next he took the marijuana from the closet shelf and sat down in front of the commode and began tearing the half pound into handfuls small enough to flush. When he finished he walked to the window and looked out. The police were gone and he wasn't going to be arrested, at least not yet. He didn't know whether he wanted to laugh or cry. He'd flushed all his drugs and pot away. He packed his car, leaving Saul's scales in the top of the closet, and ten minutes later he was on the highway to Nashville.

CHAPTER THIRTEEN

Henry followed the interstate to Gainsley then turned onto State Highway 44. The interstate had ruined the business along the highway, particularly the bars and motels near the river. All the motels had closed and only two bars remained open, one on the Texas side and one on the Oklahoma side.

Two hours after leaving Fort Worth Henry was pulling into the driveway at his grandmother's home in Joneston. He hadn't been home in more than a year and he hadn't called in more than a month except to see if she'd gotten the album he'd mailed her.

"What a nice surprise," she said, as she opened the door. "I wasn't expecting to see you drive up. Come in here. Are you hungry?"

"No ma'am. I'm sorry if I woke you up. I know it's early."

"Nonsense. I should have been up already." Lahoma hugged Henry's neck and asked if he was staying.

"I'm just passing through on my way to Nashville. I thought I'd spend a few days with you if you don't mind."

"You know I don't mind. I wish you'd move back here and settle down. Maybe find a nice girl." She turned and walked to the kitchen. Henry followed and took a seat at the table while she started making coffee. "How many eggs you want Henry?"

"I'm not hungry. Maybe I'll eat later."

"You need to eat Henry. I've never seen you this thin. You look like you've been in a concentration camp. You're nothing but skin and bones and you look sickly."

"I'll eat later. I promise. Right now I'd just like some coffee."

Five minutes later Lahoma poured Henry a cup of coffee then asked if he'd like her to cut his hair.

"No. Ma'am."

"Henry you look like one of those California hippies. You looked so nice when you came home from the Navy. At least let me trim it and get it out of your eyes. It won't take but a minute."

"Maybe later," Henry lied. "How's Mother? Has Charlie beat her to death yet?"

"She's fine I guess. I don't see her much but she calls from time to time to ask about you. I gave her your phone number. Please let me cut your hair. I just can't hardly stand to see it long and shaggy like that and please try to eat something. You've lost so much weight and it's not healthy. You don't look healthy. You look like you've been in a hospital."

"I'm fine Grandmother. I promise you I'm fine."

"Let me fix you some eggs and biscuits and gravy. Please."

Henry knew she wouldn't be happy until he ate or tried to eat. He agreed to two eggs and toast. Lahoma poured him a fresh cup of coffee then turned on the stove and started heating the skillet. She stood behind him and gathered Henry's hair together at the base of his neck.

"Let me cut just this much," she said.

"I don't want a haircut," Henry snapped. He immediately felt guilty for being short-tempered with his grandmother. "I wore my hair the way somebody told me to wear it for four years," he explained, "and I've had enough haircuts to last a lifetime."

Lahoma broke two eggs into the skillet and placed two slices of bread in the toaster. A few minutes later she set the food down in front of Henry and took a seat across the table from him. "I won't say anymore about your hair but I wish you'd stay here instead of running off to Nashville. I know you want to write songs but you don't even know anyone in Nashville."

"I have a friend who plays guitar for Ernest Tubb."

"Couldn't you live here and send your songs to your friend?"

"I don't think it works that way. Pete can't be on the road with Tubb and pitching my songs too, even if he wanted to."

"What about your friend Wynn? Won't he record anymore of your songs?"

"He would if he had a label."

Henry ate the two eggs and one piece of the toast. Now he wished he had one of those diet pills he'd flushed down the commode. He'd had little sleep the past few days and eating had made him sleepy. He kissed Lahoma's cheek and asked if she'd mind if he lay down for a while.

"Are you alright?" she asked.

"I'm fine. I'm just tired from the trip."

"A two hour trip wore you out? I worry about you Henry. It'll take you a week to drive to Nashville."

Henry woke up shortly after two in the afternoon. Lahoma was busy with alterations and didn't notice he was awake until he asked her if she wanted a fresh cup of coffee.

"Are you hungry?" she asked. "It won't take but a minute to make dinner."

Henry gave his standard answer, "I'll eat later," then asked if he could use the telephone.

"This is your home Henry. I don't know why you think you have to ask."

He looked in the telephone book for the number of Harvey Pike's parents then dialed the number. Harvey's mother told him

Harvey was living in Hardmor and gave Henry a number and an address. Henry called the number and after several rings a girl answered. He could tell by the tone of the voice that he'd woke her up.

"Is Harvey home?"

"He's sleeping."

"Wake his worthless ass up."

"I can't. He wouldn't like it."

"I don't give a rat's ass what he likes. Tell him I'm on my way over to drag his fat ass out of bed."

"I can't tell him that! Who are you anyway?"

"I'm Henry Ridge. Tell him I'm on my way over there."

Henry hung up before the girl could reply. He called again forty-five minutes later from a telephone booth in Hardmor.

Harvey answered the telephone. "Where you at hare-lip?"

"I'm at the Texaco station near the interstate. I thought I'd better call and see if you'd hauled your carcass out of bed yet."

"If anybody else had woke me up I'd be kickin' their ass."

"Hell Harvey it's damn near supper time."

"I don't give a damn what time it is. Do you know where I live?"

"Your mother gave me an address off Refinery Road."

"Take a right off the old highway and I'm at the Sandalwood Apartments. They're brand new and they're the only apartments out here. I'm in one-o-eight."

Ten minutes later Henry was knocking on Harvey's door. A pretty young redhead wearing a short terry cloth bath robe and a black eye answered the door then returned to her place beside Harvey on a large, gray, over-stuffed sofa. Harvey stood up and gave Henry a quick hug then pointed to a gray over-stuffed chair and told him to sit. A coffee table sat in front of the sofa. A razor blade, a rolled hundred dollar bill and a small pile of white powder was on the coffee table. Harvey appeared thinner than Henry remembered but he was still well muscled. He was suffering from premature baldness and the hair was missing from two-thirds of his scalp.

"Goddamn look at you," Harvey grinned. "I'll bet you don't weigh a hundred pounds and twenty pounds of that is hair. Roni, this skinny thing is Henry Ridge. The best friend I ever had."

Roni, the redhead, sat on the sofa Indian style, with her legs underneath her. Her bathrobe was open enough to reveal most of her breasts and Henry could see enough to know she was a true red head. He wanted to stare a little longer but he forced his eyes away. The girl was with Harvey and Harvey was his friend. Henry wanted them to remain friends.

"You want coffee or beer or whiskey?" Harvey asked.

"Coffee sounds good."

"Roni get Henry a cup of coffee," Harvey ordered. Roni stood at once and walked to the kitchen. She returned with a large mug of black coffee and placed it on the table near Henry. Harvey bent over the coffee table and cut out a section of the white powder then cut this section into four lines, each one about three inches long. He rolled the hundred dollar bill into a cylinder the shape and size of a small drinking straw, snorted two lines, one in each nostril, then offered the rolled hundred to Henry. Henry scraped the two lines into a small pile then used the razor blade to pick the powder up and drop in his coffee.

"What am I drinking?" Henry asked. "Coke or Speed?"

"Coke," Harvey answered, "and you're the first person I've ever seen that drinks it."

"You need to get out of Oklahoma more Harvey."

"So what the fuck are you doing back? I heard you was writin' songs and partying with all those country stars."

"You heard wrong. I've had a couple songs recorded by Wynn Stewart and that's about it. I have seen some parties though. Right now I'm just on my way to Nashville. I stopped to visit my grandmother for a couple of days."

"I got your album around here someplace. We use it to roll pot. I didn't figure you'd mind." Harvey was teasing Henry and Henry knew it. He doubted Harvey had even heard the album.

"When you leaving?" Harvey asked.

"Probably Monday."

"I wish you'd hang around a while. I'll even let you fuck Roni while you're here."

The remark caught Henry by surprise and he nearly choked on his coffee. "Roni might have something to say bout that."

"Roni does what I tell her to do. She knows what'll happen if she don't"

Henry had an idea where Roni got her black eye and he tried to change the subject. "What are you doing now Harvey? I know you well enough to know you couldn't be melted and poured in a job."

"I'm in business with some old friends of yours, the Holton brothers. As a matter of fact Leon's due by here sometime today."

"I thought they'd moved to eastern Oklahoma. Up in the mountains somewhere."

"They did but Leon likes to spend most of his time down here partying. About the only time Josh and Jake come around is during Pioneer Days in Mayetta." Harvey stared at Henry for a few minutes then asked, "Ain't you the least bit curious about what we're doing?"

"I figured you'd tell me sooner or later. You never could keep a secret. If I had to guess I'd say you're dealin' coke."

"That shows how much a hare-lip knows. Roni get my box," Harvey ordered. The redhead walked to the bedroom and returned a moment later with a cigar humidor large enough to hold fifty cigars. She set the box down in front of Harvey and asked him if he wanted her to roll a joint. "I want Henry to," Harvey answered, then shoved the box over to Henry and raised the lid. The humidor was filled with marijuana buds.

"Good pot will kill the coke," Henry commented.

"So fuckin' what! We'll just snort some more coke or in your case drink some more coke."

Henry picked out a bud nearly six inches long and half that wide. The bud was sticky and had a strong 'pine' smell. Henry tore a sizable chunk from the bud and began shredding it. The plant stuck to his fingers and left a dark green residue on his fingertips. "You sure this isn't part of a pine tree?" Henry had never seen marijuana like this.

"Wait till you smoke it. It'll tear your lungs up. The Holtons grow this and it's the best fuckin' pot in the state!"

"What are ya'll charging for this?"

"Three hundred a pound when they buy a hundred pounds or more. We don't deal in ounces at all."

Henry finished rolling the joint then lit it. The first toke sent him into a coughing spasm. When the joint was passed back to him he took a smaller toke. He offered the joint to Roni and Henry saw her look at Harvey before she accepted it. The joint kept going out and had to be relit every time it was passed. Halfway through the joint Henry said he'd had enough. He picked up the coffee mug and asked if he could get a refill. Henry intended to get the coffee himself but before he could push himself out of the chair Roni jumped up and took the mug from his hand. Harvey pulled a small, brown vial from his shirt pocket, unscrewed the top, then added a small amount of cocaine to the cocaine already on the coffee table. Roni returned with Henry's coffee as Harvey was cutting four more lines. He snorted two lines then offered Henry the other two. Henry added one line to his coffee then offered the other line to Roni. Roni asked Harvey's permission and Harvey nodded yes. Henry watched her snort the cocaine and remembered how Charlie's hunting dogs cowered every time Charlie fed them.

The telephone rang and Roni answered it then gave the receiver to Harvey. A moment later Harvey gave the receiver back to Roni and announced that Leon Holton was on his way over. Fifteen minutes later Leon walked in carrying a green military style duffel bag. He put the bag down near the kitchen door then smiled when he recognized Henry. "Goddamn Rabbit. We were just talking about you the other night at home. Daddy was wondering what happened to you. As soon as he found out you had an album out with your songs on it he had to have one. He's got it ordered from the Ernest Tubb Record Shop in Nashville. You're gonna have to come home with me for a few days. Mom, Dad, Josh, Jake, they'd all love to see you."

"I was planning on leaving Monday for Nashville."

"What's your hurry?" Leon asked. "Nashville ain't going nowhere. We got a lot of catchin' up to do."

"My funds are extremely limited. I stay a few days and I won't have the money to leave."

"Don't worry about money," Leon said. "I guarantee you'll make at least ten thousand a month if you'll go back home with me. I guarantee you'll make at least that much and nothin' hard about it. Easiest money you'll ever make. Did Harvey tell you what we got going?"

"He told me you developed a green thumb."

"I'm growing the best fuckin' pot in the world," Leon bragged, "and I can't grow enough."

"Let me think about it," Henry said.

"While you think about it Harvey and I will do a little business." Leon pulled the duffel bag over to the front of his chair and opened the top. The strong 'pine' smell told Henry what the duffel bag contained.

"Harvey," Leon said. "I don't mind Henry being here but the whore needs to go someplace else."

"Henry," Harvey asked, "would you mind taking Roni somewhere for an hour or so?" He reached in his pants pocket and pulled out a wad of money, peeled off a fifty dollar bill and offered it to Henry.

"I've got money," Henry told him, "just tell me how long you want us gone."

"Just an hour or so."

Roni came into the kitchen and stood near Henry. She'd changed from the bathrobe into a blue denim skirt and a paper thin T-shirt covered by a man's denim shirt.

"Do you have any suggestions on where we can kill a couple of hours?" Henry asked her as he was pulling out of the parking lot.

"Go left to the first stop sign then take a right. That will take us to the lake road. I know a place where we can go skinny dippin'."

"If I remember right there's a bar on the lake road near the city limits."

"The Knave of Hearts. But why would you want to go there?" Roni asked. "Wouldn't you rather buy some beer and go to the lake?" Roni ran her hand up the inside of Henry's thigh.

"There's a Stop 'n' Go across the street from the bar that sells beer."

Henry didn't answer and tried to ignore Roni's hand. A few minutes later he pulled into the bar's parking lot and parked next to an old Chevrolet Impala. Roni's hand had gotten him aroused and he had to make an adjustment in his pants before entering the bar. This seemed to amuse Roni. Inside the bar they saw two men sitting together at the bar nursing Black Label beers. A fat middle-aged blonde was stocking the beer boxes. Henry led Roni to a booth in the corner and ordered a beer for himself and a diet Coke for Roni. Roni sat down close to Henry and continued rubbing his thigh. "Why don't you like me Henry?"

"I do like you," Henry answered. "What makes you think I don't?"

"Then why don't you fuck me? I know you want to."

"You're Harvey's girl and Harvey's my friend. And even if we weren't friends I wouldn't like to think about having to fight that big son-of-a-bitch. If Harvey came after me about the only thing I could do is ask for a moment to make my piece with God before he killed me. Ain't no pussy worth fightin' Harvey over."

"Harvey wouldn't care if you fucked me. He makes me fuck the Holtons."

"He makes you huh?"

"He makes me fuck all three of 'em! I'll have to suck Leon's dick when we go back. And the last Pioneer Days Josh and Jake came down with Leon and I had to fuck and suck all three of 'em for a week. All the fuck they did was snort and drink and smoke and take turns with me!"

"Tell me if I'm wrong but I get the idea you might enjoy it."

"I like the sex. I just wish Harvey wouldn't hit me. I don't mind being slapped a little now and then but Harvey uses his fists and they hurt. He likes to watch me suck somebody's dick then he beats me because he says I enjoyed it too much."

"Why don't you leave him? There's a lot of men out there who likes girls that gang bang that won't beat you."

"You don't understand. I love Harvey. I just wish he wouldn't beat me with his fists. Besides, he said he'd kill me if I ever tried to leave him and I believe him." Roni ran her hand further up Henry's thigh and squeezed a testicle. "Why don't we go to the lake? Josh Holton says I have good pussy. He says it's pretty too."

"Girl I don't doubt that every inch of you is pretty and I'd love to see you naked and I know Harvey's no where around but I'd still be expectin' him to come chargin' out of the trees about the time I dropped my pants. I never could look over my shoulder and enjoy sex at the same time."

"Harvey would never know if we didn't tell him."

"Harvey would know."

"But how? I promise I won't tell him."

"By the shit eatin' grin I'd be wearin'."

Two beers and an hour later Henry drove Roni back to Harvey's apartment. Harvey and Leon sat on the couch in front of a fresh pile of cocaine watching Looney Tunes with the volume turned down. Leon offered Henry a beer and Harvey offered him cocaine. Henry dropped the powder in his beer and swished the liquid around in the can. Leon glanced at Roni then suggested the three men talk in the kitchen and leave Roni in the living room. "Harvey can I change the TV station?" she asked.

"NO!" Harvey yelled.

Leon lit a joint and passed it to Henry. Henry took a small toke and passed it to Harvey.

"How much money you got in your pocket?" Leon asked Henry.

"Enough to get to Nashville and eat a few days."

Leon pulled a roll of money from his shirt pocket and slid it across the table to Henry.

"I'll give you that if you'll come back to Poteau with me. Just come and visit and look around. That's all you have to do."

"I don't know how much money's there," Henry told him, "but I'll bet you can get a whole lot of people a whole lot cheaper."

"But I can't get people I can trust."

"Sure you can."

"Goddamn it Rabbit they ain't you! You're damn near part of the family! If you're worried about the law, don't be! We're so fuckin' far back in the hills you need a map to find us! You could be driving a new car and walking around with enough money in your pockets to buy anything you wanted."

"I got people in Nashville expecting me," Henry lied, "and I don't need a new car or a bucket of money."

"You're a fuckin' idiot," Harvey told Henry. "You used to have a little sense but you're a fuckin' idiot now."

"Why don't ya'll let me think about it? When you going home Leon?"

"Sunday. You can follow me if you want to."

"I'll think about it. Right now I need to get back to Joneston."

"Are you coming to Hardmor tonight?" Harvey asked. "You know you can stay here if you want."

"I won't be back tonight. I wanna spend some time with my grandmother. But I'll be back tomorrow."

Harvey gave Henry a large bud of marijuana and Leon offered him money again. He refused the money and hid the marijuana in his boot. It was nearly dark before Henry arrived back at his grandmother's.

"Are you hungry?" Lahoma asked.

"I ate in town," Henry lied, "but I would like a cup of coffee."

"Did you see Harvey?"

"I saw him and Leon Holton too."

"I wish you'd stay away from them, especially that Harvey."

"Harvey's just different Grandmother."

"He's crazy Henry! He's been that way since he came back from that damn war! I hear stories every week about him. I hear stories about those Holton brothers too. I also heard Orville Holton had a heart attack a while back."

"Leon didn't mention it. He wants me to move to Poteau and help out on their farm."

"What did you tell him?"

"I told him I was on my way to Nashville."

"I wish you'd stay here."

"Once I get settled maybe you could come up and we could go to the Grand Ole Opry."

"I'm too old to drive that far."

"You could take a bus. Be there over night."

"I'm too old to ride a bus all night."

"I'll come and get you."

"I can hear the Opry on the radio. I don't have to go to Nashville."

Henry carried his coffee out to the back porch, sat down and rolled a joint. Lahoma came out a few minutes later and sat down in a chair beside him. He made no attempt to hide the marijuana figuring she'd find out sooner or later and it was best to get it out in the open now.

"When did you start rolling your cigarettes?" She asked, then sniffed the air a couple of times. "What kind of tobacco is that? It smells like you're smoking ragweed."

"It's marijuana," Henry half whispered.

"What did you say?" Lahoma was on her feet. "It sounded like you said marijuana. Oh Lord Henry! You're not using dope are you? Please tell me you're not on dope. That stuff makes people crazy."

"Do I look crazy to you? If I hadn't told you what it was you'd have sat here half the night guessing. It's no worse than a shot of whiskey or a large glass of wine."

"But it's against the law. They lock people up who smoke marijuana. You're not using cocaine or that other dope, I forget what they call it..."

"You talkin' about heroin?" Henry was having trouble keeping a straight face. "Nothin' but marijuana Grandmother. I promise. Nothin' but marijuana."

"But you can go to jail for it Henry."

"If you'd rather I not bring it around you I'll understand and I'll leave it in my truck."

"I don't want you to hide anything you do Henry. But promise me you'll be careful.....and if we go anywhere you'll let me do the driving."

They spent the next two hours on the back porch talking before the mosquitoes drove them inside. A few minutes before she retired to bed she told Henry, "I think if I had to choose between you drinking beer and smoking that marijuana then I'd pick the marijuana. I wish you'd give them both up but I can't see that the marijuana's done anything to you and I can always tell when you've been drinking."

Lahoma telephoned Erica early the next morning and asked her if Charlie would throw a fit if Lahoma brought Henry by for a visit. Erica said she'd ask and hung up. A moment later Erica called back and said Charlie wouldn't mind as long as it wasn't too late in the evening. Lahoma told Henry about the plan when Henry woke up and stumbled into the kitchen. She called Erica back that afternoon to see if Charlie had changed his mind. Erica assured her Charlie wouldn't be upset and a few minutes later Lahoma and Henry were on their way to Mayetta.

When they pulled into the driveway they saw Erica and Charlie sitting in the front yard on a pair of folding beach chairs, a large cooler of beer between them. A fifty gallon drum sat behind Charlie and to his left. Several empty beer cans were strewed around the drum. Erica stood and hugged Henry then walked to the front porch and returned with two more folding beach chairs. Henry sat his chair on Erica's left and Lahoma put hers on Henry's left facing Charlie.

Henry, Lahoma and Erica made small talk for several minutes and Erica smiled like a new mother the entire time. Erica offered Henry a beer and he accepted it. Charlie sat silent and drunk, staring at Lahoma, then Erica, then Henry, then he exploded. "Who the fuck said you could drink my beer you fuckin' hare-lip?" Charlie was on his feet trying to steady himself. "Go buy your own beer you ugly little piece of shit!"

"I gave him the beer Charlie." Erica mumbled. "You sat right there and heard me offer it to him."

"It ain't your fuckin' beer either bitch!" Henry wanted to throw the can of beer at Charlie's head but he offered to pay for it instead. "I don't want your money you rabbit lookin' piece of shit! I just want your ugly ass out of here! I'm fuckin' tired of lookin' at you!"

Henry wanted to hurt Charlie but instead he turned and walked toward the car thinking the whole visit had been a mistake. Lahoma followed him. Once seated in the car he looked back toward his mother. She sat on the edge of the lounge chair with her head down and her hands covering her eyes and Henry could tell she was crying. Charlie was back in his lounge chair staring at Erica and drinking his beer.

"That was a short visit," Henry said, trying to make light of it.

"I'll go to hell because of Charlie," Lahoma told him.

"Why would you go to hell because of him?"

"The thoughts I have. All the times I've wished him dead. I've even thought about paying someone to kill him. I'd never do it but the Bible says evil thoughts are sins also and Charlie's turned me into a sinful woman."

Henry did the supper dishes while Lahoma finished some alterations then he walked outside to finish a joint he'd started earlier. Later Henry and his grandmother watched the Glen Campbell Hour on television. Lahoma spent the entire hour telling Henry how nice she thought Glen Campbell looked and how nice she thought Henry would look if Henry had his hair cut just like Glen Campbell's.

Henry had forgotten he'd told Harvey and Leon he'd be back in Hardmor that night until Harvey called a few minutes after nine p.m. Henry told him he'd see them the following day.

Henry was sitting on the front porch the following morning smoking a joint and drinking a cup of coffee when Leon Holton pulled into the front yard on a black Harley-Davidson motorcycle. Lahoma heard the Harley and came outside to see what was making so much noise. She hadn't seen Leon in years but she recognized him right away. "Why Leon," She purred, "what a nice surprise. Would you like some coffee or a glass of tea?"

"No ma'am."

"How's your folks? I heard Orville had a heart attack. How's he doing?"

"Daddy's doing good. Our biggest problem with him is getting him to take it easy. He never did like people doing for him or waiting on him."

"You tell Mona and your daddy I said hello. I'm going back to my sewing and let you boys visit."

The two friends spent the next two hours on the porch smoking marijuana and talking. Leon spent most of that time telling Henry about the wonders of Poteau, Oklahoma, the town closest to the Holton land. He talked about all the available girls and the parties. Finally Henry asked him why he hung around Harvey when there was so much in Poteau.

"Business mostly. I set up the deliveries and Harvey collects the money. I try to keep it as far away from home as I can and I don't normally carry more than I smoke. I brought that duffel bag down with a hundred pounds in it for Harvey to trade for cocaine. We use a horse trailer for most of our loads and we pay others to haul it."

"Sounds like you and Harvey have a good thing going."

"Everybody's getting rich but you Henry. We ship as much as a thousand pounds a week during harvest at three hundred a pound. You do the math. You could work for us two or three months a year then sit on your ass the rest."

"It's tempting Leon but that's a lot of jail time if you get caught."

"You think I'd be doing this if I thought I was going to get caught? Do you think the folks would? Daddy thinks it's stupid to try and outlaw something you can grow in the backyard. He don't see that it's any worse than moonshine. But he don't want to make a career of it either. Just another two or three years or so."

"Then what?" Henry asked. "I can't see your daddy sittin' around on his ass whittling."

"No, I can't either but I can see myself sitting around whittling. I don't care if I ever do another day's work at anything," Leon said, rising from the chair. "I guess I'll head back to Hardmor and go by Harvey's and get my dick sucked. You had any of Roni yet? If you haven't then you don't know what you've missed. That girl likes it."

"I never did like standing in line."

Henry waited until nearly dark before driving into Hardmor. He'd talked to Harvey earlier and agreed to go to Dotty's, a bar just off the interstate. He knew if he drove to Harvey's first Harvey would insist that he ride with him and he wanted to be able to leave the bar when he felt like it. If he rode with Harvey then he'd have to wait until Harvey was ready to leave. He drove to Dotty's and called Harvey from the bar. Harvey sounded angry. "Why the fuck didn't you come by here? Leon and I have been waiting half the fucking day!"

"I didn't think it was that big a deal whether we met at your place or the bar. I didn't think it'd piss anybody off."

"You act like you're too fucking good to hang around with your old friends."

"You know that's bullshit Harvey! You start talkin' that trash and I'll just turn around and head back to Joneston!"

"Here," Harvey mumbled, "Leon wants to talk to you."

"Henry," Leon said, "don't pay any attention to Harvey. He's just in one of his moods. Stay where you are and we'll be there in a minute."

The night was early and only a handful of people were at the bar. Henry was standing alone at the far end of the bar when Harvey and Leon walked in. Both men ordered beer then walked over to where Henry stood. "You finally got your ass out here," Harvey sneered, "I was beginning to think we'd have to go and get you."

"Hell Harvey it's early yet. There won't be a crowd for another hour or so. Where's your lady at?"

Harvey's face turned red. "You mean the whore! She's where the whore oughta be! Why? You wanna fuck her?" Harvey tore a key off his key chain and threw it on the bar. "Here's the fuckin' key! Go fuck her!"

"Easy big boy." Leon was talking to Harvey like he'd talk to a guard dog. "Henry didn't mean nothing and you know it. Just fucking settle down."

"I'm not after Roni, Harvey," Henry told him. "You don't have a thing I want. Besides that we go back too many years for you to be comin' in here jumpin' my ass." Henry finished his beer. "Maybe I oughta find another bar."

"You ain't going nowhere hare-lip," Harvey ducked his head and stared at the bar. "You know I didn't mean nothing. I'm just......it's just the dope talking."

Henry ordered three more beers and a shot of Jim Beam for each. A moment later Harvey announced he was going to the men's room to piss.

"I've heard Harvey goes crazy on occasion. He's not going crazy tonight is he?"

"I hope not," Leon answered. "He just got his feelings hurt because you didn't come by when you got into town."

People slowly drifted in and an hour later the bar was nearly filled to capacity. Harvey and Leon 'table hopped' and Leon tried to dance with every pretty female in the bar regardless of whether they were alone or not. The men gave Harvey and Leon a wide berth while the women gave them the eye. Harvey had lost a few pounds and most of his hair but he was still tall and well-muscled and Leon was lean and tall.

Mike Bryce came over to the bar where Henry was standing while Leon danced and Harvey sat at a table flirting with an attorney's wife. Henry hadn't seen Mike in years and he invited Mike to join the group. "I can party with you Henry,"

Mike told him, "and I can get along pretty well with Leon but I don't want to be around that crazy son-of-a-bitch Harvey. I don't guess Leon told you what happened one night when Harvey and I went drinking. The bastard tried to kill me. We're having a drink at the bar and the next thing I know something hits me in the side of the head and knocks me on my ass. Then the crazy bastard tried stomping me through the floor. I couldn't work for two weeks. He broke a couple of my ribs and fucked my right arm up good not to mention what he done to my head. There was no reason for it Henry. No reason at all. We're just standing there one minute having a drink and the next minute he fucking goes nuts. You be careful around him. I know you think he's your friend but I've known him longer than you have and he went off on me."

"I hate to hear that Mike. I know at one time you were close as brothers."

"He's different now. He came out of the Army fucked up and he's been fucked up ever since." Mike took a drink of beer then asked Henry to walk over to a table with him. "I want you to meet my wife."

Henry followed Mike to a table where an overweight blonde and two men sat. "Henry this is my wife Marsha and those two ugly hillbillies with her are Eddy Creeley and Walter Travish. I'll see if we can find you a chair."

"I don't think there's a vacant chair in the building."

Henry heard a commotion at a table near the back. Everyone turned around to look. Leon and Dotty, the bar's owner, a small gray haired lady that wouldn't weigh eighty pounds soaking wet, were standing between Harvey and a 'cowboy'. Dotty was pointing toward the front door and ordering Harvey out.

Leon was trying to persuade Harvey to leave but Harvey didn't want to go.

"Call the law!" Dotty yelled to her bartender. "I'm sick of this Harvey! Every time you come in here you start trouble! Now get out right now or I'll let the law handle your sorry ass! And I don't want you back in here again!"

Leon half pushed, half led Harvey to the front entrance. Leon looked around, spotted Henry and yelled, "come on we're leaving!"

Henry followed Leon and Harvey out to the parking lot. Harvey leaned against the car and glared at Henry. "We're going to Rebel's," Leon said.

"That's the biker bar on the highway isn't it?" Henry asked.

"Just past the city limits on the right," Leon answered.

"I'll see you there shortly." Henry walked back into the club and returned to Mike's table. An empty chair now sat on Mike's right and Henry sat down. "I wonder what set Harvey off?"

"He don't need no reason," Eddy answered. "He's been barred from most of the places around here."

"I know bars where they meet him at the door with a shotgun," Walter commented. "He'll get his head blowed off some night. He'll fuck with the wrong person and they'll put an end to his bullshit."

"He wasn't that way when me and him were runnin' wild," Henry told them. "Hell Mike you knew him better than I did. He'd fight, he's always been ready to fight but he didn't really go out of his way lookin' for one. He used to be a lot of fun to hang around with."

"The motherfucker's crazy," Mike said. "I think he always was crazy but we just didn't notice it. They say Viet Nam fucked him up but you're Viet Nam vets and you're not that fucked up."

"No but we're getting there, ain't we Eddy?" Walter asked.

Eddy grinned and nodded then asked, "Why don't we get out of here and go to Ellery's? I hear they've got a band tonight."

"I told Leon I'd meet him at Rebel's."

"That's all the more reason to go to Ellery's," Walter commented. "I think Harvey's barred from Ellery's."

"Marsha and I are staying here," Mike told them. "We got a young'un at home with a babysitter. We'll be headed that way when we finish our drinks."

"Wanna ride with us?" Eddy asked Henry.

"I'll follow you."

Ellery's club was slightly smaller than Dotty's and every seat in the place was taken. The three men found a place at the end of the bar near the rest rooms and stood. Ten minutes later Eddy was on the dance floor 'belly rubbing' with a pretty young brunette and Walter was trying to corner an attractive young blonde. Henry slipped out to his car and started toward Jonston. He turned off the highway onto a dirt road he'd follow home and stopped long enough to roll a joint.

Henry didn't climb out of bed until after ten the next morning. Although it was Saturday Lahoma was already working on alterations for a customer. She stopped her sewing and offered to cook Henry breakfast. He thanked her and told her he'd just wait until lunch. He poured a cup of coffee, walked out to the front porch and sat down. He fished around in his shirt pocket until he found the unfinished joint he'd started on his way home from Hardmor a few hours earlier. A few minutes later Lahoma walked out and told him Harvey was on the telephone wanting to talk to him. Henry didn't want to talk to Harvey but he didn't see any way to avoid it.

"Where the fuck did you go?" Harvey yelled. "We waited at Rebel's a goddamn hour for you!"

"I went home Harvey."

"Why didn't you fucking tell us you were going home?"

"I didn't know I was until I got in my car."

"I thought you wanted to party with us! What the fuck's wrong hare-lip? You too fucking good for me and Leon?"

"You get a little crazy Harvey."

"So? I get a little fucking crazy. You've seen me get crazy before. It never used to bother you."

"What was the fight about at Dotty's last night Harvey?"

"Nothing. I just played with a whore's tit and her old man didn't like it."

"And you think that's nothin'? That's justifiable homicide in a lot of Oklahoma courts. You're lucky he didn't shoot you. You got mad at me for just asking about your lady."

"I told you that was just the dope talking. You're welcome to fuck Roni anytime you want to. You can drive over and fuck her now if you want to. I don't care. She's just another whore."

"Not all of these good ole boys have such sophisticated attitudes Harvey. You oughta remember that."

"If you want to lecture my ass then why don't you drive over here and do it? If you wait till Leon gets here you'll have an audience."

"What time do you expect Leon?"

"Who knows? Whenever he gets up. He found him a whore last night at Rebel's and went home with her."

"I'll be by later."

"Now don't tell me you're coming and then don't show up."

"I'll see you later Harvey."

Henry waited until the middle of the afternoon before driving into Hardmor. He stopped at a Stop 'n' Go store for a pack of cigarettes and saw Eddy Creeley pull in as he was leaving. Eddy asked where he was going. Henry told him he was on his way to Harvey's and asked Eddy to go with him.

"I'm going over to Walter's," Eddy answered, "and even if I wasn't you couldn't pay me to go to Harvey's. I can't enjoy myself if I'm having to watch him, wondering when he's going to go off on me. Why don't you follow me to Walter's? He's got a big house with a pool table and if I know Walter he'll have beer and maybe a bottle of Bushmill."

"I told Harvey I'd be by."

"If you change your mind this is Walter's address." Eddy wrote an address on the back of a book of matches and gave it to Henry. "You'll see my truck in the driveway."

Henry wished he hadn't told Harvey he'd stop by. Henry liked Eddy Creeley. Eddy was Henry's height but a few pounds heavier and barrel chested. He wore a four inch brim Stetson, starched Wrangler jeans, western cut shirt and expensive looking round-toed cowboy boots. He had an 'air' about him that gave Henry the idea he could handle himself in any fight. Henry told him he'd try to get by there on his way home.

"If it's after dark," Eddy told him, "we'll probably be at Dotty's or Ellery's."

Leon's motorcycle was parked near the front door of Harvey's apartment when Henry arrived. Roni answered the door wearing her bath robe. The robe was open in front and she made no effort to close it. Harvey and Leon sat on the couch wearing nothing but their jeans. Cocaine residue covered the front of the coffee table and a marijuana 'roach' lay in the ashtray. Leon held a can of Budweiser beer and a bottle of Crown Royal whiskey and a can of beer sat on the end table to Harvey's right.

"Hey hare-lip," yelled Harvey, "we started without you. Whore get chief longhair a beer. Take this," Harvey passed the bottle of whiskey to Henry. "You got some catching up to do."

Henry took a drink of whiskey then set the bottle down on the coffee table. Roni brought him a beer and stood in front of him for several seconds with her bathrobe open before returning to the sofa. Leon picked up a joint and lit it then started teasing Roni with it, holding it out to her then pulling it back when she reached for it. Leon passed the joint to Harvey. Harvey took a hit and passed it to Henry. Henry took a hit and offered the joint to Roni. Roni looked at Harvey then Leon before accepting the joint. She took a long pull and passed the joint to Leon. A hot seed fell from the joint and went unnoticed until a small stream of smoke began rising from the sofa's cushion. Leon and Roni stood and extinguished the fire, leaving a hole the size of a dime. Harvey stared at the hole then stood and hit Roni on the left side of her face knocking her against the end table and upsetting a lamp. She lay sprawled on the floor and the left side of her face began swelling. Within seconds her cheek was swollen to more than double the normal size.

"You fucking whore!" Harvey screamed. "Goddamn stupid bitch! I oughta kill you!"

Leon had both hands on Harvey's chest pushing him away from where Roni was laying.

Henry was mad and disgusted. He was sure Roni's cheek bone was broken at least.

"You had no call to do that," Henry told him, "no call at all."

Harvey turned toward Henry and Leon stepped between them. "Since when did you give a damn about a slut like that?" Harvey screamed.

"She needs a doctor Harvey. She's hurt! And for what? For a little fuckin' hole that may or may not have been her fault. She needs to go to the emergency ward Harvey! You know how I was raised Harvey! Both of you do! I watched this bullshit every fuckin' day with my own mother and you're so fuckin' stupid you can't understand why it upsets me!"

Harvey stepped forward forcing Leon to back up while still standing between the two men. "Maybe your whore of a mother liked it hare-lip. You ever think of that?"

Henry's blood was boiling. He didn't care how big Harvey was he intended to fight him.

"You're a fuckin' coward Harvey Pike!"

Harvey tried shoving Leon out of the way but Leon managed to stay between the two.

"Get out of here, Henry," Leon ordered, "or he'll hurt you."

Henry glared at Harvey. "It'll be the last time he hurts anyone. He ever lays his hands on me I'll kill him." Henry looked at Roni and asked, "Would you like me to take you to the emergency ward?"

This triggered another outburst from Harvey and he again tried to shove Leon out of his path. "You ain't taking the whore anywhere you little punk piece of shit!"

"Get out of here!" Leon yelled. "Just get the fuck out!"

"Roni, do you want to go to the doctor?" Henry asked.

Roni looked at Henry and shook her head no. Henry left the apartment and drove back to Joneston. The following morning he packed the Studebaker, kissed Lahoma good-bye and drove to Nashville.

CHAPTER FOURTEEN

All Henry knew about Nashville were five things—it was the capital city of Tennessee and the country music capital of the world: the Ryman Auditorium, the mother church of country music was located there: the Grand Ole Opry was there and Tootsie's Orchid Lounge was there.

The trip took fourteen hours and Henry had decided early on to get a cheap motel room and wait until the following day to go downtown. He changed his mind as soon as he got a good look at the room he rented at the Dickerson Road Motel. He unpacked his car then took two of the motel's towels and tried to plug what appeared to be rat holes in the wall near his bed. An hour later he was sitting in Tootsie's nursing a long neck bottle of beer.

Tootsie's Orchid Lounge was located at 422 Broadway, across the alley from the Ryman Auditorium, home of the Grand Ole Opry, and was considered the most famous country music bar in the world. The place was owned and ran by Hattie 'Tootsie' Bess, an unofficial den mother to the stars and 'wannabbes' alike. She was well known for her big heart (she had a cigar box filled with thousands of dollars of unpaid tabs) and for the hat pin she carried and often used to convince troublesome patrons to either behave or leave.

It was nearing midnight and the groups of tourists wandering up and down Broadway were thinning out. Henry had noticed a man sitting in the corner when he entered Tootsie's earlier. Henry had ordered his second beer and the man in the corner was still sipping the same beer he'd had in front of him when Henry entered. The man had long curly hair, a black beard and mustache, large, blue, saucer-shaped eyes and a 'shit-eating' grin. He appeared to be studying everyone who entered the bar and Henry had seen the man glancing at him from time to time. Finally the man left his barstool and sat uninvited on the stool next to Henry. Henry assumed the man was 'queer'.

"Nice night ain't it?" The stranger asked, still grinning from ear to ear. Henry couldn't help but smile back.

"Yeah it is," Henry agreed.

"You know what would make it nicer?"

"What?"

"Another beer."

Henry laughed. He didn't know the man's name and the man was bumming a beer. Henry ordered two more beers and studied the man. He appeared clean, his clothes weren't ragged or dirty and he seemed harmless.

"I'm Stewart Donaldson," the man said, extending his hand. "My friends call me Bogie."

Henry shook the man's hand. "I'm Henry Ridge and my friends call me Henry."

Bogie's smile widened, "I like you Henry Ridge. You're all right. If I had something to smoke I'd invite you outside."

"I've got a cigarette if you want one but I don't think we have to go outside to smoke."

"Don't fuck with my head Henry Ridge. I know a toker when I see one."

Henry bent over and looked under Bogie's barstool. "What are you looking for?" Bogie asked.

"I just wanted to see if your balls were draggin' the ground."

Bogie laughed. "Let's finish this beer and get out of here."

"If I go anywhere it'll be to my room….alone." Henry was certain the man was gay.

"Where you staying Henry Ridge?"

"At the Dickerson Road Motel."

"Bad neighborhood. Where you from?"

"Oklahoma."

"You planning on staying awhile?"

"I was."

"Well Henry Ridge this is your lucky night. I know where you can get an apartment tomorrow if you got the money."

"I've got ninety dollars."

"That's not enough Henry Ridge. Ninety dollars won't last long at a motel, even one on Dickerson Road."

"I'll get by."

"I'm sure you will Henry Ridge. I'm sure you will. But I've got an offer I'd like for you to consider. I need a ride to Madison and you need a place to stay until you can get enough money for an apartment. Why don't you stay with me until then? I've got a furnished apartment in Madison and nobody there but me. We can go by the motel on the way and pick up your stuff."

"I don't know you from Adam and we just met a few minutes ago. Why would you do that for me?" Henry was more certain than ever that the man was gay.

"Do you believe in karma Henry Ridge?"

"Call me Henry for God's sake and no, I don't even know what the fuck karma is."

"Well Henry, when you help someone and later on someone helps you or when you act like an asshole and later on someone down the road treats you like an asshole, that's karma. Simply put, it's getting what you give or what goes around comes around."

"If you're queer you picked the wrong fellow."

Henry saw Bogie's eyes twinkle and his smile broaden. "If I was queer," he said, "I think I'd pick someone with more than ninety dollars. Now do you want a place to stay or not?"

Ten minutes later they were sitting in Henry's car smoking a joint. Twenty minutes later they were on their way to the motel to pick up Henry's belongings. Henry hoped he wasn't making a mistake. In the ten minutes they spent smoking the joint he learned that Bogie had made the trip from Oak Park, Illinois to Nashville to try and make a career as a country music entertainer or songwriter or possibly both. He had left his wife and baby with the promise that if he didn't make it in a year he'd return home to Oak Park. He'd been in Nashville more than three years and he was still chasing the 'neon rainbow'.

Henry asked Bogie about jobs in the area and Bogie assured him he could be working in a matter of days if he wanted to. "Worthan Bags is always hiring," he said. "You walk in and put in an application and you'll be working in a day or two."

"I'm figuring it's not much of a job if you quit."

"It's not hard as far as the work goes. It's being there at seven in the morning. I'm not much of a morning person. A lot of people come to Nashville needing a job in a hurry and they go to work there until they get on their feet then start looking for something else."

"Where you working now?" Henry asked. He saw that twinkle in Bogie's eyes again.

"I'm between jobs."

Bogie's idea of a furnished apartment was a couple of folding chairs, two large mattresses, one on the living room floor and one on the bedroom floor, and two upended cardboard boxes that served as end tables. The apartment came with a stove and refrigerator.

"So this is what folks in Illinois call a furnished apartment," Henry commented. "I'd hate like hell to have to live in an unfurnished one."

Bogie walked to the bedroom and returned a moment later with a sheet, blanket and pillow. "You can sleep in the living room," he said, throwing the bedding down on the mattress. "I'm sorry I can't offer you a four poster bed to sleep on."

Bogie's tone of voice gave Henry the impression that his feelings were hurt and that was the last thing Henry wanted to do. The man offered him a place to stay and help finding a job. Henry put his hat on an 'end table' and told Bogie his apartment was a lot nicer than the room at the Dickerson Road Motel. He rolled a joint and the two men sat on the edge of the mattress and talked and smoked until Bogie announced he was going to bed. Henry thanked him again then pulled a twenty dollar bill out of his pocket and offered it to him. Bogie refused the money but Henry insisted he take it and stuck the bill in Bogie's shirt pocket. After Bogie went to his bedroom Henry pulled his shirt and boots off then spread the blanket over the mattress. He kept his pants on still not totally convinced that Bogie wasn't gay.

Bogie was sitting in a chair drinking coffee and watching Henry when he woke up. Bogie handed him a small white sack. "There's a half dozen White Castles and a cup of coffee if you want 'em."

"Coffee sounds good," Henry said and pulled the large Styrofoam cup of coffee out of the sack. "What time is it?"

"A little after nine."

"You told me you weren't a morning person."

"I meant the early 'get up at five' kind of morning person."

Henry rolled a joint and the two smoked it. The marijuana gave Henry an appetite and he ate three of the small hamburgers. Bogie carried his coffee to the sliding glass door and slid the curtain back far enough to look outside.

"The neighbors should be coming out soon," he said. "There's three sisters that live in the corner apartment and they like to lay in the sun every morning for two or three hours. Another neighbor, Teresa, usually joins them. She has a two year old girl and the oldest sister, Mattie, has a boy about the same age. I'll introduce you."

Henry joined Bogie at the door and looked outside. He saw four young bikini clad women and two toddlers near the pool. He followed Bogie outside and to the pool.

"Henry, this is Teresa and that's her pretty little daughter, Jenny." Teresa appeared to be in her early twenties. She was dark haired with big breasts and a big ass and a bikini that couldn't cover her. Next he met the Conner sisters. Mattie, the oldest and the mother of the other toddler, Jeremy, was in her late twenties, blonde and well built. Margie, two years younger, was plump with light brown hair. Edie, the youngest, was in her late teens, plump, blonde and very friendly. Teresa asked the sisters if they'd keep an eye on her daughter then she and Bogie disappeared into her apartment.

"They'll be gone for awhile," Mattie told Henry. "You might as well sit down in her chair. Where you from?"

"Oklahoma. Just got into town last night."

"You a picker or a writer?" Edie asked.

"I'm a writer. Is it that obvious?"

"Everybody's a writer or a picker or a singer," Mattie said with a hint of sarcasm. "The boy that sacks groceries, the cashier at the restaurant, the janitor, they all come to Nashville."

"And what brought you to Nashville?" Henry asked.

"Nothing brought us," Edie answered. "Our daddy used to play at the Opry before he retired."

"How did you get hooked up with that weasel Bogie?" Mattie asked.

"You can tell my sister doesn't like him much," Edie said.

"I think he's a damn snake. He waits for Teresa's husband to go to work then he slithers over to her apartment for a few hours." Mattie's right breast slipped out of her bikini top exposing her nipple. She looked down, saw her nipple, covered it and looked at Henry. "Did you see anything?"

"Not a thing," Henry lied.

Mattie lay back and closed her eyes. Margie was sleeping and Edie was yawning. Henry stood up, intending to walk back to Bogie's apartment.

"Do you drink beer?" Mattie asked. "I know it's early but I have some beer at the apartment if you'd like one. I can get the girls to watch the kids."

"I'd love a beer," Henry answered. He followed Mattie around the building to a corner apartment where they spent the next two hours talking and drinking beer. He learned that Mattie's parents originally came from West Virginia and moved back when her father quit the Opry. Every weekend the parents drove down to Nashville usually arriving late Friday night and leaving early Sunday afternoon. The sisters worked the small bars around the Nashville colleges. Mattie and Margie played flattop guitars and Edie played tambourine. The three sisters took turns singing lead while the other two sang harmony.

"We're not getting rich," Mattie told him, "but we make enough to pay the bills. That's more than some folks are doing."

Margie decided she'd had enough sun and returned to the apartment. Henry thanked Mattie for the beer and the conversation and walked back to Bogie's apartment. He rolled a joint, smoked it then decided to return to the pool and wait for Bogie. When he stepped outside he saw Bogie walking toward the apartment. "Were the neighbors nice to you?" Bogie asked.

"Nice enough."

Henry walked to a Quik Sak store a half block away from the apartments and bought a local newspaper, The Tennessean, and two six packs of beer. Bogie had neither a radio nor a television and nothing to read but a four month old Playboy magazine. Henry had planned to read everything in the paper except the business section but after two joints and three beers he dozed off while reading the horoscope. Two hours later Bogie opening a beer woke him.

"Nothing happening now," Bogie commented, "but we may find a party later. I know a few pickers around here and if there's nothing going on here we'll pay someone a visit. We'll go to Broadway if nothing else."

"You wouldn't happen to know Pete Mitchell would you?"

"Everybody knows Pete," Bogie answered. "When he's not on the road he's in one of the bars downtown. Is he a friend of yours?"

"I knew him in Fort Worth. I heard he's with Ernest Tubb now."

"He picks with Jimmy Newman too. I haven't seen him for a few weeks but if he's in town he'll be on Broadway in one of the bars."

Henry and Bogie smoked a joint then Henry asked to use the shower. Bogie told Henry again to consider the apartment his home as long as he wanted. When Henry came out of the shower Bogie was gone. He looked outside and saw Bogie talking to a tall, stout man near the pool. The man walked inside the apartment adjacent to the pool and Bogie returned to his own apartment and told Henry there would be no need to hunt a party tonight.

"The manager likes to cook hot dogs a couple of times a week and invite anyone in the apartments. Usually anywhere from two to three dozen people show up. Every teenage girl around here will show up. The Conner sisters always show up and wait until you meet the manager's daughter. While he's cooking hot dogs she's giving head. She won't fuck anyone because she's scared she'd get pregnant and her daddy would kill her but she'll suck your dick till you squeal. I kind of feel sorry for the man because I think he knows what she's doing. He has to, everyone else knows. While he's cooking wienies she's sucking them. After the party breaks up he spends half the night hunting for her. He hasn't caught her with anyone yet but some night he probably will and then I'll feel sorry for the man he caught. I think she's worth the beating though."

"Just how old is his daughter?" Henry asked.

"Lisa's fifteen going on thirty."

"You sound like you speak from experience. Please don't tell me I'm living with a child molester."

"If you look at it like that then most of the men here are child molesters. I don't know anyone that's turned her down yet and I don't think you would either once you see her."

"You're wrong Bogie. There's some lines I won't cross."

Henry's remark seemed to touch a nerve with Bogie and for the next hour they drank beer and talked little. Henry rolled another joint and after they finished smoking they walked out to the pool. A dozen or so tenants were already near the pool including the Conner sisters. A small grill had been placed between the pool and the adjacent apartment. The tall stout man was at the grill rotating wieners. Bogie introduced Henry to the man at the grill. "Henry this is Larry Byrd, the manager. Larry this is Henry. He's staying with me until he gets on his feet."

"It's nice to meet you Henry." The man extended his hand and Henry shook it. "I've got some vacant apartments I can show you when you're ready."

"As soon as I go to work I'll take you up on that offer."

Bogie led Henry a few feet away from Larry and the grill and pointed toward a small group of girls. Four of the girls appeared to be in their early teens. All were scantily dressed in tight short shorts and T-shirts. A tall, big breasted blonde appeared to be in her late teens.

"There's the manager's daughter, Lisa."

"Which one?" Henry asked. "I'd like to know who to avoid."

"See the tall big-tittied girl with long hair? That's Lisa. You still want to tell me you'd turn that down?"

"She looks older but I don't give a damn if she looks forty. If she's fifteen I won't touch her. I don't understand how you could get a hard on with a fifteen year old child. I've got socks older than her."

"Well I hope it don't bother you if I get some head tonight. If she offers it I plan to take it. If I don't someone else will. She ain't a fucking virgin Henry. You probably have the only dick around here she ain't sucked."

"This is your apartment. If it bothers me I can leave. Besides, you're the one that has to face yourself in the mirror every morning."

"I just don't want you thinking I'm some kind of pervert."

"You are a pervert Bogie. You're a nice pervert, one of the nicest perverts I've ever met, but you're still a pervert. You've got all the scruples of a Yankee pig but you're a nice guy."

"Just as long as it doesn't bother you."

The two men walked over to where the Conner sisters and Teresa were sitting. Jeremy stood near his mother Mattie and Jenny was sitting on the lap of a short fat man sitting on the lawn chair near Teresa. The four women were dressed as scantily as the teenage girls. All wore short shorts or short cut-offs and T-shirts with the exception of Edie who wore a tank top that exposed most of her breasts. None of the ladies wore a bra. Bogie introduced the short fat man as Teresa's husband, Dan. Henry shook the man's hand then turned his attention toward Mattie. Mattie seemed glad to see him and offered him a beer from a large cooler.

"Find a chair and sit down," she said, handing him a cold can of beer. "Do you always wear that hat?"

"Never without it. There doesn't seem to be a lot of chairs around. You don't mind if I just sit on the grass do you?" Henry sat down Indian style beside Mattie.

"What are you doing hanging around that pig?" Mattie asked, pointing toward Bogie.

"You talking about Bogie? Bogie's alright. A little perverted maybe but he's been nice to me."

"He's a pig," Mattie said. "We caught him peeking in Edie's bedroom one night."

"Maybe he was high and confused. I think he's harmless though."

"He's a pig. I like to get high but I don't peek in people's windows when I do."

"I've got a little pot," Henry offered, "if you'd like to smoke one. We could slip over to Bogie's apartment."

"I'm not going near that pig's apartment. Besides I've got my own smoke. If you want to we'll go to my apartment later."

Henry heard someone strumming a guitar and looked around to see where the music was coming from. "That's 'Ears'.

He's over by the grill tuning up," Mattie said. "There's a lot of people here trying to break into music and they'll be passing the guitar and singing. Maybe we can get you to do some of your songs."

"I don't think so."

Henry saw Bogie walk to his apartment and return with an old flattop Martin guitar. Another man carrying a fairly new Yamaha flattop walked up to Mattie and asked if she'd perform that night. She introduced the man to Henry as Jerry McPhearson. "Everyone calls him 'Ears'," she said. Henry could understand why. The man had the biggest ears he'd ever seen on a head. The way the man smiled it was apparent to Henry that the nickname didn't bother him in the least. 'Ears' worked with a carpenter's crew while he was trying to make a name as a writer and performer. Next Mattie introduced him to Rodney, a songwriter working as a machinist and his live-in girlfriend, Emma, and Joe, a roofer trying to make it as a guitarist and songwriter and Anna, an Ohio native trying to make a name as a performer while working at the Madison Dry Cleaners, then Matt, a songwriter at heart and a construction laborer by necessity. Matt was also Edie's part-time lover.

Henry watched the group pick and sing their creations, some good, several bad and every now and then something excellent that he wished he'd written. Every few minutes someone would ask Mattie to sing and she always introduced Henry then told them "maybe later". He watched Matt and Edie disappear for an hour and watched the manager's daughter disappear with one man, return a few minutes later and then disappear with another man while her daddy cooked and dispensed weenies. Finally Mattie asked Henry if he'd like to slip away to her apartment and smoke a joint. Henry said he'd love to and Mattie asked Edie to watch Jeremy and keep an eye on her chair.

"So what do you think of Nashville?" Mattie asked as they sat at her kitchen table drinking a beer and smoking a joint.

"I haven't seen much of it yet but I like what I've seen so far. The folks I've met seem nice enough."

"Don't let some of the people fool you," she warned. "This is a cutthroat town. People will walk all over you to get what they want, including your friend Bogie."

"Why do you stay here then?"

"It's the only place to be if you're in music. Me and my sisters can make a living here. We can't make squat in West Virginia."

"I'd like to come out and hear you some night."

"We're working Thursday, Friday and Saturday night at the Red Nail on Gallatin Road. You can ride with us if you want to. You wouldn't mind helping with the equipment would you?"

"It'd be my pleasure."

They finished their beer and the joint then returned to the pool area. Matt was singing a song he'd written called 'Jesus and George', comparing Jesus to the country music legend George Jones. The lyrics were perfect but Henry knew the song would never be recorded. The Baptist controlled Tennessee the way they controlled Oklahoma and the rest of the South. The song would be considered blasphemous.

Henry wasn't impressed at all with Anna. She looked good and Henry was sure she'd give every man in any audience a 'hard on' but her material was mediocre. Bogie took his turn next and sang a song he'd written for the daughter he'd left in Chicago called 'Scarlett In Diapers'. Henry was impressed. The song was far better and more original than anything he'd heard in a long time and he told Mattie what he thought. "I didn't say he couldn't write," she replied. "I just said he's a pig."

Bogie's next song, 'Dixie In The Morning', about a man living in the city with a lady named Dixie, made Henry want to tear up everything he'd written. The wild-eyed, free-spirited pervert could write circles around him. He made a comment to Mattie about not being able to understand why Bogie's songs weren't being recorded. "They're as good if not better than anything on the radio now," Henry told her.

"Politics Henry," Mattie answered. "If people don't like you they won't do your songs. Your pig friend Bogie offends too many people. He's walked into some of the publishing companies drunk and fucked up, he's called more than one publisher an idiot or worse, he'll fuck anything, young, old, married or single. He's a pig. Look in the dictionary under pig and you'll probably see a picture of him."

"What did he do to you to make you despise him so much? And don't tell me a little window peekin' was all he did."

Henry struck a nerve in Mattie. She looked around, located her son and yelled, "Come on Jeremy we're going home." She stood, picked up her son and the chair and said, "Good night Henry," and walked away.

Apartment regulations forbid any outside noise after ten p.m. and at ten p.m. exactly the manager called an end to the gathering. Small groups wandered off to continue their get together inside an apartment. Bogie invited anyone who wanted to come back to his apartment and Ears, Rodney and his wife, Emma, Joe and Anna accepted. The group sat on the mattress and drank beer and passed the guitar. Ears, Rodney and Henry had marijuana and the three men took turns sharing what they had with the others. Everyone but Bogie and Henry had to work the following day and around midnight the group broke up and everyone returned to their own apartments. Bogie went to bed and Henry stepped outside and lit a cigarette. He heard foot-steps and saw Anna coming up the sidewalk.

"Did I leave my cigarette case here?" she asked.

"I didn't see it but that doesn't mean it isn't here. We can go in and look." After ten minutes of searching they decided the cigarette case wasn't there.

"Maybe you left it at your boyfriend's apartment," Henry suggested. He didn't even know if she had a boyfriend.

"I just left there. It isn't there. Can I have one of your ciga-rettes? I'll just have to wait until tomorrow to find my case or buy some more. My boyfriend's asleep and I don't want to wake him."

"You said you just left there. He can't be asleep already."

"He fell asleep as soon as he rolled off me."

"Damn," Henry half mumbled, "that's hard to believe." Anna was a beautiful girl with big breasts, small waist and a perfect ass. Henry was fairly certain she was also sexually frus-trated. "Would you like to smoke a joint and talk?" He asked, trying not to sound like a dirty old man.

"I can't. I have to work tomorrow but thanks for the ciga-rette."

Bogie left for Teresa's apartment shortly after nine a.m. the following morning. Henry knew he'd be gone for a few hours and was trying to decide what to do. He knew he should be try-ing to find a job but since it was Wednesday he'd decided the best time to put in an application for work would be Monday. He was brushing his teeth when he heard someone knocking on the sliding doors. Anna was standing there holding a cup of cof-fee. "I didn't see a coffee pot last night and I thought you might want this," she said.

"I thought you worked at a dry cleaners."

"I called in sick. I'm not imposing am I?"

"Not at all," Henry answered. "Come on in."

Anna sat down on the corner of the mattress and Henry sat down next to her, placing the cup of coffee on the floor. He asked her how her career was going and struggled to make small talk and keep her interested enough to stay until he could figure out what she wanted. If she wanted a friend, someone to talk to and he made a pass at her he risked losing a potential friend. If she wanted to be more than friends and he didn't make a pass at her he still risked losing a potential friend because she would find someone else to meet her needs, the needs her boyfriend wasn't meeting. Soon the discussion turned toward the subject of problems.

"My biggest problem," Anna told him, "is I can't say no. All a man has to do is touch my boob and I lose control and I can't help it."

It took a second for the statement to reach Henry's brain and another second for Henry's hand to reach her breast. Two minutes later they were on the mattress naked and Henry was nursing her breasts like a starving calf. Two hours later she was kissing him good-bye and Henry was pleading with her to call in sick the next day. "Maybe I'll come back this afternoon if Bogie isn't here."

"I'll lock him out. He never carries a key."

"I wish you had your own apartment Henry."

"I'll have one soon I promise." Henry had decided not to wait until Monday. He'd put in an application tomorrow. The quicker he went to work the quicker he'd have his own place.

The manager didn't cook hot dogs that evening but a small group still gathered near the pool to pass the guitar and sing or listen to others pass the guitar and sing. The apartment complex was made up of five two-storied buildings each containing twenty apartments, ten on the first floor and ten on top. Each apartment could be entered through a door in the hallway or through the sliding glass doors at the back of the apartment. The glass doors on the bottom opened to a small patio connected to a sidewalk. The top apartments opened to a small balcony. People sat in front of their apartments or on their balconies every evening the weather permitted and talked or listened to whomever was performing or simply watched the other people moving about.

Bogie returned from his daily visit shortly after two the next afternoon. Henry had hoped that Anna would return but she hadn't. Now the two men were sitting outside drinking beer and Bogie was trying to talk Henry into waiting until Monday to look for work. "I'll bet that bitch Maggie has something to do with it," Bogie said. "I'll bet she's been telling you I'm a sorry piece of shit."

"She didn't use those words exactly but that's not the reason I'm going into town tomorrow. I need my own apartment and I need a job to get one."

"What's wrong with staying here and splitting the rent?"

"You don't have any furniture and I'm kind of partial to a bed. You're a nice guy and I hope you won't be offended if I tell you that after two days I'm already tired of your living room." Bogie had that hurt look on his face again. "It's nothin' personal Bogie. I appreciate you puttin' up with me and I'll always feel like I owe you for it but I just need my own apartment."

Henry waited until mid-morning then drove into Nashville and asked an attendant at a Texaco station for directions to Worthan Bagging. After stopping two more times to ask directions he pulled into the parking lot and asked a gate guard for directions to the company employment office. After asking two more people for directions he was standing at a desk asking a receptionist for an application for employment. Fifteen minutes later he was seated across a desk from an older man wearing a suit, tie and very little hair. Five minutes later he was hired and told to report for work at seven a.m. Monday morning. After stopping several more times to ask directions he was on his way back to the Madison Center Apartments. He stopped at the White Castle and bought a dozen hamburgers then at the Quik-Sak for two six packs of beer. Bogie was still at Teresa's when he returned to the apartment. Henry ate six of the burgers and chased it with two beers. He rolled a joint and stood at the door smoking it. Mattie, Margie, Edie, Mattie's son Jeremy and Teresa's daughter, Jenny was at the pool area. For a moment he thought about walking over and visiting Mattie then decided to walk to the pay phone and call his grandmother. Edie called out a good morning as he walked to the phone and Mattie and Margie ignored him.

Lahoma scolded Henry for waiting three days to call her but seemed happy that he'd found a job. He gave her the name of the apartments and Bogie's apartment number in case she needed to get in touch with him. Back at the apartment he finished the joint then took a nap.

Bogie woke him an hour later and Henry told him about his trip to Nashville and Worthan Bagging. "Why didn't you come to Teresa's and get me?" Bogie asked. "I'd have gone with you. We could have gone downtown."

"I didn't think you were interested in going to Worthan's."

"I wasn't. What shift did they put you on?"

"I need to be there at seven Monday morning."

"If you're smart you'll take the bus."

"Why would I take a bus?" Henry asked. "I've got a car."

"The bus is thirty-five cents. I know damn well you spent more than seventy cents in gas and you'd have gotten there in half the time. You oughta save your car for weekends or when you want to go to music row and push your songs."

"Would you like to ride with me tomorrow?" Henry asked. "I'd like to look around a little."

"Sure. I'll show you the best places to get rejected. The ones with coffee and doughnuts. If you're lucky you'll have time to fill your stomach before they call you in to hear your tapes."

"If they don't like your songs I doubt they'll want any of mine. From what I heard so far you write circles around me."

"They've taken a lot of my songs," Bogie told him. "They said they wanted them. They just haven't done a fucking thing with them. But I'm always welcome to their coffee and doughnuts."

"You've about got me convinced that I'm wasting my time."

"Oh no, don't get that idea. You never know what a publisher's thinking although most of the writers I know agree that they never have an original thought. They'd rather you bring them a song that sounds like something that's already on the radio. You play an original song for one of them and they'll hurt themselves trying to get to the other side of the room."

"You sound like you don't care much for publishers."

"I don't. I think they're all assholes. But I like their coffee and doughnuts."

Bogie was already at Teresa's when Henry rolled off the mattress and started dressing. The two men had decided the previous evening that they'd wait until after the traffic thinned out before driving into Nashville. Henry had decided to buy a coffee pot while they were out. He was dressed and on his way to the White Castle when Anna showed up. "I called in and told them I was having car trouble," she said as she unbuttoned her blouse.

Thirty minutes later she was on her way to work. Henry had her drop him off at the White Castle where he bought a large coffee to go and carried it back to the apartment. Bogie was waiting on him. "We'd better hurry or the doughnuts will be gone," he said.

"I'll buy us some doughnuts," Henry offered.

"It's not the same. These doughnuts are probably the only payment I'll ever get out of those people."

"So it's a matter of principle."

"You might say that."

There were publishing companies in nearly every run down house on Sixteenth and Seventeenth Avenues. Bogie took Henry to Coal Miner's Publishing and had planned to take him to Surefire and Barron and Longhorn Publishing. Henry had four songs on a reel-to-reel tape and while he played the tape for the publishing agent Bogie ate every doughnut he could lay his hands on. Henry came out of the meeting and announced that Coal Miner's Publishing had taken all four songs. He was excited and sure that he'd have a song on the radio soon and wanted to celebrate. He drove them to lower Broadway and parked near the Music City Lounge. Inside the bar he ordered both a beer.

"I know you're excited," Bogie said, "and I don't want to burst your bubble but…."

"But what?"

"Just because they took your songs doesn't necessarily mean they'll do anything with them."

"Then why would they take them?"

"They liked them and they may even demo them but I wouldn't start counting my money yet. They could sit on a shelf and somebody may record them or they could sit on a shelf and sit on a shelf and sit on a shelf and…."

"I get the picture."

"I think they've got about forty of mine and I haven't had a song out yet. They got us over a barrel Henry. We have to take our songs to someone and they know it. But every now and then someone gets a song recorded. If the song reaches the top forty they'll drag every song they've got of yours off the shelf and record them. It's just getting that first song out."

"I thought I had my foot in the door when Wynn recorded my songs."

"You did have with Wynn."

"You sayin' I should have stayed in Texas?"

"No, I'm saying you should have stayed with Wynn. Someone with Wynn's talent can always find a new label."

Henry and Bogie had two more beers at the Music City Lounge then walked up Broadway to Demon's Den for two more then down a few doors to Tootsie's where they had several more.

Henry asked about Pete Mitchell at every bar. Everyone knew him but no one had seen Pete for a few weeks. Around six that evening both men were tired of the tourists and decided to return to Madison and continue drinking and getting high. They stopped at the Quik-Sak and bought beer and when they pulled into the apartment's parking lot Henry realized he had forgotten to buy a coffee pot.

The crowd near the pool was slightly larger than the previous nights although the Conner sisters were absent. While the sisters were doing their act at the Red Nail, Teresa was babysitting for Mattie. Jeremy, Mattie's son, played in the grass with Teresa's daughter, Jenny, a few feet from where Teresa sat with her husband, Dan. Bogie opened a beer and started toward them but noticed the manager's daughter, Lisa, standing alone. Henry watched Bogie walk over to where she stood and speak to her briefly. Lisa nodded her head and looked over at her father turning hot dogs at the grill. Bogie walked back to his apartment and Lisa walked the opposite way and disappeared around the corner of the building. A few minutes later Henry saw her reappear from around a corner two buildings away then walk back toward Bogie's staying as close to the building as she could. She stepped through the sliding glass door and Henry didn't see either of them again for nearly fifteen minutes when Bogie walked over with a fresh beer to where Henry stood talking to Anna, her boyfriend Dave and Ears. Lisa returned to the pool area a few minutes later and was talking to Joe and Rodney.

"You sure like to live dangerously," Henry whispered to Bogie.

"I don't know what you're talking about," Bogie whispered back.

At ten p.m. the party broke up and Joe, Rodney, Emma and Anna followed Bogie and Henry back to Bogie's apartment to drink beer and smoke a few joints. Anna's boyfriend, Dave, had gone back to their apartment an hour earlier. Joe, Rodney and Emma left shortly after midnight leaving Henry and Anna at the apartment. Henry hoped Bogie would go to bed and leave him alone with Anna but Bogie was tireless. An hour later Anna announced she was leaving and Henry walked outside with her. "I wish you could stay," he told her.

"I could if you had your own apartment."

"I promise I'll have one soon."

Teresa's husband, Dan, didn't work weekends so Bogie had to find other ways to amuse himself. He was easily bored and when Henry asked if he wanted to accompany him on a small shopping trip Bogie jumped at the chance. "What are we going to buy?" He asked.

"I'm buying us a coffee pot and a clock radio and I need some more reel-to-reels."

Bogie knew where the nearest stores in Madison were and an hour later they were back at Bogie's apartment waiting for the coffee to finish perking. Henry plugged in the radio and set the time then they spent the next two hours making a demo of two of Henry's songs. The first song was an up-tempo take-off on the old Conoco Oil slogan called 'I've Got The Hottest Brand Going'. The second song was an idea he'd gotten from Saul Carter. Saul had been talking one evening about prison life and the men he met while serving time for manslaughter. He told Henry he'd met men who could cut their mother's throats and laugh about it but if you mentioned a Mexican whore tears would come to their eyes. Henry wrote 'Juarez' a song about a cold hearted man who joked about killing his best friend in a barroom brawl but when another inmate mentions a weekend spent in Juarez with a pretty senorita the killer gets melancholy and whines and stares through the bars. Henry thought the songs would be perfect for Waylon Jennings and intended to pitch them to Waylon's publishing company, Baron Music. Monday afternoon Bogie would take the bus into town and meet Henry at the bus stop on Seventeenth Avenue in front of the Country Music Hall of Fame. They'd walk to Baron Publishing and try to see Tommy Jennings, Waylon's brother and the head of Baron Publishing.

Saturday morning the manager came to the apartment and asked a nervous Bogie to give Henry a message. Lahoma had called the previous evening and said she needed to talk to him. Henry walked to the pay phone and called her collect.

"You have a letter here from Capitol Recording Company and I need an address to send it to you."

"What's in it?" Henry asked.

"It's your mail, Henry. I don't open your mail. It's a long envelope. It could be a check."

Henry gave her Bogie's address, assured her he was eating properly and he loved her then returned to the apartment. He was sure the check would be a big one and he told Bogie he wanted to celebrate. "I've got thirty-eight dollars and we're low on pot. I figure that will get us enough beer, pot and White Castles to last until my check gets here."

Bogie knew a marijuana dealer a few blocks from the apartment. Henry bought an ounce of the weed for fifteen dollars then stopped at the White Castle for a dozen hamburgers and the Quik-Sak for a case of beer. Another dealer came by that afternoon to tell Bogie about some 'speed' he'd just purchased for re-sale. Bogie told the dealer about Henry having a check coming soon and asked to purchase speed on credit. The dealer refused at first then allowed them to buy twenty dollars worth, ten pills, with the promise they'd pay him Monday afternoon.

The grill was going that night and Bogie and Henry were 'speeding' their asses off. The pills made Henry and Bogie both horny and Henry watched Bogie slip off with Lisa early in the evening. Henry tried talking to Anna and all she said was, "you got that apartment yet?" He tried talking to a couple of other females who appeared to be unescorted and discovered their husbands were nearby. When the party broke up nearly a dozen people made their way to Bogie's. Henry watched Bogie take another young lady named Roxie back to his bedroom while Henry sat with the company and listened to the guests sing the same songs he'd heard them sing at the pool area every night. Sunday morning Henry and Bogie were still awake, sitting in Bogie's apartment drinking coffee and speeding, Bogie with his 'shit eating' grin and Henry with a hard on and 'my world sucks' attitude.

Monday morning Henry decided against taking the bus to Worthan Bagging. He'd wait for his check to arrive and use the money to get an apartment and any left over to buy a bed and a sofa and he'd worry about a job when the money was running low. The check didn't arrive Monday but the speed dealer did. Bogie promised him the check would be there the following day and Bogie was right. Henry tore open the envelope and nearly fainted when he saw the amount the check was made out for: four dollars and fifty-eight cents.

"What am I going to do?" Henry asked, showing Bogie the check.

"Shit man! What am I going to do? I've got a man coming by today expecting money. Money you promised we'd have."

"I didn't promise your friend shit."

"No but you let me believe the check would be a little bigger than four fucking dollars!"

"Four dollars and fifty-eight cents," Henry reminded him.

"I guess I'll have to go to Manpower tomorrow and sit with the winos and hope I can work somewhere."

"I should have gone to Worthan's," Henry commented.

"I guess there'll be two of us at Manpower tomorrow. I just won't be answering the door or going out tonight."

"All you owe the man is ten dollars."

"I seen him cut a man for less," Bogie replied.

Bogie refused to answer the door the rest of the day or join the others at the pool area. Henry decided to stay inside too since the dealer knew Henry was staying with Bogie. The dealer came by early that evening, knocked at the door a few times then left. An hour later he came back and stood outside the door and hollered, "I know you're in there and you'll have to come out sometime!" The following morning they were catching a bus into town. They arrived at Manpower a few minutes before six a.m. and the place was already full of unwashed alcoholics.

"Whatever you do don't pull out your cigarettes," Bogie warned. "If you do every man in here will want one." A short stocky man carrying a clipboard called off several names and told those men to follow a man wearing a blue uniform and matching baseball cap. A few minutes later he called three more names and gave them a slip of paper with the name of a foreman on it and told them a van would transport them to the work area. After forty-five minutes Bogie and Henry were the only two left. Both men were ready to give up on working that day when their names were called and they were told they'd be transported to a construction site to work as laborers.

Henry and Bogie were taken to a site west of the downtown area to work with a crew building apartments. They spent the next eight and a half hours at the site working eight of the hours with a thirty minute break for dinner. The two men spent the thirty minute dinner break watching the others eat then returned to work driving stakes for setting forms and hauling plywood and lumber to the crew. The job paid three dollars an hour and the men from manpower were paid each day when they returned to the Manpower office.

Henry and Bogie walked toward Tootsie's with twenty-four dollars each. They arrived back at the apartment with less than ten dollars between them. The speed dealer was waiting. Henry saw Matt and Anna near the pool talking to another tenant and he walked over, leaving Bogie to talk to the dealer. He apologized for his dirty appearance and told Anna he'd been working at a construction site to earn enough money for an apartment. Matt overheard the conversation and told Henry if he'd known Henry and Bogie needed a job he could have got them jobs with the construction company he worked for. "They don't pay but five dollars an hour but they always need laborers," Matt told him.

Henry asked Matt to check with his foreman the next day. "I'll check with him but I know what he'll say. He's always complaining about needing more laborers. Why don't you and Bogie just go to work with me in the morning?" Henry said he would talk to Bogie.

Henry walked to the apartment to take a shower and get a cold beer. He first checked the mailbox and found a letter from his grandmother. He opened the letter and found a short note and a letter from Broadcast Music Inc. He opened the letter from BMI and found a check for eight-two cents, royalties from air play for the two songs Wynn had recorded. Bogie entered the apartment and asked Henry if he had twelve dollars. Henry told him he only had a little over eight dollars. Bogie took the eight dollars and left the apartment.

Henry's first check for four days work was one hundred and thirty-two dollars and six cents. He planned to take the money needed and rent his own apartment but Bogie and he decided to have a few drinks on Broadway first then Henry could talk to the apartment manager the following day. Two days later they staggered home and Henry had less than forty dollars left. The apartment would have to wait another week. The following week they found a good deal on an ounce of marijuana and two grams of cocaine. The next paycheck went for beer, speed and rent for Bogie's apartment. Five weeks later the foreman caught them smoking a joint behind a stack of lumber and fired them both. Anna had given up on Henry ever having his own apartment and hardly spoke to him.

The summer ended and so did the pool parties. October was cold and windy and Henry and Bogie were working at Manpower just enough to pay rent, buy beer, marijuana, an occasional hamburger and cheap speed when available. He hadn't been on music row or pitched a song in weeks and he was growing tired of Nashville.

Henry and Bogie were in the apartment smoking a joint and listening to Conway Twitty when Edie's boyfriend Matt knocked on the patio door. "Henry, please go get Mattie and take her to apartment seventy-eight. They're going to gang bang Edie and I can't stop them!"

"Why don't you go tell Mattie?"

"I can't. She'd kill me. She's gonna blame me for this."

Henry pulled on his hat and coat and asked Bogie if he'd go with him. Bogie refused. "The last time I got involved in matters of the heart a man knocked me out of my chair. Besides maybe Edie wants it."

"She don't want it!" Matt screamed. "For God's sake she's scared to death!"

"Show me the apartment," Henry said. "No need to bother Mattie."

Henry didn't bother knocking on the door. Inside he saw Edie standing in a corner, naked and crying. Four young men he'd seen around the pool a few times were sitting on the couch and a fifth man Henry had never seen was standing near the bedroom door with Edie's clothes in his hands. "Give her back her clothes," Henry ordered, "I'm taking her home."

"She's not going anywhere," the man holding her clothes yelled. "She owes us some pussy!"

"Yeah," one of the other men agreed. "She said she'd fuck us all if we got her high and that was six joints ago."

"Well, she lied and now she's going home. Give her back her clothes!"

"That was our last six joints and she's not going anywhere until we get our pussy! If you want her clothes why don't you come over here and take them?"

"We can fight," Henry told the men, "and I'll more than likely get my ass whipped. But someone will call the law and someone will have to tell them why there's a naked girl in here crying her eyes out. Then on the way to jail you can tell 'em all about the pot you smoked."

"Let it go Barry," a skinny, blond haired man sitting on the couch yelled, "she ain't worth it! Give the pig her clothes." Barry threw the clothes at Edie and glared at Henry.

Henry didn't turn his back until Edie was dressed and the two were walking back toward Edie's apartment. "You won't tell Mattie will you?" Edie asked.

"I won't tell her but she'll probably hear about it anyways. But she won't hear it from me or Bogie."

"Thanks Henry. I like you. You're not much older than me. Why don't you ever invite me to your apartment?"

"I thought you and Matt had something going on between you."

"Not anymore. Not after tonight."

Mattie heard about the incident before noon the next day and sent Edie to Bogie's that afternoon to tell Henry she wanted to see him. He followed Edie back to her sisters' apartment and Mattie invited him in for a beer. "I heard what you did for Edie and I wanted to thank you."

"It wasn't that much Mattie."

"Have you got plans for Saturday night?"

"Nothin' special," Henry answered. "Why you askin?"

"Marge and Edie are working a college bar near Vanderbilt and I'm staying in with Jeremy. I thought I might fix you a home cooked meal to show my appreciation for you taking care of baby sister."

"You don't have to go to that kind of trouble."

"I want to."

"Then tell me what time you want me here."

"The girls will leave around six-thirty. Anytime after that."

"Seven-thirty?"

"Make it eight."

Henry arrived a few minutes after eight. Mattie told him to help himself to a beer while she put Jeremy to bed. Henry walked to the refrigerator and looked around the kitchen. He didn't see anything that appeared to be cooking. He carried the beer back to the living room and sat down on the sofa and waited. Mattie came out of the bedroom wearing a blue negligee, her bra and panties clearly visible. She walked around the room turning off every light except the one on an end table near Henry. Then she sat down and put her head in Henry's lap. Soon they were both naked and Henry was climbing aboard. He mounted her twice more in the next three hours.

He met her parents that weekend and the sisters led their parents to believe that Henry was only a friend. Even Margie went along with the lie and soon he was spending five nights a week with Mattie and sleeping at Bogie's apartment on weekends when the parents were visiting. Mr. Conner was a tall friendly man with little to say. Mrs. Conner was a large woman who quoted the Bible while taking Valium and washing it down with sun tea. Both parents wanted their daughters back in West Virginia and every weekend tried to talk them into moving. Henry stood on the porch with the sisters every Sunday to wave good-bye to their parents as they started the trip back. Sunday nights he returned to Mattie's bed.

Often Bogie would show up at a window unannounced while Henry and the sisters played cards or watched television. At first one or more of the sisters would scream when they saw his bushy-headed, wild-eyed face pressed against the window but soon Margie and Edie learned to laugh at his intrusions. Mattie cursed him every time. One night Bogie showed up at the window while Henry sat at the table with Mattie and her parents. Mrs. Conner grabbed a broom and ran outside and chased him off before anyone could explain who he was. When Mrs. Conner returned to the table she brought up the subject of the sisters moving back to the family farm.

Henry and Bogie continued to work at Manpower three or four days a week and although Henry was spending more time at Mattie's he continued paying half the rent on Bogie's apartment.

A few days before Christmas Bogie suggested they get a tree for the holidays. When Henry told him they had trees for sale on a corner lot just off Gallatin Road Bogie said he wanted to cut his own. On a cold, bone numbing day Henry drove them a few miles east of town and past several farm houses and ranches until Bogie spotted a small fir growing a few yards off the road. Henry stopped the car and Bogie climbed out carrying a hacksaw he had borrowed from a neighbor. Bogie climbed through the barbed wire fence while Henry looked around. A moment later they heard dogs. Henry looked up the hill toward a farm house and saw a man coming down the hill carrying a rifle and following a pack of dogs. "Oh Lord, Bogie, you're gonna be knee deep in dogs in a minute!"

Bogie kept sawing away and the farmer and his dogs were less than a hundred yards away when Henry heard the tree snap.

Bogie crawled through the fence, grabbed the tree and threw it in the back seat of the car. Henry heard a rifle shot and his back tire exploded. He didn't stop the car until the rubber was falling off. "I hope you're fuckin' happy. That five dollar tree cost me a good tire!"

"Don't look at it that way, Henry. It's Christmas. Be thankful that old man missed us and hit the tire."

"I think that old man hit what he was aiming at. Now we gotta get out in this freezin' fuckin' weather and change a tire. That'll just about take care of my Christmas spirit."

Henry received another royalty check for six hundred and twelve dollars and invited Bogie to a night out. Four days later they were back in Madison broke. Henry vaguely remembered a midget school teacher from Kentucky and fourteen dollar snifters of brandy at the King of The Road. Bogie remembered too much. "She rode you piggy back into every bar in town." Mattie didn't talk to him for a week.

Henry had his clothes stolen the second week in February. The apartment complex had its own laundry room where the tenants could wash and dry their clothes. He usually waited until he was down to his last set of clothes before doing any laundry then he would put on his oldest, most ragged shirt and pants while he washed his better clothes. Like most of the tenants he'd leave the laundry room while the clothes were washing, returning to place them in the dryer then leave while they dried. This day when he came back to remove his clothes from the dryer they were gone. All Henry had left to wear besides his hat, boots, vest and coats were the clothes he had on. Mattie told him where a 'thrift store' was and loaned him ten dollars. He bought four pairs of second hand jeans and four second hand shirts. He refused to buy second hand underwear.

Henry was lying in bed with Mattie listening to the rain. The rain had been coming down steady and hard this Wednesday morning and he was glad to be in a warm bed with a warm body beside him. They'd had sex a few minutes earlier and Mattie waited until he finished his cigarette before reaching up and turning out the lamp near her side of the bed. She snuggled close to Henry and both were asleep in minutes. The next thing Henry knew something was hitting him hard on his head. Mattie turned on the lamp and they both saw Mrs. Conner standing at the foot of the bed with the broom raised back over her shoulder. She swung the broom again catching Henry on the side of the head and ordered him to get out. She swung again and Henry ducked and jumped out of the bed naked, grabbing what clothes of his he could find as he ran toward the door with Mrs. Conner behind him swinging the broom at his head and hitting him several times in the back. He stopped on the porch and tried to pull his pants on but Mrs. Conner ordered him off the porch and took another swing at his head. Henry left the porch and stood on the sidewalk naked in the rain wearing his hat and holding his pants, shirt, underwear and one boot. Mrs. Conner stepped out on the porch holding a small bundle containing his vest, coat, socks and boot. She threw the bundle at Henry and it landed in a puddle of water at his feet. She ordered Henry to "never return to this apartment for any reason," then slammed the door and locked it.

Henry picked the bundle up and finished dressing in the rain. He walked to Bogie's cold and thoroughly drenched. When he opened the sliding glass door and turned on the light Bogie, not knowing who it was and thinking Henry would be at Mattie's, came around the corner with a claw hammer in his hand. "Please don't hit me with that," Henry pleaded. "I've been hit on enough tonight."

"What happened? You piss Mattie off?"

"No," Henry answered, "but I think her mother's a little upset."

Bogie sat down on the mattress Indian style grinning from ear to ear. "So the mother made a surprise visit. Tell me all about it. I may write a song about you yet. What did Papa Conner have to say?"

"I didn't see anyone but the mother. All she said was get out, damn you and stay out!" Henry removed his clothes at the door and spread them out on the floor to dry then put on a pair of dry pants and a dry shirt.

"Look at your back," Bogie remarked. "Did she do that?"

"Do what?"

"Your back is scratched all to hell."

"That must be from the broom she was beatin' me with. She chased me clear out to the sidewalk."

"What are you going to do now?" Bogie asked.

"About what?"

"About Mattie."

"Right now I'm goin' back to bed. I'll talk to Mattie when her mother climbs back on her broom and flies back to West Virginia."

The rain quit that afternoon and the following morning a U-Haul truck backed up to Mattie's porch. In a few hours the apartment was empty and the family gone. Henry never saw Mattie again.

Henry had been in Nashville a little over a year and knew a number of struggling songwriters, singers and musicians. Bogie had introduced him to several people and two or three nights a week they'd find someone's home to visit that was always ready to drink, smoke, toke and pass the guitar. Henry heard better music at these gatherings than he heard on the radio. He didn't try to sing, he knew he couldn't carry a tune in a bucket, but when the guitar was passed to him he'd ask Bogie to play the music while he recited two or three of his recitations.

Early one morning while driving back to their apartment they were pulled over by a patrol car. Bogie had two joints in his shirt pocket and he immediately started eating them. The officer saw what Bogie was trying to do and tried to open the car's door. The doors were locked and the officer pulled out his nightstick and threatened to break out the window. Henry unlocked the door but by the time the officer pulled Bogie from the car Bogie had swallowed the marijuana. Both men were arrested and charged with possession of a controlled substance and destruction of evidence and Henry's car was impounded. At the station the two men were separated and taken to two different cells. Neither man knew where the other man was being held. Three days later the jailor came to Henry's cell and told him he was being released.

When Henry walked out of the station Saul Carter was waiting for him. "How did you know I was in jail?"

"Don't worry about how I knew. Just be glad I did. You ready to go get your car?"

"What about my friend Bogie? I hate to just up and leave him here."

"Your friend got out a couple of days ago."

"I don't have the money for the impound charge."

"I'll loan you the money and you can pay me back later."

"I may have to mail it to you," Henry said. "I think I'm gettin' out of Nashville."

"Not having much luck, huh?"

"They take every song I pitch 'em and that's as far as they go. I got more songs scattered out in this fuckin' town than I can remember and that's all my songs are doin', just layin' around scattered. After we get my car you can follow me to the apartment. I got some beer in the icebox if Bogie didn't drink it all. Might even be able to scrape up a joint."

The impoundment fee was seventy-five dollars. Saul paid the fine and Henry turned the Studebaker toward Madison. Thirty minutes later they were at the apartment drinking Henry's beer and smoking Saul's marijuana while Henry read a note Bogie left him. 'I'm sick and tired of waking up sick and tired. Come and see me sometime if you can. You're always welcome. Your friend Bogie'. At the bottom of the note was a Chicago address and telephone number.

"Looks like your friend had the same idea you had," Saul commented. "I take it he didn't have much luck here either. You got any money to get you to where you're going? Do you even know where you're going?"

"I'm broke Saul. I figure I'll call my grandmother and get enough money for gas to get me to Oklahoma then figure out later where I'm going from there."

"I'll loan you the money to get to your grandmother's. Have you ever considered living in New Mexico?"

"Is that where you're at now?" Henry asked.

"I've been there a few months. You'd like it and you might even make some money. The Texas law has your number. You go back to Texas and I promise they won't leave you alone."

"Speakin' of the law how did you get out of jail? The last time I saw you at Park Plaza they were loadin' you in the back of a car."

"I was out in two hours. Everything was gone when they busted my room. All they found were a few seeds."

"I'm glad you didn't think I had anything to do with it."

"The thought occurred to me for about a second but I already had a good idea who snitched me out."

"Who was it?"

"You didn't know him but he won't be snitching on anyone else."

"Give me your address and phone number in New Mexico. I won't promise you I'll move there but I will think about it and I will pay you back regardless."

Saul wrote the information on the back of a business card and gave it to Henry. "I've got some business in North Carolina so give me a few days before you call." He left a few minutes later and Henry was still wondering how Saul had found out he was in jail.

CHAPTER FIFTEEN

Henry rolled down the driver's side window and hung his left elbow outside the car. He had two joints in his pocket and he planned on smoking one as soon as he was out of the city. When he passed a sign on Interstate 40 West that read 'Memphis 194', he lit the first joint and stayed in the right lane driving five miles over the speed limit. Three hours later he crossed the Mississippi River into Arkansas. He lit the second joint and stayed high all the way to Fort Smith. He continued following Interstate 40 into Oklahoma stopping for coffee every time he bought gas and eating an occasional pimento cheese or tuna salad sandwich. He made the seven hundred and fifty mile trip in less than fourteen hours, arriving at his grandmother's house shortly after eight a.m.

Henry hadn't talked to his grandmother since Christmas. He'd often thought of calling her but he hated calling collect, promising himself he'd call when he had the money. When he did have money he usually spent it on beer or drugs or a night or two or three in Nashville.

Lahoma had seen him pull into the driveway and was waiting near the door. She hugged his neck and told him how much she'd missed him then took a step backward and slapped him hard on his left cheek.

"That's for not calling me you ungrateful pup! Not one call since Christmas Henry! Not one call telling me you're still alive! I've never been to Nashville but I know they got telephones in Nashville! Not one call in months! You oughta be ashamed of yourself! I deserve better than that!"

"I'm sorry Grandmother," Henry mumbled.

Lahoma slapped him again. "No you're not! Quit lying to me Henry! If you came home to lie to me you can crawl back in your car and hit the road! Now come inside and I'll fix you some breakfast. You're nothing but skin and bones....and hair! I don't suppose they have any barbers in Nashville either or maybe all the phones are in the barber shops."

Henry apologized again for not calling and Lahoma told him a few more times how rude and inconsiderate he was. Henry promised again that regardless of where he was he'd call at least once a week. When Henry asked about his mother Lahoma started crying.

"Your mother has cirrhosis of the liver. If you'd have called once in awhile you'd know that."

"Mother's a beer drinker. I've always heard that cirrhosis was a hard liquor disease."

"Well you heard wrong. The doctor told her to quit drinking or she'd die." Lahoma continued crying, dabbing at her eyes with a well-worn Kleenex. "She won't quit Henry. She's skinnier than you and looks older than me and she still won't quit. She's killing herself and there's not a thing I can do about it."

"If I thought she'd listen to me I'd try to see her. I'd probably have to get the sheriff to go with me. But if she won't listen to you then there's no way she's gonna listen to anything I have to say."

"She won't listen to anyone Henry, not even the doctor."

"Is there any chance that bastard Charlie would let us see her? Maybe if we talked to her together we could make her listen."

"I've been to their place a few times. The last time I tried to see her Charlie told me to leave. He said my visits upset her too much. He's got her right where he's always wanted her, totally under his control."

"He's always had her there Grandmother. She hasn't had a thought of her own in twenty years."

Henry wanted to return to Fort Worth. Saul had advised him to stay out of Texas but Henry missed the bars and 'after hours' clubs and the music. He planned on looking Wynn up as soon as he was settled but first he'd need to acquire enough money to get him there and to rent a room when he arrived. He had originally intended to borrow the money from his grandmother. He'd borrowed money before and had always paid her back, although it sometimes took several months to do so, but now he was too embarrassed to ask her. He had never realized a telephone call from him meant that much to her.

Thelma Pike, Harvey's mother, came by the following morning and Henry got another lecture on calling home. "Your grandmother called that number you gave her in Nashville and you never called back unless you thought she had money for you. The last few weeks she didn't know if you were dead or alive. She's going through a lot with your mother and if you can't or won't stay around to help her then the least you could do is not make it any harder. Your fingers aren't broken and you have no excuse for not calling every once in a while."

Henry promised he'd call more often then asked about Harvey.

"He's in Hardmor and that's about all I know. He doesn't call any more often than you do and he never seems to be at home if I call him."

"I need a temporary job, Mrs. Pike. You wouldn't know of anyone who needs some fence mended or some land cleared would you?"

"I know a couple of places where you could probably get a full time job if you wanted."

"I hate takin' a full time job when I know I'll be quittin' soon."

"You're just like Harvey, cut from the same cloth. Your home town isn't exciting enough for you. Well I've heard there's a produce warehouse in Hardmor where they hire winos and derelicts to unload trucks. I can't remember the name of the place but it's right off the railroad tracks so you shouldn't have any trouble finding it and they pay by the truck."

Henry woke early and drove into Hardmor. He had no trouble locating 'Wells' Produce' and was parked and in the warehouse before eight a.m. He gave his name to the dock foreman and was told he'd have to hang around and wait until another truck arrived. He looked around and saw half a dozen men sitting or napping near the loading dock. Several more men drifted in, giving the foreman their names then settling down to wait. Around ten a.m. a truck backed up to the dock and the foreman called off the first four names from his list. A half hour later another truck backed into the loading area and the foreman began calling a new set of names from his list. Henry's name was the third one called. The truck was filled with stalks of bananas with each stalk weighing as much as eighty pounds or more. The stalks were carried on a worker's shoulder, one stalk at a time, to a walk-in refrigerator and hung from the ceiling. It took nearly four hours for Henry and three others to unload the truck. Two of the men drew their pay as soon as the last banana was hung. Henry didn't know for sure but he'd have bet money they were headed for the nearest bar or liquor store. Less than thirty minutes later another truck loaded with hundred pound sacks of onions backed up to the loading dock and Henry's name was called again. Henry helped unload a third truck that afternoon and then drew his pay. He'd earned twenty-six dollars. Another few days of work and he'd have enough money to leave for Texas.

Henry left the warehouse a few minutes after four p.m. and walked toward his car. Half way across the parking lot he saw a man leaning against the Studebaker. He recognized the man at once as Harvey Pike. He didn't know if Harvey was there to fight or just pass the time of day. Harvey straightened up as Henry neared his car and Henry's heart skipped several beats. If Harvey wanted to fight the parking lot was the perfect place. There wasn't anyone around to pull him off Henry. Henry stopped a few feet from Harvey, who stood in front of the driver's door, and tried to act like seeing Harvey in a parking lot near the railroad tracks was nothing to be concerned about.

"Hello Harvey. To what do I owe this pleasure? I know you're not here lookin' for a job."

"Mother called and said you were in town and might be here. I just wanted to talk to you."

"Your mother told me you didn't take her calls."

"Okay shithead. So she left a message. I still wanted to talk to you and tell you I was out of line the last time I saw you. Hell Henry we're friends. Even friends disagree every now and then."

"I can forget anything you said about me Harvey, that's no problem. But you had no right to utter a fuckin' word about my mother."

"I didn't mean nothing by it. We were both pissed off. I had so damn much crank in me I didn't know what I was saying. You said some shit to me that day too that I know you didn't mean."

"I meant every fuckin' word I said Harvey."

Harvey's face reddened and his eyes narrowed and Henry

felt his knees trying to buckle under him. Then Harvey started laughing. "That's what I like about you Hare-lip. You've got more balls for a skinny guy than anyone I've ever known. I could squash you like a bug and you'd still cuss me. I don't have any friends like you."

"You've got the Holton brothers. They're your friends. Or did you chase them off too?"

"They still come around but they're not friends like we are. We go back a lot of years Hare-lip. Why don't you follow me back to my place and we'll have a drink and burn one?"

Henry gave in. "I think I can remember how to get to your apartment. Why don't I meet you there later?"

"I've moved since the last time I saw you. I'm renting a house off Tuffet Road. Turn left off the highway on Tuffet Road and go about three miles. It's a white house on the right."

"I can't stay long Harvey and if you start actin' crazy I'll walk out."

"I told you it was the crank talking the last time." Harvey sounded irritated and Henry hoped he wasn't making a mistake by agreeing to visit him. "I'll see you in a few minutes then," Harvey said, then turned, walked to a new Ford pick-up, climbed in and drove off.

Henry sat in the Studebaker and smoked a cigarette before driving toward Tuffet Road. He found the house, pulled into the driveway and parked his Studebaker behind the Ford pick-up Harvey had driven. He knocked on the door and was surprised to see Roni answer the door wearing the same bathrobe she'd worn on Henry's last visit. The belt was tied loosely and the robe open enough for Henry to see several bruises on her thighs. She smiled and stood close enough to the door to brush against Henry when he entered the house. Henry followed her into a large living room where Harvey sat on a chocolate brown leather couch. A can of Budweiser, a rolled joint and a small pile of white powder lay on the coffee table in front of Harvey.

"Sit down Hare-lip," Harvey said, patting the area on the couch next to him. "Roni get Henry a beer."

Henry sat down in a tan chair on Harvey's right. Roni brought Henry a beer and sat down Indian Style in the area Harvey had patted for Henry to sit in. Harvey lit the joint and passed it to Henry. Henry took a long toke then passed it to Roni. Roni glanced at Harvey before taking the joint. 'Nothing has changed,' Henry thought. Harvey cut out four lines from the pile of powder, rolled a hundred dollar bill into a straw, snorted two lines, then passed the straw to Henry. Henry used the straw to scoop up one line of the powder and pour it in his beer, then passed the straw to Roni. She glanced at Harvey for approval and Henry saw Harvey nod his head. Roni snorted the line and passed the hundred dollar bill back to Harvey.

"I see you're just as weird as ever," Harvey said. "You're the only motherfucker I know that drinks his cocaine."

"Hell Harvey you wouldn't want me around if I wasn't weird."

"You're probably right." Harvey cut out two more lines and snorted them both without offering Henry any. "Why'd you leave Nashville Hare-lip? They didn't like your songs?"

"I don't know what the fuck they like Harvey. Maybe that's why I left. Or maybe I just miss Texas."

"You going back to Texas?"

"As soon as I make enough money to buy gas, pay rent and eat every once in a while. Another few days unloadin' trucks and I'm gone."

"You don't have to work with those fucking winos. I'll give you the money. Fuck Henry we're friends. Hang around here a few days."

"I don't want your money Harvey. Grandmother told me

a long time ago that the best way to lose a friend is to borrow money from 'em or move in with 'em."

"I don't suppose you'd mind me giving you a little coke and smoke to take with you?"

"Grandmother didn't say a thing about coke or smoke."

"I'll give it to you when you're ready to leave. That way I know I'll see you again before you leave."

"I'll be back in town the next few days working."

"If you're planning on coming back in tomorrow why don't you just spend the night here? Now don't get spooked! I'm not asking you to move in. Just hang around tonight and get fucked up. Maybe talk old times."

"I smell like onions and I didn't bring a change of clothes with me."

"I've got a washer and dryer and a shower." Harvey took Henry's beer from the coffee table and poured enough cocaine for several lines in the can. "Drink this and think about it while Roni rolls another joint."

"I'll need to call Grandmother." Henry called and told Lahoma he was staying in town with a friend.

"You're not staying with Harvey are you?"

"I'm just staying with a friend."

"I guess you're big enough to make your own mistakes," Lahoma said, then hung up the phone.

Harvey loaned Henry a bathrobe that fit Henry like a circus tent. Henry handed Roni his clothes then took a hot shower and returned to the living room. Two fresh lines of white powder and two joints lay on the table.

"I've got to go out for a while on business," Harvey said. "Just make yourself at home. There's whiskey in the kitchen if you get tired of beer. I'll be back as soon as I can."

Henry waited until Harvey left then told Roni she was

welcome to both lines of cocaine. Roni snorted the lines immediately. Henry lit the joint and passed it to her. Roni took a toke, passed the joint back to Henry, then opened her robe and pointed to a scratch an inch or so above her pubic hair. "Do you see where I scratched myself?" She asked, spreading her legs. "It itches."

Henry tried not to look. He hadn't had a woman in weeks and the last thing he needed was Harvey walking in and catching him with Roni. "Maybe you need to put something on it," he suggested.

Roni left the couch and stood in front of Henry with her bathrobe open, then she knelt in front of him and started massaging his testicles. Henry grabbed her hands. "You're crazy girl. If Harvey walks in he'll beat us both to death."

Harvey returned two hours later. The two friends stayed up the next three days and nights smoking marijuana, drinking beer and whiskey and using cocaine. When he announced he was leaving Harvey insisted Henry take an ounce of marijuana, a small vial of cocaine and the hundred dollar bill Harvey had used for snorting the drug. Henry accepted the gifts and drove back to Joneston. He told Lahoma he'd be leaving for Texas the following day then fell across his bed and slept till morning.

Henry expected Lahoma to try and talk him out of leaving and was surprised when she didn't. He ate the eggs, bacon, biscuits and gravy she cooked him for breakfast then loaded his car.

"Promise me you'll call when you're settled and promise you'll call me at least once a week. Call collect Henry. I don't mind."

Henry promised he would and shortly after eight a.m. he left for Fort Worth. Less than two hours later he was at the front desk of the Park Plaza paying his first weeks' rent. The clerk, a middle-aged woman, was a stranger to Henry. Henry asked about Beth, the young woman who was working as the day clerk when he left for Nashville and was happy to learn she was still working there as a night clerk. He also learned that Jody Payne and Bobby Wayne still had rooms at the Park Plaza.

Henry unpacked the Studebaker then called room service and ordered a pot of coffee. He knew it was too early to be knocking on anyone's door and he figured he had at least two hours to kill before anyone he wanted to see would be awake. He mixed a small amount of cocaine in his coffee and sipped it as he rolled a joint then turned on the television and watched an 'I Love Lucy' rerun. Thirty minutes later he was restless. He left the room and walked to Beth's room and knocked on the door. Beth came to the door and it was apparent to Henry that he'd woke her up. She stepped outside, pulling her door shut behind her and told Henry she had another man in her apartment but would be happy to have him visit later when her company was gone. Henry returned to his room and tried to watch television but the cocaine had him wired. He walked to the door every few minutes and looked outside to see if anyone he wanted to see was moving about. A few minutes after noon he saw Jody Payne walking toward the restaurant. Jody seemed surprised when Henry followed him into the restaurant and sat down across the table from him. He ordered a late breakfast and Henry ordered coffee.

"I thought you were in Nashville," Jody said. "When did you get back in Fort Worth?"

"A couple of hours ago."

"So, how's it been going with you?"

"I'm happy to be out of Nashville. How's it going with you?" Henry asked. "Where you working?" The last Henry had heard Jody had been picking lead guitar for the singer Sammi Smith.

"You won't believe it man," Jody answered, grinning from ear to ear. "I'm playing lead for Willie Nelson and I wouldn't trade places with Jesus." Henry was impressed. Every musician Henry knew wanted to work with Willie and every writer Henry knew wanted to write like Willie.

The forty year old Nelson had been an icon and a legend in country music for years. First as the writer of such classic masterpieces as 'Night Life', 'Family Bible', 'Crazy', 'Funny How Time Slips Away' and 'Hello Walls'. He had his first hit as a singer in 1962 with 'Touch Me'. The song reached the country Top Ten and in 1964 Willie was invited to join the Grand Ole Opry. He had numerous single and album releases on the Liberty label and RCA label but failed to reach the top of the charts again. Tired of Nashville bureaucracy he returned to Texas in 1970. In 1973 he released an album titled 'Shotgun Willie'. The album contained Willie's version of the Bob Wills song 'Stay All Night, Stay A Little Longer'. The song reached the top twenty chart and the public 're-discovered' Willie. Willie worked Panther Hall regularly and Henry had met the singer and his band backstage at the dance hall several months earlier.

"We're doing a show in Austin Friday," Jody said. "Would you like to go?"

"Hell Yeah!"

"Pack enough for the weekend. We won't be back before Monday." Jody shoved his plate aside and sipped his coffee. "Have you seen Bobby yet?" He asked.

"Not yet. I thought it might be a little too early to knock on his door. Have you seen Wynn Stewart lately?"

"Wynn moved to Nashville. You knew he remarried didn't you? Married Doris Massey."

"Cliff's daughter? The pretty blonde? I wish I'd have known that while I was there. What's Clay doing?"

"He's in Minneapolis with Perry Michaels. They're working with Charles Dean at The Flame Club. I think they're due back soon." Jody told Henry he had some things to do and they agreed to meet later at Rustler's Rest. Henry walked back to his room and waited for Beth's company to leave.

Henry had fifty-two dollars in his pocket Friday morning. He asked Beth to hold thirty- five of it for next week's rent and at noon climbed into the passenger side of Jody's Cadillac. Less than four hours later they were pulling into the driveway of Paul English, Willie's drummer. The show that night was at the Austin Civic Center and was a private, black tie affair. Willie would be presented with an award for his charity work and Darrell Royal, Danny Thomas and several politicians, including the mayor of Austin, would be attending. While the band members were having their measurements taken for tuxedos, Henry and Darrel English, Paul's son, were asked to take the band's equipment to the Civic Center and unload it. After unloading the equipment Darrel drove them to Bobby Nelson's, Willie's sister and pianist, for a short visit then back to the Civic Center. When they returned the band was waiting.

During the show Henry took advantage of the bar backstage while Willie and his band performed for the Austin elite. Danny Thomas, waiting for his turn to take the stage, came over to the bar and stood a few feet from Henry. Henry didn't want to bother the entertainer and stood there silent, sipping a whiskey and water. After a moment or so Danny Thomas turned toward Henry, stuck out his hand and introduced himself. Henry shook his hand and mumbled something he hoped didn't sound silly. A second later Danny Thomas said that was his cue, told Henry it had been a pleasure to meet him then walked on stage.

The show ended around eleven that night and the band helped Henry and Darrel load the equipment then Jody and Henry drove back to Paul's home. Diane, Paul's pretty wife, went out of her way to make Henry feel welcome, showing him where he could sleep and shower. Henry did little sleeping and the following day they climbed aboard a tan Open Road recreational vehicle with bassist Bee Spears and his lady and the newest member of the band, harmonica player Mickey Raphael. Two hours later the bus arrived at the John T. Floores Country Store, an old building that appeared to be half store and half barn. A crowd had already started gathering and by the time Willie took the stage the crowd numbered in the hundreds. On the way back to Austin a part of that crowd rode in the RV. Henry guessed close to thirty people were on the bus, sitting or standing where they could and often walking on each other's toes. In Austin the crowd disembarked at Paul's house and the party continued.

The following afternoon they returned to the Floores Country Store in San Antonio. The crowd was as large as the previous night but Henry would remember little of it. His head was spinning from the whiskey, speed and marijuana. After the show they returned to Paul's and midmorning the following day Jody and Henry left for Fort Worth, arriving at the Park Plaza early in the afternoon. Henry hadn't closed his eyes for more than two hours during the past four days. He thanked Jody for taking him along for the party then walked to his room, smoked two joints and fell asleep.

Henry had been back in Texas nearly two weeks and he hadn't worked a day. The cocaine Harvey had given him was long gone, his marijuana was running low, the car needed gas, he needed cigarettes and he had less than two dollars. To top it all off a homeless alley cat had crawled in Henry's car one night and had a litter of kittens in the back floorboard behind the driver's seat. Henry found the kittens but the mother wasn't around so Henry assumed the kittens were abandoned. He placed the five newborns in a plastic sack then tied the sack tightly cutting off the air to the kittens. Henry considered this to be more humane than leaving the kittens to die from the elements or the vermin. He dropped the sack in a nearby dumpster and started back to his room when he spotted the mother cat watching him from a few feet away. The cat followed Henry to his room meowing all the way then sat in front of the door and meowed all night. The cat finally left Henry's door but she would suddenly appear several times a day when Henry left his room and follow him and meow. The cat knew he had taken her kittens and she wanted them back.

Henry returned to Manpower and worked two days as a laborer with a construction crew. He returned to his room expecting to see the cat waiting for him and was surprised the feline was nowhere in sight. 'She's probably out gettin' pregnant again', Henry thought.

That evening Henry drove to Rustler's Rest where he bought a dozen diet pills. He took two of the pills and danced with a pretty half Apache lady, newly divorced and new to the Fort Worth night life. At closing time she invited Henry to her apartment and Henry accepted but first he wanted to return to his room long enough to roll a few joints. What marijuana he'd brought with him earlier he'd smoked with two of the band members. She gave Henry her address and he promised he'd be there within the hour. He returned to his room and rolled four joints then emptied his pack of Camels and placed the joints and two diet pills inside before replacing the cigarettes. He took the remaining eight diet pills and placed them in a pair of socks, rolled the socks up and returned them to the drawer. He placed

the Camel pack in his shirt pocket, returned to the Studebaker
and started the motor.

Unknown to Henry the mother cat had crawled back in
the Studebaker and was curled up asleep on the back floorboard
behind the driver's seat, the same location where she'd had her
litter. The cat remained calm until he pulled onto the interstate
and sped up. Then the cat decided she wanted out of the car. She
screeched and jumped on Henry's neck, knocking his hat into
the passenger seat and digging her claws into his hide. Henry
screamed and tried to grab the cat and keep the car on the road.
He stopped the car in the middle of the interstate and the cat
jumped out the driver's side window and ran across the interstate and into the darkness. Henry was glad it was early morning
with little traffic on the road. He picked his hat up and placed it
on his head then rubbed his neck and saw blood on his hand. He
continued driving and had gone less than a quarter mile when he
was pulled over by a city patrolman. The patrolman walked over
to Henry's car and asked him to step out.

"I saw you weaving," the officer explained. "Have you been
drinking sir?"

Henry explained about the cat while the officer checked
Henry's driver's license, his neck and the contents of Henry's
pockets. The officer believed him and Henry was replacing his
wallet, pocket knife and money when another patrol car pulled
over in front of Henry's Studebaker and a heavy set older patrolman got out and walked over. The older officer pointed toward
Henry's cigarettes laying on the hood of the car and asked the
younger officer, "did you check the cigarette pack?" Before the
younger officer could answer the older officer grabbed the Camel pack and tore the top off. He held the pack under the younger
officer's nose and said, "this is why we tell you to always check
the cigarettes. Place him under arrest and I'll talk to you later

at the station." Henry was taken to the Tarrant County Jail, body searched, sprayed with bug killer then ordered to dress in an orange jump suit with Tarrant County Jail stenciled on the back in large letters. He was taken before a judge five hours later, charged with possession of a controlled substance and ordered held on five thousand dollar bond. He didn't know anyone with that kind of money but he wasn't going to waste his one phone call. He called Beth at the Park Plaza and asked her to hold on to his belongings. Mid afternoon the jailor came to his cell and told him he'd been bonded out. Henry dressed and retrieved his property, minus the pills and marijuana, and found a young, well-dressed attorney waiting for him.

"I'm Bob Patterson, Mr. Ridge. Toni Stockton asked me to do what I can for you. Ms. Stockton put up the money for your bond. You're in a difficult position Mr. Ridge and I want to be honest with you about your situation. You'll probably have to do a few months time with the county. Do you understand?"

"They want my company for awhile."

"That's one way to put it. You'll have a few days to take care of business."

"How did Toni know I was here?"

"You'll have to ask her Mr. Ridge."

"What about my car? What's it going to cost to get it back?"

"Your car has been impounded Mr. Ridge. They'll try to keep it and sell it at auction. What model car is it sir?"

"A 1958 Studebaker."

The attorney looked like he wanted to laugh. "You just might get it back for the impoundment fee."

Henry left the station, walked to the nearest pay phone and called Beth at the Park Plaza. He asked her if she'd called Toni on his behalf.

"Clay came by looking for you," she answered. "I told him you were in jail. Maybe he called Toni."

"Are you busy?"

"No, why?"

"You sure you don't have company?" Henry teased.

"You talk like I have company all the time."

"If you didn't have to work tonight I'd be trying to keep you company."

"I don't go to work for four hours."

"It'll take me about half that long to walk home," Henry said.

"Why don't you just cut the shit and say you need a ride Henry? I'll be there in ten minutes."

Henry and Beth took a shower together, had five minutes of sex then lay in bed and smoked pot until Beth announced she had to dress for work. Henry returned to his room and called Toni. "Thanks for getting me out. I promise I'll repay you some way."

"Don't worry about the money Henry. What do you plan to do now? Bob Patterson says you'll probably get jail time out of this because of the diet pills."

"I know what I'd like to do. I'd like to disappear but I can't do that to you."

"Do what? I told you not to worry about that money. I'm not. Do you have somewhere you can go?"

"I've got a number in New Mexico."

"Then go for it! I'd rather know you're in New Mexico than sitting in jail. Just keep in touch. When you plan on leaving?"

"Before daylight. Beth gets off work at four in the morning. I'm gonna ask her to drive me to the city limits."

"Do you need anything? You got enough money to eat on?"

"I've got a few dollars and a little pot. I'll make it."

"If you need anything else you let me know."

"Do you have a gun?" Henry asked.

"A gun? You're not planning on doing anything stupid are you? Why would you want a gun?"

"There's this cat I'm thinkin' bout shootin'."

CHAPTER SIXTEEN

Henry had Beth take him to Interstate 20 West less than an hour after sunrise. He'd taken two diet pills earlier and given Beth two pills. He had four pills and four joints rolled up in a Glad sandwich bag and hidden in his right sock and less than twenty dollars in his pocket.

Henry didn't like the idea of occupying a Texas jail even for a few months and he was running like a rabbit. If they wanted to keep him in a cage they'd have to catch him and he was smart enough to know he wouldn't be hard to catch. Any lawman that spotted him and decided to run a radio check on him would almost certainly arrest him and he'd be returned to a Tarrant County jail cell. He wouldn't feel comfortable until he was out of Texas and Texas was a damn big state. New Mexico seemed a long ways away.

His first ride took him twenty miles to Weatherford, Texas. He didn't catch another ride for an hour and he spent that hour with his thumb pointed west and his head rotating like a swivel hook while he sucked on a joint and watched for the law. The marijuana took the edge off the speed, making the wait for a ride more bearable. Finally a car occupied by two teenage couples pulled over a few yards in front of Henry. Henry placed his duffel bag in the car's trunk then climbed into the passenger side beside a pretty, young brunette.

"I'm Matt," the driver said, "and this is Carol. Those two lovebirds in back are Larry and Denise. We're just riding around and we can't take you far but we thought you might want to get high." Denise leaned over the seat and offered Henry a drink of Boone's Farm strawberry wine. The wine was cold and Henry took a long pull before passing the bottle back.

"You folks like to start early," Henry commented. He'd already decided not to tell them he was probably higher than they were or to mention what he had hidden in his boot.

"We started last night," Carol replied. Matt lit a joint and passed it to Carol. "This ought to get your head right," Carol told Henry, passing him the joint.

Matt took the next exit and followed the service road to a dirt road. He turned right and for the next two hours they rode the back roads, talking, drinking wine and smoking joint after joint. Henry remembered they opened at least four more bottles of wine but he couldn't remember how he wound up in Mineral Wells, Texas, a tiny town off state highway 180. He knew he didn't leave the interstate to reach New Mexico but there he was in 'downtown' Mineral Wells, a wide awake drunk, confused and bound to draw the wrong kind of attention.

Henry looked around trying to get his bearings. He could see a strand of lamp poles off in the distance and he knew they were probably the lamp poles that lined Interstate 20. The poles didn't appear to be more than a few miles away if he walked cross-country. He looked at the sun and guessed the time to be close to noon then climbed a fence and started walking, certain he'd be back to the interstate in a short couple of hours.

Henry walked through bull nettles, cacti, briars and anything that punctured the skin. He tripped and fell in countless holes and gullies and twice walked into sections of a collapsed barbed wire fence hidden in the tall weeds. He climbed other barbed wire fences and spent an anxious half hour watching a bull walk parallel across a field from him while the bull eyed Henry like he was a strange new heifer. He continued walking, carrying his duffel bag, then dragging it, tripping, falling and cussing, certain he'd die in someone's cow pasture. The 'short two hour walk' took nearly four hours and by the time he reached the interstate he was scratched, bruised, itching, dehydrated, half hung over and ready to walk in front of a truck. He threw the duffel bag on the ground and sat on it. He was too tired to stand and hold his thumb up too. A short time later a salesman picked Henry up and took him to Abilene. A young gay man picked Henry up in Abilene and gave him a ride to the next exit. Then two 'good ole boys', who liked to drink and throw their bottles at any sign they passed, gave him a ride to Odessa. Henry spent the next thirty minutes on the side of the rode before a 'hippie' couple in a Volkswagen van picked him up and took him to Monahans. After smoking a joint with him they warned him to avoid Pecos, Texas. "Don't take a ride unless they're going through Pecos man. You don't wanna get caught hitchin' in Pecos. The Pecos pigs don't like hitchers man."

Henry's next ride took him passed Pecos to Van Horn, Texas where he spent an hour staring at a dark, empty highway before smoking a joint and crawling in a culvert to sleep a few hours. The sun and the traffic woke him and he crawled outside with his duffel bag and stood for several minutes before walking to a truck stop intending to buy a cup of coffee and return to the highway. The manager of the truck stop met Henry at the door and informed him they didn't want his kind inside bothering the customers for a ride. Henry told the man all he wanted was coffee and offered to stay outside if the man would bring him a cup. The manager agreed and Henry gave him a dollar bill. The man returned in a few minutes and handed Henry the coffee then told him to get off his property. Henry walked back to the highway intending to drink his coffee while he waited for a ride. He'd no sooner stuck his thumb out when a United Van Lines truck stopped. Henry spilled his coffee attempting to climb into the cab. The driver offered him a cup of coffee from his thermos bottle and he gladly accepted. In a little more than three hours he was at the Mesilla Valley Truck Stop near Las Cruces. He walked inside expecting to be asked to leave and ordered a cup of coffee. He sipped the coffee and waited until he needed a re-fill before walking to a pay phone near the front and calling the number Saul Carter had given him in Nashville.

Dan Cross, a pianist Henry had met at Saul's room in the Park Plaza, answered the telephone. Although it was midmorning Henry could tell by the tone of Dan's voice that the telephone had woke him. Henry apologized for disturbing him and asked for Saul. Dan told him Saul was at a lady's apartment and asked Henry if he wanted to leave a message. Henry told Dan he was at the truck stop and asked for directions to Saul's intending to walk to the address and wait outside until Saul came home. Dan told him to stay where he was and he'd come and get him. Fifteen minutes later he was in Dan's car telling Dan about his run-in with the law.

"I called Saul," Dan told him, "and he's glad you're here. We have an apartment a few miles out of town. It's only two bed-rooms but Saul said you wouldn't mind sleeping on the couch."

Dan turned right off the highway and followed a black top for a quarter mile before turning right onto a dirt road leading to a cotton field. In the middle of the field sat a red brick duplex apartment. "We're here," Dan announced, "just make yourself at home."

Henry unloaded his duffel bag then pointed to a row of cotton stalks. "I hope you don't expect me to pick any of that."

"You don't have to do a thing you don't want to do," Dan answered.

Henry removed his boot and took the sandwich bag from

his sock. He lit a joint and passed it to Dan then took two diet pills and offered the other two to the pianist. Dan swallowed the pills and offered to make coffee while they waited for Saul to arrive. Twenty minutes later Saul came in, smiled at Henry and said, "I hate to say 'I told you so' but I told you so. You should have came here when you left Nashville. How'd you like that Texas jail?"

"I didn't care much for it. But what am I supposed to do here? Don't look like they have a lot of publishers in Las Cruces."

"Don't worry about a job," Saul said. "There's no one pushing you to go to work. You oughta be able to hustle enough to get by."

Henry lit another joint and passed it to Saul. While the three men smoked and drank coffee Henry learned that Saul and Dan worked with a band fronted by a local singer, Jerry Nicholson. The band worked three nights a week, Friday through Sunday, at the El Corral, a popular country bar on the west side of town. The rest of the week they worked where they could, sometimes at bars in El Paso or Alamogordo and occasionally at a private party.

Saul drove Dan and Henry to the El Corral that evening. Although the band wasn't working, the bassist, Elwood Guillen, and the drummer, Tim Heister, were there. Elwood was tall, thin, likable and nineteen, old enough to be in the bar but too young to buy his own beer. Tim Heister was in his mid twenties, stout and quiet. Elwood looked like he'd came straight from the farm and Tim looked like he'd rather be somewhere else.

Saul introduced Henry to Tony Rizzo, a bearded transplanted New Yorker who'd had enough foresight to see the value in Indian jewelry. Tony had set up a shop in a building behind the police station to manufacture 'genuine Indian' jewelry for resale to the tourist traps between El Paso and California.

The first few weeks Henry worked with the band, loading and unloading the band's equipment. While the band played Henry drank, danced and smoked marijuana with unescorted ladies, often going to the lady's apartment for an hour or so of sex and returning in time to help load the equipment. What few dollars he'd had when he arrived in New Mexico were gone and he was now dependent on the band for his cigarettes, drugs, beer and what little food he consumed. Anytime he mentioned the subject of finding a 'real' job Saul or Dan would hand him a few dollars and tell him not to worry about it. "You're the best roller we got," Dan told him, "and ain't no one can get more pot from a bag of seeds and stems than you can. Hell Henry that's worth something."

Tony Rizzo overheard Henry and Dan discussing jobs during a break one night at the El Corral. When the band went back on stage Rizzo came over to Henry's table and sat down. "I heard you talking to Dan," Tony said. "If I'd known you wanted a job I'd have said something earlier. You can come to work for me if you want to."

"I've never made jewelry."

"There's nothing to it," Tony assured him. "Be there at eight Monday morning and I'll put you to work."

"I've got this one problem," Henry said. "I'm living in the middle of a cotton field a few miles out of town. I'd have to ask Saul or Dan to take me to work and they'd rather support me than leave a party or crawl out of bed that early."

"I don't know what to tell you. You got a job if you want it but you'll have to come up with your own transportation."

"I think I have it figured out if you'll hear me out. A lady told me there's a small trailer for rent a few blocks from the El

Corral. I'd just be a fifteen or twenty minute walk from your shop. All I need is a small advance."

Tony laughed. "Will you listen to the hare-lip. I offer him a job and he's already trying to hustle me for money." Tony put his hand on Henry's shoulder and squeezed hard. "You know I'm just teasing you don't you? How much do you need?"

"The rent's sixty a month."

"Is that all? I tip the waitresses more than that. Here take a hundred, get the trailer and come to work when you're settled. You can pay me back later. Just don't take too long getting settled."

Dan drove Henry into town Monday afternoon and Henry rented the trailer. He liked the location. He was within walking distance of work and the El Corral.

The crew at the jewelry shop were young, the majority younger than Henry and nearly half were female. At one table the ladies cut the silver needed for a particular order, sometimes a thousand bracelets, a thousand rings or a thousand pairs of earrings. The silver pieces were then passed to the 'soldering table' to be shaped and soldered together before being passed to the 'crimpers' who placed the right amount of sawdust beneath the turquoise setting to give it a respectable height before crimping the silver edge down tightly to hold the stone. Next it was sent to the 'finishing' table to be sanded and buffed before being thrown in a box to be counted later.

Tony also did repair work. The majority of the repairs were cracked or broken stones. Henry was assigned to a table near the back where a large box of jewelry needing new stones was placed on his right and a box of turquoise stones was placed on his left. His job was to remove the bad stone, find a new stone near its size and grind it down until it fit the setting. Once the stone was the proper size, he'd drop a small pinch of sawdust in the setting, add the stone, then run the crimper around the outer edge of the setting until the silver border secured the stone.

Workers were allowed to drink alcohol as long as they could do their job. The shop had a party atmosphere with good rock music coming over two speakers in two corners of the building and everyone talking, drinking and flirting while they made 'genuine Indian jewelry'. The workers were allowed two twenty minute breaks, one at ten a.m. and one at two p.m. and a thirty minute lunch break from twelve p.m. to twelve thirty p.m. During the breaks the majority of the crew sat behind the shop and smoked marijuana, ate their meals and watched the traffic come and go at the local police station.

Henry liked living in Las Cruces. The city had a population of sixty thousand and sat on the Rio Grand River in the Mesilla Valley, thirty-five miles northwest of El Paso, Texas. It boasted a number of bars and dance halls and was also home to the New Mexico State University. Pretty young women and drugs were everywhere. And Henry liked working for Tony Rizzo. Tony often dropped by the shop and on occasion would bring a bottle of Crown Royal whiskey and sit across the table from Henry. More than one day Henry staggered home from work, fell across the bed and passed out. Tony also invited Henry to supper at least once a week.

Henry never refused an offer to eat with the Rizzo family. He considered Jane Rizzo to be the finest cook in Las Cruces.

The weather turned cool then the weather turned cold and Henry started looking for another car or pick-up. The cold was a dry cold but when the wind blew down the back of Henry's neck it was hard to tell the difference between dry cold and wet cold. He bought a 1964 Volkswagen Beetle for three hundred dollars. The car was missing a bumper and had a couple of small rust holes in the floorboard. The previous owner had installed a homemade sun roof that sometimes stuck and refused to close. Henry took the car to Al, a mechanic he'd met at Tony's house one evening. Al covered the floorboard with a thin sheet of tin and made a bumper from a four by four wooden beam. Henry bought a used radio and two speakers and had them installed then drove the car home and parked it on the street near his trailer. The next morning the radio was gone. The following night the thief or thieves returned and took the speakers.

Buck Adkins came to the shop the last week of March. Buck was a stout, bearded man wearing a well-worn, rolled-brim, Stetson hat, brown leather coat and rough out boots. Tony left Henry's table and stepped outside with Buck for several minutes. When they returned Tony turned down the stereo and asked for everyone's attention. "Buck's looking for a couple of men to cut wood with him. Any of you men wanna be a woodcutter?" Two men at a soldering table volunteered and Buck asked if anyone else was interested.

"What about you Henry?" Tony asked. "If you don't like the mountains you can come back here and I'll give you your job back. I think you and Buck will hit it off though."

Henry decided to accept the offer and Tony introduced him and the two other men, Greg and David, to their new boss.

"Be ready to go at daylight," Buck told them. "It can get cold in the mountains at night so come prepared. We'll meet here at six tomorrow morning."

Henry paid another month's rent then packed his duffel bag with enough clothes for several days. The following morning he left the trailer at five thirty a.m. and walked to the shop. Buck was already waiting in a three quarter ton, extended cab, four wheel drive Ford truck. The truck's bed was loaded with tents, mattresses, Coleman lanterns, blankets, chain saws, canned goods, ice coolers, tools, twenty gallons of gas, forty gallons of water, a case of oil, a case of kerosene, a case of whiskey, twenty pounds of beans, cooking supplies, a pound of marijuana and five cartons of Camel cigarettes. Greg and David arrived twenty minutes late and insisted on taking Greg's two year old Pontiac Firebird instead of riding with Buck.

Buck drove northwest toward the Sacramento Mountains and two hours later turned off the highway onto a small paved road and followed the road for several miles up into the mountains. A half hour later he turned off the paved road onto a dirt road and followed the dirt road as far as he thought Greg's Pontiac could follow. He stopped near a clearing and the truck was unloaded and three tents were pitched. The two larger tents were for sleeping quarters and were tall enough to stand in and wide enough to accommodate a double mattress and sleep two people. The smaller tent would be used for storing supplies.

At noon they took a break and Buck passed out cellophane wrapped chicken salad sandwiches. Thirty minutes later they were back at work digging trenches around each tent, then digging a latrine and finally digging a large 'garbage pit' to bury their waste.

"There's bears up here men," Buck warned. "And if they smell food they're gonna visit us. We keep our food covered and our trash buried so we won't have to worry about any uninvited guests."

The tents were up, the mattresses placed inside, the supplies unloaded and put away in the smaller tent, the digging completed and Greg and David decided to quit. "We changed our minds," David told Buck. Henry and Buck watched the two climb in Greg's Firebird and start down the mountain. Buck started laughing.

"That's funny," he said. "That's real funny, those two quitting like that. I told Rizzo I didn't expect you to last a day but

I figured they'd stay with me for awhile anyways. Two big husky fellows quitting and a skinny, long-haired, hare-lip staying. Rizzo was right about you Henry. He told me you'd stay around long enough to see if you liked it. Now that they're gone we don't have to worry about that piece of shit car. Tomorrow morning we'll move the camp a little higher up the mountain."

Thirty-two year old Buck Adkins was born and raised in Las Cruces. He'd worked as a cowboy, carpenter, grave digger and a truck driver but preferred working in the mountains. He lived in Las Cruces with a pretty red-headed hair dresser named Leanna Hickman and often went weeks between jobs. Leanna supported Buck's free spirit, even purchasing the four-wheel drive truck Buck used. Buck drove the truck but the title was in her name. Slow to anger and quick to laugh he liked whiskey, marijuana, women and a good time. He wore a full beard and was tall, barrel-chested and muscled. Henry liked Buck and he liked Buck's attitude.

The following morning the truck was loaded and the camp moved higher up the mountain. Henry walked ahead of the truck moving any rocks or logs in their path while Buck drove. A half hour later they came to a meadow and Buck stopped the truck and announced they'd be camping here. Henry could see a small pond where the mountain and the meadow met. The pond was fed by the melting snow from the mountain top and the overflow from the pond formed a small creek that ran down the mountain on the far side of the meadow.

Buck dug a fire pit and cooked a breakfast of bacon, eggs and coffee. After eating breakfast and smoking a cigarette the truck was unloaded, the tents pitched, trenches, latrine and garbage pit dug and supplies put away. Buck dug the fire pit several inches deeper and lined it with rocks then cleared the ground around the pit of anything that could catch fire and burn. Then he broke out the whiskey and marijuana. "Tony said you came from Texas. I wouldn't advertise that fact up here."

"I'm originally from Oklahoma," Henry told him. "I was livin' in Fort Worth before comin' out here. Why? They got somethin' against Texans up here?"

"Three years ago a family from Texas let a camp fire get out of hand and start a fire. Nearly two dozen homes were burned to the ground along with a sizable portion of mountain. If you're smart and one of these ridge runners ask where you're from you'll tell them you're from anywhere but Texas."

The following day Buck had Henry erect two tripods near the edge of the tree line while Buck serviced the equipment. Buck owned two fourteen pound Stihl MS-440 chain saws with twenty inch guide bars and two nine pound Stihl MS-170 chain saws with fourteen inch guide bars. The heavier saws were used for cutting trees as close to ground level as possible and the smaller saws used for trimming the branches from the trees. The chain saws were placed in the truck every evening.

The area they were cutting in was an area that had suffered the fire three years earlier. The trees that remained alive were considered 'scorched' although Henry couldn't find more than a handful that showed any sign of being in a fire. The state allowed the trees in the burnt area to be cut for personal use and issued a limited number of permits each year. The permits cost two hundred and fifty dollars and the purchaser had to sign a statement that the trees were for his own use and would not be sold to anyone else. Buck knew the permits were in great demand and had purchased his permit weeks earlier.

The two men would cut for two or three days then Buck would put the saws away in the truck and they'd carry the trees they cut and trimmed back to the camp and stack them near the tripods. After a significant amount of poles were stacked they would be placed on the tripods one by one and the bark would be removed with a 'skinning' knife, a double handled blade that resembled a small cross cut saw.

The third morning, shortly after daylight, Buck filled his cast iron Dutch oven with raw beans and water and buried the container in the coals of the fire. After breakfast and a joint they returned to carrying the cut trees back to the camp site and stacking them. At noon Buck called a break for lunch and the two men dined on beans, bacon and biscuits. As they were eating Buck pointed toward two yellow buses in the distance making their way up the mountain on the paved road. Henry asked Buck about the buses and Buck told him he'd heard they had a youth camp at the top although he'd never seen it. A few minutes later they returned to work. An hour later Buck decided to call it a day.

They both wanted baths and Buck reasoned the best time to face the freezing pond water was when the sun was high. They walked to the pond carrying towels, clean underwear and soap. Once undressed they stepped in the pond and stood as close to the edge as they could. The water only came to their ankles and their feet were already growing numb. They both knew it would be nearly impossible to splash oneself sufficiently to soap their bodies and then rinse the soap off. They stepped out of the pond and stood their shivering. "Why don't you go first?" Henry suggested. "Show me how you mountain men take a bath."

Buck started laughing. "Now you know why mountain men don't bathe a lot. But I've got an idea how we can do this." Buck yelled, jumped far enough out in the pond where the water was waist deep then turned around and started splashing Henry. Henry ran toward the meadow. "Come on you hare-lipped wussy!" Buck yelled. "You scared of a little water?"

Henry turned, ran and jumped in the water. He lost his breath for a moment and heard Buck laugh. Buck stood in the water up to his waist shivering. "There's no way I can splash myself and I don't figure you can either. We'll have to soap up and splash each other when we're ready to rinse off." A moment later they were running toward the campfire wet, naked and carrying their clothes. Buck added wood to the fire and they sat for several minutes wrapped in blankets trying to stop their teeth from chattering. Henry's long wet hair felt like icicles against his back. A few minutes later they stopped shivering enough to dress. As Henry was pulling his underwear on a park ranger stepped out from behind a tree. The ranger startled Henry but Buck seemed to be expecting him. The ranger walked around the camp checking each tent, the latrine and the garbage pit then checked Buck's driver's license and cutting permit.

"We probably won't see him again," Buck said as the ranger left. "As long as he didn't see any fire hazards or garbage laying about he'll leave us alone."

"Reckon how long he's been watching us?" Henry asked.

"There ain't no telling," Buck replied.

Supper was beans, corn, hot dogs and biscuits. After supper the food was put away and the garbage buried. Buck opened a bottle of Jim Beam whiskey and asked Henry to roll a couple of joints. Two hours later they were on their second bottle when they heard something in the brush near the camp. The first thing Henry thought was 'bear'. Then four young women stepped into the clearing.

"I'm Lisa," a tall blonde announced, "and that's Julie and Pam and Eve. We're counselors from the girl scout camp. We just put the girls to bed and were walking around when we thought we smelled marijuana." Henry passed a joint to the brunette named Julie and Buck offered the girls whiskey.

"How close are we to your girl scout camp?" Buck asked.

"It's a few miles," Lisa answered, "if you follow the highway. It's just a half mile or so if you walk up the mountain."

The girls stayed at the camp drinking whiskey and smoking marijuana until nearly daybreak. The next night eight young women showed up at camp. The third night only Lisa and Julie returned. "We flipped coins to see who'd come," Lisa explained.

Lisa spent the night in Henry's tent and Julie shared Buck's bed. Every night for the next ten nights they came to the camp and stayed until first light. Then one morning Henry and Buck saw the yellow buses descending the mountain and knew they'd be sleeping alone again.

The two men 'skinned' the poles they had cut and stacked the poles to the side. They'd done a minimum of work with the counselors around every night but Buck was ready for a break anyways. They drove to Ruidoso, dropped off their laundry with an attendant at a laundromat, got drunk, picked up two ladies in a bar, retrieved their laundry, bought another case of whiskey, then returned to camp. The ladies stayed two weeks, laying in the sun, drinking whiskey and smoking pot while the men worked, then made themselves available to either man at night. After returning the ladies to Ruidoso Buck bought another case of whiskey and a few other supplies then they returned to camp alone.

Buck had a buyer for the poles before he bought the permit and Buck and the buyer had worked out the details for taking delivery of the wood. Buck would call when he had a respectable amount ready for pick-up and the buyer would send a truck and a couple of 'helpers' to the camp to load the poles. Buck had called the buyer on their last visit to Ruidoso. A truck would arrive at the camp in five days.

The morning the truck was due Buck drove down the mountain to the highway and waited. The driver of the truck had no idea where to turn off the highway and Buck would have to lead him up the mountain to the campsite. The truck arrived later than planned and it was mid- afternoon before Henry heard Buck's truck coming into camp followed by a flat bed logging truck. It took the helpers less than three hours to load four hundred and ten poles. In five weeks of drinking, smoking, whoring and sporadic working they'd earned two thousand and fifty dollars. They followed the truck back to Las Cruces and Buck picked up the money. After deducting expenses and putting enough money aside to finance the next trip Buck split the remaining money evenly with Henry. Buck went home to Leanna and Henry returned to his trailer. The first thing he did was take a hot shower and dress in fresh clothes. He walked next door to his landlord's and paid two months rent then walked to the street to his Volkswagen. He tried starting the car and found his battery had been stolen. He walked to the El Corral, got drunk and woke up in bed with a woman several years older than him. Buck came by the trailer that evening and asked Henry if he was ready to return to the mountains. Henry told him he was ready anytime. The following morning Buck was beating on Henry's door before daylight. Henry, hung over from two nights of drinking, slept all the way to camp.

They'd been back in camp less than a week and had nearly two hundred poles 'skinned' and ready for pick up. Buck was restless, horny and ready for Ruidoso. Henry had more than two hundred dollars left and Buck's money was burning a hole in Buck's pocket. They drove to Ruidoso Downs Racetrack that morning and were broke and back in camp before dark.

Two nights later Henry woke to a roar that curled his toenails and a tearing sound, like canvas being ripped. He heard

Buck screaming. "Bear! Bear! Get in the truck! Get in the truck!" Henry reached the truck a second behind Buck and climbed in the passenger side. Buck locked his door then reached across Henry and locked Henry's door. He turned on the truck's lights and they sat and watched through the windshield as the bear tore Henry's tent and mattress to shreds then turned toward the supply tent. Buck's tent was nowhere in sight. The bear roared again and swatted canned goods and ice coolers high over the meadow and into the trees. Henry glanced at Buck. Buck looked ready to cry. "That cooler had the pot in it," he said. "I hope he don't find the whiskey." The bear sniffed around, swatted a few of Buck's cast iron pots to parts unknown, then disappeared into the woods. Neither man made a move to leave the truck.

"I guess we ought to get out and check the damage," Buck suggested.

"You go first," Henry said.

"There's nothing to worry about," Buck told him. "That bear's probably two or three mountains away by now."

"What if he's hangin' around waitin' on one of us to get out of the truck?"

"A bear's not that smart."

"Then why did you lock the doors?"

Henry and Buck spent the better part of the day trying to put the camp back in some kind of order. All three tents and both mattresses were ruined and canned goods and kitchen ware was scattered all over the meadow and half the mountain. Two bottles of whiskey were unbroken and Buck was feeling down about the bottles that didn't survive until he found the cooler with his marijuana inside, intact and untouched. Henry found his duffel bag hanging from a tree branch. The leather vest he'd had hanging from the tent pole was shredded. His hat and shirt were never seen again. His right boot lay near the edge of the meadow and his left boot in the brush.

As Buck was making a list of what would need replacing the park ranger they'd met on their third day in the mountains appeared from behind a tree holding a can of pork 'n' beans.

"Looks like you fellows had company," the ranger remarked, handing the beans to Buck.

"I can't understand why," Buck replied. "We had our food covered and our garbage buried."

"He probably just wandered in," the ranger said. "He's probably the same one that hit that youth camp a couple of nights ago. There wasn't anyone there but they still haven't found all their garbage cans. I'm just glad no one was hurt." The ranger walked around a moment, wished both men better luck then left.

Henry waited a moment then asked Buck, "do you figure he knows we got pot and whiskey here?"

"He knows," Buck answered.

The two men drove into Las Cruces the following day and Buck dropped Henry off at the El Corral while he talked to the buyer about an advance on the next load to replace the tents and buy supplies. Buck was back at the El Corral in less than an hour.

"The bastard wouldn't let me have but three hundred! He wanted to know what I did with the two thousand."

"What did you tell him?"

"I told him it was none of his business!"

"I wish you'd have gotten more," Henry said. "I need a new hat. I feel naked without one."

"We'll get you one as soon as we sell this next load."

"But I feel naked now."

"We'll have a drink then buy what we can and get back to camp."

"I can't cut wood without a hat Buck. Where I come from a hatless man is a shameful sight and an object of scorn."

Buck laughed. "If anybody didn't know better they'd think you was serious."

Leanna Hickman came through the entrance and walked straight to the bar and faced Buck.

"Hi sweetheart," Buck said, giving her his best smile, "I was just getting ready to call you. A bear tore up our camp and we came in to buy new tents and a few other things then we're going back."

"Give me the keys," she said, in a way that sounded like a growl to Henry.

"What are you talking about?" Buck asked, grinning from ear to ear. "What keys?"

"The truck keys." Leanna's lips didn't appear to be moving when she spoke and her teeth were clamped together. Her voice was little more than a whisper but everyone in the bar heard her.

"But sweetheart, I need that truck for work. I can't cut wood without it." Buck tried to put his arm around Leanna but she knocked his arm away.

"Maybe one of your whores has a truck you can borrow. Now give me my keys!"

Buck put on his best 'I'm shocked' look and cried, "Whores, what whores? I've been working my ass off for God's sake. Just ask Henry. There are no whores where we're camping. Go on, ask Henry there! Henry tell her we haven't been with any whores!"

Leanna turned toward Henry, still clamping her teeth and growled, "Don't lie to me Henry. I like you but if you lie to me I'll never speak to you again."

Henry mumbled something about not being able to think without a hat then ordered another beer. Leanna turned back to face Buck. Her teeth relaxed and she almost grinned then she slapped Buck hard enough to stagger him. "People saw you in Ruidoso asshole and those whores told everyone in Ruidoso about the two weeks they spent with you two! I have friends who live in Ruidoso! Did you think I wouldn't hear about it? Are you that damned stupid Buck? I want those keys and I want them now!"

Buck knew he was beat. "Can I keep the truck long enough to go back and get what's left of my camp?"

"Two days Buck! You've got two days! Not three days! Not four days! Two days! And you keep your whores out of my truck! I'll have your shit packed and sitting on the porch when you get back!"

Henry helped Buck pack what was left of the camp onto the bed of the truck. Most of it would be thrown away at the first dumpster but it was important to Buck that they leave a clean camp behind. The following day Henry was back at the repair table in Tony's shop. He asked for an advance and bought a new hat and a battery for his car. Three days later Buck showed up at Henry's table and laid one hundred and fifty dollars in front of him. "That's from the wood we cut," Buck explained. He stayed on Henry's couch a few days before taking a job driving a truck for the highway department.

Henry tried to call his grandmother at least a once a week, usually from the pay phone at the El Corral and usually collect. The calls were always short, just more or less 'how are you' and 'I love you' and Henry liked to make the calls early and get it out of the way before settling down to the serious business of getting drunk or high or both. He thought tonight's call would be no different.

"Henry is that you? Thank God! I didn't know who to call to find you."

"What's wrong Grandmother?"

"Your mother's in the hospital in a coma."

"I'll be home before morning." Henry hung up and drove to the trailer and packed his duffel bag then drove to Tony Rizzo's house to tell him he wouldn't be at work. He had enough money to get to Oklahoma and he wasn't worried about money to return on but Tony had his wallet out before Henry had finished speaking. He held six twenty dollar bills out to Henry.

"I've got enough money to get home," Henry said, "but I appreciate the offer."

"Take it anyways," Tony insisted. "If you don't need it you can give it back later."

Henry had been in Las Cruces more than a year and this was his first trip home. He knew Texas had warrants out on him for skipping bond and if he was stopped by any lawman in any part of Texas he'd be arrested. He also knew he had nearly six hundred miles of Texas to cross in a Volkswagen 'bug' with a front wooden bumper and a homemade sun roof.

Henry crossed the Red River into Oklahoma ten hours later and felt the muscles in his ass relax. The trip home had been tense and nerve racking, especially going through Fort Worth and he was ready to smoke a joint and drink a cup of his grandmother's coffee. He arrived at Lahoma's before daylight and wasn't surprised to find her awake and waiting for him on the front porch. Henry hugged her for several seconds then followed her into the kitchen. She handed Henry a cup of coffee and the two returned to the front porch and sat down.

"How's Mother doing?" Henry asked. "Do they think she'll come out of this?"

Lahoma started crying. "They have her on life support

Henry. They have a feeding tube in her. And she knows what's going on around her. She can't move and she stares straight ahead and she cries all the time. Her mind works but her body doesn't. Oh God Henry, I can't imagine what she's going through. I pray every day God will take her that night. She's suffering Henry. If she was unconscious it would be easier but she knows what's happening to her. She knows she's dying and she cries all the time."

"How long has she been like that?"

"Charlie found her four days ago on the bathroom floor unconscious. She opened her eyes three days ago and we thought she might come out of it but she hasn't. The doctors don't think she will."

"You suppose Charlie had anything to do with it? Maybe he hit her too hard?"

"I thought about that and I brought it up with the doctor. The doctor said he warned your mother about something like this happening. He told her she had to quit drinking or die. He couldn't find anything that made him think she was beaten. Charlie's taking it hard Henry. In spite of how he treats her he loves her. They have to chase him out of her room when they clean her up. The rest of the time he sits in a chair beside her bed and holds her hand."

"As far as I'm concerned he's the reason she's in that bed. He may not have beat her this time but he beat her enough in the past. You sound like you feel sorry for him."

"I do Henry. I've hated Charlie since before you were born but I can't do nothing but feel sorry for him now. He loves your mother and he's holding her hand and watching his world collapse around him. You need to quit hating Henry. It's like poison and it hurts no one but you. Charlie's suffering too."

"He's not suffering near as much as he should. You feel

sorry for him if you want too but I'd rather just keep hatin' the bastard's guts."

"Charlie's got no one but your mother Henry. When she's gone he'll have no reason for living either. He's watching his whole world slip away and he's scared."

"When can I see her?"

"You can see her anytime I guess. I've tried to wait until after nine to give the nurses time to do what they have to do. That gives me time to try and cry myself dry so I won't cry in front of her."

Henry refilled his cup and checked the time. "What room is she in?" Henry asked.

"Two-forty."

"It's a forty minute drive so I think I'll go ahead and go unless you'd rather I wait for you."

"No need to wait for me," Lahoma answered. "I know my way."

Henry stood outside the door of room two-forty for several minutes before entering. His mother lay in bed on her back, eyes wide open, staring at the ceiling. Charlie sat in a chair near the head of the bed facing the door and holding Erica's hand. Upon seeing Henry he leaned over whispering something in Erica's ear. Henry saw the tears form in her eyes and roll down her cheeks. Charlie nodded and Henry ignored him. He stood a moment staring at his mother then he left the room. He felt useless here. He felt his coming home had served no purpose.

Henry left the hospital and walked outside to the parking lot. He lit a cigarette and leaned against his car waiting for his grandmother to arrive. Ten minutes later Lahoma pulled into the lot and parked next to his Volkswagen. "Have you seen your Mother?"

"Yes ma'am and I wish I hadn't."

"I know it's hard Henry. But at least your mother knows you're here. Dr. Conway wants us to come by his office and talk to him."

"What about?"

"I'll let him tell you."

Henry and his grandmother met Dr. Conway in the hall outside Erica's room. The doctor suggested they go to his office and talk. "I think Mr. McCarthy should be there too," he said. Henry and Lahoma waited outside in the hallway as Dr. Conway walked into Erica's room, leaned over and said something to Charlie. Charlie looked at Erica then back to the doctor and shook his head. Dr. Conway pulled Charlie to his feet then half led, half pulled Charlie out into the hallway and down the hall to an office. Inside the office Dr. Conway told them that a decision had to be made.

"What kind of decision?" Henry asked.

"I think we need to talk about when to remove the feeding tube. I know it's a difficult decision and I know you'll need time to discuss it."

"There's no chance she'll come out of this?" Lahoma asked.

"In my opinion there isn't."

"You think we just oughta let her die?" Charlie whined. "Let her starve to death? I won't let you do it. I've heard about people being like that and coming out of it."

"No disrespect intended Mr. McCarthy but I'm sure the people you heard about didn't have advanced liver disease."

Lahoma had her head bowed crying into a wet tissue and Charlie had his head bowed crying into the palm of his hand. Henry felt like he should be crying but he couldn't. He wanted to cry, felt he almost had a duty to cry but he couldn't force a single tear.

"What do you think Mr. McCarthy?" Dr. Conway asked Henry.

"It's not my decision and my name is Henry Ridge."

"I'm sorry. I just assumed......"

"The decision is my grandmother's."

"If you think it's best Dr. Conway then go ahead," Lahoma told him.

"No goddamn it!" Charlie yelled. "I won't let you do it!"

"You don't have any choice Charlie!" Lahoma yelled back.

"We've been together more than twenty years! That gives me some rights!"

"If you were concerned about rights," Lahoma answered, "you would have married her! As far as I'm concerned you don't have any rights!"

"Maybe you need time to discuss this further," Dr. Conway suggested.

"There's no need Dr. Conway," Lahoma answered. "This discussion is over unless Charlie has the money to hire a lawyer and fight it in court."

Charlie stared at the floor. "Go ahead," he mumbled. "I won't fight you."

"Is that your decision too Mr. McCar...er...Mr. Ridge?"

"I told you before Dr. Conway it's my grandmother's decision."

Charlie returned to Erica's side and Henry walked Lahoma to her car. Outside Lahoma broke down and started crying uncontrollably. "I'm being punished Henry. I don't know what I did to God but He's punishing me. I wish it was me in that bed instead of your mother. Oh God how I wish it was me!" Lahoma dug around in her purse for a used Kleenex. Henry pulled his bandana from his back pocket and offered it to her. Lahoma blew her nose and offered it back and Henry told her to keep it. "I shouldn't have talked to Charlie that way," she said. "God knows he's hurting too but I just can't stand to see her like that. She's suffering, God knows she's suffering and there's nothing I can do for my daughter except let her die. I know this is hard on you too Henry."

Erica's feeding tube was removed and four days later she was dead. Charlie stayed at her side during that time holding her hand and sobbing while Lahoma sat near the foot of the bed and fought back her tears. Henry accompanied his grandmother to the hospital every day but spent most of the time in the parking lot smoking cigarettes and feeling like a heartless bastard for his lack of tears.

The body of Erica Madeline Ridge, age forty-six, was cremated two days later. Lahoma told Henry that Charlie had agreed to scatter her ashes above the Red River that weekend at an informal service to be attended by a few family friends. When the weekend arrived Charlie refused to relinquish the ashes.

Monday morning Henry left for Las Cruces. A week later he called his grandmother and was told Charlie's body was found floating in the Red River. No note was found and opinions were divided on whether it was an accident or a suicide.

His mother's ashes and the earthen urn that contained them were missing.

CHAPTER SEVENTEEN

Henry had been in El Paso with Anne, a waitress at Jupiter's, a small rock bar on the city's east side. He wasn't comfortable partying in Texas, but Anne had long, silky legs that reached nearly to her neck and an uninhibited outlook on anything sexual. The two days of anxiety had been more than worth it. He was back in New Mexico now, less than twenty miles from his trailer, when he saw the hitchhiker. She was female and wearing the shortest shorts he'd ever seen. Henry hit the brakes and pulled over. The hitchhiker trotted to the car and threw a small canvas bag in the back seat then climbed in the passenger seat.

"Where you headed and what's your name?" Henry asked.

"Lucy and I'm going to Bakersfield to see my mother."

Lucy's shirt only covered the top two thirds of her breasts and when she raised her arms to pull her hair back her entire breasts were exposed. Henry nearly ran off the road. Lucy smiled and sat with one leg folded under her revealing enough to let Henry know she wasn't wearing any underwear.

"I can take you as far as Las Cruces."

"Do you live alone?"

"Yes ma'am. Can't find anyone who can put up with me."

"I can't believe that." Lucy cooed, pulling her hair back and giving Henry a view of two thumb sized nipples on two cantaloupe sized breasts. "I've never been to Las Cruces. Is it nice there?"

Henry took the bait like a brain damaged carp. "Would you like to see Las Cruces? Maybe rest a couple of days? I rent a trailer, it's kinda small but you're welcome to stay as long as you want."

"I think I'd like that," Lucy answered.

Fifteen minutes later they were at Henry's trailer. Lucy started pulling off her clothes before Henry had the trailer door shut. He led her to the bedroom and less than thirty minutes later he had agreed to drive her to Bakersfield, California to see her mother.

Lucy was a pleasure to travel with. She performed oral sex on Henry while he drove and was willing to pull off on a dirt road and have sex anytime he wanted. The second night of the trip they were nearing Palm Springs when Henry saw a club off the highway with a marque that read 'Willie Nelson Live'. He took the next exit and followed the service road to the club. At the back door of the club he was met by two Hell's Angels working as security guards. Henry scribbled his name on the back of an old business card he found in his wallet and asked the bikers to take it to Willie's lead guitarist, Jody Payne. A few minutes later Jody came to the door and asked the bikers to allow Henry and the lady in. After the show they drove to the motel where the band was staying and spent the next two hours visiting with Jody and Randy (Poodie) Locke, Willie's road manager, before the group had to leave for a show in San Francisco. Lucy had fallen asleep and Jody suggested that since the room was paid for until noon Henry let her sleep. Henry lay down beside her and slept until the maid came to service the room. They left the motel shortly after ten a.m. and at three p.m. were only a few miles from Bakersfield. Lucy reached into her bag and pulled out a pair of shorts and a T-shirt and changed clothes while Henry drove. The shorts were several inches longer than the shorts she'd been wearing and the T-shirt covered all of her breasts and stomach. Henry assumed she was changing for her mother. Thirty minutes later they pulled up to a trailer on the south side of the city and Lucy jumped from the car. The trailer door opened and a big, muscled giant of a man came outside and grabbed Lucy and the two kissed and pawed one another for several minutes before the man pried himself away and asked, "Who the hell is that?"

"He picked me up outside of town and gave me a ride," Lucy told him. "Dutch this is Henry. Henry this is my boyfriend Dutch." Dutch reached out a ham sized hand and offered it to Henry and while Henry shook his right hand Dutch's left hand massaged Lucy's ass.

"Thank you for giving my woman a ride," Dutch said, then turned to Lucy and asked, "How's your mother doing?" Henry wanted to laugh but first he wanted to get out of there. He made a mental note to run over the next female hitchhiker he saw.

Henry had taken Interstate 10 from Las Cruces and followed it to Interstate 5 in Los Angeles and then north to Bakersfield. He decided to take Interstate 40 to Flagstaff then turn south to Tucson and Interstate 10 and avoid the traffic he'd encountered traveling through Los Angeles. An hour later he stopped in Keene, California and filled the car with gas and added a quart of oil. The Volkswagen had started using a quart of oil for every tank of gas but Henry didn't think he needed to worry as long as he checked the oil when he refilled the tank and didn't let the oil get too low. He'd have the car looked at when he returned to Las Cruces. He was crossing Tehachapi Pass, less than a hundred yards from the top of a mountain, when he heard a loud clanging noise and the car sputtered, shook a few times, then died. Henry tried restarting the car then stepped outside to check the motor. The motor looked fine but the large growing oil stain under the car told Henry the motor was blown. He felt like he was deserting an old friend as he gathered his maps and a few other items from the car and stuffed them in his duffel bag then stuck out his thumb and waited. A few minutes later he was in the cab of a truck relating the story to the sympathetic driver.

Henry hitchhiked all night and was standing by the side of the road in Tucson at mid- morning the next day. He'd been warned once by an Arizona State Trooper to get off the highway or go to jail. The temperature was already in the nineties and the only place to go was the middle of the desert so Henry chose to ignore the trooper and stay on the road.

Henry saw the driver of the brown Ford pick-up pass him and look back and thought nothing of it. His long black hair usually drew attention from the local cowboys and Tucson had more cowboys than cacti. The Ford took the next exit and circled back then pulled over several feet in front of Henry. The driver stepped out before Henry reached the pick-up and he recognized him as Billy Moore, the cowboy from Oklahoma.

"I thought that was you," Billy said. "I wasn't sure though with all that long hair. What the hell are you doing out here on foot? It's hot enough we got jack rabbits running around with canteens around their necks."

Henry told Billy about Lucy and the trip to Bakersfield while Billy continued driving east.

"Was it worth it?" Billy asked.

"If you're askin' me if a car was worth a fine piece of ass you'll have to give me a while to think it over."

"You got time for a steak and a beer?" Billy asked.

"I seem to have nothin' but time."

Billy took the Mustang Road exit off Interstate 10 and followed a dirt road to a bar called Little Abner's. He introduced Henry to the bartender, Steve, a husky man with hair nearly as long as Henry's and a gold earring in his right ear, and Gayla, a thin, pretty waitress who wore her hair in a long braid. Several other people were drinking, eating or shooting pool and they all seemed to know Billy.

Billy ordered two beers and a steak dinner and insisted on paying. After the beer he told Henry he had to return to work at the Lazy K Bar guest ranch and he'd be back later to check on him if Henry wanted to hang around and rest awhile. Before leaving the bar he called Steve and Gayla over to the side of the bar and whispered something. A few minutes later Gayla sat an inch thick T-Bone steak in front of Henry and a shot of Jose Cuervo Tequilla.

After Henry finished his meal Steve asked him if he'd like to lay down on a cot in the back room. "Billy told me you'd been up all night," he explained, "and it may be a few hours before he gets back here."

Henry accepted the offer and fell asleep at once. He was woke up a few hours later by Billy shaking him and asking if he was going to sleep all night.

"What time is it?" Henry asked.

"It's after six," Billy answered. "You've been sleeping awhile. You ready for a drink?"

Henry walked out front and found the bar full of people and for the next few hours he drank tequila and shot pool with Billy and several of his friends. Shortly before midnight he found himself drunk and engaged in a discussion with Billy about the length of his hair.

"Why do you want hair that long?" Billy asked.

"I wore my hair the way Uncle Sam told me to for four long ass years either in a crew cut or a burr. I promised I'd never let anyone tell me how to wear it again."

"I might be able to get you a job around here if you'll cut your hair."

"I got a job in Las Cruces."

Billy called for two more shots of tequila then asked Henry what kind of job he had in Las Cruces.

"I repair jewelry."

"Don't sound like much of a job to me. I thought you wanted to cowboy." Billy ordered two more tequilas.

"I did until I got kicked 'tween the eyes."

"Hell that happens. You can get hurt on most near any job. Probably get hurt repairing jewelry if you tried."

"I got a good boss too," Henry mumbled. The tequila was hitting him hard and he was having trouble remembering what they were discussing. Billy ordered two more shots.

"Well if you're happy fixing rings then I guess you oughta stay with it. Now me, I'd rather be in a saddle. Two more tequilas Steve."

Henry woke up on a pallet on the floor of a small cabin. He'd had a horrifying nightmare about being sheared like a sheep and his head hurt. He had trouble focusing his eyes and when he finally did get his eyes in focus he noticed a long thin strand of hair hanging down the right side of his face. He was afraid to touch his head, afraid of what might not be there and afraid to look in the mirror and find out he hadn't been dreaming. He had to piss like a pregnant race horse and he staggered to the bathroom and faced the mirror and wanted to scream. His head was bald in places and his remaining hair ranged in length from an inch or two to scattered strands two feet or longer in length. Henry felt sick and it wasn't from the tequila.

The small room contained a single bed, dresser and card table with three folding chairs. An electric coffee pot sat on the edge of the dresser with two white coffee mugs. Henry poured a cup of coffee and sat down at the table. A small alarm clock near the bed showed the time to be nine twenty. He sipped the hot coffee and tried to remember the previous evening. Bits and pieces of the night came back to him and he vaguely recalled helping Billy search a 'tack' room until they found a pair of sheep shears. He remembered returning to Little Abner's and wondering why Steve, Gayla and a few others couldn't look at him without laughing. He didn't remember leaving the bar and coming here.

The door opened and Billy walked in like a man who hadn't consumed half the tequila in the Tucson area and told Henry he had some bad news. Even with Henry's new hair cut he couldn't find anyone who needed another hand.

"I thought I could get you on here at the Lazy K doing something but they said they can't afford to hire anyone just now."

Henry placed his hat on his head and the hat fell down over his ears. The 'haircut' had cost him two hat sizes. "You wouldn't happen to have a strip of leather laying around would you?" Henry asked. "My hat seems to have grown."

Billy searched the bottom dresser drawer and came up with a three foot strip of suede.

"How much do you need?"

"Just enough to place inside the sweat band. A foot or so."

Billy cut the strip and handed Henry a piece. Henry placed the strip in the sweat band and placed the hat on his head. "This'll do. It's not snug but it'll keep my hat off my ears. Now could I ask you for a ride to the highway?"

Billy drove Henry back to Interstate 10 apologizing all the way for the haircut and not being able to find Henry a job. Henry thanked him for the night at Little Abner's and for trying to get him a job. "And don't worry about my hair. It'll grow back eventually."

The times Henry had hitchhiked most of his rides had came from truckers or young 'long hair' drivers. The 'rednecks' hardly ever picked up male hitch hikers. Now with his hair gone the 'longhairs' wouldn't pick him up. He spent eight hours on the side of the road before four, very drunk, black men gave him a ride to Lordsburg, New Mexico. Six hours and three more rides and he was back in Las Cruces walking back to his trailer.

Henry called Leanna Hickman the following morning and asked if he could drop by her hair salon. An hour later Henry was waiting patiently for Leanna to quit laughing.

"What happened to you?" Leanna asked. "You run into another bear?"

"Can you fix my hair?" Henry asked.

"I doubt anyone can do that but I can even your hair up to where it's all the same length." Leanna went into another laughing spasm. "Has Rizzo seen it yet?"

"No."

"I'd like to be there when he does."

"How long will it take to grow back."

"Too long for you to go into hiding if that's what you're thinking."

Henry offered to pay Leanna and Leanna refused the money. He walked to the jewelry shop and tried to enter the building without attracting a lot of attention. Everyone in the shop was staring at the door waiting for him to enter.

"Leanna called," Tony said. "Take your hat off."

"Fuck you. Start that shit and I might just quit."

"You'll always come back but take your hat off and I won't care if you work or not. I'll pay you for the entertainment."

Henry sat in his recliner smoking a joint and watching 'Barbary Coast'. His hair had grown back enough to cover his ears and reach his shirt collar. Two weeks earlier Saul, Dan, Elwood and Tim had left Jerry Nichols and the El Corral for a job in Galveston, playing at a club near Galveston Beach. Saul and Dan had done their best to talk Henry into moving with them but Henry liked it right where he was.

"Strange pussy and I hear the dope's good," Saul had told him. "It'll give you a chance to use that Merchant Marine card you carry around or do you just carry that to impress people?"

"Nobody but you and a few others even know I have the thing," Henry answered, "and I like it here. I like the people, I like the weather, I like my boss, I like the pot, I don't particularly care for Texas. You seem to forget that Texas wants to throw me in a cage. I'll miss yall and I'll think of yall every time I smoke a joint but I'm staying here."

Henry took another pull on the joint and tried to remember the plot of Barbary Coast. His mind was on Liz, one of the prettiest girls in town, more than William Shatner or Doug McClure. He'd bought an ounce of good marijuana earlier from his neighbor and Liz was on her way over to Henry's trailer to cook him a spaghetti dinner. Henry was thinking how good life was when the door flew open and a fat detective yelled, "Police! Freeze!" A short Hispanic deputy leveled a gun at him. Henry didn't move until the detective ordered him to stand. While the detective handcuffed him the Hispanic deputy and three others started tearing his trailer apart.

"You don't have to do that," Henry told them. "All I have is an ounce of pot and it's under that chair."

A small white skinny deputy placed a gun to Henry's ear and told him, "I'd advise you to keep your fuckin' mouth shut." Henry clammed up but the deputy continued threatening him. Bringing the gun down to the base of Henry's skull he whispered, "I hope you make a run for it."

"You must think I'm an idiot," Henry answered.

While the three lawmen inside kicked in his television, broke his house plants, radio, kitchen ware and tore to shreds as much of his clothing as they could two other deputies were outside dumping the garbage can and digging up the yard. A few minutes later they placed him in the backseat of a patrol car and drove him to the Dona Ana County Jail. He was fingerprinted and photographed then placed in a cell with three other men. A metal table and benches sat in the center of the cell. Three Hispanics sat on bunks to Henry's right.

"What's your name kid?" A short, dark haired man sitting on the bunk asked. "What they got you for?"

Henry knew he'd been wrong about the number of Hispanics. There were two Hispanics. The man asking questions was Italian. Henry guessed him to be in his sixties. "The name's Henry and they caught me with an ounce of pot."

"You're cute white boy," one of the Hispanics commented. "Maybe we could get better acquainted later."

"You leave him alone!" The Italian yelled. "Come over here Henry."

"No thanks. I'm not fuckin' any Italian either." Henry stepped forward a few feet until he stood in front of the mouthy Hispanics. "And let me tell you somethin' you ugly little wetback! You lay one fuckin' finger on me and you'd better not go to sleep again or you may wake up with something sticking in your throat!"

The Italian laughed. "Come over here kid. I just wanna talk to you. My name's Tony. Tony Alvarico. I like you. I like the way you told that piece of shit where to get off at."

Henry shook the Italian's hand but declined the offer to sit next to him on the bunk. "Suit yourself," Tony said, then stood and walked to the commode and pissed.

The second Hispanic waited until Tony's back was turned then whispered to Henry, "You better stay away from that old man. He's loco. Even the guards are scared of him."

Tony returned to his seat on the bunk and Henry asked him why he was in jail.

"Murder."

The jailor announced 'lights out' and Henry wanted to move to a bunk near the wall, as far as he could get from the mouthy Hispanic. Tony asked Henry to stay and talk.

"How'd you get busted?" Tony asked. Henry told him about the raid on his apartment.

"There's something not right," Tony said. "The pigs don't usually do that kind of search unless they're sure they'll find something. And I don't mean an ounce of weed. You been pushing dope?"

"I just buy what I smoke and I can barely afford that much."

"Let me think about this," Tony said. "We'll talk in the morning. And don't worry about that loud mouth Mexican. He knows if he bothers you I'll tear his fuckin' heart out."

The jailor came after Henry at seven a.m. and told him the Judge was ready to see him.

"There's something not right about this," Tony remarked. "They don't hold court this early."

Henry was led to the Judge's office and the charges were read. The Judge asked Henry how he pled. Henry knew enough to know a person never pled guilty, even if the person was caught red handed. "Not guilty your Honor." The Judge sentenced Henry to six months in the county jail.

Back at the cell Henry was given a small plastic bag containing a toothbrush, tube of toothpaste and a small bar of soap. The jailor told him when he wanted to shave he'd have to check out a safety razor and shave while the guard watched. Henry emptied the bag on his bunk then carried the toothbrush over to the window and started filing the toothbrush handle down to a point by rubbing it against the rough cinder block window sill while staring at the Hispanic who'd commented on his ass the night before.

"What're you doing kid?" Tony asked.

"Puttin' a point on this toothbrush. I may want to leave it in somebody's throat."

"Come over here and talk to me. No one's gonna bother you with me here."

Henry liked Tony Alvarico. He wasn't sure if he believed a thing the man said but he knew the other prisoners were scared of him and even the jailors showed him a certain amount of respect. Tony never missed a chance to tell a lawman that he'd kill him if he ever got his hands on him.

"What are they gonna do to me? Give me another thirty years? They've already given me three hundred and thirty."

"How does anyone get three hundred years?" Henry asked.

"Three hundred and thirty. Listen kid I'm what they call a mechanic. You know what a mechanic is?"

"I'm sure you're not talking about working on engines," Henry answered.

"I took care of problems for certain people. I was in Albuquerque taking care of a problem and someone snitched me out. I made the hit and when I came out the pigs were waiting. The Judge gave me three hundred and thirty years. I could have got a lot less if I'd snitched a few people out but I wouldn't. I hate a fuckin' snitch. I can smell one. I knew you wasn't a snitch when you came through that door. You may not know it kid but someone snitched you out or you wouldn't be here. They told the pigs

what they wanted to hear. Either that or the pigs were so fuckin'
stupid they got the wrong house." Tony took a scrap of paper
and started scribbling on it. "You ever been to Florida?"

"A time or two," Henry answered. He decided not to mention his brig time with the Navy.

"I have a club and restaurant in Fort Lauderdale. When
you get out of here go to this address and give anyone there this
note and they'll set you up."

Henry read the note. An address and name of a club was
at the top and a message underneath that read "this is Henry, a
friend of mine. Set him up with an apartment, a job and a car.
Tony."

"Why are you doing this?" Henry asked.

"Because I like you and the way you're going now you'll
wind up in prison as somebody's punk."

"An ounce of pot is a long ways from a prison sentence,"
Henry argued. "That ounce of pot got you here but I heard you
threaten to kill that Mexican son-of-a-bitch that first night and
I don't doubt you would kill him and that'll get you a one way
trip to prison. You understand what I'm saying? You may have
handled that the other night but prison is a lot different. If I
didn't know you and they brought you into Leavenworth I'd be
wanting your hole too. I'm not going without a hole for three
hundred years kid. The only chance you'd have in prison is if
you told the baddest motherfucker in there that you'd be his
punk if he kept the others away. Otherwise they'd be standing
in line to fuck you."

"They'd have to kill me first."

"No they wouldn't kid. No they wouldn't. All they'd have
to do is break a few bones. Then when you heal up they'd stretch
your asshole again. Get smart kid. Take that note and go to
Lauderdale when you get out of here."

"I'll think about it."

"You better think hard on it. I've been thinking about the way your bust went down. You say they dug up the yard. They don't do that unless their snitch tells them the drugs are there. All you had was an ounce and they hit you like a major player. Where'd you get the weed?"

"From a neighbor."

"That explains it. They hit the wrong house and they know it. That explains the early court too. You're an embarrassment kid. They fucked up and they know it."

"How does anyone get three hundred years for a murder?" Henry asked. "I've heard of people getting twenty or thirty years or even life but not three hundred."

"It wasn't one murder. The snitch tied me to fourteen others."

"How did you end up in Las Cruces?"

"They put me here to wait for a Marshall to come and escort me to Leavenworth."

The mouthy Hispanic was released after breakfast. Henry, Tony and the remaining Hispanic, Jorge, played hearts with a deck of cards nearly as old as the jail. Dinner was two slices of white bread, a slice of bologna, a small helping of beans and a small paper cup of lukewarm unsweetened tea.

Jorge was released an hour later. Henry and Tony played cards until supper then talked until after 'lights out'.

Tony Alvarico was wrong about them sending a Marshall to escort him to prison. They sent two Marshalls the following day and Tony Alvarico was gone before breakfast.

Tony Rizzo came to the jail during visiting hours and brought Henry a carton of cigarettes. He asked Henry if he wanted anything else.

"I'd like a drink of whiskey and a joint the size of my thumb but I'll settle for something to read."

Henry spent the rest of the day staring out the window at the traffic below or playing solitaire. That evening he watched the neon lights come on above the bars, restaurants and motels. Shortly after lights out they locked a drunk in Henry's cell and Henry spent the next hour listening to him puke then another hour listening to him dry heave and ask God to take him. The following morning the drunk was released. Shortly before noon the jailor brought Henry four paper back books Tony Rizzo had brought to the jail.

Henry spent the next week reading and watching prisoners come and go. Most were Hispanics arrested for public drunk or drunk driving or domestic violence and most were only there overnight.. Jorge was back in jail two days after being released for trying to break into his ex-wife's apartment.

Ten days after being sentenced the jailor came back to the cell and led Henry to the office of the Police Chief. Henry saw his wallet laying on the Chief's desk and his Merchant Mariner identification card laying next to it. The Chief picked up the card and leaned back in his chair. "According to this card here Mr. Ridge you're a seaman," the Chief said. "As far as I know we don't have any ports around here so I can't see how you'd have any reason to be here. Now here's what we're going to do. We're going to help you get to a port. We've even bought you a ticket for Houston. There's a bus leaving in the morning and I want you on it. Do you understand me ?"

"Sounds like I'm being run out of town."

"We're just giving you an opportunity to get out of jail early."

"Can you give me a few days to take care of a few things?"

"I'm in a good mood Mr. Ridge. Today's Friday, I'll give

you until Monday morning. The bus leaves around ten and I'll have a deputy waiting to make sure you're on board when it leaves. And one more thing Mr. Ridge......don't come back to Las Cruces. You've worn out your welcome here."

Tony Rizzo threw Henry a party Saturday night that lasted into Sunday afternoon. Sunday evening Henry called Galveston and talked to Saul Carter. Monday morning Liz drove Henry to the bus station and under the watchful eye of a deputy Henry boarded the 10:10 to Houston.

CHAPTER EIGHTEEN

Henry's bus arrived in Houston shortly after midnight. Three hours later Saul and Dan arrived. "I'm sorry we wasn't here when your bus came in," Saul said, "but we had a gig at a private party and we needed the money. You been waiting long?"

"Not too long. I appreciate you coming after me."

"Hell we're glad you're here," Dan told him. "We're renting a five bedroom house on the beach and there's plenty of room. I wanna warn you though that the house wobbles a little. That's the only reason we can afford it. The house may fall into the gulf with the next strong wind but the house has to be occupied for the owner to collect insurance. He charges us twenty-five dollars a month and we pay our own utilities."

Henry threw his duffel bag into the back of the ten year old Volkswagen van the band bought for hauling them and their equipment to whatever bar they were working.

"Do you know any of the local shrimpers?" Henry asked.

"We know a few," Saul answered. "Why?"

"I need a job and I thought I'd try shrimping."

"You ever work a shrimp boat?" Dan asked. "I've heard it's hard work."

"No, but I can learn anything."

"Why are you thinking about a job?" Saul asked. "You just got off the bus. You can help us if you want. We're not getting rich but we're not doing without much either."

"You can't afford to support me and my habits."

"We did it in Las Cruces," Saul teased, "but if you're serious about going to work on a boat we know a snapper fisherman that has trouble keeping a hand. He's a nice guy and he likes to drink and get high."

"If he's a nice guy why does he have trouble keeping a hand?"

"He likes to go out and work his ass off, doesn't come in until he has all the snapper his boat will hold, then he might take the next month or two off."

"Sounds like my kind of boss," Henry said.

An hour later Saul turned off the highway and drove toward the beach then turned right a hundred yards from the gulf and followed a small road passed several houses finally coming to a house at the end of the road that sat on stilts out in the water. A jerry-built set of stairs led from the beach to the front door of the house. Inside, a large kitchen was on the right and a large living room was in the center of the house. There were three bedrooms to the left of the living room and two bedrooms on the kitchen side. Henry walked out on the back porch and looked around. The porch extended over the water and the Gulf of Mexico ran under the house.

"You can have the bedroom over here," Dan said, pointing to a door nearest the kitchen. "Are you hungry or had you rather get high?"

"I'll eat later," Henry told him, "and I brought five joints from New Mexico with me. Where's Tim and Elwood?"

"Tim's got a girlfriend he stays with most of the time and Elwood's in bed. That's where I'm going after we smoke a joint."

"I appreciate you and Saul picking me up."

"Don't think a thing about it," Saul said. "You'd have done the same for either of us."

Saul, Dan and Elwood were already awake when Henry crawled out of bed shortly before noon. Dan had been out earlier and bought four hamburgers and Henry was the only one who hadn't eaten. He ate his hamburger and sipped a cup of hot coffee then the three men shared a couple of joints. Saul suggested they go out for a drink at a local bar. A few minutes later they were sitting in a small bar a few blocks down the beach from the house. The bar was nearly full.

"Is it always like this?" Henry asked.

"Everyday and the nights are even better," Saul answered. "I've never been in here that there wasn't a crowd. We'll be picking here this weekend."

Dan elbowed Henry in the side and pointed to a tall, husky man with brown hair. "That's Randy, the snapper fisherman we told you about."

Randy made his way toward the bar stopping several times to hug a girl's neck or shake a man's hand. He saw Dan and came over to the table and tried to hug him. Dan appeared embarrassed and Henry got the idea Randy knew Dan was embarrassed and probably tried to hug Dan every time he saw him.

"Damn it Randy," Dan said, "I've told you before they talk about me enough without you trying to hug me." Randy laughed and tried to hug Dan again. Henry liked Randy immediately.

"I was telling Henry here that you might need a hand on your boat," Saul said.

"I do need a hand. You ever work a snapper boat Henry?"

"No, but I can learn anything."

"There's not that much to learn. I'll be going out in two or three days. How can I get hold of you?"

"He's staying with us," Elwood answered.

"Then I'll let you know when I'm ready to go out. Right now I see a woman that needs my attention. It was nice meeting you Henry." Randy staggered toward a young blonde sitting alone at the bar. He called ten days later.

Randy came from an upper class family who had lived in the area for generations. His father was a prominent doctor in Galveston and his mother was a school teacher. Both parents had once had high hopes for their son but Randy was a free spirit and liked to work only when necessary and play anytime he could. The life of a fisherman suited him perfectly. He owned and lived on a thirty foot fishing boat he called the 'Tramp'. When working he fished eighteen to twenty hours a day until he had every hole and container on the boat, including the ice chests, filled with snapper. After selling the fish and paying the crew and a few debts he'd party until he was broke again.

Henry borrowed money from Saul and purchased a pair of deck boots and a knit cap then Saul drove Henry to the docks. Randy introduced Henry to the only other crew member, Bo, a man in his early forties who had worked with Randy off and on for years. Randy and Bo laughed when they saw Henry's duffel bag.

"You might as well send that back with Saul," Randy advised. "All you need to carry is a toothbrush."

Randy pulled the 'Tramp' around to the fuel docks and filled the boat with fuel and the lower containers with ice and purchased beer, cigarettes and groceries, mostly canned goods, then ran full throttle for three hours before slowing down to two or three knots. Randy studied the Loran, or 'fish finder' as Bo called it, while Henry and Bo cut several spoiled mackerels into chunks about two to three inches square. After cutting several mackerel into bait size and filling two large metal buckets with the parts they baited their hooks and waited.

The hooks were attached to the lines of two metal reels located mid ship on the boat, one on the starboard side and one on the port. Each line contained fifteen hooks and was weighted down with a piece of lead weighing approximately one pound. The line was held loosely in the palm of the hand as the line was dropped and one could feel the metal weight hit the bottom. The line was then reeled back until the weight was two or three feet off the bottom. After the reel was set the line would be raised slightly with the hand and held across the palm. This enabled the fisherman to know when he'd hooked a fish. As more fish took the bait the line would become heavier. When the fisherman thought he had enough fish hooked he reeled the line in and unhooked the fish. After hitting a second school of snapper Randy would set the boat's motor in neutral and help. While two men fished the third man 'gutted and gilled', slicing the stomach open and grabbing the gills and pulling, bringing the stomach contents out with the gills. The snapper were tossed into laundry baskets until they fished the location out then Randy would slowly troll the area until the Loran registered another school of fish. While Randy trolled, Henry and Bo would take the snapper through a hatch to the ice below deck. One man would shovel the ice from a bin leaving only a layer of ice on deck. The other man would layer the fish on the ice while the shovel man covered each layer until all the fish were iced down. Then it was back to fishing.

Randy was good at his chosen profession, locating fish quickly enough to work almost non-stop and taking a break only long enough to eat or answer the call of nature. The meal was always the next fish caught and beans or eggs. They worked without knowing the time of day and quit when Randy was tired and wanted to sleep and went back to work when Randy was rested, usually no more than four or five hours after they lay down.

The work was steady but not back breaking and Randy allowed his crew to drink beer and smoke marijuana as long as it didn't interfere with their work.

The 'Tramp' stayed out two weeks before Randy decided to return to Galveston. Everything on the boat that could hold fish had fish in it. More than twenty-one thousand pounds of red snapper and four hundred pounds of flounder. Henry's pay was six hundred dollars, fifty pounds of snapper and a hundred pounds of flounder.

Randy told Henry and Bo he'd call in a few days when he was ready to go back out to sea. Henry called Dan from a phone booth near the dock and asked him to come and pick him up.

The closest thing to personal hygiene Henry had experienced aboard the fishing boat was brushing his teeth twice a day and washing his hands before eating. He still wore the same clothes he'd worn when he went aboard. The smell of fish blood, guts and gills had permeated his clothes and his skin.

Dan drove his car up next to the dock and Henry walked out carrying the fish then returned for his duffel bag. Dan had placed the fish in the trunk and Henry climbed in the passenger side of the car. Dan fanned the air in front of his nose, "Damn Henry, I think I'll put you in the trunk and let the fish ride up front. You smell more than a little ripe."

"I reckon I do need a bath."

"Just please leave your window down."

Henry felt like he was still on a boat and everything was swaying. At the beach house he took a long, hot shower and changed clothes but he could still smell fish. He took another shower and the smell was still there. He asked Dan to take him to a shopping center where he bought four new pants, a half dozen long sleeved knit pull over shirts and a Greek fisherman's cap. He was disoriented from the two weeks spent on a constantly rocking boat and he walked like a drunk man. Back at the beach house he smoked a joint and had trouble standing without support and he still smelled like fish when they went out later to the bar.

Dwight 'Daffy' Dawson came by the beach house on a Sunday morning. He was thin with an unruly head of hair and a beard to match. Saul introduced him to Henry. "Here's the man you wanna work for," Saul said. "He's a shrimper. You won't make much money but you'll party your ass off."

"I try to have a good time," Daffy bragged. "Life's too fucking short to take serious."

"I heard you took a woman shrimping with you," Dan said. "I also heard she's suing you."

Daffy laughed. "She says she's pregnant and I'm the pappy. There were four of us on board and she fucked us all but she names me. One of my hands, Sherman, was so scared she'd name him he took off for ports unknown."

"Henry's looking for a job," Saul said.

"You ever work a shrimp boat?" Daffy asked.

"He's been working for Randy," Saul answered.

"Well you can relax awhile if you're waiting for him to go back out. My boat's in dry dock now having some work done on the motor but I'll keep you in mind when I'm ready to go."

"You have any idea how long that will be?" Henry asked.

"Ten days, maybe two weeks. It'll be before Randy goes out again. I can guarantee that."

Henry saw Randy nearly every day at the bar and every time he asked when they'd be going back to work it was always the same answer, "in a day or two". He saw Daffy a few days later and asked him when he'd be ready to go shrimping and got the same answer, "in a day or two". A day or two stretched to three weeks and Henry was broke. The nights were already turning cold and Henry needed to work.

Daffy came by the beach house the second Monday in October. The band was off that night and Henry, Dan and Elwood were drinking beer and sharing a joint. Daffy asked Henry to step out on the porch. "You wanna make some money tonight?"

"That depends on what the job is," Henry answered.

"I've got an insurance job. A friend of mine wants a boat burned and it has to look like an accident. That means I have to have a crew. I'll pay you three hundred dollars for a couple of hours of your time."

"As bad as I need the money," Henry answered, "I'd hate to spend the winter in a Galveston jail. Thanks for considering me but I think I'll pass on it. When you finally get ready to go shrimping I'll load like a huntin' dog."

"If I thought there was any chance of going to jail I wouldn't do it. There's no way they can prove the fire was anything but accidental after the boat sinks. Bo said he'd help and we'll just go out like we're going to work. You'll be back before daylight. I'll give you four hundred to help us."

"You make it hard to say no Daffy but I got a gut feeling about this. I hope I'm wrong and I wish you luck."

Tim came by the house shortly after ten a.m. Henry and Saul were sitting at the kitchen table drinking coffee and smoking a joint. Elwood was still in bed sleeping. "Did you hear about Daffy?" Tim asked. "He's in jail. The Coast Guard arrested him for arson."

"What happened?" Saul asked.

"He set fire to an old junk shrimp boat called the Laura

Anne. The idiot didn't see the Coast Guard boat and they saw the whole thing. He dumped gas or something at the stern and lit it. I guess he thought he'd have time to radio for help before they had to abandon the boat but the fire spread to the cabin as soon as he lit the match. They had to jump into the water and the only thing that saved them from freezing was the fact that the Coast Guard had seen it all. I heard they let them flop around in the water for a while before they picked them up."

"Well Henry," Saul said, "I don't think you need to wait on Daffy to go shrimping anytime soon. They'll pull his license for this."

"Was Bo with him?" Henry asked.

"Bo was and some beach bum Daffy found."

Henry was tired of waiting for Randy to run out of money. He asked Dan to give him a ride to the docks.

"It's cold on that water this time of year Henry. Why don't you just kick back until spring? We've got pot and beer and food most of the time and you'll earn your keep."

"I feel like a bum Dan. Yall pay for everything and I know it don't bother yall but it bothers me."

"It shouldn't bother you. We're friends and if it was reversed you'd do the same thing for us."

"I appreciate it but I've already made up my mind."

"I don't guess there's any talking you out of it. If you still want to go tomorrow I'll take you."

Henry packed two pairs of pants, two shirts, two pairs of long johns and a half dozen pairs of socks into a small over night bag he'd borrowed from Elwood. His duffel bag, Stetson hat, boots and remaining clothes would stay in the house. He wore a wool peacoat, the fisherman's cap and deck boots. His knit cap and working gloves were in a pocket of the peacoat.

Four packs of cigarettes were in the other pocket. At eleven a.m. Dan drove Henry to the docks.

"Would you like for me to hang around somewhere close in case you don't get hired?"

"No need in that," Henry answered. "If I don't have a job before dark I'll call you to come after me. If I do get a job I'll call you and tell you what boat I'm on."

Henry started at the end of the dock and went from boat to boat asking if they needed a hand. A couple of boat captains expressed an interest until they learned he'd had no experience working on a shrimp boat. Finally at a fifty five foot, double rigged trawler named the Jerron Marie, he made the captain an offer he hoped the captain couldn't refuse.

"I'll work for nothing," Henry told him. "Just my room and board. If I make a hand then you pay me the next time we go out." The captain, Jerry Stelman, a tall, bald, whale of a man in his early forties, agreed to take him aboard.

Jerry Stelman grew up on a shrimp boat. His father had been a shrimper and his father before him. He owned his own boat and had two men working for him when Henry came aboard: Robert, a small, quiet man in his early thirties and Toothless, a big man in his sixties who loved to tell jokes and often told the same joke several times a day. Both men had worked for Jerry for years.

The cabin of the trawler had three bunks counting the bunk in the captain's quarters. Henry was told he'd have to sleep on the floor of the engine room. He left his bag in the engine room then walked to a telephone booth near the end of the dock and called Dan. Then he called his grandmother. An hour later the crew of the Jerron Marie was taking on fuel, picking up supplies and loading the trawler's hold with ice. Then Jerry turned the Jerron Marie toward the gulf.

"We'll be running for a few hours," Robert told him. "You

oughta lay down and get as much rest as you can. I'll wake you for supper."

"It's daylight yet. I don't think I could sleep."

"You'll learn to."

Jerry was a beer drinker and carried beer on the boat. He allowed the crew to drink as long as it didn't interfere with their work. But he made it clear he wouldn't tolerate drugs, even marijuana. Not because of any great aversion but simply because he could have his boat confiscated if anyone aboard was caught with drugs of any kind. Henry had to respect another man's property, especially when that property was essential to supporting the man and his family. He walked over to the rail and when he was certain no one was looking he threw the six joints he'd brought with him into the gulf.

Henry drank two beers and walked down to the engine room intending to try and take a nap. The noise was intolerable and the engine room was freezing. He walked back to the cabin and sat down in the small booth where the crew ate their meals. Robert and Toothless were in their bunks.

"Can't sleep?" Toothless asked.

"Too noisy," Henry answered, "and colder than a well digger's ass."

"You think that's cold," Toothless said. "I seen it get so cold the water backed up under the bridge to get out of the wind." Henry laughed and Robert moaned. Henry would understand why after he'd heard Toothless repeat the line a dozen or so times.

Robert cooked the supper meal and while the four men ate at the small table Jerry told Henry that he'd be expected to cook too.

"We rotate cooking so every fourth day you'll be expected

to do the honors. I'm not going to ask if you know how to cook or not. I just expect you do. But if you can't cook or if you cook something we can't eat, and we can eat most anything, then this will be your last trip with me."

Around midnight Henry descended the stairs to the engine room carrying two wool blankets. He spread one on the floor then lay down fully dressed, wearing his hat and gloves, and pulled the other blanket over him. The noise of the engine made Henry believe that no one could sleep under these circumstances but sometime later he finally dozed off. The next thing he remembered was Jerry yelling down in the engine room, "get your ass up! It's time to go to work!" The outriggers were lowered and the nets dropped and thirty minutes later Henry was back on the floor of the engine room trying to fall asleep again. Four hours later Jerry's yelling woke him up again. They were taking in the nets.

Robert and Toothless were already working the lead line, the line that led to the heavy towing cables that dragged the 'doors' of the nets along the bottom of the gulf, stirring up schools of shrimp. When enough of the towing cable was on deck the cable was wrapped around a winch and the nets hauled up. Once the 'doors' were secured, the 'lazy' line allowed the nets to be brought aboard and held over the deck and emptied.

The drainage slots on both sides of the deck were covered and the nets emptied. Several species of aquatic life fell out of the nets with the shrimp. Crabs, turtles, flounder, sheep head, salt water catfish, scorpion fish, stingrays, eels and several more varieties Henry was unfamiliar with. Toothless handed Henry a wooden box about four inches deep to sit on. The box reminded Henry of the wooden cases Nehi and Coca-Cola used to use. Henry, Robert and Toothless sat in a circle around the catch with their legs spread.

"Just reach out and get an armload and pull it toward you and start looking for shrimp," Toothless explained. "When you find one just take his head like this," Toothless held his thumb and index finger together and snapped, "and pop his head off. But be careful what you grab. There's critters in there that can hurt you. You get hold of one of those hardheads the wrong way and he'll spear you with a barb. And it hurts too. It'll make a grown man cry like a baby." A bushel basket sat between Robert and Toothless and another between Henry and Robert. The three men wore tight rubber gloves. Toothless talked non-stop and Henry had already learned how to tune him out. He was surprised that after a few minutes he was able to keep up with Robert and Toothless. 'Heading' shrimp wasn't much different than pulling cotton. Jerry came over to where the three men sat and said, "Henry, you lied to me".

"I don't know what you're talking about," Henry replied.

"You told me you'd never worked a shrimp boat. Ain't nobody comes on board raw and head shrimp like you do."

"You just never had any cotton pickers in your crew before."

The three men filled sixteen bushel baskets with shrimp then Henry and Robert descended to the hold and shoveled ice on the shrimp while Toothless stayed on deck and lowered the baskets with a hoist. Then the covers from the drainage slots were removed and the 'trash' fish pushed over the side. The sting rays were thrown over using the eye sockets for a handle and the eels were led to the openings. Flounder and snapper were kept and iced down with the shrimp.

The sun was up when the nets were lowered again and the men gathered in the cabin. It was Toothless' day to cook and he'd already started the coffee percolating and the bacon frying. After a breakfast of bacon, eggs and toast Henry returned to the engine room and lay down. For some reason the engine didn't seem as loud as it had and the room didn't seem as cold. He pulled on his leather gloves and lay down and fell asleep at once.

Henry didn't know how long he slept but he felt like it couldn't have been more than a few minutes. He heard Jerry yelling from the top of the ladder leading to the engine room. "Come on goddamn it! Get your lazy ass up! We're bringing in the nets.!"

Henry's hands hurt. The shrimp antennae were like needles and the rubber gloves the men wore while 'heading' shrimp were easy to puncture. His fingers were stiff and sore and when he removed his gloves he saw his hands were festered in places. He eased his gloves back on and climbed the ladder to the deck. Robert noticed him rubbing his hands and assured him his hands would be all right.

"You got a little fish poisoning is all. A couple of more days and you won't even think about your hands. Get you some coffee, that'll help."

Less than five minutes after they started bringing in the nets Henry had forgotten about his hands. They no longer felt stiff and sore but every time Henry would lay down to sleep, whether it was one hour or four hours, his hands would fester and stiffen again. A few minutes of work and they were nearly as good as ever.

The eighth day out Henry cried like a baby.

Henry, Robert and Toothless were sitting in a circle 'heading' shrimp. Henry and Robert were drinking beer, stopping every few minutes to wipe the fish blood and guts off the top of the can and take a drink. The day was cool but the sun was bright and Henry had been daydreaming about a girl he'd known in Fort Worth. Suddenly he felt his whole body stiffen with more pain than he'd ever felt in his life. The barb of an Atlantic Croaker, more popularly known as a 'hardhead', had punctured his right index finger to the bone. Henry stood and screamed, the hardhead hanging from his finger. He felt big tears running down his cheek and he didn't care. He was hurting and he didn't give a rat's ass if the whole world saw him bawl. His toe nails hurt, his teeth hurt, his hair hurt and every inch of skin hurt. He hopped from one end of the deck to the other. Robert caught him and grabbed the hardhead, jerking down, pulling the barb out of Henry's finger and taking a chunk of Henry's meat with it. Toothless continued 'heading' shrimp, looking up long enough to say, "I told you to watch for those hardheads. Don't let it embarrass you. I've seen bigger men cry. But I don't think I ever saw one that could hop as good as you."

Henry cried a little more. His finger had already swollen to twice its size and every time his heart beat it sent another jolt of pain through his body. Jerry put his arm around Henry and led him to the cabin. He took a box of baking soda from the cabinet and told Henry to hold his right hand over the sink. He then took a clean cloth and filled the cloth with a thick layer of baking soda and applied it to the injured finger.

"That baking soda will suck some of the poison out," Jerry explained. "You just sit here and keep that on your finger until you feel like you can work."

Less than an hour later Henry was back in the circle heading shrimp. His finger still throbbed but the pain was bearable. He didn't daydream much after that.

Jerry was subject to mood swings and often tried to take his frustrations out on Henry. Henry had already made up his mind to hunt another job on another trawler as soon as they were back in port. One moment Jerry could be a man's best friend and the next moment you were ready to go over the side to get away from him. Henry was certain they'd be fighting before they returned to port and he was equally certain Jerry would whip his ass good. He mentioned this to Robert one night when Robert was on the wheel and Henry wasn't ready to sleep. Jerry was in bed in his cabin and Toothless was snoring in his bed.

"I don't know why he's like that," Robert said. "Every time he gets a new hand he tries to brow beat them so bad they quit as soon as we tie up. But he likes you kid. You don't take none of his shit and he respects that. There won't nobody blame you if you quit though."

"I have nightmares about fightin' that big bastard."

Robert laughed. "You don't have to worry about fighting him. You wouldn't make a pimple on his ass in a fight and he knows that. I've seen him take on three men at a time but he won't fight anyone smaller than him."

"I still think I'll be better off huntin' another job. At least I have experience now. I'll always be grateful to him for that. And I appreciate you and Toothless for puttin' up with me."

"You're a good hand kid. I hope we don't lose you."

"I think I'll go lay down now. Good night Robert."

"Good night kid."

The third week out Jerry decided to change locations. The nets were brought in and two hours later they were dropping the nets near an abandoned oil rig. Two days later they snagged an old oil drum and tore a net and spent the next day repairing it. Robert, Toothless and Jerry had experience repairing net and Henry didn't. While the three men repaired the net Henry held the net for whoever needed it held. The work was tedious and while he held the net for Jerry he started to doze off. A sharp pain across his left knuckles woke him. His hand hurt. Jerry had hit him across the knuckles with the heavy plastic 'net needle'. Henry dropped the net and started cursing. "Goddamn you Jerry!"

"You shouldn't have dozed off! I'm not paying you to sleep!"

"You're not paying me at all!"

"You're eating ain't ya? Now pick up that net!"

"You crack my knuckles again and I'll lay you out with the first thing I can get my hand on!"

"You threatening me you long haired little hare-lip?" Jerry dropped the needle and stepped toward Henry.

Robert stepped between them. "You shouldn't have cracked his knuckles. I'd get pissed off too."

Jerry sat down and picked up his needle. "Sit down kid and pick up the net. We're wasting time."

"Are you done crackin' my knuckles?"

"Doze off again and you'll find out."

Thirty-two days after leaving port the Jerron Marie turned toward Galveston. During the return trip the outriggers were raised and the trawlers scrubbed from stem to stern. Later Henry, Robert and Toothless sat in the cabin drinking coffee while Jerry was on the wheel.

"Toothless," Jerry yelled from the pilot house, "come take the wheel for a minute!"

Jerry sat down next to Robert, across the table from Henry and ordered Henry to get him a cup of coffee.

"Get it yourself."

Jerry and Robert laughed. "You made a good hand kid," Jerry said. "You got a smart mouth but you're a good hand. You got a job if you want it. I'll pay you a nickel a pound."

"Things would have to change," Henry told him. "I don't like being cussed and insulted."

"That's just my way of working. Robert and Toothless

knows that. They know I don't mean nothing by it. Now do you want the job or not? Don't tell me you do and then not show up when we go back out. You got a job, a paying job, but I need an answer now."

"I'll stay on."

"Good, now get me a cup of coffee."

"Get it yourself."

The shrimp were unloaded at a processing plant and the flounder and snapper were divided four ways. Jerry had also put aside fifty pounds of shrimp for each man. Robert's wife arrived to take him home and a few minutes later Toothless' wife was near the dock honking her car's horn. Henry told Jerry he'd be back in a few minutes and walked to the telephone booth near the dock and called Dan. Jerry was drinking a cup of coffee when Henry returned to the boat. "Is your friend coming after you?" Jerry asked.

"Yes, but it'll be awhile. His roommate has the car and he'll have to wait until he gets back."

"If you need a place to stay you can stay on the boat. There's plenty of food and you can pick any bunk you want while we're tied up. Fact of the matter is I'd like to have someone on the boat. We'll be leaving out in ten days, that's the day after Thanksgiving." Jerry handed Henry a folded bill and said, "Take this."

Henry unfolded the money and saw it was a hundred dollar bill. "You don't owe me no money."

"You earned it kid. The next trip out you'll earn a lot more than that."

"I can buy some new deck boots now."

"Hold off on buying those boots."

"Why?"

"Just hold off kid. I've got my reasons."

Henry spent nine days with the band. Tim's girlfriend

Nicole cooked the shrimp and fish for Thanksgiving dinner at the beach house and after dinner everyone sat around smoking marijuana and drinking spiked eggnog. The band was working that night and Henry wanted to go to the club with them but he knew Jerry would be leaving port early the following morning and he didn't want to risk missing the boat. He asked Dan to give him a ride to the dock. Dan offered Henry a small bag of marijuana to take with him but Henry refused it.

"I'd love to have it but I can't gamble with Jerry's boat. I will take a couple of joints to smoke tonight."

Later Henry lay down in Robert's bunk and fell asleep. He woke up shortly before daylight when Robert came aboard. "I hope you don't mind me using your bunk."

"Not at all. Just don't get too attached to it."

Jerry and Toothless arrived together less than a half hour later. Jerry was carrying a small single size mattress and a pair of deck boots.

"Here kid," Jerry said as he flipped the mattress off his shoulder toward Henry, "this is yours. You'll have to sleep in the engine room but at least you'll be off the floor and here's some deck boots. Throw those others away."

"I intended to buy deck boots."

"I figured you'd get another cheap pair so I bought you these."

"What do I owe you?"

"Nothing if you do your job."

The Jerron Marie stayed out for nearly twenty-six days then stayed in port until after New Year's day. The second trip out Henry caught his finger between the boat and one of the heavy net 'doors'. The 'door' snapped his tendon leaving his finger stiff and unable to bend. After a few days he adjusted to the stiff finger and hardly noticed it until someone called attention to it. But the stiff finger prevented him from making a fist with his right hand and this bothered him. He'd be nearly useless in a fight and he lived in a world where fights were common.

He earned over four hundred dollars for the second trip. Jerry still cursed him but it no longer bothered Henry. Each man on the boat knew how to do his job without being told but yelling and cussing were a part of Jerry's nature and Henry accepted it.

Henry's third trip with the Jerron Marie was thirty-three days and Henry earned nearly nine hundred dollars. The crew was given ten days off and Henry called Dan to come and get him.

Dan introduced Henry to a girl at the club named Mindy but everyone called her Hamburger. She'd gotten the name as a teenager when she'd lived with a heroin addicted mother and had to fend for herself. At one point in her young life she'd been so desperate she was exchanging sex for hamburgers. She was off the streets now and had been for years, working in a financial services office, but the name had stayed with her. Henry didn't care what they called her and he cared even less about her past. He liked Hamburger. She was fun to be with and she never seemed to notice the fish smell Henry couldn't scrub away.

Dan told Henry one evening that the band had an offer to work the 'motel circuit', touring and playing in Holiday Inns around the country. The tour wouldn't start for a few weeks and he was certain the band would accept the offer. Later that night they were standing at the bar waiting for the rest of the band to arrive. Henry had two more days before returning to the Jerron Marie and he planned on making the most of it. Hamburger was working late and would be meeting him later.

A tall, stocky man in a black cowboy hat and black duster

with red trim walked up to the bar and stood next to Henry then deliberately elbowed him in the side. The man wanted a fight but he was several pounds heavier and several inches taller than Henry and Henry had no desire to fight him or anyone else, especially when his right hand had a stiff finger that prevented him from making a fist. Henry picked up his beer and moved down the bar. The stranger followed and elbowed Henry again.

Henry looked up at the man and asked, "Do I know you? Did I do something to piss you off?" Dan had been on stage checking the band's equipment. He heard the commotion and left the stage and was walking toward the bar.

"I don't like long-haired queers," the stranger sneered, "especially long-haired, hare-lip queers! Why don't you take your ugly ass out of here queer?"

"I don't think so!" Henry answered.

The stranger grabbed Henry by the front of his shirt. Henry picked up an empty long neck beer bottle from the nearest table and hit the man across the nose. The man released Henry's shirt, shook his head a couple of times then came after him again. Henry backed up several feet then picked up another bottle and threw it at the man's head. The bottle put a new crease in the man's hat and bounced off his head like a rubber ball.

"What's going on here?" Dan demanded to know.

Henry saw the man's right hand disappear then reappear a second later holding a Buck knife and facing Dan. Henry stepped forward and tried to grab the stranger's hand and the man turned toward him again. Henry never saw the knife come around but he felt his chest explode in pain as the four inch blade tore his chest open from his left shoulder to his right nipple. Henry looked down and saw the front of his shirt already soaked in blood. An ambulance was called and Dan instructed Henry to lay down and not move. Ten minutes later Henry was in the back of a speeding ambulance with an IV in his arm. He was taken to the hospital emergency room and given an injection. When he awoke Saul, Dan, Tim, Nicole and Hamburger were standing near his bed. A nurse came in a moment later with a needle.

"It's for the pain," the nurse explained.

"But I'm not in that much pain," Henry said.

"You will be when that other shot wears off."

"What happened to that bastard that cut me?" Henry asked.

"He disappeared," Saul answered, "and if he's smart he'll stay disappeared."

The shot made Henry drowsy and Saul announced that they were going to leave him alone to rest and would return tomorrow. When Henry awoke Dan and Hamburger were sitting in the room.

"Do you need anything?" Dan asked.

"A joint and a beer."

"I don't think they allow that here."

"A cup of coffee then." Hamburger offered to get it. "I need you to do me a favor Dan, if you don't mind."

"I'll do anything I can. Just name it."

"I'm supposed to be going out day after tomorrow. Would you mind calling Jerry Stelman and tell him what happened and tell him I'll try to make the next trip?"

"I'll call him tomorrow."

"When you're done with that would you do me another favor?"

"Sure, what is it?"

"Come back and get me."

"The doctor wants to keep you a few days."

"I can heal just as good at the beach house."

"We'll see how you feel."

Dan came by the following afternoon on his way to the club and Henry asked what Jerry had to say. "He did a lot of cussing Henry."

The following day Henry insisted on being released. The doctor refused to release him, lecturing him on the dangers of a chest infection. Henry informed the doctor he was leaving with or without his permission and the doctor finally relented, asking Henry to promise he wouldn't leave the hospital until he returned with a prescription. The nurse changed Henry's bandage then Henry dressed and waited for the doctor to return. Forty minutes later the doctor entered the room carrying a small sack of bandages, a large bottle of the iodine solution they used on his wound and a prescription for two weeks of antibiotics. An hour later Henry was in bed at the beach house smoking a joint and drinking a beer, Hamburger sitting in a chair near the bed.

Henry spent the majority of the next week on his back, only leaving the bed to use the toilet, brush his teeth and sponge bathe. Hamburger came to the house after work and Saul or Dan were usually around during the day. After a week Henry started leaving bed for several hours a day. The wound was still red and ugly but he felt the danger of infection was over. Fourteen days after leaving the hospital he returned to have the stitches removed. The wound was dark pink and the doctor thought it best to leave them in a few more days. Henry persuaded Hamburger to remove the stitches when they returned to the house.

Henry had nearly eight hundred dollars put away and he asked Saul and Dan if either knew where he could buy a used pick-up at a reasonable price.

"There's a man comes in the club a couple of nights a week

that has a place off the highway," Saul answered. "I'll point him out to you the next time he comes in."

The following night Henry went to the club with Hamburger. They ended the night parked on the beach in the backseat of Hamburger's car. The following morning Saul handed Henry a business card while they were drinking their midmorning coffee. "This fellow said to come and see him and he'll fix you up with a truck."

Saul offered to give Henry a ride and an hour later Henry had purchased a 1966 Chevrolet half ton pick-up for five hundred dollars. The following morning he told the band he was leaving.

"Where you going?" Dan asked.

"To Oklahoma and see my grandmother. Maybe I'll run into yall at a Holiday Inn some night."

"Have you told Hamburger?"

"Not yet. I figured I'd call her tonight."

"Call when you get to Oklahoma and let us know you made it." Dan handed Henry a half ounce bag of marijuana.

Henry made the trip from Galveston to Joneston in under eleven hours. He hadn't been home an hour when Saul called.

"I was going to call you tomorrow," Henry said. "I figured yall would be out at the club tonight."

"Have you called Hamburger?"

"I was going to call her later."

"You're an asshole Henry. A real asshole."

"What did I do to piss you off? If it bothers you that much I'll call her now."

"That girl really cares about you Henry. When she came by this afternoon and found out you was gone she threw a fit. Nicole had to call a doctor she knew and they had to give her a sedative."

"Why the hell would she throw a fit over my leaving? I

barely knew her. I swear Saul I had no idea she'd take it like that."

"There's a lot you don't seem to know! But you should have had the courtesy to call her!"

"I'll call her goddamn it!" Henry lied and knew he was lying. He'd planned on calling her in a day or two but Saul's call had changed his mind. The last thing Henry wanted to hear was a hysterical woman.

CHAPTER NINETEEN

Henry was happy to see his grandmother again but he was surprised at how much she'd aged since he'd seen her last. Her hair had turned solid white, her face was thinner and she seemed to move a little slower. He felt guilty for not coming home more often and decided to stay in Oklahoma at least through the summer and possibly longer. A week later he was starting to get restless and decided to call Harvey Pike. No one answered at Harvey's so Henry called Eddy Creeley. Eddy invited him out to Walter Travish's fishing camp and Saturday morning Henry made the trip to the east side of Lake Milor. Eddy and Walter sat at a card table drinking coffee.

"Somebody said you were sailing the high seas," Walter commented.

"I was working my ass off on a shrimp boat."

"What happened?" Eddy asked. "You get homesick?"

Henry told them about the fight then asked about Harvey.

"That motherfucker's crazy," Walter answered. "Sticking anything he can get in his veins. Coke, meth, horse tranquilizer—if he can get it in a needle he'll stick it in his arm. If you're half smart you'll stay away from him. If you do see him don't bring him out here."

"He still got that girl with him?"

"You talking about Roni?" Eddy asked. "He broke her arm and she took off for parts unknown. He's threatened to kill her if he finds her. You can do what you want but Walter's right. If you got half a brain you'll stay away from him."

An hour later James Moon and Gary Mellons, two un-
employed construction workers, showed up at the camp with a
bottle of tequila. That afternoon more friends arrived and a col-
lection was taken. Henry and Eddy drove into town to a liquor
store and returned with four more quarts of tequila. Four days
later Henry returned to Joneston long enough to check on his
grandmother and grab a couple of changes of clothes.

Henry was broke. He took a job delivering furniture for
a local store and quit after the first paycheck then took a job
'swamping' a bar three days a week, Friday, Saturday and Sunday,
at thirty dollars a day. The job was fairly easy and he could set
his own hours as long as the bar was clean for the five p.m. opening. He spent most of his time at Walter's fishing camp drinking,
smoking and occasionally taking a woman out to spend a little
time in one of the three tents Walter had set up. Two or three
times a week he drove to Joneston to see his grandmother.

Henry and Eddy drove to Norman, Oklahoma one weekend to attend a Willie Nelson concert and visit with Jody Payne
and some of the other band members. A few weeks later he took
a young lady to a Willie Nelson show in Fort Worth. But Henry
was getting more and more restless. Then Saul called the fourth
of July. "I heard you'd quit playing Popeye. When you coming
to Albuquerque?"

"Let me think a minute. What have I lost in Albuquerque?
I can't think of a thing Saul."

"You might be happy to make the trip. They're filming a
movie here. I might get you a part in it. My roommate and I have
parts in it."

"How did you talk your way into a movie?"

"I can't answer that on the phone. You'll have to come to
Albuquerque. If you need money I'll send you the money."

"I've got money."

"When you leaving?"

"Monday."

Henry stopped at a service station in east Albuquerque and called the telephone number Saul had given him. He followed Saul's directions to an apartment building off West Central Boulevard and saw Saul standing on a third floor balcony. "Come on up! Apartment three twelve!"

Apartment three twelve looked big enough to Henry to park his truck in. The living room was spacious, the kitchen bigger than most entire apartments, three large bedrooms and a bathroom big enough for a small family to live in. Henry was given the bedroom to the right of the bathroom.

"The movie must pay pretty good Saul. You're not making pornography are you?"

"No, I'm sorry to disappoint you but it's not porno. They're filming a movie based on that C.W. McCall song, 'Convoy'. Sit down and I'll get your head right." Saul pulled a film canister from his shirt pocket and emptied it into four lines. Henry walked into the kitchen and returned with a Budweiser and dropped his two lines into the beer and drank it.

"My roommate Thad should be back soon. He knows you're driving in and wants to meet you."

"How did you hook up with a movie crew?" Henry asked.

"I can't tell you yet. I promised Thad I'd wait until you two met. I can tell you this though the movie's not paying for this apartment."

"Then you're dealing cocaine."

"I didn't say that!"

"You don't have to say it Saul. Anyone with a brain can figure it out. Remind me to not tell you any secrets I want kept. How much you sellin'?"

Before Saul could answer, the door opened and a stocky

man in his early thirties entered. Saul introduced Henry to his roommate Thad.

"Saul's told me about you," Thad said. "He told me how those Texas cowboys used to give you hell about your hair and how you bounced a few of 'em off the wall. Did Saul tell you what we got going?"

"He wouldn't tell me nothin'. You know how Saul is."

"Saul trusts you but I wanted to meet you first. We have parts in this Rubber Ducky movie driving trucks as part of the convoy. We got the parts because they sent a movie scout in to find a drug connection while they're filming here. Saul and I heard about it and figured we could sell it to them as easy as anyone else. I never dealt coke but I knew where to buy it. Saul knew how to deal it but didn't know where to get it. Now we're selling nearly more than we can handle. We're dealing as much as two ounces a day, a gram at a time, to the movie crew."

"How much a gram?" Henry asked.

"A hundred," Thad answered.

"That's twenty-eight hundred an ounce. What's an ounce cost you?"

"Between sixteen and eighteen hundred, depends on who we're dealing with."

"Two thousand a day. What would I get out of it?"

"A commission," Thad answered. "Ten dollars for every gram you deliver. There's no selling to it. They come to you. You'll sell at least twenty grams a day maybe more depending on how busy Saul and I are."

"Well what about it?" Saul asked. "Wanna hang around a while? We might be able to get you a part in the movie."

"You can keep your movie part. I don't like cameras pointed at me."

Thad left the apartment and returned a moment later with

a well-built lady in her late thirties wearing a T-shirt a size or two too small and a pair of denim shorts.

"Emily," Thad said, "this is Henry. He'll be staying with us awhile."

"Oh good," Emily cooed. "Now I have three men down the hall I can fuck when I want to."

A few minutes after seven the following morning a limousine pulled up to the apartment and Saul and Thad climbed in. Henry was invited to ride with them but chose to take his truck and follow the limousine to the movie's location. An hour later they arrived at a small town with less than two dozen buildings.

The town had been scouted and chosen for its old jail. Several years before a new jail had been built some distance away and the old jail was simply shut down and the doors locked. A scene in the movie called for Kris Kristofferson to drive his truck, the Rubber Duck, through the jail and rescue an old friend. EMI, the company producing the movie, had bought the old jail and cleaned it up. They'd also bought several more buildings they planned to demolish.

Kristofferson had filmed his part of the movie and returned to touring with his band. Ernest Borgnine, Burt Young and Ali McGraw were still on the set.

Saul introduced Henry to the associate producers, lighting and wardrobe personnel, stunt men, gofers and anyone else that used cocaine. He knew who would want two grams a day and who would want as many as five and he had the grams weighed out and in his pocket. When Saul and Thad were called to take their places in the trucks Saul handed Henry several packets of cocaine and told him, "Just hang around. When they want more they'll come to you."

Being called didn't mean you were being filmed anytime

soon. As the company filmed a scene with a multi-colored bus full of 'Jesus freaks' Saul and Thad sat and waited. By Henry's count Saul and Thad sat through six joints, a gram of cocaine and several beers while the 'Jesus freaks' rode back and forth on the highway singing at the top of their lungs the only gospel song everyone on the bus knew at least one verse of: We Shall Gather At The River. Two hours later they quit filming for the day and Saul and Thad crawled out of their trucks without having faced a camera the entire time.

Two weeks later Henry was bored with movie making. The money from cocaine was good but the standing around watching others stand around was occasionally depressing. Saul, on the other hand, was convinced he could be the next Paul Newman if only given a chance. He chased Ali, Burt, Ernest and several more all over the site trying to get them to listen to the movie ideas he had that were guaranteed to be a hit especially if he had a starring role. They started dodging every time they saw him approaching and soon Henry's greatest daily amusement was watching everyone avoid Saul.

The nights were good. Emily was a constant visitor making herself available at anytime to anyone and Thad brought at least one new woman home nearly every night and anyone he brought home returned. Cocaine, whiskey and sex were like a magnet to several young women.

Elvis was dead. That night Henry, Saul and Thad mourned in a way they believed the King would appreciate: with a few ladies, several grams of cocaine and countless 'long live the King' toasts.

Filming ended in October and EMI threw a 'wrap up' party at the Hilton Inn. Henry woke up the next morning in a strange room with a young lady he didn't remember meeting.

The cocaine dealing continued. They lost the majority of

their customers when the film crew left town but during the time the crew was in town they also acquired a number of local customers. No customer was allowed at the apartment. When someone wanted cocaine they called the apartment and Henry, Saul or Thad would meet them in the parking lot of the Hilton Inn. No customer knew where the dealer lived.

The 'Grateful Dead' were in town for a concert and Saul had received a call earlier that a few of the 'roadies' wanted cocaine. Saul had a lady on the way over and Thad and Emily were 'entertaining' a local coed from the University of New Mexico. Henry volunteered to make the delivery.

The 'roadie' was waiting at the back door of the auditorium with the money and five minutes later Henry was back in his pick-up and on his way home.

He saw the lights from the police cars a block before he reached the apartment. He took the next left and parked in back of the apartments then walked around toward the front staying in the shadows until he could see the apartment. Police were everywhere. The front door was wide open and he could see Saul sitting on the floor near the door with his hands cuffed behind his back. He could see a pair of pretty legs on the balcony and assumed it was either Emily or the coed.

Henry walked back to his pick-up, started the motor and turned toward Oklahoma. There was nothing he could do for Saul, Thad or either lady. He was leaving a new hat, new boots and all his clothes, except what he was wearing, and a thousand dollars hidden in a pair of socks in a drawer. He had nearly eight hundred dollars in his wallet and another six hundred in his shirt pocket from the sale of the cocaine to the roadies.

Henry made the trip to Joneston in twelve hours looking over his shoulder most of the time. He knew Saul and Thad would never give his name to the law but he wasn't sure about the women. He wasn't sure if there was anything in the apartment with his name on it or not but he knew over the years he'd given several copies of his lyrics to Saul.

Henry crossed into Texas expecting roadblocks to be set up and waiting for him at the state line. A few hours later he crossed into Oklahoma and wanted to get out and hug the earth. He spent two days at Lahoma's watching the road for lawmen. On the third day he decided to leave for Galveston and find work at sea. He stopped for the night in Freeport, Texas and rented a room at the Schooner Inn then walked out to the lobby and bought a copy of the Texas City Sun newspaper to check the local television listings. Back in his room he rolled a joint and decided to check the want ads and found an advertisement for a Merchant Seaman to work for a shipping company.

The following morning he called the number in the advertisement and was invited to put in an application at their home office in Port Arthur. Two hours later he was in the office of the Trinity Oil and Towing Company filling out the paper work. The following morning he was sent to a doctor's office for a physical and that afternoon was told to report to the Captain of the oil tanker S.S. Voyles. He had applied for a job as deck hand but was assigned a room and told to report to the galley cook at five a.m. with the promise that as soon as an opening became available with the deck crew he would be transferred.

The S.S. Voyles was a twenty year old oil tanker that had originally belonged to Mobil Oil. The four hundred foot ship was what seamen commonly called a 'rust bucket'. More rust than paint covered the tanker. He asked a dock hand if his pickup would be safe on the docks. He was told no one would bother his truck but the battery would be down before he returned. "There's a boat repair shop a couple of blocks west," the dock hand said. "For a hundred a month they'll park your truck and start it once a week to keep your battery up." Henry drove his truck to the shop then returned to the ship. He spent the next hour walking around getting acquainted with his new home. That evening he walked to a telephone booth near the dock and called his grandmother.

Henry's starting salary was sixteen hundred dollars a month with a dollar and a dime a day deducted from his pay for room and board. A new hand was expected to stay aboard four months before taking his first leave. After the first leave you were only required to stay three months to request leave. Each month spent aboard ship earned ten days paid leave.

Henry's duties were helping the cook serve the men their meals then cleaning the kitchen and galley. The rest of the time he could do as he pleased. The ship had a 'no drinking on board ship' policy and hard liquor was strictly forbidden but beer was tolerated as long as a man was discreet and could still do his work. Henry was also pleased to learn there were several marijuana smokers among the forty crew members.

The ship sailed a week later for an oil refinery near Santa Isabela, Puerto Rico. They stayed four days and Henry hated leaving the little fishing village. From Puerto Rico they sailed to Aruba for three days and Henry seriously considered quitting the ship and becoming a beach bum. They then sailed for Free-port, Bahamas for four days then north to New York, then Boston, Philadelphia, Charleston, Jacksonville and Miami. Henry didn't meet a port he didn't like.

Henry had resented working in the galley when he first came aboard but soon determined it was one of the better jobs on ship. The deck crew had to stand quarterdeck watches, even in port. That meant they had to leave whatever they were doing on shore and report back at a certain time and be sober or close to it. Henry had all night from around six p.m. to five a.m. to report back to ship.

When the ship reached Miami Henry had been aboard forty-two days and he requested leave. Four days later the leave was approved and Henry caught a cab for the airport. That night his plane touched down in Beaumont, Texas and he caught a cab to the bus depot. He was in Port Arthur before noon and in his truck and on the road to Oklahoma an hour later.

Henry met Eddy and Walter at Misty's early Saturday evening. They had two beers each then drove to the Beer Barrel to hear a local band called T.B. and the Lungers. They hadn't been in the bar thirty minutes until a fight broke out. Henry didn't know who started the fight but he wound up in a corner hitting anyone that came near him. It took several men to pull Eddy off John, the bar owner's son, and the three friends left the bar minutes before the police arrived. They drove back to Misty's and within an hour the news of the fight had reached the crowd at Misty's and the three men learned they were barred from the Beer Barrel.

Sunday afternoon they returned to the Beer Barrel thinking tempers would have cooled and they'd be welcomed back. Eddy and Walter were allowed back inside but Henry wasn't. Someone had given the owner's wife a black eye and she claimed it was Henry. He didn't remember hitting her, he didn't believe in hitting women, but he had to admit he might have hit her in all the confusion and not known it. The three drove to Ellery's and sat at the bar drinking beer. Eddy started laughing.

"I'm glad you think it's funny," Henry said.

"I think it's funny you got barred for something you're not sure you did."

"Hell, I don't even know what started it."

"I know what started it," Walter answered. "It started when Eddy punched out John."

Henry grinned and shook his head. "I take it you had a reason to punch him out."

"The best reason in the world. I wanted to. I've been wanting to smack that counterfeit son-of-a-bitch for a long time."

Henry spent the next three weeks at the fishing camp during the day and the bars during the night. He tried to spend a respectable amount of time with his grandmother and was embarrassed by the little time he did spend with her.

He received his vacation pay, more than twenty-one hundred dollars, a week before he was due to return to work.

The Beer Barrel was having a party that Saturday night featuring several bands and discounted prices on beer and drinks. Ladies would be admitted free and everyone Henry knew planned to attend. He felt sure he'd be allowed back in the bar but word came back to him quickly that he wouldn't be allowed to attend and if he "showed his hare-lip" anywhere near the premises he'd be arrested. Even the band couldn't change the owner's mind.

"I wore the knees out on a pair of pants trying to get him to let you back in as a favor to Eddy," T.B. told him. "He'll let Walter in and he'll let Eddy in but he says he'd shoot you on sight."

"Everyone in five counties will be there," Henry commented.

"Not everyone," T.B. laughed. "It don't appear that you'll be there."

Henry was going to attend the party at the Beer Barrel. He didn't know how but he made up his mind he'd find a way. It was either that or spend a long Saturday night alone on a bar stool waiting for the party to break up.

Saturday afternoon Henry was sitting at the fishing camp

drinking beer with Eddy and Walter when Chop Halfditch, the harmonica player for the Lungers, and his girlfriend, Rita Ballou, drove into camp. A few minutes later the subject turned to the upcoming party.

"Maybe if I wore a false beard or somethin'," Henry said, "maybe they wouldn't recognize me. Wear a different hat and clothes."

"What do you plan on doing with your hair?" Chop asked. "You've got the longest hair of any man around here. Your hair will give you away. You'd have to dress up like a woman to get away with it."

"Why not dress him like a woman?" Rita asked. "I could get Jan and Anne to help me. I'll bet one of them has a dress he can wear and a little make-up will cover his lip."

Eddy, Walter and Chop told her she was crazy. Henry liked the idea.

"We'd better get started," Rita said. "It's almost two and the band starts at nine. If you want to do this we'll go see if Jan and Anne are home and meet the others later."

Henry drove Rita to the apartment of the Fisher sisters, Jan and Anne. When Rita told them what she and Henry were planning they both insisted on helping any way they could. "Just don't let me get in the line of fire tonight," Jan said.

The girls started at the top, washing Henry's hair then putting it in rollers. Then they pierced Henry's ears and inserted two circular gold studs. They next shaved his underarms and then his legs from the knees down. They were picking out the underwear when Chop and Roaring Rob, the bands guitarist, arrived at the apartment. Both men started laughing at the sight of Henry in his underwear, legs shaven and hair in rollers. "You're gonna be one ugly woman," Roaring Rob commented.

A couple of joints and a fair amount of Crown Royal later

and the two men left for the Beer Barrel to set up their equipment.

Henry took a shower and put on one of the sister's bathrobes. The next hour was devoted to teaching Henry how to walk in low-heeled pumps. Then Henry's eyebrows were plucked and make-up applied. Make-up cake and lipstick were used to conceal the small indentation in the center of his top lip. He donned a pair of panty hose and a small hand towel was placed in the seat of the panty hose to give Henry more ass. A bra was strapped on and the cups stuffed with wash cloths. A red dress had been chosen for his evening ensemble and he was zipped into the dress and the bra adjusted. The rollers were removed and his now curly hair was combed and styled, to cover part of his face, and sprayed. Henry looked in the mirror at the tacky earrings, red dress, red purse and red shoes and commented, "All I need now is a pimp." They'd spent nearly four hours getting him ready.

Rita, Jan and Anne showered and were dressed and ready by eight p.m. They decided it would be best to wait until there was a crowd at the club before trying to get Henry in. They waited until after ten p.m. before leaving the apartment in Jan's car. When they arrived at the Beer Barrel Jan pulled a pair of lady's horn-rimmed glasses from her purse and told Henry to wear them until they got inside. They followed four other women through the bar's entrance and found a table in the corner. Two local ladies sat on one side of the table and Henry took a seat facing the band and the crowd. Rita, Jan and Anne sat across the table from the other two ladies and to anyone entering the club it appeared Henry was with the other women and not with Rita, Jan and Anne.

During the band's first break Chop and Roaring Rob came

over to the table. They couldn't quit snickering and Rita finally told them both to leave the table before they gave Henry away.

Eddy and Walter entered the bar forty-five minutes later, spotted Rita and the Fisher sisters and took a seat at a table on the other side of the club. Walter walked over to their table and stood near Anne. An empty chair was all that separated Henry and Walter and Walter didn't recognize him. "Where's Henry? What'd he do? Wimp out? I don't blame him. He'd never have gotten away with it. I guess I can tell Eddy it's safe to move around. Henry threatened to do something to repay Eddy for getting him barred. He's sitting over there scared to death Henry's gonna walk over in a dress and grab his balls or something."

T.B. and the Lungers played their last song of the set then left the stage to let another band take their turn. Chop walked over to the table where Eddy sat and leaned over and whispered in his ear while pointing in Henry's direction. When Walter arrived back at the table Eddy pointed toward Henry and both men started laughing. Henry saw John, the club owner's son, a few feet away watching Eddy's table. A few minutes later John left the club.

Henry had been at the club for three hours consuming drinks bought by horny 'cowboys' who thought the strange lady in the red dress was cute. His bladder was full but he didn't have the nerve to use the ladies room and he sure couldn't use the men's.

Bill Mitchell, an old friend of Henry's from Joneston, not knowing the true identity of the lady in red, and getting drunker by the minute, had bought Henry a number of drinks and asked him each time to dance. Henry had turned him down each time but since the bar would be closing soon and Henry knew how to two step backwards and Bill had been such a gentleman he decided to have one dance with him. They danced to the Kitchen Pickers rendition of 'From A Jack To A King' and after the dance ended Bill bowed slightly, tipped his hat and said "Thank you ma'am."

"You're welcome Bill," Henry replied. Bill recognized Henry and his eyes got as big as saucers but Henry didn't have to worry about his old friend giving him away. Bill was too embarrassed. "You tell anyone about this," Bill warned, "and I'll cut ya'. I'll cut ya' from asshole to ankles. I swear to God I will."

Henry smiled and whispered, "It'll be our little secret Bill."

Henry walked back to his table. The three ladies were standing and ready to leave. Henry picked up his purse and followed the women outside. John was walking back inside as they walked across the parking lot. A moment later he ran out the door and caught them at the car. "Hey hare-lip!" He yelled. Henry turned and faced him. John outweighed Henry by forty pounds or better and Henry was wearing a dress. "I'm gonna whip your rabbit ass!"

Henry held up his hand, bent at the wrist and tried to sound feminine. "Why John are you mad at little ole me?"

Before John could answer a voice behind him asked, "You wouldn't hit a woman would you fat boy?"

John's face turned white. He was unaware Eddy and Walter had followed him outside and were standing behind him. "This is none of your business Creeley."

"I'm making it my business," Eddy told him.

"Why don't you let the fuckin' hare-lip fight his own fight?"

"Cause he's Walter's date." Eddy couldn't make the remark without laughing and soon everyone but John was laughing.

"Fuck all of you," John said, walking back toward the club.

"I'll see to it that none of you get back in here again and I'm gonna have the hare-lip arrested!"

"Well this is another fine mess you've gotten us into," Walter teased, doing his best Stan Laurel imitation. "Where should we go now?"

"It's just a little after one. We could go to Ellery's," Henry suggested.

"Don't you want to change clothes first?" Eddy asked.

"Ellery's would be closed by the time I changed and got back out. Besides I've already ruined a pair of panty hose."

Less than a dozen people, including Ellery and the bartender, were at the club. Henry had to piss more than ever and once inside the club he walked straight to the men's room. Two 'cowboys' were standing at the trough shaped urinal and Henry stepped up to the trough between them, lifted his dress, pulled down the front of his panty hose and started pissing. The 'cowboys' pissed all over their legs and most of the walls trying to get their penises back in their pants and exit the men's room at the same time. Henry walked out of the men's room and found everyone staring at him including Ava, a lady he'd dated several months earlier. Eddy, Walter, Rita, Jan and Anne were sitting at the bar talking to Ellery. Ellery was shaking his head, laughing and mumbling, "I don't believe it. I just fuckin' don't believe it." Henry walked over to where Ava sat with two other women and asked if he could buy her a drink. Ava stood and screamed, "Get away from me you sick son-of-a-bitch! You're crazy! You need help!" Ava grabbed her purse and started for the door. "I never want to see you again you sick bastard!"

Henry couldn't resist. "I guess a head job's out of the question?"

"Fuck you Henry you sick son-of-a-bitch!"

Henry sat down at the bar next to Jan and asked, "Is that any way to talk to a lady?"

Ellery's closed at two a.m. and the crowd drove over to Jan's so Henry could change his clothes. A few minutes later he left for Joneston taking the back roads. He'd scrubbed as much make-up off his face as he could but he knew he hadn't gotten it all off and he'd had too much to drink to try and explain it to a state trooper.

Henry crawled out of bed shortly after ten a.m. He heard his grandmother talking and laughing with someone in the kitchen and when he walked in he saw her drinking coffee with Sheriff Wesley.

"Here's my little granddaughter now." Lahoma and the sheriff were grinning. "Lydell was just telling me the strangest story about a man in Hardmor that runs around in a dress." Lahoma and the sheriff started laughing.

"You're not mad?" Henry asked.

"Of course I'm not mad but the sheriff knows someone that is."

"Henry," the sheriff had his head down trying to stop grinning and look serious, "I got a call from Chief Collins in Hardmor wanting you arrested. Dan McDonald, the owner of the Beer Barrel, woke him up this morning complaining about you. I know you did it as a joke but this McDonald character isn't laughing. I told him I'd have a talk with you and you wouldn't go back to the Beer Barrel. Collins says McDonald intends to shoot you if you come on his property again. Collins told Mac-Donald if he didn't want to shoot you to call him and he'd come out there and shoot you himself. Do you understand what I'm saying? Stay out of the Beer Barrel."

"Do you have the dress you wore?" Lahoma asked.

"I gave it back to Jan. Why do you ask?"

"I thought you'd model it for Lydel and me." Lahoma and the sheriff started laughing.

CHAPTER TWENTY

Henry left for Port Arthur the following day. He took a room at the American Inn and the next morning drove his pick-up to the boat repair shop then walked two blocks east to the home office of Trinity Oil and Towing. He was told his ship, the S.S. Voyles, would arrive in Philadelphia the following day and would be in port for four days before sailing for Miami. Henry was on a plane to Pennsylvania before dark and in Philadelphia before the bars closed. The S.S. Voyles sailed the same course every time with little variation, spending the majority of the time in the Caribbean. Henry was soon wearing sandals, denim cut-offs, T-shirt and a blue derby he'd purchased in Puerto Rico. He didn't need warm clothing until they were on the east coast during the winter months.

Henry didn't take his leave three months later opting instead to take his vacation pay and continue working. Six months and three days after boarding the ship in Philadelphia Henry applied for leave. Leave was granted when the ship arrived in a snow covered New York City the first week in February. He left his derby, cut-offs and T-shirts aboard ship and went shopping for winter clothing purchasing a gray ankle length cashmere coat, two gray vests, four solid colored flannel shirts with banded collars and a new Stetson fedora. He caught a cab to the airport and the following afternoon was in his pick-up and on the road to Oklahoma stopping near Grainsley at a western clothing store and buying four pairs of Wrangler jeans and a new pair of boots. A few days later Henry met a former homecoming queen ten years younger than him named Leah Scragg. Henry knew her father, John Scragg, from the small bar John owned on Commerce Street in Hardmor called the Derrick Club. The two men had always gotten along until Henry started dating his daughter. Now he was making it clear to anyone in earshot that he didn't want a long-haired, hare-lipped seaman, particularly one named Ridge, dating daddy's little girl.

Leah liked money and downers, particularly Quaaludes and Valium. Henry took her shopping during the day and bought her drugs in the bars when they went out at night. A few days before he was due to return to the ship she told him she'd fallen in love with him and would wait faithfully for his return. It was all Henry could do to keep from laughing. He didn't believe or expect any girl to wait a week, let alone three months, for his return. Leah was too pretty and too popular to sit at home while her friends partied.

On his next leave she told him she was pregnant. She swore there was only one other man besides Henry who might be the father and the other man had made it clear he didn't want the baby. Leah broke down in the motel room and started crying uncontrollably.

"I don't know what to do," she sobbed. "It's too late for an abortion and Richard won't marry me and daddy hates your guts. I don't know what I'm going to do."

Henry had spent his life following one rule. When he came to a point where he had to make a difficult decision he always asked himself one question. What would Charlie do? Then Henry did the exact opposite. Charlie had never married Erica, Henry's mother, or admitted Henry was his son. Henry in turn had always denied that Charlie was his father. If Henry was the father he didn't want the baby to grow up being called a bastard.

Two weeks later they were married at the Lake Milor Chapel. Lahoma, several members of Leah's family and a few of Henry's friends attended. Leah wore a white dress and her stomach was already protruding enough to make it difficult for Eddy and Walter to refrain from laughing. The reception was held at the Derrick Club where Henry got quite drunk and tried to ignore the 'drop dead and go to hell' looks John Scraggs gave him.

The marriage was in trouble from the start. Leah's mother had found a house for the couple to live in less than two blocks from her house and John Scragg had already arranged for Henry to go to work in the oil fields as a roughneck. Henry informed both parents that he had no intention of quitting his job with Trinity Oil and Towing and only agreed to live in the house until after the baby was born. Henry returned to his job and four months later received a letter telling him he had a daughter named Anna Marie. He requested leave and returned to Oklahoma to meet his daughter.

Henry had entered into the marriage thinking that if the marriage didn't work out he wouldn't suffer any heartache. He liked Leah but knew that living without her wouldn't be difficult. He assumed he'd feel the same way toward the baby girl.

But Henry was wrong. One look at Anna Marie Ridge and he was hooked. He loved the girl as soon as he laid eyes on her. He didn't give a damn if Leah had fucked every man in the state. This was his daughter. This girl would have his name. Lahoma loved Anna as much as Henry did. They spent the next three weeks showing her to everyone they could and for the first time in years he regretted leaving Oklahoma. The month had been too short. He kissed his wife and his perfect daughter and drove to Port Arthur.

Three months later Henry requested leave as soon as he'd accumulated enough days at sea. He arrived home two days before Christmas with a stuffed, life-sized donkey. Anna started crying as soon as Henry carried it inside the house and wouldn't stop crying until he carried the stuffed animal outside and sat it on a garbage can.

Snow fell the following night and continued for two days. The weather was too cold to take his daughter walking or visiting friends. Henry played in the floor with Anna for most of the month until he left for Port Arthur the third week in January.

Henry waited until early afternoon before leaving planning to stop at a motel around dark. Ten hours later he was less than a hundred miles from Port Arthur and had already decided to drive on in. The highway was deserted and even though it was well past midnight he wasn't particularly tired.

Henry didn't see the quarter ton delivery truck until it went around him at a high rate of speed then pulled back in front of his truck, locking the delivery truck's back bumper with the front bumper on Henry's truck. He didn't remember anything else until he woke up with his pick-up laying on his right leg and two ambulance attendants telling him to lie still and remain calm.

Henry saw a bone sticking out of his left boot and his right leg was pinned beneath the side of the pick-up's bed. He didn't feel any pain and he knew he should be feeling something. He felt like he could hop away if he could free his right leg.

"What did you give me?" Henry asked the female attendant.

"Nothing," she answered, "you're in shock."

Henry started trying to pull his right leg free. The male attendant stopped him. "You're doing more damage to your leg," he said.

A fire truck arrived and the ground around the truck was watered as they drained the gas from Henry's truck. After the gas was diluted enough to prevent it from igniting a cutting torch was rolled over near where Henry lay and the section pinning his leg was cut from the truck and lifted off. He was taken by ambulance to a Bay City hospital and carried to the nearest emergency room. A doctor handed him a clipboard and asked him to sign the top form. "We may have to amputate both legs to save your life," the doctor told him. Henry signed the form.

For the next three days Henry was in and out of consciousness. He awoke the fourth day laying in bed in a cast from the waist down. He raised his head to see if he still had his legs. Both legs were in a cast and the right leg had a dozen or so metal rods protruding from the knee to the ankle. The two ambulance attendants were standing at the foot of the bed.

"I remember yall", Henry said. "Thank you for what you did last night."

"You mean four nights ago don't you?" The male attendant asked. Both attendants were smiling. "You've been out of it."

"I hope I wasn't any trouble to you. I know I got you out in the middle of the night."

"Don't apologize please. We were just doing our job."

"You sure you didn't give me a shot of somethin' ?"

"Your brain did that," the female attendant answered. "We called your wife. She said she'd try to get here to see you."

"If she can't get here in four days she's not coming. Would you please call my grandmother?"

""If you'd like to call her yourself they'll bring you a telephone but you'll have to ask them for one."

Henry was transferred by ambulance to a charity hospital. The building was old and infested with bugs and mice. A new hospital was under construction and the older hospital would be closed upon completion. He was placed in a ward on the fourth floor with five other men. Most were there for minor injuries. Four had torn ligaments or tendons and one had damaged his knee cap. All five were bikers.

The nurse brought Henry a bed pan and placed it on the night stand near the bed. Henry looked around and knew he'd never be able to use the thing. A few minutes later Dr. Martin and Dr. Pollack came into the ward and went from bed to bed discussing each chart and talking with each patient.

"You're a lucky man," Dr. Pollack told him as he stood at the end of Henry's bed and read his chart. "Dr. Goodwin built you a right leg. Don't get too attached to it though. You'll most likely lose it within the year. And you may be in a wheelchair for awhile."

"You can keep your wheelchair doc. I'll be dancin' the two-step in six months."

"I like your attitude," Dr. Martin said.

"I'd like to talk to you about that bed pan doc. I don't think I can use it. I've noticed a couple of walkers in here and I was wondering if I'd be allowed to use a walker and go to the bathroom instead of trying to squat in bed."

Dr. Pollack looked over at Dr. Martin and Henry saw Dr. Martin nod slightly. "If you think you can manage a walker then I'll tell the nurse to bring you one when you want it."

Henry's cast covered him from his waist to the soles of his feet with a section cut out in back for body functions. He could see the stitches from the corner of his eye on the left side of his face and he could feel stitches on the right side of his neck. He'd asked to see a mirror but the nurse refused to bring him one.

"You don't want to see your face honey," she told him. "Take my word for it. I'll bring you a mirror in a few days."

It took more than half an hour for Henry to inch the walker to the bathroom less than twenty-five feet away. He closed the door and lowered himself on the toilet seat and wiggled around until he felt he could have a bowel movement without making a mess. He looked around the room hoping he'd see a mirror. The room had only a sink and a toilet.

Mike Roach, a Houston attorney, visited Henry that afternoon. Henry had no idea who'd sent the lawyer to him but he was glad they had. Thirty minutes later He signed his name to a document allowing Attorney Roach to pursue a lawsuit against the delivery company that owned the truck responsible for injuring Henry.

Henry spent more and more time on the walker. His wallet, bandana and pocket change had been sent with him and placed in the night stand next to his bed. He wore the bandana around his head Indian fashion to keep his long hair out of his way as he tried to maneuver the walker farther and farther from his bed.

He never saw his hat or duffel bag again.

Henry was on the walker inching his way to the hall with the intention of finding out how far they'd let him roam before bringing him back. At the door to the ward he peeked out in the hall and saw a young black man mopping the floor. The man looked at Henry and asked, "What's up Geronimo?"

"The name's Henry. I'm just taking an afternoon walk."

"My name's Carl and it looks like you're doing more dragging than walking. Why don't you ask them for a wheelchair? They'll bring you one if you ask."

"I've always heard that once you get in a wheelchair you stay there." Henry looked at Carl's eyes. They were bloodshot. Carl was high on something. "Could I talk to you for a minute?"

"Hey we're talking now ain't we?"

"I was wondering if you could get me some pot. I'll make it worth your while."

Carl jerked his head up and stepped back away from Henry. "Man I don't fuck with that shit. That shit'll get me fired."

"Carl I know you can tell by looking at me that I'm not a narc and I can tell by looking at you that you're high on something. If you can get me an ounce of pot I'll buy you an ounce for your trouble."

Carl looked in both directions down the hall, leaned on his mop a minute and then said, "That shit's expensive. I'm not saying I can get any but if I could I'd have to have the cash first."

"I'll give you the money now."

"Let me think about it bro. I know where your bed is."

Carl came by Henry's bunk a few minutes after three p.m. Henry pulled the drape around his bed so the others wouldn't be able to see him giving Carl the money.

"It's thirty dollars an ounce," Carl whispered. "You still buying me an ounce?"

"I said I would. Can you pick me up a couple of more things? I need some rolling papers and a box of cigars."

"What kind of cigars?" Carl asked.

"Anything that stinks."

The man on Henry's left had shattered his knee cap when he wrecked his motorcycle on a two lane highway with too much gravel to take a curve at eighty-five miles an hour. He'd been operated on the day Henry arrived at the ward and had been given morphine every four hours for pain. The first few days he'd sleep for three hours after being given a shot then scream for a shot for the last hour. The nurse told him time and again that the screaming did nothing but bother the other patients and he could scream till hell froze over and he still wouldn't get a shot but every four hours. And he still screamed. A few days later he was sleeping two hours then screaming two. Today he'd slept an hour and screamed for three.

The biker had a pretty red-headed wife named Terri that he verbally abused at every opportunity. Terri came by every day and stayed until late at night. One night during one of the rare moments her husband wasn't screaming Henry told her, "You know that's the drugs talking don't you."

"That's not the drugs," she whispered, watching her husband for any sign he wasn't asleep. "He's that way all the time."

"Why do you put up with it?" Henry asked. "I know men who'd cut their arm off to have a lady like you."

"I'm not putting up with it anymore. As soon as he's out of the hospital I'm going back to Shreveport."

Henry woke up around three in the morning and saw Terri performing oral sex on her husband. Before Henry could look away Terri turned and saw him watching. She continued as though Henry had never seen her and Henry continued watching.

Two days later the biker had gotten on enough nerves to be transferred to another ward. His knee was doing fine but now they had to wean him off the morphine. Terri handed Henry a small slip of paper before she pushed her husband's wheelchair out of the ward. Henry looked at the paper and saw a telephone number for Shreveport.

Carl delivered the marijuana, cigars and rolling papers a few minutes after 6 a.m. "Man you need anything else you let me know."

"You'll be the first. I know you took a chance and I appreciate it."

Henry pulled the drapes around his bed and rolled five joints. He asked aloud if anyone wanted to get high and four patients answered yes. He threw each man a joint then he threw each man a cigar to smoke and hide the odor.

Henry had just finished a joint when the courier arrived with the large manila envelope and asked Henry to sign his name at the bottom of a form on a clipboard. Henry opened the envelope and read the papers from a lawyer named Clark Jameson stating he was representing Leah Ridge and Henry was being sued for divorce. Henry puffed on his cigar a moment then lit another joint.

Three weeks and three days after arriving at the hospital the doctors informed him he could be released if he had anyone to assist him at home. He knew his grandmother would be happy to take care of him but he also knew she couldn't make the trip to Houston to get him. She could barely find her way around Mayetta. Henry called Eddy that evening and Eddy agreed to drive to Houston and get him but he couldn't make the trip until Saturday, two days away. Henry told him he'd call him later collect and tell him what motel room he'd be in. He had no intention of staying in the hospital any longer than he had to. He told the doctor he had relatives in Houston he could stay with until his ride from Oklahoma picked him up. To his surprise the doctor believed him. The following morning he was rolled outside with a set of crutches and his personal belongings sitting across his lap to a waiting taxi. He told the driver to take him to a cheap motel that didn't have rats and only a limited number of bugs. He rented a room for two nights at the Gulf View Motel. The place was cheap enough, sixteen dollars a night and Henry didn't see any rats and only a few dozen or so roaches but the wall near his bed had a large hole that he was sure wasn't man made. He ordered a pizza delivered to his room then called his lawyer in Houston and told him he was out of the hospital and would be at his grandmother's home in a few days. The lawyer assured him they'd keep in touch. He then spent the rest of the day eating pizza and trying to watch television and the hole in the wall near his bed at the same time. That night he shoved as much of a pillow as he could into the hole and tried to sleep. Henry had paid for the room until Sunday morning and wasn't expecting Eddy until late Saturday night but Eddy and Walter arrived shortly after nine a.m. Saturday morning. The two men had left a couple of hours after Eddy had gotten off work and had borrowed Chop's car then driven all night to Houston. They made him a bed in the back seat, stealing a pillow from the motel, then started back to Oklahoma. While Henry slept most of the way they rotated the driving, catching naps in the passenger seat. Ten hours later they were at Lahoma's and Henry was carried inside. Eddy and Walter stayed a few minutes then announced they were both going home to get some sleep. They promised they'd see Henry the following day.

Henry had left the hospital wearing the same thin pants and gown the hospital had given him. The following morning Lahoma made him breakfast then informed him she'd be going out for an hour or so. She returned two hours later with four sets of gray sweat pants. The casts and the rods protruding through his legs made it impossible to wear his wranglers. Later that day she made him a pair of gray leather 'booties' to wear over the casts on his feet.

Eddy and Walter came by late that afternoon with a bottle of Old Bushmill and a twelve pack of Coors. A few minutes later Chop and T.B. came by with another twelve pack on their way to the Buzzard's Roost, a local bar near the river, to pick and sing for all the beer the band could drink.

"Why don't ya'll come out to the Roost?" Chop asked.

"I'd rather not," Henry answered. "I'd just as soon nobody sees me this way."

"You're going to be that way for a while," T.B. commented. "You planning on hiding out here until you heal? Everybody in the county knows about your wreck."

"Give me a few days to get used to these crutches then maybe I'll come out and hear yall."

T.B. leaned over and whispered something in Chop's ear and Henry saw Chop nod his head up and down. "Mrs. Ridge!" T. B. yelled, "We're taking Henry with us for a while if that's okay with you!"

Lahoma came to the door and answered, "That's fine. I think it'll do him a world of good."

Chop picked Henry up like a new bride and carried him to the car and placed him in the back seat. "Eddy, Walter, you coming with us?" he asked.

"We'll follow you," Eddy answered.

T.B. laid Henry's crutches in the back seat with him then climbed into the passenger seat. At the bar Chop carried Henry in and sat him at a table with Eddy and Walter. Henry asked for his crutches.

"You won't need them," Chop replied. "One of us will carry you anywhere you want to go."

"What if I need to piss?"

"We'll carry you to the men's room."

"You do that a couple of times and we'll be the talk of the county."

Chop brought Henry his crutches.

The following Monday Henry gathered his medical records and Lahoma drove him to the Veteran's Hospital in Oklahoma City. He'd called a couple of days earlier and they'd given him an appointment for nine a.m. The trip took nearly two hours one way and once they reached the city and Lahoma found herself in bumper to bumper traffic Henry started having doubts they'd make it. His grandmother drove fifty-five and was a nervous wreck, often staying in the passing lane while others cursed as they sped around her and she slowed down to a crawl when she had to change lanes to reach an exit. They reached the hospital more than two hours after leaving Joneston and while Henry sat in a chair Lahoma gave the lady at the counter his name. Lahoma was told to take a seat and Henry's name would be called soon. Henry used part of the time filling out an application for disability and more than seven hours later, at a few minutes before five p.m., he was called in to see a doctor.

The doctor took his records, asked a couple of questions then told him to make an appointment to return in a month. He was out in less than ten minutes. The return trip, with Lahoma driving, was as nerve racking as the earlier trip had been.

A few days later a new Cadillac pulled into Lahoma's drive and a handsome man in his late sixties got out and walked toward the front porch. The man wore a white hat with a three inch brim and a cattleman's crease, ostrich quill boots and a tailored, western cut, tan suit. Henry had seen him from a distance several times and knew he was a customer of his grandmother's. He tried to stay out of the way when his grandmother was with a customer but today she called him into her sewing room.

"Henry this is Charles Murray. He's an attorney."

"Proud to meet you sir," Henry said, shaking the man's hand.

"Your grandmother tells me you need a lawyer."

"I do but did she tell you I'm kinda broke at the moment?"

"I didn't say anything about money. You can pay me when you get it. When's the last time you saw your wife?"

"January twenty-six."

"You have a daughter too I'm told."

"Yessir."

"Have you tried to see her?"

"No sir."

"Why not? Don't you want to see her?"

"I'd give my eyeteeth to see her but as long as I'm in this cast I can't take care of her properly and I don't want to burden my grandmother."

"Lahoma did you tell him it would be a burden to help him with his daughter?"

Henry received a letter in the mail notifying him that the Veteran's Administration had approved his disability and he would receive four hundred and ninety dollars a month until the doctor released him or he had a job.

Two weeks later Henry and his attorney went to court while Lahoma stayed home. They arrived at the courthouse several minutes early and were already seated when his wife Leah walked in accompanied by her mother, her lawyer and her new boyfriend, Ronnie Woodson, a drug dealer Henry had met briefly at Ellery's a few months earlier.

Leah's lawyer, Clark Jameson had a reputation for trading his legal services for sex with some of his poorer clients. Henry had heard from several women how Clark would make a 'date' with a female client then park down the street from their house at the appointed time and flash his headlights off and on until the woman came out to the car and climbed in the passenger side. Henry wondered who was paying Clark's legal fees—the drug dealer or Leah. He wouldn't have given a rat's ass either way if his daughter hadn't been in the middle.

Henry's crutches lay behind him, out of sight, against the waist-high petition that divided the court room, separating the general audience from the lawyers' tables and the judge's bench.

Henry took the stand, raised his right hand and swore to tell the truth. The judge asked several questions and took notes concerning Henry's medical condition and his income. Then Clark Jameson questioned Henry.

"When was the last time you saw your wife Mr. Ridge?"

"The day of my wreck, January 26th."

"You haven't talked to her since then?"

"I spoke with her on the phone trying to see my daughter but I haven't met with her in person."

"So you haven't been by the house at all since January 26th?"

"That's right."

Clark Jameson called Mrs. H. A. Scragg to the stand. Leah's mother raised her right hand and swore to tell the truth.

"Mrs. Scragg when was the last time you saw Mr. Ridge?"

"Two nights ago when he came to the door and he demanded to see his daughter. I told him she was asleep and asked him to come back later."

"What did he say or do then?"

"He called me a lying whore and then he hit me."

"After he hit you what did he do?"

"He took off running."

"No more questions."

Charles Murray stood and asked Henry's mother-in-law to repeat her story. Then he asked Henry to show the court his right leg. Henry placed his leg on the table top and removed his 'bootie' then unzipped the pants leg and revealed the cast. "Can you run on that leg?" His attorney asked.

"I don't think so."

Attorney Clark blushed and Leah ducked her head. Judge Thomas was angry. "Mrs. Scragg I'm holding you in contempt of court and you're lucky I don't charge you with perjury. Do either of the attorneys have any more questions?"

"Only one," Charles Murray answered. The attorney pointed at Leah and asked, "Henry do you want to be married to this woman?"

"No sir."

The divorce was granted and Henry was given visitation rights for every other weekend, every other holiday, including Christmas, and three weeks during the summer. He was ordered to pay one hundred dollars a month for child support until he was able to return to work. H.A. Scragg was ordered to return to court August 1st to answer to contempt charges. Henry left the courthouse humming 'It's Such A Pretty World Today'.

Henry called his ex-mother-in-law's house Friday evening to arrange picking up his daughter, Anna, the following morning for her weekend visit. According to the court Henry had custody of his daughter from nine a.m. Saturday until five p.m. Sunday. Leah's mother answered the telephone and informed Henry that he'd never see his daughter then slammed the telephone down. Henry waited until Monday morning then called his lawyer's office and spoke to Charles Murray. Henry told him about the call and he told Henry he'd look into it and call him back. That afternoon shortly after three p.m. the attorney called back.

"I talked to their lawyer, Mr. Jameson, and he told me that his client said you never called. According to him they had your daughter dressed and ready to go and you never showed up."

"They're lying," Henry replied.

"I know they are but what it boils down to is it's your word against there's. They could do this every week. Do you have a tape recorder?"

"No, but I can have one in a couple of hours."

"Good. Get a recorder then go to the Radio Shack in Hardmor and tell the salesman you need to make a recording of a telephone call. He'll sell you a little gizmo simple enough even your daughter could use it. Call your ex-wife again and ask when you can see your daughter and record the conversation."

Henry bought a forty dollar cassette tape recorder and a device with a recording jack on one end of a small electrical cord with a suction cup on the other. He placed the suction cup on the receiver end of Lahoma's telephone and plugged the jack into the recording outlet of the recorder. Friday afternoon he turned the recorder on and called his ex-mother-in-law's home and asked to speak to his ex-wife.

"She's not here!"

"I need to set a time when I can come and get my daughter."

"You'll never see Anna you son-of-a-bitch!" H.A. yelled then slammed down the phone. Monday morning Henry called his attorney and told him he had a tape and told him what was on it. Charles asked Henry to drop it off at his office and thirty minutes later Henry was handing it to Charles Murray's secretary. He then drove to Walter's fishing camp and spent the next two days drinking with Walter and several friends. He returned to Lahoma's Thursday and she had a message for him from his attorney. Charles informed Henry that they'd have to go back to court again for visitation rights and the nearest court date possible would be at least three months.

Henry had another problem. His right leg was starting to smell and something was trying to push through the cast a few inches below the knee. Henry asked his grandmother if he might borrow her car and drive to the hospital for his next appointment. The car was an automatic and Henry could use his left foot as easily as his right. Lahoma didn't relish the idea of driving in city traffic anymore than Henry relished the idea of riding with her in city traffic. She agreed to loan him her car. Henry waited eight hours at the Veteran's hospital before a doctor could see him. Henry's cast was removed and the source of the odor revealed. He had a bone sticking out of his leg halfway between the knee and the ankle. The resulting hole was infected with dried pus covering the area beneath the wound. An X ray was taken and revealed the presence of osteomyelitis, an infectious disease of the bone often of bacterial origin that is marked by local death and separation of tissue.

"Apparently a piece of bone broke off," Dr. Neils informed him, "and has worked it's way to the top."

"It oughta be simple to remove then. When can you do it?"

"We can't," the doctor answered. "It's not life threatening. You'll have to live with it until you have that leg removed."

"Have you smelled this thing?" Henry asked. "Do you know my grandmother and me spent two hours the other night looking for a dead mouse before we figured out it was my leg that was smelling? You tell me I have to live with that?"

"We can cut your leg off."

"You can cut my leg off but you can't remove a piece of bone that's stickin' up and winkin' at you?"

"I'm sorry but that's the way it is. When you're ready to have that leg removed come back and I'll cut it off. Until then there's nothing I can do."

The doctor called a nurse in and ordered a new cast be placed on Henry's leg leaving an opening for the hole and the bone. Henry drove back to Joneston still smelling like a dead rat. Lahoma was angry and she had an idea. A friend of hers, Marilyn Cobb, had a daughter, Jeannie, that worked as a reporter for the Hardmor Inquirer. Lahoma called Marilyn and asked her friend to call Jeannie about the possibility of her doing a story on Henry and the Oklahoma City Veteran's Hospital. An hour later Marilyn called back and told Lahoma that Jeannie would meet with them at her desk in the newsroom of The Hardmor Inquirer at two p.m. the following afternoon.

Jeannie Cobb started the interview by telling Henry that she would be researching anything he told her and if he lied to her she'd tell the world that he'd lied. Henry agreed that would be fine and answered every question she asked. Before the interview was over she asked a photographer to take a couple of pictures of Henry.

The Sunday edition of the paper featured a front page picture of Henry above a caption that read 'VA Refuses Treatment For Vietnam Veteran'. To Henry's surprise the Veteran's Administration in Oklahoma had confirmed everything Henry had told the reporter and the spokesman for the hospital had concluded his statement with "Mr. Ridge has an unrealistic outlook on his medical situation."

Monday morning shortly after nine a.m., Henry received a call from Washington, D.C. An ambulance would be waiting in Hardmor Tuesday morning to take him to the VA Hospital in Oklahoma City for treatment for his leg.

He packed an overnight bag with a pair of pajamas, razor, toothbrush, toothpaste, hair brush, a carton of Camel filter cigarettes, a box of Dutch Master Panatellas, two packs of Zig Zag rolling papers and an ounce of pot. He met the ambulance at the Veteran's Center, more popularly known as the 'old soldier's home', in Hardmor and less than two hours later was being carried on a stretcher to the sixth floor of the Oklahoma City Veteran's Hospital. Because his leg was infected he was given a private room. He turned the television on and found a station that played old movies. He was in the middle of a Lash La Rue film when a Dr. Graves came in with Henry's chart. He poked and prodded at Henry's leg before ordering an IV inserted into his right arm. He asked the doctor when they planned on removing the bone fragment from his leg.

"We have to take care of the infection first," the doctor told him. "You'll be receiving penicillin for the next several days until we have the infection under control. In the meantime stay off that leg. I'll have a wheelchair brought in if you want."

Henry asked the doctor to shut the door when he left. As soon as the doctor was gone he rolled a joint then hopped over to the window pulling his IV pole with him. He lit the joint and took several long drags before pinching it out and returning to bed. Back in bed he lit a cigar and started puffing until the room was full of cigar smoke. Ten minutes later the police came into his room. The marijuana smell was gone and all the officers could smell was cigar smoke.

"We've had a report you were smoking marijuana in here," the officer told him.

"All I'm smoking are these cigars. You can search my room if you'd like to." Henry had his marijuana hid under his mattress and he was hoping they wouldn't ask him to leave the bed while they searched it. The second officer looked in the small closet and the drawer of Henry's night stand then the first officer apologized for bothering him and both officers left. Henry called the nurse as soon as they left and asked for the wheelchair the doctor had offered him. He placed the pole with the IV in front of him and wheeled down the hall toward the visitor's lounge. He was high and in no mood to lay in bed. The head nurse stopped him a few feet from the nurse's station. "Ya smoka dope," she said in a German accent," and I tella the police. You can't smoka that stuff in here."

"I was smoking a cigar," Henry replied.

"I neva smella cigar like that. Ya smoka dope and ya betta stop."

Henry spent the next hour rolling up and down the hall talking to other patients as bored as he was. He returned to his room and smoked the rest of the joint he'd rolled earlier then sat in the wheelchair watching Rawhide and puffing his cigar. Twenty minutes later the police returned. Henry had removed the marijuana from under the mattress and had it hid in the bottom of his left sock.

"We've had another report that you're smoking pot," the officer told him as they turned his mattress up on it's side.

"I told you before they're smellin' my cigar." The officers finished searching the room then left.

Henry smoked another joint the following morning a few minutes after the doctor had made his morning visit. He finished the joint, hid the marijuana under the night stand, lit a cigar, turned on the television and waited. A few minutes later the police returned. This time they removed his mattress and checked the bed frame. They found nothing and left again. Henry smoked another joint a few minutes after eating lunch. He lit a fresh cigar and waited. After an hour a young black nurse came into his room and started laughing. "You're something else white boy. The head nurse called the police again about you smoking that wacky tobacco and they wouldn't come. They told her that she was smelling your cigars. She's madder than a wet hen. You got it made now. You can smoke that shit in the hall and the police won't come."

"I'm just smokin' cigars," Henry replied.

"Don't lie to me white boy. Your eyes tell on you. If I knew I wouldn't get caught I'd be in that bed smoking it with you. You be careful white boy."

Henry told his grandmother not to try and visit him while he was in the hospital. It wasn't that he didn't want to see her but her driving worried him and he wasn't sure she could find the hospital without someone with her.

Henry had trouble sleeping and soon was spending a good portion of the night prowling the halls in his wheelchair pushing his IV pole ahead of him. When Dr. Graves heard this he ordered a shot of Valium be given to Henry at ten p.m. every night to help him sleep.

"White boy this is gonna knock your ass out," the young black nurse told him as she injected the narcotic into his arm. The shot made Henry high but it didn't knock him out and a few minutes later he was rolling down the hall with a mannequin used for CPR instruction sitting on his lap like an old girlfriend. The following morning, after talking with the nurses, Dr. Graves ordered Henry's Valium dosage increased.

Two weeks later Dr. Graves informed Henry he would be released the next morning. Henry's infection was down and the drainage from his leg had nearly ceased. But he still had a bone protruding from his right leg. "Aren't you going to remove that bone?" Henry asked.

"We will later," Dr. Graves assured him.

"How much later?"

"A few months."

"But I'm already here. Why can't you do it now?"

"They'll schedule you an appointment in a few weeks and we'll take care of it then."

Henry called Eddy and asked him if it would be possible for him to pick Henry up in front of the hospital the following morning. Eddy told him he'd take off work and be there as early as he could. At nine thirty the following morning Henry was standing by the front entrance and the next thing he remembered he was on a stretcher headed to the emergency room. He had no idea what had happened to him. All he knew was he had an unbearable pain in his back and his tongue hurt. In the emergency room he tried to talk to the nurse "Plain ahm in plain," he heard himself moan. "Otts in otts uh plain." Henry's tongue felt the size of a baked potato. A pretty middle-aged nurse leaned over him and said, "I know you're in pain Mr. Ridge but I can't give you anything right now. You've had a seizure and until we find out what caused it we can't give you anything."

"Plain," Henry moaned again. "Otts uh plain. Peas shood me. Dust shood me. Ahm in plain. Otts ah plain."

X rays were taken and blood drawn from his arm and he was returned to the same bed he'd left a short time earlier. Eddy was waiting for him in the room. "I talked to the nurse and she said you had some kind of seizure."

"Plain. Ahm in plain. Shood me. Peas. Plain. Otts uh plain."

"She said you won't be getting out today."

"Plain. Ahm in plain."

Henry spent the next thirty minutes begging Eddy to find a gun and put him out of his misery. Finally a nurse returned with a syringe. "You've had an allergic reaction to the penicillin Mr. Ridge." She inserted the needle in Henry's left arm. "And you fractured a disc in your back. This shot oughta help you."

The pain was gone in seconds and Henry's eyes were getting heavy. He didn't remember Eddy leaving and he didn't know how long he slept before the pain returned and woke him. He pressed the button for the nurse and examined his tongue with his fingers while he waited for her. He knew now why his tongue was sore and swollen. He had bitten a hole in it.

The nurse gave Henry another injection and when he woke up a few hours later the pain had lessened. Three days later they released him again. His back was still sore and his tongue still hurt but the cast was gone.

CHAPTER TWENTY-ONE

Three months after his divorce, Henry was back in court. Charles Murray called Henry's ex-mother-in-law, H.A. Scragg, to the stand and asked her if she'd ever denied Henry the right to see his daughter.

"No," she answered.

"You've never cursed him and slammed the phone down?"

"No."

Charles Murray held the cassette up where everyone could see it and asked, "Do you know what this is Mrs. Scragg?"

"It looks like a cassette."

"Do you know what's on this cassette?"

"No. I've never seen it before."

"It's a tape of a conversation my client had with you on April eleven. Do I need to play it for the court?"

H.A. dropped her head and stared at her lap. "No," she mumbled.

"No more questions."

Judge Thompson spent the next few minutes scolding H.A. Scragg and telling her that regardless of how she felt toward Henry Ridge she couldn't deny him the right to see his daughter.

Saturday morning Henry arrived at H.A.'s house shortly after nine a.m. The front door opened and Anna, now thirty-two months old, walked out to where Henry stood. No overnight bag, no change of clothes, nothing, not even a toothbrush. That didn't bother Henry. He had the time of his life buying

Anna denim pants, a red blouse, red cowboy boots, a Tweety Bird toothbrush and Barbie doll panties. Then he drove to Joneston.

Lahoma hadn't seen her great granddaughter in more than nine months. She'd already picked out several patterns of dress material she thought would look pretty on Anna. Henry showed her the items he'd bought and told his grandmother how they'd sent Anna off for the weekend without so much as a change of clothes.

"They know what they're doing. This way you'll be buying her clothes and anything else she needs. Maybe you should keep what you buy her here. I can wash her dress and we'll change her before you take her back."

"I can't do that even if I have to buy clothes every time I have her."

"I don't think I could do it either. I don't even know why I suggested it."

Henry took Anna walking.

A month later Henry drove into Hardmor to pick up his daughter for the third weekend visit. This time his ex-wife, Leah, walked out carrying a small canvas bag with Anna walking behind her. The bag contained a change of clothes and Anna's toothbrush. She handed the bag to Henry then asked to borrow a hundred dollars.

Henry paid his child support at the County Clerk's office. The money was then sent to his ex-wife. He'd already paid this month's child support. "You should have gotten your money by now. I paid it more than a week ago."

"I got the child support but I need to borrow a hundred if you have it. You can skip next month and we'll be even."

"I'll write you a check for fifty. That's all I can afford."

"I'd rather have it in cash."

Henry lowered his voice, "And I'd rather have some way of proving I gave you the money."

"Why are you acting this way Henry?"

"I reckon it's because I don't trust you any farther than I can throw your mother. Do you want the check or not?"

Leah took the check and Henry took Anna walking.

Henry had visitation with his daughter every other weekend and every other holiday. The twice monthly visits were hardly a problem other than his ex-wife wanting money every time he picked up his daughter. But the holidays were different. H.A. didn't want Anna to have any holidays with Henry. H.A. argued and cursed and it worked on the Fourth of July but it hadn't worked since. Henry had his daughter Labor Day and Leah had her Thanksgiving. Henry had to threaten to take them back to court before they agreed to let Anna spend Christmas with him.

Henry's infection grew worse until the pus was draining from the hole around the bone more than it had when he was admitted to the hospital nearly a year earlier. He had kept his monthly appointments thinking each time they might admit him to the hospital and remove the bone protruding from his leg. They always sent him home with a promise of 'soon, maybe in a few more weeks'. Now the smell of rotten flesh permeated his clothes and his skin. Even after taking a shower he could detect the odor of pus. The corner of Lohama's sofa where Henry usually sat smelled like pus. Finally, eleven months after releasing him from the hospital, Henry was readmitted.

Henry spent the first two weeks hooked up to an IV until the doctor had his infection down. He was then taken to surgery and the fragment removed. He awoke in his room with the IV back in his arm and a towel covering his right leg. He raised up enough to lift the towel and saw that his right leg was split down the center and the bone exposed. The bone fragment was gone. Dr. Graves entered the room accompanied by another doctor. He removed the towel and as they studied the wound said, "Henry, this is Dr. Sighe. We borrowed him from the Knee and Joint Clinic long enough to operate on your leg."

"Thank you doctor. I appreciate it."

"You may not be so thankful when you're back in a year or two having it removed," Dr. Graves told him.

"You don't think I'll keep it any longer than that? With that piece of bone out I thought it would heal."

"You have osteomyelitis and there's no cure for it. Later on that infection could turn cancerous. In the meantime leave that towel off and let it get some air and if you feel like you just have to get into that wheelchair and roll around the halls keep that leg elevated as much as possible and cover it with the towel. I wish you'd just stay in bed and watch television or read a book."

"When you plan on sewing me up?"

"In a few days."

Henry waited about ten minutes after the two doctors left before working his way into the wheelchair and rolling over to the window and smoking a joint. He lit a cigar and rolled toward the nurse's station expecting to see the police arrive at any moment but the police didn't come.

A week later Henry was back in surgery. When he awoke he was in a ward with several other men, his leg bandaged and elevated. A large portion of the back of his calf was missing.

Henry had carried a hard cover copy of Henry David Thoreau's Walden and Civil Disobedience. He'd read the book years earlier and had agreed with Thoreau on several things, particularly Thoreau's opinion that a person had a duty to resist laws that seem wrong to a majority of the population even if that person had to break that particular law or laws at every opportunity. Henry didn't believe marijuana laws were fair. He didn't believe the government had any right to tell a person what they could grow in their own little garden. He didn't believe a person should be sent to prison for smoking marijuana when the prisons were overcrowded and murderers, rapists and child molesters were being released. In some states a man could do more time locked in a cage for possessing marijuana than most murderers and rapists. Henry felt he almost had a duty as an American to smoke marijuana. He also had another reason for carrying the book with him. It was a good place to hide part of his marijuana.

The night before surgery he rolled five joints. He placed the bag of marijuana in a spare pair of socks and placed this in his overnight bag with his underwear. The five joints he placed several pages apart in the book and then closed it and sat on it awhile until the joints were flat and unnoticeable.

Henry looked to his left and saw the book laying on top of the night stand. He picked it up and flipped through the pages. All five joints were there. He checked the night stand drawer and found his cigarettes, cigars and lighter inside. He took a cigar, removed the wrapper and lit it. Next he pulled the serving tray located on the left side of the bed around until the tray lay across him. He raised the tray several inches to an eating position then took a joint from the book and lay the book on the left side of the tray. He placed the ten inch high plastic water container on the right of the tray and his drinking glass on the container's left. He could move his head to the right and the water container blocked him from the view of the other patients and any visitors they might have. He could move his head to the left toward the book and see most of the ward. He puffed on the cigar a few times creating as much smoke as possible then moved his head to the right behind the container and lit the joint. He took several long tokes then moved his head to the left and took several puffs of the cigar. He smoked half the joint then put it out and replaced it in the book. Then he sat upright and swung the tray away from the bed. He heard someone in the ward remark, "I don't care what you say I smell pot." Henry was high.

Four days later Henry was released from the hospital and told to return in six months to have his leg examined. "Unless something happens or you change your mind and decide you want your leg removed," Dr. Graves told him, "we won't need to see you but twice a year."

Henry had to return to Oklahoma City three weeks later to give a deposition concerning the accident. Henry's lawyer, Attorney Roach, was suing the driver and the company he was working for and the insurance lawyers wanted to question Henry and look at his leg. Henry met the lawyers in a conference room at the Hilton. Two hours later he was on his way home.

The first week of April, four years, four months and three days after the accident, Attorney Roach called and told Henry the insurance company had made an offer of one hundred thousand dollars cash and five hundred dollars a month for the rest of Henry's life. The lawyer advised Henry to accept it and Henry did. A check would be mailed to Henry with his name and Attorney Roach's name on it also. Henry was to sign the check and mail it to the attorney. Attorney Roach would deduct what he was owed and send Henry a check for his part. Henry did as he was told and a few weeks later a check arrived for his share of the one hundred thousand. The check was for forty-one thousand and Henry felt robbed. The manila envelope also contained an itemized list of the expenses the lawyer and his associates had incurred. Henry was charged for every cup of coffee, every meal, every motel, every drink, every first class ticket, every cab fare and every other fuckin' thing they could squeeze on the list. But Henry knew without the lawyer he'd never have gotten a dime and he held his anger.

Henry deposited the check in the Mayetta First National Bank then told the president of the bank that he wished to pay anything his grandmother owed the bank. Lahoma owed five thousand on a home mortgage and eight hundred on her car. The car title and the deed to her home were placed in a large white envelope. He purchased a 1976 Chevrolet pick-up truck he had looked at earlier then drove to Joneston and gave the envelope to Lahoma telling her it was an early Christmas gift. Lahoma looked at the deed and the car title and told Henry he shouldn't have done it. Then she sat down and cried.

Henry had spent half his life wanting out of Oklahoma and now all he wanted was ten acres of his own land near Red River. He talked to an old friend from Joneston, who had a real estate office in Mayetta and two days later he was the proud owner of ten fenced acres less than five miles from his grand-mother's home. Thursday night he drove to the horse sale and bought a small paint mare for his daughter Anna. The following day Walter borrowed a horse trailer and drove to the sale barn to load the horse and deliver the animal to the ten acres Henry had purchased. Henry followed in his pick-up truck. In the pick-up bed was a large galvanized bathing tub, a small galvanized tub, a mineral block and a salt block, a hundred pound sack of sweet feed and a hundred pound sack of bran. The galvanized bathing tub was placed a few yards away from the corner of the fence facing the road. The smaller tub was tied securely with baling wire to the top of the two corner poles. The salt block and the mineral block were placed a few yards out toward the center of the field. Henry took an empty one pound can of Folger's coffee and filled it with sweet feed then dumped the sweet feed in the small bucket. Next he took a can of bran and dumped it in with the sweet feed and mixed it. He decided that wasn't enough food and he added another can of sweet feed and a half can of bran. Since the field had no well Henry would have to haul water from his grandmother's until he could have a well dug.

Anna would be five in a few days and he hadn't told her about the pony. Saturday morning he drove into Hardmor and picked her up then drove to the ten acres. The mare started immediately toward the feed bucket. Henry filled the feed bucket and held Anna while she petted the horse. She was still too frightened of the animal to stand on the ground although the paint was gentle enough for Henry to place Anna on the mare's back for a moment.

The following morning Henry drove his daughter back to the field to feed and water the horse. This time she didn't seem as frightened and asked Henry to put her on the paint's back. 'She'll be riding soon', Henry thought to himself. He would take her shopping for a saddle the next weekend he had visitation.

Henry had heard stories about his ex-wife Leah. She'd lived with the drug dealer until he grew tired of her stealing and forging checks and threw her out. H. A. wouldn't allow her around Anna except to come over and beg money from Henry every other Saturday when he came to pick Anna up. He knew his support money was going to H. A. and she was also receiving an Aid to Dependent Children check from the county. He also knew she liked to guzzle Jack Daniels and watch soap operas while Anna played alone in H.A.'s postage stamp size backyard. He confronted H.A. when he took Anna home and she came out on the porch.

"Give me a kiss," Henry told his daughter, "then run inside while I talk to your grandmother. I'll see you in twelve days."

"What do you want to talk about with me Henry? If you have something to whine about you oughta take it up with Leah."

"I know Leah doesn't live here. Everybody in the county knows she doesn't live here. But my daughter deserves at least one parent. She shouldn't be raised by a whiskey guzzling grandmother. I bought some land and I'll be building a home for Anna. I'm not taking anyone to court for custody, I wouldn't put Anna through it, but Anna will be twelve in seven years and then she'll be able to choose where she wants to live. I intend to make sure she has a home if she decides to live with me."

Henry spent the next few days at Walter's fishing camp, driving back and forth each day to feed and water his horse. Often as many as a dozen or more people showed up at the camp to drink, smoke and enjoy each other's company. When it rained you could count on Gary Vines and Jimmy Moon, two construction workers for an industrial pipe laying company, to show up early and stay late. And a good rain could mean a few more days off waiting for the ground to dry out. Eddy was there often and T.B. liked to lay around the camp while the rest of the band worked their day jobs. Henry and the others liked the location because you were far enough away from the law to have a good time and there was no reason to drive away drunk when you had a choice of three tents to sleep it off in.

Henry drove to Hardmor the second Saturday of September to pick up Anna for his twice a month visitation. H.A.'s car and two other cars were parked in the driveway but no one came to the door when Henry knocked. He knocked louder, then checked the door and found it locked. He knocked again, louder, and still didn't get an answer. He drove to a small mall four blocks away and used the pay phone to call H.A.'s home. Still no one answered. He drove to a small café off Highway 44 and sat down at a booth and ordered coffee. Every fifteen minutes he called H.A.'s house. No answer. After an hour and four cups of coffee he drove back to the fishing camp. He'd call his attorney Monday morning and let him handle it.

Henry drove to Mayetta Monday morning and called his attorney from a café two blocks from the attorney's office. Charles Murray told him he needed to come to his office. Henry was there in less than five minutes. He barely had time to sit down before a stocky black man in a charcoal gray suit entered the office and told Henry he was under arrest for child molestation. Henry went for the man and Attorney Murray stepped between them.

"Who are you calling a child molester you black son-of-a-bitch!"

"Calm down Henry," the attorney said. "Brandon's just doing his job. There's no need to cuff my client Brandon. He knows his rights and I've already made arrangements with a bail's bondsman."

After Detective Brandon Grant left the office Henry sat down in a chair. His head was pounding and he was pissed. He'd been accused of something he considered the lowest, most despicable act a man could commit.

"This is serious Henry," the attorney told him. "I won't lie to you and tell you it isn't."

"When can I see my daughter?"

"Your visitation has been suspended until we go to court."

"When will that be?"

"A few weeks if we're lucky."

"What am I expected to do? Just sit around with my thumb up my ass? When was I supposed to have done this?"

"I don't have all the details. I didn't know about it until a few minutes before you called. But you're not helping by calling Brandon a black son-of-a-bitch."

"I didn't call him that because of his race. If he'd been green with purple polka dots I'd have called him a green and purple polka dotted son-of-a-bitch! How the hell do they think they'll get away with it? Anyone who knows me knows how I feel about anyone who'd hurt a kid. I'd kill a man if I thought he was even thinking about puttin' his hands on Anna! I don't understand how they think they can get away with it! The truth will come out!"

"Don't bet on it," the attorney advised. "In any other crime you're presumed innocent and they have to prove your guilt. In child molestation cases you're presumed guilty and you have to prove your innocence."

"That doesn't sound Constitutional to me."

"It isn't. Welcome to the real world. Now cool off and let me handle this. I'll call you when I find out more."

"I guess I ought to tell my grandmother."

"She already knows. I called her earlier looking for you."

"How did she take it?"

"She's madder than a wet hen but not at you."

"Aren't you going to ask me if I'm guilty?"

"I know you aren't and I'll tell you why. If your grandmother thought for one minute you were molesting her granddaughter she'd have shot you herself."

"Tell me how much this is costing and I'll write you a check now."

Charles Murray gave Henry an amount and watched for a reaction. There was none. Henry didn't care what he had to pay to see his daughter. He'd just have to build a little smaller home for Anna than he'd planned.

Henry drove to Joneston. Lahoma was sitting on the front porch when he pulled into her driveway. Normally she'd have been sewing at this time of day. "Why are they doing this Henry? Don't they know they're hurting Anna? Anyone who's ever seen you with that child knows you'd never do anything to harm her and there's not a soul in this country believes you could ever do what they've accused you of."

"I think I scared Leah's mother. I told her I was going to build a home for Anna and I think she believes I was about to try and get custody from Leah. Leah doesn't see Anna more than an hour or so a week and H.A.'s living off child support and a county check. If I take Anna she'd have to go to work and miss her soap operas. You couldn't melt that old drunk and pour her into a job."

"You've got the best attorney around. Thank God for that."

"He thinks a lot of you Grandmother."

"I think a lot of him. Charles Murray's a good man."

Henry decided to stay at his grandmother's instead of returning to the fishing camp. He wanted to be where his attorney could contact him and there were no telephones at the camp. Mid afternoon Lahoma called Henry in and told him his attorney was on the line. "They're claiming you molested Anna on the twenty-seventh of last month."

"When was the twenty-seventh?" Henry lost all track of the days staying at the camp. The only days he'd kept track of were every other weekend and often he couldn't tell you the date of the weekend without looking at a calendar. He counted the days back and smiled. "You're not going to believe this Mr. Murray but those fools picked a Saturday when I wasn't with my daughter. I had visitation the Saturday before and the twenty-seventh I was at a friend's fishing camp with a dozen or so others."

"Make a list of everyone who can testify to where you were on the twenty-seventh and bring it by the office."

Henry had the list in Charles Murray's office within an hour. Then he drove to the fishing camp.

Henry's trial was set for the first Monday in October. More than twenty people had offered to go to court on Henry's behalf including Eddy, Walter, Chop, T.B., Gary and Jimmy. A special Judge had been called in from Tishomingo named William Sanderson. As the witnesses crowded into the small courtroom the Judge asked the District Attorney what kind of evidence he planned to submit to the court. The District Attorney explained that Anna wouldn't testify and they intended to submit the grandmother's testimony as that of the granddaughter.

"Is that all you have?" Judge Sanderson asked. The Judge pointed at Henry and said, "This man shouldn't even be here! Case dismissed!" The trial was over before all the witnesses could be seated.

Henry turned to his attorney and asked, "Does this mean I can see my daughter this weekend?"

"No, we'll have to go back to court again."

"I don't understand. The judge threw the case out. Why can't I see my daughter?"

"A court order suspended your rights and it will take a court order to restore them."

"I reckon they'll take their time settin' a court date for that too."

"They won't get in any hurry," the attorney agreed.

Henry's next court date was the third week of January. A blizzard had covered southern Oklahoma with several inches of snow. The weather was below freezing and the roads were hazardous. The normally fifty minute drive to Hardmor took Henry more than two hours. When he arrived at the courthouse the District Attorney stated that they weren't sure anyone would drive from Joneston to Hardmor in a blizzard and they would need time to call the other party and instruct them to come to court. It took more than two hours to find out whose bed his ex-wife was in that morning.

"I'm just curious," Henry asked his attorney. "If they'd shown up and I hadn't do you suppose they'd have delayed court to hunt me down?"

"I think you know the answer to that."

Court lasted less than twenty minutes. Charles Murray asked that Henry's visitation be restored and his ex-wife's legal aid attorney, Larry Fallon, argued that Henry was unfit to see his daughter unsupervised. The judge agreed with Fallon.

"I have some questions about Mr. Ridge's character and I'm ordering that all visits be supervised and limited to every other Saturday from nine a.m. to five p.m. Attorney Fallon suggests that all visits take place at the children's shelter or at Henry's grandmother's home with the grandmother present when the daughter is visiting."

Henry had his choice of sites to visit his daughter every other Saturday. He could meet her at the children's shelter or he could take her to his grandmother's. If he chose the shelter Anna would be taken there by H.A. and Henry wouldn't be able to leave the shelter with his daughter. This meant he wouldn't be able to take her walking or to the lake. Henry had driven by the shelter and wasn't impressed. The yard was small and sandy, with little grass and only a merry go-round and a set of swings to play on. He knew Anna wouldn't enjoy spending a Saturday at the shelter. If he wanted to take his daughter to Joneston he'd have to have his grandmother accompany him when they picked Anna up and accompany him when he took her back to H.A.'s. At Lahoma's they wouldn't be able to do anything unless

Lahoma was with them. Henry knew his grandmother had no desire to walk a dirt road for several hours or lay on a lake beach in hundred degree weather.

"This sucks," Henry told his lawyer. "If I take her to the children's shelter she'll start hating the visits and if I take her to Joneston my grandmother might start hating the visits."

"Your grandmother would offer to do it. Take Anna walking just don't take her into town alone. Don't worry about taking her to the beach. Summer's a while away and we'll go back to court again in a few weeks."

Lahoma accompanied Henry on the trip to Hardmor to pick up his daughter. The day was perfect for walking, a rare February day with the temperature in the mid sixties. Minutes after arriving at his grandmother's Henry and Anna were on the dirt road walking. They'd gone less than a quarter mile when a pick-up pulled alongside Henry.

"You better get back to your grandmother's hare-lip!" The man in the pick-up was H.A.'s younger brother and Anna's great uncle, Larry Wilson. In the truck with him was his frizzy, red-headed wife, Bertha. Larry was a drunk and a coward and Henry knew he was trying to provoke him. Larry wouldn't open his mouth to anyone that would fight back. He wanted Henry to do something they could force Anna to testify to in court later. Henry had another idea.

"You know you can't be alone with her you long-haired bastard! You better get your ass back to the house right now!"

Henry looked down at Anna and smiled, "Your Uncle Larry's a silly man ain't he?"

Anna laughed and looked around Henry's leg at the couple in the pick-up and yelled, "You're a silly man Uncle Larry! A silly, silly man!"

Larry Wilson hit the gas and spun his tires throwing dirt on Henry. Henry had shielded Anna and the small rocks and sand had peppered his back. Soon the pick-up and Larry were out of sight.

Henry knew he'd hear about it later. He didn't expect any more trouble that day and saw no reason to cut their walk short. An hour and a half later they returned to Lahoma's. They'd barely gotten through the door before H.A.'s car pulled in the driveway. Larry Wilson sat in the passenger seat and frizzy-headed Bertha sat behind him in the back seat. H.A. stormed up the front porch and beat on the door. Henry was in the kitchen fixing Anna some hot chocolate. He saw Lahoma hang up the phone and go to the door.

"I'm taking Anna back with me!" H.A. yelled. "You're not supposed to leave her alone with that bastard! I'm demanding that you send her out now!"

"You don't come to my door and demand nothing!" Lahoma slammed the door in H.A.'s face. Larry Wilson stepped up and took his turn beating on the door. Henry left the kitchen and started toward the front door.

"Get back in the kitchen Henry!" Lahoma ordered. "I won't have you or anyone else fighting around that child. I've already called Charles so just stay in the kitchen with your daughter."

H.A. and Larry were still on the front porch demanding that Anna be sent out when the sheriff arrived a few minutes later. He threatened to arrest H.A., Larry and frizzy-headed Bertha for public drunk if they didn't leave at once.

Henry spent the summer days at the fishing camp and the summer nights in a bar. He missed his daughter and, frustrated with the judicial system, was drinking as much as a quart of whiskey a day.

The fishing camp was nearly twenty miles from Hardmor and a lot of nights Henry wasn't sure he wanted to make the drive. A quarter mile from Ellery's was a dirt road that ran all the way from Hardmor to the Red River. Ten miles down the dirt road was an old cemetery with a pair of giant oak trees on both sides of the entrance. If Henry didn't want to make the drive to the fishing camp he took the dirt road toward the river. He parked at the entrance to the cemetery where the trees would shade him when the morning sun came up and he could sleep until the heat woke him. If the weather was cold he carried two blankets behind his seat. If he needed to be up early he'd park across the road in front of the gate to a cow pasture. The rancher fed his cattle early, between five and five-thirty a.m. and would have to wake Henry to move his pick-up so the rancher could get through the gate and feed his cattle. The rancher was friendly and never seemed upset at the inconvenience.

Most of Henry's friends had received drunk driving tickets at one time or another. They liked to take the interstate or one of the state highways and get home faster and often they went to jail for driving under the influence. Henry never saw a cop on the dirt road and he never received a DUI. His friends started referring to the cemetery entrance as 'Ridge's Corner'.

Henry was sitting in a bar off Highway 44 listening to T.B. and the Lungers. The band had agreed to play for all the beer they could drink and T.B. had asked Henry to come out. Henry always enjoyed hearing his songs being performed especially when the crowd danced to them. Tonight the crowd was small but the night was early yet..

Henry saw Larry Wilson shooting pool with three 'cowboys' and pointing his way. He tried to ignore the group and turned his attention back to the band. A moment later he was knocked from his chair and ended up on the floor with the three 'cowboys' on top of him. He pulled his buck knife from his back pocket and grabbed someone's ear, cutting it nearly off. The cowboy directly on top of Henry screamed and stood up taking the other two with him. The band had quit playing and now T.B., Chop and Bob were facing the three who'd jumped Henry. A young blonde-haired 'cowboy' was holding his ear and yelling, "I need to find a doctor! The bastard nearly cut my ear off!"

"Take it outside!" Henry heard someone yell. He turned and saw the bartender standing there with a small baseball bat in his hands. "I've already called the law! If you're smart you'll get your ass out of here!"

The 'cowboys' left by the front door. Henry told T.B. he'd see him at the fishing camp then slipped out the side door. His white shirt was covered in blood and he decided to drive to Joneston.

A few days later Henry sold his horse and land to a neighboring farmer for slightly more than half of what he'd paid for the land alone.

Henry went back to court in September. Again he was denied unsupervised visits with his daughter.

"What do we do now?" Henry asked his attorney.

"That's up to you," Charles Murray answered. "We can wait a few weeks and go back to court again but I think you're wasting your time and money. I don't think Judge Thompson will ever let you see Anna unsupervised."

"Then I'll have to take Judge Thompson out of the picture."

Henry had thought often about what he was planning to do. Without the whiskey he found it impossible to sleep and on nights when he stayed in Joneston with his grandmother he found himself walking the floor, angry at the world and sleeping only an hour or two and then back up and walking the floor. He often thought that if he was half a man he'd walk in the Judge's office or the District Attorney's office and knock someone out of their chair. He knew the only problem with acting like half a man is the other half would have to be an idiot. Anything he did would have to be legal.

Henry drove to the K-Mart in Hardmor and bought two white poster boards then drove to the fishing camp hoping Walter would have the rest of what he needed.

"I need a piece of molding," Henry told Walter.

"What for?"

"I'm going to town and protest."

"You're shittin' me."

"I've never been more serious in my life."

Henry took one piece of poster board and laid it on the hood of his truck. He took a black magic marker and wrote his statement in large letters. He took the second poster board and wrote another statement. Walter handed him a piece of one inch by two inch molding nearly six feet in length. Henry nailed one poster board to one side and the other board to the other side of the molding. When he held the sign up one side read 'Judge Thompson Is A Jackass' and the other side read 'DA Collins Is An Ambulance Chasing Idiot'. He planned to be in front of the Hardmor courthouse the following morning at eight a.m.

Henry was amazed how word could spread from a fishing camp with no phone service to half the county's population. That evening at Ellery's several people asked if the rumor they'd heard was true. Would Henry be picketing the courthouse tomorrow morning? He told them they'd have to come see for themselves.

He arrived early and parked across from the courthouse at a bail bondsman's office. Henry had never met the bondsman but the man had sent word he wanted to meet him. Henry carried the sign inside the man's office and stood it in a corner. He then spent the next ten minutes drinking coffee and listening to the bail bondsman tell him how corrupt the county judicial system was. At exactly eight a.m. he stepped out of the office holding the sign up and crossed the street to the courthouse. He looked around and saw a small crowd of two dozen or so gathered at one corner of the courthouse and across the street another dozen or so. At another corner two deputies stood with their arms folded across their chests blocking the sidewalk. He headed for the deputies thinking he might as well get it over with.

"What the hell do you think you're doing?" A deputy demanded to know.

"What the hell does it look like?" Henry answered. "I'm exercising my constitutional rights."

The crowd had grown and the deputies looked around at the number of people gathered. Then they walked away. Henry walked around the courthouse with the sign held high. He saw several old 'friends' cross the street to avoid the possibility of him wanting to speak to them. Henry would be 'hotter than a pancake' to anyone walking a fine line between 'felony' and 'misdemeanor'. Too hot to be seen with. No one could ever recall hearing anyone publicly call a county judge a jackass or a district attorney an ambulance chaser and an idiot. They were certain no one had ever put it on a sign and walked around carrying it until they drew a crowd.

A reporter with the Hardmor Inquirer showed up about ten a.m. and asked Henry a number of questions then walked into the courthouse. A news crew from the local television station arrived a few minutes later and interviewed him. A few minutes before noon a news crew from a television station in Ada, Oklahoma, a hundred miles northeast of Hardmor, interviewed Henry for nearly ten minutes. He had the same message for all of them. "He was not a child molester. The district attorney was either too lazy or too incompetent to investigate and Judge Thompson was a jackass and a drunk who wasn't fit to judge a pie eatin' contest. Judge Sanderson had thrown the case out before anyone could be seated. He wanted to see his daughter." After the Ada news team left Henry quit his protest. He felt like he had got all the attention he would get that day.

The story made the front page of the Hardmor Inquirer the following day. A large picture of Henry carrying the sign with the 'Judge Thompson Is A Jackass' side to the camera accompanied the article. The reporter quoted Henry nearly word for word and Henry was pleased with the story until she quoted the district attorney. The DA stated that Henry had never paid child support and Henry was upset that he couldn't see his daughter until he paid his child support. Henry gathered every receipt and cancelled check he had saved and drove the fifty minute trip to Hardmor in thirty minutes. He parked in front of the newspaper's office and walked inside and over to the desk of Deanna Maldrin, the reporter who'd interviewed him the previous day. He laid the receipts and checks on her desk and told her, "Why don't you total that up and see if I owe any child support?" Deanna took a pad and added the figures then half giggled "I guess they were wrong."

"I don't guess you'd be willing to print that in your paper would you?"

"I can't call the district attorney a liar Mr. Ridge. Everyone at that courthouse is a friend of mine."

"What mail order college did you get your journalism degree from?"

"I think you'd better leave Mr. Ridge."

Henry spent the night at the fishing camp where a small crowd had gathered to drink, smoke and congratulate him for making the front page of the local paper. The story had not run on the Hardmor television station but several people told Henry the Ada station had shown his interview. A few apologized for avoiding him explaining how they couldn't afford to be seen with him until their probation ended or their legal problems were resolved.

Henry woke up in a tent with a young lady he'd met at a biker wedding. Phoebe was a gang banger and had sex with four others before crawling into the tent with a very drunk Henry. All Henry remembered was waking up sometime later with Phoebe on top of him. He slipped out of the tent without waking her and got dressed. It was barely daylight and no one else in the camp was up. Henry drove to Joneston.

Lahoma was sitting at the kitchen table drinking coffee when Henry walked in. Yesterday's paper lay in the center of the table. Henry didn't know how she felt about what he'd done until she looked up and smiled. "The phone's been ringing off the wall. You've got a lot of supporters Henry. I wish your grandfather could have been here to see it. I'm not sure how Charles Murray's taking it though. He called yesterday morning and he wants you to call him as soon as you can."

Henry called his attorney's office. "I wish you would have discussed it with me first Henry. I think you've shit in your own nest."

"I didn't do nothin' illegal."

"You didn't help yourself either," Attorney Murray told him. "Did your grandmother tell you about the bounty Joe Scraggs has on your head?"

"Not yet. I just got home a few minutes before I called you. Where did you hear about a bounty? I haven't heard nothin' in Hardmor about any bounty."

"It may just be whiskey talk Henry and then again it might not be. A client of mine came into my office yesterday and told me about being in a bar with Joe and a few others and hearing Joe offer a thousand dollars to anyone who killed you. He honestly believes you molested his granddaughter. Like I said, it may have just been the booze talking but be careful Henry. Protect yourself and don't be calling the Judge and the DA anymore names. At least not in public."

Henry went back to court the following February. He had a new Judge, Leo Cardinal, and his ex-wife, Leah, had her favorite divorce attorney, Clark Jameson. This would be Henry's final attempt at regaining his original visitation rights. He was running out of money.

Henry wore Wrangler pants with grey boots, white shirt and grey vest. He wore his hair in a French braid and he was the first person Attorney Murray called to the stand. Henry raised his right hand and swore to tell the truth.

"State your name and address please," Attorney Murray said.

"Henry Ridge, Joneston, Oklahoma."

"Is that your grandmother's home?"

"Yes."

"Are you asking this court to allow you specific visitation rights to your daughter?"

"I haven't seen my daughter in nearly two years."

"If allowed visitation where would you take your daughter?"

"I'd take her to my grandmother's in Joneston."

"How much room is in that house?"

"There's three bedrooms."

"How many people reside there?"

"My grandmother and me."

"Are you now employed?"

"I draw a disability check as part of an insurance settlement."

"Are you aware of your ex-wife's residence at this time?"

"She moves around a lot but I've heard she lives with a drug dealer."

"Where is your daughter residing at this time?"

"At her other grandmother's."

"And how long has she resided in the home of her other grandmother?"

"Since our divorce. Four years. . .maybe five."

"Is your daughter in fact residing with her mother at all?"

"No sir."

"To your knowledge, has any order ever been entered in this case or any other giving custody to the grandmother?"

"No sir."

Attorney Murray sat down and Attorney Jameson stood to take his turn at questioning Henry.

"You testified you're residing at your grandmother's?"

"Yes sir."

"Isn't it true you also spend a lot of time at a fishing camp?"

"I wouldn't say a lot."

"Answer yes or no Mr. Ridge."

"No, I don't spend a lot of time there."

"Isn't it true you spend more time in a tent than you do at your grandmother's? Or sleeping at the entrance to the Criner Hill Cemetery?"

"Of course not!"

"Answer yes or no Mr. Ridge. Judge please instruct Mr. Ridge to answer with a simple yes or no."

Judge Cardinal was grinning like a shit eatin' possum. 'The bastard thinks this is funny' Henry thought. 'I'm fightin' to see my daughter and this redneck is lovin' every minute of it'.

"Is it true you like to dress up like a woman?"

"Not all the time."

"Answer yes or no!"

Judge Cardinal leaned toward Henry and told him, "Mr. Ridge you will answer each question with a yes or no. Do you understand me?"

"I understand. You can bet I understand." Henry now believed Judge Cardinal had decided this case before he ever took the bench.

"I'll ask you again," Attorney Jameson continued, "Do you sometimes feel the need to dress like a woman?"

"I wouldn't call it a need…."

"Answer yes or no Mr. Ridge!"

"No!"

"You've never worn a dress in public?"

"I've never felt a need."

"But you did wear a dress to a bar one night. A bar you knew you weren't welcome at. Is that right Mr. Ridge?"

"That's right." Henry didn't care what the attorney asked. He knew he couldn't win. The judge had made up his mind before Henry ever opened his mouth.

Clark Jameson snickered then said, "I have no more questions for Mr. Ridge."

Attorney Murray called Leah Scragg to the witness stand. "Your name please."

"Leah Scragg."

"Are you the mother of Anna Marie Ridge?"

"Yes."

"Is your daughter now residing in the home of your mother?"

"Yes, she is."

"Ms. Scragg, are you at this time under any care for alcohol or drug dependency?"

"Yes sir, I am."

"During the term of your custody of your daughter have you been hospitalized for these problems?"

"Yes."

"When was the last time?"

"It's been three years."

"Where are you living at this time?"

"I reside with my mother."

"How long have you been residing with your mother?"

"Well, ever since Henry and I have been...when we were separated and before we were divorced I've lived there. The only times I've been gone was when I was in treatment."

"Has Henry been allowed to visit his daughter?"

"Yes, sir, he has."

"When was the last time?"

"I'm not sure. Henry said two years but I'm not sure. My mother would know."

"Do you know a man by the name of Parker Thomason?"

"Yes sir, I do."

"Were you living with him in 1985?"

"No sir, I wasn't."

Attorney Murray ended his questioning and Attorney Jameson began the cross examination. "Ms. Scragg, you will concede to Judge Cardinal that at one time you had an alcohol dependency?"

"Yes sir."

"And did Henry Ridge also?"

"Yes."

"You will concede to Judge Cardinal that at one time you had a chemical dependency for drugs?"

"Yes."

"Did Henry Ridge?"

"I believe so, yes."

"Did you receive treatment for these problems?"

"Yes sir."

"Did Henry Ridge?"

"Not to my knowledge."

"Your ex-husband, under oath, has told the Judge that you reside with another man. Is that true?"

"No."

"On a daily basis, who takes care of your daughter?"

"I take care of her sixty percent of the time. My mother does help me a very lot. She does help me."

"Do you live with her?"

"Yes."

Leah Scragg left the witness stand and Attorney Murray called Lahoma Ridge to testify.

"State your name, please."

"Lahoma Ridge."

"And how are you related to Henry here?"

"He's my grandson."

"Is Henry a good parent to his daughter?"

"Yes. He's a real good parent."

"Do you feel there would be a problem with him having regular parental visitation with his daughter?"

"No, I don't."

"Have you been with Henry when he attempted to visit his daughter?"

"Yes, I have."

"And has there been difficulty?"

"Yes. We weren't very welcome and it was kind of insulting sometimes."

"Has your son been denied visitation rights?"

"Yes."

"Whenever you helped Henry go to and from these attempts, where was his daughter?"

"I don't know. We weren't allowed to see her."

"I believe that's all, Judge."

Attorney Jameson started his cross examination with, "Good morning Mrs. Ridge, I just have a few questions. Do you think Henry would be a good parent?"

"Yes sir, I do."

"He's lived with you for the past three or four years, right?"

"Yes sir."

"Does he pay you anything for room and board?"

"I don't ask him to but he does whenever he wants to."

"Isn't it true he's never bought groceries or paid a nickel in rent?"

"He doesn't have to. He paid off my mortgage."

"Are you aware of the serious allegations that have been made against your grandson?"

"Yes, sir."

"Does that concern you ma'am?"

"Not in the least."

"That's all I have for now. You may step down. Your honor I'd like to call Ernie Phillips to the stand." Ernie Phillips walked to the witness stand and was sworn in.

"State your name."

"Ernest Marlowe Phillips."

"What is your occupation?"

"I'm Clinical Director of Southern Oklahoma Mental Services."

"Did you have the opportunity to interview Anna Ridge, the defendant's daughter?"

"Yes sir, I did."

"And in your opinion did Mr. Ridge molest his daughter?"

"Yes."

"What made you arrive at that conclusion?"

"She said 'my daddy plays with my bobo'."

"She used the term 'bobo'?"

"Yes."

"Were you able to determine what the child was referring to by using the word 'bobo'?"

"Yes. I asked her and she pointed to the low pelvic area and said 'that's my bobo'."

"In your opinion are children usually pretty honest?"

"Yes."

"Did Anna Ridge appear to be coached?"

"No."

"No more questions."

Attorney Murray walked toward the witness stand. "Mr. Phillips, have you worked with cases before where there have been alleged fondling and molestation charges?"

"Yes, I have."

"How many?"

"Several hundred."

"Of those several hundred, how many did you interview personally?"

"I can't be sure, there's been so many."

"Have you ever met the defendant?"

"No sir."

"Have you ever talked to the defendant, by phone or any other means?"

"No sir."

"Did the defendant try to initiate a conversation with you?"

"Yes sir."

"And you refused to meet with him?"

"Yes sir."

"Why?"

"I was afraid it would cause me to change my opinion."

"That's all the questions I have for this witness. I would like to call H.A. Scragg to the stand." H.A. Scragg took her place on the witness stand. "State your name please."

"Harriet Abigail Scragg. Most people call me H.A."

"And you're Leah Scragg's, formerly Ridge's, mom; is that right?"

"Yes."

"Is Anna Ridge living in your home?"

"Yes."

"Is your daughter, Leah, residing in the home with her?"

"Yes sir."

"And how long have they been living there?"

"Since they've been divorced."

"Did your daughter ever live with Parker Thomason?"

"No."

"Have you ever asked for custody of Anna because of your daughter's drug and alcohol problems?"

"No."

"Do you have any concern at all about Anna being with your daughter?"

"No."

"The same question as to your ex-son-in-law. Would you be concerned?"

"Yes, I am afraid for him to be with Anna."

"That's all. Your witness Mr. Murray."

"Hasn't Leah tried to remove Anna from your home and you denied her?"

"Not to my knowledge."

"And you don't think your daughter's continuing bout with alcohol and chemical dependency affects your granddaughter?"

"It would affect her if she didn't try to do something about it."

"Since the divorce, has Leah ever had Anna on her own?"

"She's always been in her custody."

"I mean outside your home."

"I'm telling you she has always lived with me. She and Anna have always lived with me."

"Haven't you continuously refused to allow Anna to see her father?"

"Heavens no!"

"Your Honor the defendant rests."

Judge Cardinal asked if there were any other witnesses to be called. When no one responded he called for a recess to deliberate his decision. Court had been in session less than ninety minutes. Twenty minutes later court resumed.

"The court still has concerns about the character of Henry Ridge," Judge Cardinal announced, "and I place great stock in Mr. Phillips' opinion. I don't think the Code of Civil Procedure as it relates to child visitation allows me to make an order for a less restricted visitation. So anyway, that's the decision of the court."

The next morning Henry drove to the fishing camp to tell Eddy and Walter that he was leaving town. "I've run out of money and when you're out of money you're out of lawyers."

"Where you going?" Eddy asked.

"Nashville. I'm gonna look up my old friend, Wynn Stewart and try to get a foot back in music. That's the only chance I have to make enough money to hire another lawyer."

Henry walked into the Surf Lounge on Nashville's lower Broadway a few minutes after 2 p.m. Two men, one tall and husky the other short and thin, stood at the far corner of the bar, drinking beer and talking.

He chose a stool near the middle of the bar and ordered a beer. When the barmaid set the beer in front of him he asked her if she knew how he might contact Wynn Stewart.

"Wynn Stewart! Wynn Stewart is dead! Hey Rusty," she yelled to the husky man. "When did Wynn die? Was it four or five years ago?"

"At least five." The man moved down the bar and introduced himself to Henry. "I'm Rusty Adams. Did you know Wynn?"

"We were friends and I was lucky enough to have him record a few of my songs." Henry extended his hand and said, "I'm Henry Ridge."

"Henry, Wynn died about five years ago from a heart attack. He'd just gotten a new booking agent and a new bus and he was going on the road the next day. He walked into his mother's house and sat down in a chair and when she checked on him a few minutes later he was gone."

"I'm gonna miss him. He was a good friend....and what a voice! The world won't see another talent like Wynn again. I guess there's nothin' keeping me here now. I might as well head south."

CHAPTER TWENTY-TWO

For nearly twenty years Jody Payne had invited Henry to visit his home whenever Willie was off the road and the band had a few days off and 'hang out'. Thru the years he'd invited Henry to Austin, Texas, Venice, California and Nashville, Tennessee. A few weeks earlier Henry had visited Jody and the others on the band bus after a Willie Nelson concert in Norman, Oklahoma. Jody was living in Alabama now and had a small bar near Mobile called 'Jody's Crystal Lady Saloon'. He invited Henry to visit and Henry had decided to take him up on his offer. He'd stay a few days and hang out and party with his friend and figure out where he was going from there.

Willie was having a problem with the Internal Revenue Service and the government had ordered him not to play any more concerts until the matter was resolved. In the meantime they'd confiscated everything that Willie owned and had audited the band members. Not being allowed to work with Willie had caused every member a hardship. Jody was home full time working his bar and booking out at other bars such as the Flora-Bama in order to pay his bills.

Henry turned south on Interstate 65 then lit a joint and rolled down his window. Three joints and eight hours later he pulled into a Western Inn motel located across the bay from Mobile and rented a room. He walked next door to a Waffle House and ordered a hamburger and a cup of coffee then returned to his room and showered. It was nearly midnight so he decided to smoke a joint and go to bed and call Jody the following day. At ten a.m. the following morning he smoked a joint and called Jody at home. Jody informed Henry he was less than a mile from the Crystal Lady and gave him directions to the bar. They agreed to meet there at noon. Henry called his grandmother and gave her the number to the bar then checked out of the motel. He drove up the causeway looking for a cheaper place to stay. He had a little more than eight hundred dollars on him. He couldn't afford to stay at the Western Inn at fifty-seven dollars a night.

The Woody Motel stood on stilts on the east side of the causeway. Customers climbed a set of stairs to get to the office and the rooms. Henry rented a room then unloaded his truck and parked it where he could watch it. The motel was old but had an affordable weekly rate. He turned on the television and noticed everyone on the screen was green. He flipped through the channels and was ready to go to the office and demand a better television when he flipped to the Playboy channel. Henry had never been a big fan of pornography but something about a green couple with green genitalia and dark green pubic hair and nipples struck him as funny. He smoked a joint and watched a couple have sex and decided he'd keep the television.

Jody was at the Crystal Lady when Henry parked in front. A cute, small-chested, brown- haired lady was working behind the bar. The two friends hugged then Jody introduced him to the bartender, "Henry this is Pascagoula Patsy. Patsy, this is Henry Ridge."

"You from Mississippi?" Henry asked.

"I lived there twenty years ago."

"And they still call you Pascagoula?"

"Only Jody does."

Henry remembered another pretty girl he'd met in Mississippi twenty-five years earlier. He cupped the bottom of Patsy's face and stroked her chin. Patsy jerked her head back and slapped his hand. "What are you doing?" she demanded to know.

Henry smiled and answered, "Just checkin' for whiskers."

Henry followed Jody to his home an hour later and met Jody's pretty wife, Vicki and their ten year old autistic son, Austin. The Payne's house sat on five acres of land complete with a barn and two ponds stocked with catfish. The two friends drank beer and listened to a tape of a few songs Jody intended to record for a new album. Henry waited until Jody excused himself to take a shower and get ready for the night then he thanked Vicki and returned to the Crystal Lady. Several soldiers were drinking beer and playing pool when he walked in. Henry drank beer and flirted with Patsy. Two hours later Jody and Vicki arrived at the club.

A small stage was located on the right side of the club and Jody spent several minutes checking the band equipment before walking over to the bar. "I hope we have a good crowd tonight," he said.

"How's your crowd been?" Henry asked.

"We've had some good nights and some not so good nights. A lot of military people come here but my job with Willie is the only thing keeping us afloat. If we don't go back on the road soon I may lose the bar." Jody walked behind the bar and pulled a shoe box out and sat it down in front of Henry. He opened the box and started laughing. The box was full of slips of paper. "These are the unpaid tabs. If anyone didn't know better they'd think the first thing we did was bar the paying customers."

"You've talked about having your own bar since I met you in Texas."

"I wanted a place to play with my own band when I was off the road. I've got a good band here, the 'Slightly Trashy' band and Vicki and I have a lot of friends."

"I like your bar," Henry said, "and your bartender too."

"Gayle and Jessica, our other bartenders ought to be here soon."

"And I'm going home," Patsy announced. "I'm tired."

"I wish you'd hang around and two step with me," Henry told her.

"I don't know how to two step."

"I'll be happy to teach you."

"I'll stay for a little while."

Patsy was a quick learner and after a few minutes they were two stepping like they'd danced together for years. At closing time Henry tried to talk Patsy into going back to his room and watch green people have sex. Patsy refused and Henry returned to Woody's alone. He smoked a joint and chug-a-lugged two warm beers while watching two green men 'sandwich' a shapely green lady. He fell asleep and two hours later a nightmare woke him. He'd dreamed he'd been abducted by aliens and taken aboard their mother ship where he was gang raped repeatedly by little green men with huge green penises.

"I'm watching too damn much TV." Henry thought to himself.

Patsy Lee Edwards had been married twenty-four years to a shipyard worker and divorced less than six months. She'd had a twenty-one year old son, David, killed by a hit-and-run driver as he worked on his Harley Davidson late one night. She'd adored her son and wasn't interested in a relationship with any man. When she wasn't working she could usually be found at the dog track or a bingo parlor.

Henry was at the bar every morning shortly after Patsy arrived. He helped her and Vicki ready the Crystal Lady for opening and they became friends. Three weeks later he talked Patsy into sharing his bed at Woody's. Two days later he checked out of Woody's and moved into her apartment.

Patsy was smart, pretty, strong-willed and jealous as a pit bull dog. A week after Henry moved in with her they were at a local bar where Jody was booked that night. A young lady was showing Henry a little too much attention in Patsy's mind and Patsy was watching. The lady hugged Henry briefly and Henry felt something fly past his ear and hit the wall. Patsy had thrown a can of beer at his head.

"What the hell are you doing?" Henry demanded to know. "You nearly hit me in the head!"

"I'm sorry," Patsy cooed sweetly. "My aim's a little off to-day. Hug her again and I'll see if I can do a little better." Later that night Henry wrote a song called 'Patsy Lee Won't Tolerate Me Anymore'.

Patsy was born in Biloxi, Mississippi to a bookkeeping mother and an Air Force father stationed at an area air base. Her parents divorced while she was still a baby and her mother had moved them down the coast to Pascagoula. Without leaving a forwarding address she might as well have moved them to the moon. Patsy hadn't seen her father in over forty years and her mother still lived in the same house in Pascagoula.

But damn Patsy was aggravating. Henry told Jody one night, "We've been together thirty days and we've had thirty-one fights." The least little thing set her off and she'd throw Henry's clothes out in the front yard then go to bingo or the dog tracks. But Henry couldn't keep away from her and four months later they stood before a judge at the courthouse and said their "I do's". The following month Patsy threw his clothes out the win-dow five times. Henry told her one day while hanging his clothes back in the closet, "I've got clothes I haven't worn but once or twice and you've damn near worn 'em out throwing them out the window." But he couldn't leave her.

One night they were at the Crystal Lady when one of her ex-husband's co-workers came into the bar and Patsy hugged him.

"I'm going home for a while," Henry told her. "There's somethin' that I wanna do."

"What?" Patsy asked.

"I'm gonna throw your clothes out the window for huggin' that man's neck."

"But he's just a friend I've known for years."

"A neck is a neck is a neck."

A week after their marriage they drove to Pascagoula to visit her mother, Ethyl. Patsy told him the neighborhood used to be a nice place to live until the gangs moved in. The former neighbor on the east side of the house had a stroke and his wife sold the house and moved closer to the nursing home he was in. The new neighbors were using the side of Ethyl's house to dispose of their beer cans and Ethyl was too intimidated to confront them about it. She had decided instead to extend her back yard privacy fence out to the sidewalk

"You know I could probably put that fence up," Henry offered. "Just dig a couple of holes."

"I want it done right," Patsy snapped.

Henry didn't know whether to laugh or be insulted. "You know lady I've been called stupid more than once but you're the first person to tell me I'm too ignorant to dig a hole." But Henry wouldn't have traded her for all the cotton in Alabama. In many ways she reminded him of his grandmother: a free spirit, a good cook and honest as a country preacher. And like Lahoma, Patsy couldn't lie if you held a gun to her head. But damn she was aggravating.

Henry heard the bar's phone ringing as soon as he stepped out of his truck. The ringing continued while Vicki unlocked the door and Patsy walked behind the bar. Patsy answered the telephone then called out to Henry. "It's for you. I think it's your grandmother."

Henry took the phone and heard his grandmother ask if she was bothering him. "I've been calling all morning. I'm afraid I have some bad news. I guess there's no easy way to say this. Harvey's dead. I know how close you two were."

"How close we used to be Grandmother. What happened? Did he O.D. on that garbage he was sticking in his arm?"

"He was murdered Henry and that's about all I know right now. It's in the morning paper and it doesn't give any details other than they found him on a dirt road."

"How's his folks taking it?"

"I haven't talked to either of them. I'm going to their place when I hang up. But you know as well as I do they'll be taking it hard. Are you coming home?"

"Not unless you think I should. Harvey and I haven't exactly been friends for years."

"Do what your conscience tells you Henry."

"I love you Grandmother. Thanks for calling."

"I love you too."

The Slightly Trashy band consisted of guitarist Luther Wamble, bassist Darrel Roberts, and Harmonica player Troy Fisher. The band performed most weekends and drew a good crowd of regular customers. Three nights a week Jody sang at the Flora-Bama, a popular roadhouse on the beach that straddled the Alabama and Florida state line.

Flora-Bama patrons were well known for buying drinks for popular performers. Jody knew the reputation of the law on

Highway 59 from Stapleton to Gulf Shores and he knew you didn't have to be drunk to fail a sobriety test and receive a D.U.I. He offered Henry fifty dollars a night to do the driving to and from the Flora-Bama. Henry drank coffee while Jody performed and accepted the drinks the customers bought him. Henry liked the roadhouse and the owners, Joe Gilchrist and Pat McClellan and the rest of the staff were more than nice to him.

The Flora-Bama had been a fixture on Orange Beach for more than thirty years and had a reputation for drawing celebrities who wanted to party without being bothered by fans. Joe and Pat had a rule where you didn't talk while a performer was on stage and you didn't bother them when they came off stage.

Jody introduced Henry to the great football player, Ken Stabler and songwriters Red Lane, Hank Cochran and Whitey Shafer. During the week of the Frank Brown Songwriter's Festival Henry was introduced to Mickey Newbury, an icon whose recordings he'd heard countless nights in Texas and Tennessee. When the bars had closed and the after-hour joints had grown a bit tedious Henry and his friends would often gather at someone's apartment and smoke marijuana or snort cocaine or amyl nitrate or both and listen to Pink Floyd or Elton John or Jethro Tull or Mickey Newbury. Newbury's 'Looks Like Rain' album was the standard every country songwriter tried to imitate and none could.

Mickey invited Jody and Henry to pull up a chair and have a drink with him. Henry accepted while Jody visited with Hank Cochran. Over the next few days Henry and Mickey became friends.

When Henry wasn't at the bar he was often helping Jody do yard work at Jody's estate or helping Jody try to make repairs at the Crystal lady. The bar had several problems including heating, plumbing and electrical.

The government and Willie had resolved their differences and Willie and the band were allowed to return to the road. Their first show was New Year's Eve at a theater in Branson, Missouri and Jody asked Henry to accompany him on the fourteen hour drive. A heavy snow had blanketed the Ozarks and the local traffic was thin but over fourteen hundred people braved the cold to hear Willie and Family perform. The following day they returned to Alabama. Willie had signed a contract to perform at Branson during the tourist season and Jody was told Willie, the band and the crew would return to Branson in April. Jody invited Henry along to sell 'swag', the name given to the T-shirts, caps, bandanas and other merchandise sold at the shows.

Henry and Patsy were stocking the beer boxes one day when two tall, well-groomed men entered the bar. Both men wore wide-brimmed Stetson hats, tailored shirts, starched and ironed Wrangler pants and expensive boots. The men had short, freshly barbered hair, one salt and pepper and one red-headed. Both were husky with just a trace of a 'spare tire'. They each ordered a beer and Henry returned to stocking the beer boxes while Patsy served them.

"Excuse me," the dark-haired man said. "Is your name Henry?"

"That depends," Henry answered. "Are you a cop?"

The man smiled and answered, "No, I'm not a stinking cop."

"Do I owe you money?"

"You used to."

Henry knew then where he'd met the man. "Are you from Texas?"

"I'm Don Eads. You bought a car from me once."

"Eads Used Cars on 28th street," Henry replied. "I know

a few people that bought cars from you. This is my wife, Patsy. What brings you two to Dixieland?"

"Looking for a good investment. This gentleman here is Greg Shula, my partner. We wanted to get out of town awhile and I'd heard Jody had a bar here. We'd like to buy into something that might make us money and neither one of us has ever been to Mobile. Do you know anyone we might talk to?"

"I don't but Jody might. What are you looking for?"

"A bar, maybe a motel. I heard a shrimp boat makes money. Thought we'd check on that too."

"Either of you ever worked a shrimp boat?"

"No, but we both like to fish and we both like boating. I've got enough sense to know we'd have to hire a crew until we learned the ropes."

Jody entered the bar and recognized Don immediately. The two friends shook hands and Don introduced Greg. "What brings you here?" Jody asked.

Don told Jody what he'd told Henry earlier and when he brought up the shrimp boat Jody started laughing. "Henry can show you a boat. There's dozens around here for sell but I can't picture you on a shrimp boat."

"We thought we'd try something different," Greg said.

Don and Greg stayed another hour then returned to their motel room to shower and change. Shortly after dark they returned to the Crystal Lady. Don asked Henry if he'd act as their guide and offered to pay him for his time. Henry refused the money but consented to show them around.

The next two days the men looked at several real estate properties without finding anything they liked at the right price. The third day Henry took them to the shrimp boats to check on a forty footer. They took a quick look around then Don announced they'd seen enough.

"I can't believe anyone lives on anything that smells that bad," Greg said and Don agreed.

The following morning they returned to the Crystal Lady and met Jody's wife, Vicki, then talked to Jody for several minutes. Jody mentioned he'd be in Branson, Missouri in April.

The Gulf War drove the final nail in the Crystal Lady's coffin. A significant portion of their steady customers had been military personnel from the nearby Army and Navy bases. Without this support they had two options: go further in debt or close the bar. The third week in January, Jody and Vicki held a funeral for the Crystal Lady. Jody carried the box of unpaid tabs out to the bar and tore them up. Both considered the Crystal Lady a hundred thousand dollar education and neither had any desire to own another bar.

Jody called Henry one morning in the middle of February and said Don had called the previous night and asked for Henry's telephone number.

"Patsy and I went out for a couple of hours," Henry replied. "Did he say what he wanted?"

"He wants you to call him. He's in Branson."

Henry called the number and Greg answered. "Don should be back soon. He's out looking at bicycles. I'll tell him you called."

Henry couldn't imagine either Don or Greg on a bicycle. Nearly four hours later Don returned Henry's call. "I'm trying to get something going in Branson," Don told him. "I've already bought four of those parking lot sweepers and now I'm trying to set up a food delivery business. Jody said you'd be traveling here in April. Why don't you come early and help me? That'll give you time to get set up."

Henry told Don he'd think about it and call him back in a day or so. He talked it over with Patsy and called Don the next morning. The first week in March Henry left for Branson. Patsy would join him later.

CHAPTER TWENTY-THREE

Branson, Missouri 'live music capitol of the world' began in 1882 when Rueben Branson opened a store. During the late 1880's and early 1890's tomato canning was the largest industry in the area. In 1907 a book written about the area by Harold Bill Wright called 'The Shepard of the Hills' was published and became a best seller. Overnight people from coast to coast began flocking to 'The Shepard of the Hills' country and local tourism was born.

The first show in Branson was in 1959 by the Baldnobbers, a band named after a vigilante group of the Civil War era. In 1964 the group moved into a theater in downtown Branson and a few years later moved again to a theater on Highway 76. The Presley family had opened a theater on Highway 76 a year earlier and the Plummer family opened a theater soon after the Baldnobbers. Boxcar Willie was the first 'celebrity' to perform on a permanent schedule in his own theater.

The media 'discovered' Branson with articles in People, the Los Angeles Times and the Wall Street Journal and the CBS television show "Sixty Minutes" did a segment about the town. Branson had forty theaters, seventy live theatrical shows and more than 60,000 theater seats. Everyone from Andy Williams and Bobby Vinton to Mo Bandy and the original Baldnobbers performed in the theaters on the "strip".

Henry arrived in April and called the number Don Eads had given him. Don gave Henry the directions to the Ozark Cottages where he and Greg were staying. The traffic was thin and Henry was there in fifteen minutes knocking on the door to room #104. Greg answered the door and invited him in.

'Cottage' 104 consisted of two single beds, a small oven, small refrigerator, 19" television and a closet sized bathroom. Don informed him the two beds were taken but Henry could make a pallet anywhere on the floor. He was given a job driving a sweeper and cleaning the parking lot at the A&P supermarket. The following night he was sent to an office complex to 'sweep' a small mall just off the 'strip'.

Don had plans for a new business in Branson. Knowing how congested Branson would be in a few weeks and, assuming most tourists didn't like sitting in bumper to bumper traffic to reach a restaurant, Don planned a delivery service from the restaurant to the motels. He purchased one hundred used bicycles and ran an ad in the local paper for delivery men to ride the bicycles. He had menus printed and placed in the motels believing that most tourists, especially those driving long distances, would welcome a catered meal at the motel instead of fighting the traffic. He planned to place riders at each restaurant site ready to ride like the wind to deliver hot meals to grateful tourists.

Two weeks later, at the start of the tourist season, the rent on Cottage 104 tripled from three hundred a week to nine hundred a week. Don and Greg bought bunk beds and moved into an office they were renting.

Apartments were scarce at any price and Henry had to rent at Rockaway Beach, eighteen miles from Branson. The apartment wasn't much larger than the room at the cottage and consisted of a tiny bathroom and shower, a small kitchen and a pullout bed in the 'living room'. When the bed was out the mattress covered most of the room. When anyone questioned him about the apartment Henry would answer, "You can make coffee and take a piss without ever leaving the bed." The apartment building also sat at the top of a steep hill with Rockaway Beach below it.

Willie, Jody and the others arrived the last week in April. Willie's booking company had comfortable apartments waiting for the band and road crew.

The first week in May Willie and the band took the stage at the Willie Nelson Theater. Henry took a job selling 'swag' for Jody at the theater. Jody offered him 10% commission of the total sales. Henry was also asked to watch the back doors and keep the general public from walking on stage with Willie. Any friend of Willie's or the band was escorted back stage to the dressing rooms.

Patsy arrived a week after the band driving an old Chevrolet she'd bought in Mobile for six hundred dollars. The motor made a knocking sound and spewed black smoke the color of coal.

"How much oil did you use?"

"None."

"How long has the oil light been on?"

"A couple of hours."

Patsy followed Henry to the Rockaway Beach apartment. Before taking her inside he took her to the side of the building overlooking Rockaway Beach and pointed toward the third floor.

"That's our apartment up there. I want you to notice that anything thrown out the window would most likely end up in downtown Rockaway. Think about that. I don't want to see some hillbilly wearing my clothes."

A few days later Patsy found a job with a clothing manufacturer.

Henry tried to call his grandmother from a pay phone at the apartment's entrance. No answer. He tried again two hours later and there was still no answer. The following morning he called again and after receiving no answer he called Thelma Pike.

"Henry your grandmother is in the Mayetta Nursing Home. She nearly burned her house down and the social services got a court order from a judge."

"What happened?"

"Lahoma's memory is nearly gone. She can't remember what she was doing five minutes earlier. She put on a pot of red beans to cook then forgot about them and took a nap. A boy was driving by and saw the smoke and got your grandmother out. The fire department put the fire out but the kitchen is ruined and social services won't let her live alone."

"If I come home would they release her to me?"

"They might but Henry you can't take care of her. She needs round the clock care."

"I'll be home to see her as soon as I can get some time off. Thank you for looking out for her."

"No need to thank me. I didn't do it for you. I love Lahoma. I don't think I'd have made it without her when my Harvey was killed."

Henry met the legendary guitarist Grady Martin and the comedian Don Bowman. Grady had worked with nearly every major entertainer in Nashville, from Hank Williams to Jerry Reed, as a member of the 'A-team' of studio musicians. Don Bowman had a reputation as a brilliant songwriter, satirist and funny man. He'd had a top twenty hit nearly thirty years earlier with 'Chit Akins, Make Me A Star' and had also penned one of Henry's favorite songs 'Poor Old Ugly Gladys Jones'.

Henry's old friend from Texas, Bobby Wayne, had arrived in Branson a week ahead of Henry. Bobby had brought his pretty wife, Mimi, to Branson with the idea that he'd have his old job with Haggard back. Haggard was due in Branson soon to perform at the Willie Nelson Theater when Willie had other commitments that took him on the road.

At first Henry liked Branson but a month later all he could think of was leaving. The highways and roads were crowded with tourists driving bumper to bumper. A trip down the road for a pack of cigarettes could take an hour or more and people were elbow to elbow in restaurants and bars. The sewage plant had been built to handle thirty thousand but during tourist season the population more than tripled. Notices to boil water were common.

Don Eads returned to Texas three months later. He'd learned the hard way that Branson visitors didn't want their meals delivered. Being caught in traffic for hours was part of the 'Branson Experience'. Tourists liked returning home and boasting about their time in the Highway 76 congestion. The lesson had cost Don nearly eighty thousand dollars.

One Sunday Henry was having his usual coughing spell. He'd developed the cough a few months earlier and it had progressed from a couple of coughs and a spit to a twenty minute hacking and choking session. As soon as the cough ceased he lit a joint and coughed a few more times. Patsy watched silently with her 'you're a damn idiot' look. The telephone rang and Patsy answered it. "It's for you," she said. Henry took the telephone and heard Thelma Pike on the other end of the line.

"Henry you need to come home if you can. Your grandmother had a stroke."

"Is she alright?"

"No Henry, she's not alright!"

"I'll be home tomorrow."

Henry asked Patsy to pack enough clothes for a few days. He called Jody and told him the situation. Twenty minutes later Henry and Patsy were headed west to Oklahoma. Fourteen hours later they were at the hospital. Henry was told his grandmother had died two hours earlier.

The funeral home was crowded with everyone from a judge to the village idiot. Henry knew his grandmother was well-liked but he didn't expect this many mourners. He told Mrs.Pike the crowd surprised him.

"Your grandmother helped a lot of people."

"I didn't know."

"If your grandmother heard that someone was in need she'd take them a sack of groceries. The next day she'd take them a sack of clothes she'd stayed up half the night patching and mending. Your grandmother helped a lot of people. She just didn't crow about it."

After the service the crowd followed the hearse to the Criner Hills Cemetery. The small Joneston cemetery her husband and son were buried in had exceeded its limit years earlier. She was laid to rest less than a hundred yards from the place Henry's friends called 'Ridge's Corner'.

Henry and Patsy returned to Branson immediately after the funeral.

Henry was eating his fourth hot dog in six hours and after he finished the hot dog he intended to eat a Goo Goo candy bar. He'd walked out to his pick-up three times to smoke a joint and each time he'd returned hungry. Before he left the theater tonight he'd probably eat two or three more hot dogs and a couple of Goo Goo bars.

The steady diet of beer, hot dogs and candy bars was showing. His Wrangler jeans were tight and too small in the waist. Last week he'd noticed he couldn't see his belt. This week he couldn't see his boots either.

Show time was another hour away and already the place was crowded with Willie Nelson fans. Jody's merchandise was selling well and tourists were talkative. A middle-aged couple from Oklahoma spent several minutes telling Henry how much they'd admired his grandmother. A few minutes later Henry noticed a long haired, well dressed man standing to the side and watching Henry sell 'swag'. A moment later he asked Henry his name.

"Henry Ridge."

"You don't remember me do you?"

"I can't seem to place you."

"Remember Coal Miner Publishing? I used to see you there a lot. I'm Randy Krapper. I used to pitch my songs to Coal Miner's too. Are you still writing?"

"I've written a few things," Henry answered. "A lot of it for local groups in Oklahoma and Texas and New Mexico. What about you?"

"I have a publishing company now. You living here?"

"No," Henry answered. "I leave when the band leaves."

"Where are you going from here?"

"I'm not sure."

"Why don't you think about coming back to Nashville and writing for my company?"

"I'll think about it," Henry lied.

Randy extended his hand with a business card in it. "It was good to see you again Henry."

"It was good to see you too Randy."

Saturday night Henry watched a heavy set man, with legs like fire hydrants and wearing black shorts with a neon green short-sleeve shirt approach the souvenir table. He hoped the man didn't want to purchase a T-shirt. Henry wasn't sure Jody had any 'swag' that large.

"Rabbit is that you good buddy?"

"You called me Rabbit. Are you from the river country?"

The man turned the side of his head toward Henry and pointed to his right ear, "Good buddy you damn near took this off in the fourth grade."

"Sammy. Sammy Loughlin."

The two men shook hands like they were old friends. Henry didn't know whether to laugh or cuss. This person had spent years going out of his way to torment Henry. This person used to set the girls to giggling when he used Henry's pants for a flag. This was the person who used to laugh at Henry while he whipped Henry's ass.

"Rabbit, good buddy, you sure look good. How the hell have you been doing?"

"You're looking good too, Sammy," Henry replied, amazed that he could say it with a straight face. "I got no complaints, Sammy."

"That's good Rabbit. It's been a lot of years good buddy. Did you hear about your friend Harvey Pike?"

"Grandmother told me he'd been killed and that's all she told me."

"I always figured some husband or some bad ass would kill Harvey. You know he was killed by an eighty year old man that didn't weigh a hundred pounds didn't you good buddy?"

"Grandmother didn't tell me that."

"It's the damn truth good buddy. Harvey tried to pick up some woman at a bar and she let him know she didn't want anything to do with him. Well, good buddy, you know how Harvey was, couldn't take no for an answer. Anyway, good buddy, he followed her home when she left the bar. He didn't care whether she wanted his company or not so he's outside banging on a door at three in the morning until every house in the area had their lights on. Then he decided to crawl in one of her windows but he was at the wrong house. It was ole man Drucker's house. He shot Harvey three times before Harvey could get through the window." Sammy reached in his shirt pocket and pulled out a business card. "This is my house number and the other one is my office number. Call me next time you're in Oklahoma City and we'll have a drink and chase some pussy."

Henry waited until Sammy waddled into the theater intending to throw the business card in the trash but changed his mind and put the card in his wallet. Life was too short to stay mad forever and besides he might need a 'good buddy' sometime.

Willie's contract expired in November and Jody and the other band members returned to the road. Henry was out of a job now and the only income he had was his small disability check. Together with Patsy's income this gave them enough money to pay their rent and buy groceries but little else. Patsy wanted out of the area as much as Henry did but she didn't relish the idea of returning home and staying with her mother until they were able to afford an apartment. They had discussed Randy Krapper's offer to Henry to return to Nashville and write songs but they would still need money to move and live on.

Henry had paid a local pusher thirty dollars for a half ounce of marijuana and then waited three days for delivery. The pusher had come by Henry's apartment earlier and handed Henry the marijuana when Henry opened the door. The pusher refused Henry's offer to come inside and smoke and nearly ran from the building before Henry could examine his purchase. After the third joint Henry knew he'd bought 'trash weed' and he knew there was little chance he'd get his money back. He wanted to pitch a fit but the apartment was too small for the tantrum he wanted to throw and that made him want to throw another fit. He emptied the marijuana out the third floor window then walked outside and kicked the corner of the building. A beat up 1986 Buick pulling a U-Haul trailer stopped and parked across tthe street from the apartment entrance. A tall, bearded pot-bellied man climbed out and Henry recognized Saul Carter. Saul crossed the street to where Henry stood and asked, "Did that building piss you off?"

Henry started relating his sad story and Saul suggested they go to Henry's apartment. Inside Saul reached into his shirt pocket and took out two finger sized joints. Saul lit one joint and started looking around.

"Where's your coffee table?"

"In the kitchen."

Saul took a long pull then passed the joint to Henry. "I think you'll like this. I got half a ton of this shit in that U-Haul outside. How would you like a pound?" Henry's head was spinning and an old familiar buzz was back.

"You could probably sell a pound of this shit pretty quick," Saul said. "Make some money and have a little to smoke too."

"You giving me a pound?" Henry asked.

"You don't want charity. I'd be insulting you if I offered it."

"Try me."

"I'll give you a pound if you help me deliver it. You'll be home in a couple of days and have some good shit to smoke waiting on you."

"No thanks, Saul. Albuquerque scared me. How much time did ya'll do?"

"No time. They offered a deal we couldn't refuse. Sign our titles over and be out of town before sunrise. They kept the dope, the money, every fucking thing except what we were wearing."

"I'm out of that business Saul. Selling a pound is one thing, crossing state lines with a U- Haul trailer full of it is another."

"You turned into a fucking pussy Henry?"

"Well you are what you eat."

"You used to have balls. What happened?"

"They drawed up that night in Albuquerque and I haven't seen 'em since."

"What would it take to grow you a spine? I'll give up a pound of pot and three hundred dollars."

"Can't do it Saul. You like that outlaw handle but I don't. I don't like driving across country with my knees knocking and I damn sure don't like being locked in a cage with men who find me attractive."

"Five hundred dollars."

"Six hundred and a pound of pot. Take it or leave it Saul."

"I need a driver so I guess I'll take it."

"I'll need half the money before we leave." Henry wrote a note to Patsy telling her he'd call her later. He left the note, his truck keys and the three hundred dollars on the kitchen table under a salt shaker.

Three days later the men were back with the U-Haul and thirty-five cases of moonshine. Two hours later Saul was on his way to Las Cruces.

Henry called Randy Krapper that night and asked if his offer was still good. Randy told him it was and offered to let Henry and Patsy stay with him until they found a place of their own.

CHAPTER TWENTY-FOUR

Henry and Patsy started for Nashville the following morning pulling a rented U-Haul that held all their belongings. Henry knew Patsy's car probably wouldn't make it out of Missouri much less a few hundred miles to Nashville. He had her sign the title to the car and leave it on the front seat and they made the trip in Henry's pick-up arriving ten hours later. They spent nearly two hours circling Music Row before Henry called Randy for directions. Krapper Publishing was several miles from Music Row in a part of Nashville called Berry Hill.

Randy had a two bedroom apartment adjacent to the red brick publishing company. He showed Henry and Patsy to the guest bedroom and told them to make themselves at home. Patsy went to bed a few minutes later and Henry sat in the living room talking to Randy.

Henry had a pound of marijuana hid in a vacuum cleaner in the U-Haul. He didn't know if Randy was a pothead or a redneck but he wasn't going to bring it into Randy's home without Randy's approval. If Randy was a pot smoker then everything should be fine. If he wasn't a smoker he may ask Henry and Patsy to leave his property. Henry need not have worried. At the mention of marijuana Randy's eyes lit up and he smiled from ear to ear. Henry brought the marijuana inside and told Randy he'd share it with him for offering them a place to stay until they found a place of their own. Randy told him to take his time and that he and Patsy were more than welcome to stay as long as they wanted. The next day Henry unloaded the U-Haul and stored their belongings in a back room of the publishing company.

Henry had returned to Nashville thinking he'd be writing songs with Randy and using Randy's connections to 'pitch' their songs but Randy didn't appear as enthused as Henry was.

If Henry brought the subject up Randy would tell him "roll another joint and maybe we'll fuck with it tomorrow". When Randy finally looked at Henry's lyrics he had nothing but criticism to offer. "Nobody's doing songs about home or prison anymore. Roll another joint and kick back."

Henry and Patsy found an apartment a couple of miles from Randy's on Hillside Dr. The apartment they were shown was new and spotless and they were told another apartment was being remodeled and they could move into it in a couple of weeks. Henry paid a month's rent and security deposit and signed a year's lease. Three weeks later the manager called and told Patsy the apartment was ready. They drove to the apartment complex and were taken to an apartment on the north side of the building directly behind a liquor store. Bottles, used needles and condoms littered the area near the front door. Inside the carpet was dry rotted, roaches were everywhere and dried sewage covered the bottom of the bathtub. When Henry and Patsy complained and asked for their money back they were told to 'take the apartment or leave it' but their money would not be returned. They returned to Randy's and told him the news.

Two weeks later Henry ran out of marijuana and Randy's behavior changed. He began insulting Henry and told Henry his songs were too 'dirty' to be recorded.

Randy hadn't invited many visitors to his apartment until Henry's marijuana was gone. Now he had a steady stream of people during the day and he made it a point to ridicule Henry as much as possible whenever he had an audience around. One afternoon Randy had a visitor that Henry knew he'd met before but couldn't remember where or when.

"Rusty Adams this is Henry Ridge and that's his wife Patsy. Henry thinks he's a songwriter but I wouldn't put my name on anything he's written." The telephone rang and Randy stepped inside his office and closed the door.

Henry sat in the hall with Patsy and Rusty. "You look familiar," Henry said.

"You look familiar too. Are you a picker?"

"Songwriter. Wynn Stewart recorded three of mine."

"That's where we met," Rusty told him. "Lower Broadway. You came in the bar asking about Wynn." Rusty extended his hand and Henry shook it. "Any friend of Wynn's is a friend of mine. Where did you meet that asshole?" Rusty asked, pointing toward the office door.

Henry told Rusty about Coal Miner's Publishing, their meeting in Branson and Randy's offer. "He was nice for awhile. I couldn't get him interested in writing but he wasn't the asshole he is now. I had a pound of pot and when it was gone our welcome was gone." Henry told Rusty about the apartment they'd planned to rent.

"Bait and Switch," Rusty commented. "You'd need a lawyer to get your money back and he'd probably charge more than what you had coming."

"We're going to have to do something," Henry said. "Randy's made it clear he don't want me or mine here."

"Don't do anything yet," Rusty advised. "I'll talk to the manager at my apartment building and maybe we can get you in there."

The following morning Rusty called. Randy handed Henry the phone but made no attempt to leave the room. "My landlord wants to meet you two."

"Okay."

"Is asshole listening?"

"Okay."

Rusty gave Henry the directions to the Edgehill Towers Apartments on the corner of Edgehill and 12th street "Just buzz my apartment when you get here."

"Okay."

Henry told Randy that Patsy and he were going out to buy a few personal things. They were at Edgewood Towers ten minutes later. They buzzed Rusty's apartment and Rusty told them to stay where they were. A few minutes later he stepped out of the elevator and escorted them to the office and the manager's desk.

"These are the two I told you about." Rusty told the woman behind the desk. "This is Henry and Patsy."

"I'm Nellie," the lady said. "Rusty told me you two were homeless. I have a waiting list of people wanting to move here but if you're homeless I can move you to the top of the list and you can move in today. Do you have any money? We charge according to the tenant's monthly income. I'll need you to fill the papers out."

Early the next day Henry and Patsy unloaded the rented U-Haul and carried their things inside. They needed a few more items of furniture but nothing that wouldn't wait. They had their bed and television. Some time during the night someone broke a window in Henry's truck and emptied his glove box on the truck's floor looking for anything of value. Henry knew they must have been disappointed to find nothing in the truck they could trade for drugs or money.

Rusty told Henry that as a boy he'd lived in Sarasota, Florida where his mother had worked as a seamstress for the Ringling Brothers Circus. He'd studied clowning as the protégé of the late, great Emmett Kelly and it was in a circus ring that Rusty's alter ego, Koko the Clown, was born. But Rusty had music in his blood and wanted to sing. He hopped off the circus train at age fourteen and set out on his own. He soon had his own radio show in New York. This led to the Wheeling West Virginia Jamboree and ultimately to the Grand Ole Opry in Nashville, Tennessee.

The Korean War interrupted his career. He joined the army and was captured by the communist. He lost an eye due to lack of medical attention and spent the next eighteen months in a Japanese POW camp suffering from torture and eating bugs to stay alive. After the war he spent several months in a V.A. hospital. He resumed his song writing after his release. Later he fronted shows for Lefty Frizzell, Webb Pierce and Rusty's idol, Ernest Tubb, as Koko The Clown.

Rusty had a thousand stories he told and neither Henry nor Patsy believed most of them. Later they would meet people like Buddy Mize, George Toker and a few dozen more who'd been there and knew the stories first hand and they told the same stories with the same details as Rusty did.

Henry was reading an article in a local newspaper, the Tennessean, about the increased crime in Nashville due to the large number of gangs, especially the 'Bloods' and the 'Crips'. The gangs had originated in cities like Los Angeles or Chicago or Detroit and used cities like Nashville, not only for selling crack and other drugs, but to hide members wanted by the law in other cities.

Henry remembered Nashville thirty years earlier when he and Bogie often staggered through the streets. They had never been overly concerned about being hurt or robbed. Now every day the newspaper had stories about women being raped in restaurant parking lots or a tourist being robbed or raped or shot on Music Row. There were also home invasions nearly every night and afternoon killings downtown. Car thefts and break-ins were common and the first suggestion Rusty made to Henry and Patsy was to purchase a 'club', a metal bar that locked onto a steering wheel and making it impossible for anyone to turn the wheel.

Patsy found work as a cook at Eddy's Place, a small diner housed in a red mobile home near the railroad tracks. Rusty and several of his friends ate breakfast and dinner at Eddy's and business increased soon after Patsy began working there. Patsy was a good cook. She was taught by her grandmother and had been cooking southern soul food since her preteens. Rusty and several others bragged about her cooking claiming that Patsy's fried chicken was the best in Nashville.

A large portion of Henry's afternoons were spent with Rusty. Everywhere they went Rusty would run into at least one old friend and he always introduced Henry. Every Tuesday afternoon they would drive to the Ernest Tubb Record Shop on Music Valley Dr. to visit Bob Mitchell, a popular disc jockey and record promoter who invited the old timers to his radio show to play their songs and gossip. Rusty was often the hit of the show. Henry met many of the entertainers he'd listened to years earlier with his grandmother while Charlie and Erica kept company with the local drunks.

Once a month Rusty received a 'tip sheet' from Acuff-Rose Publishing. These sheets listed the names of artists recording that month along with the names of the producers and the type of material they were looking for. Rusty, tired of the garbage they were playing on so-called 'country' radio had long ago given up pitching his songs. He gave the 'tip sheet' to Henry every month and Henry would select four or five producers he thought might possibly be interested in his songs. He'd then locate the offices of these producers and deliver the demos in manila en-velopes, one song per envelope, with the producers name on the outside and Henry's name in the top left corner. He'd give the package to the receptionist and she'd place it in a pile with sev-eral other envelopes.

Henry paid fifty dollars a song to have his songs demo'd by various singers trying to break into music while bussing tables or working at the car wash. He had fourteen demos and every month he selected the songs to pitch according to the informa-tion on the 'tip sheet'.

Henry was just sitting down to the table to enjoy a large plate of Patsy's lasagna when Walter Travish phoned from Okla-homa. "What are you up to Walter?"

"Eddy and I were talking about you earlier today. We haven't heard from you for a while so I'm checking to see if you're still alive."

"I'm sorry I haven't called before Walter. How's everyone doing?"

"Good as we ever did. Eddy's working every day and I ain't. I guess you heard about the Holtons."

"Ain't heard nothin'."

"Leon made the CNN news for shooting a narc. He swears he's innocent but no one believes him. The Judge gave him a twenty-five to life and he won't come up for parole until some-time around 2020. I guess you didn't hear about Joshua or Jake either. Jake killed Joshua a few weeks back then had a wreck trying to outrun the law. I hear they had to rake up what was left of him."

"I hate to hear that. Why would Jake kill his brother? That whole family was close as bed bugs."

"Speed, Henry. Homemade crank. They went crazy on the

shit. I heard Joshua was beating Jake with a chain when Jake shot him. Mind you this is just what I heard from others."

"I'm losing my friends Walter. You and Eddy be careful. I don't wanna come home for either of your funerals."

"I have some more news. You remember T.B.? Had a band for awhile? They used to play the local dives for all the beer they could drink?"

"Sure, I remember him. He used to do a few of my songs."

"He's dead too."

"Who killed him?"

"He had a heart attack. I found him this morning on his front porch with his pecker in his hand."

"You're shittin' me."

"I wish I was. I was afraid his daughter might come by before the county moved him so I stuck his pecker back and zipped up his pants. I swear Henry I saw him smile while I was doing it. I used my ink pen to poke his pecker back in and I swear he had this shit-eatin' grin on his face."

Henry was gaining weight. He didn't know why he was gaining weight but he supposed Patsy's cooking had a lot to do with it, especially the biscuits and gravy he ate five mornings a week. Yesterday his shirt was straining the buttons and he had to lay down to fasten his pants. Today he couldn't pull his boots on. Patsy had convinced him a few weeks earlier to take out health insurance. The VA had a poor reputation with veterans and Henry knew the reason after having once waited nearly eight hours to see a doctor. He walked across the street to a neighborhood clinic where he was prescribed a diuretic pill for fluid retention. The pills helped for a few days then the fluid returned and his water retention worsened.

Henry studied the yellow pages that afternoon looking for

the name of a specialist that he could call and make an appointment with. The third receptionist he talked with recommended a heart specialist at St. Thomas Hospital. The cost was one hundred and fifty dollars a visit. Henry made a call and assured the receptionist he had the money to pay for the visit.

Henry waddled into Dr. Matthews's office the following day for an 8:30 A.M. appointment. An hour later he was at the emergency room being admitted to St. Thomas Hospital.

Henry's right chest cavity was filled with fluid and the fluid was causing his right lung to collapse making it impossible for him to draw a deep breath. A 'chest needle' was inserted in his back slightly below the shoulder blade and the fluid was siphoned from the chest cavity thru the 'needle'. He felt the results almost immediately, taking deep breaths while the fluid was removed. He was then placed in a wheel chair and wheeled to room 412. An IV was inserted in his right arm and he was handed a plastic urinal and told to use it when he needed to. When the urinal was nearly full a nurse would empty it into a plastic tub.

The following morning shortly after nine a.m. Dr. Matthews, Dr. Taylor and a nurse, pushing an empty wheelchair entered Henry's room. "We're going to do a kidney biopsy Mr. Ridge. The nurse will take you where you need to go."

Henry's blood was drawn several times a day. After a few hours Henry's arm was swollen around the IV. The IV was then moved and inserted in a different vein. The nurse stuck him four times before locating a suitable vein.

Patsy stayed until nearly ten p.m. Henry, worried about someone attacking her in the parking lot of the apartments, had tried to convince her to leave before dark. At seven a.m. the following morning she was back in Henry's room and she stayed until after nine p.m. Every day she was by his bedside.

Rusty, not sure if Patsy was drawing a paycheck, brought

her two hundred dollars one morning and laid it on their coffee table. Patsy protested and tried to give the money back but Rusty refused to take it.

Henry was released four days after he was diagnosed with kidney, liver and lung disease and was told he had to give up tobacco and whiskey.

Patsy wheeled Henry out of the room stopping at the nurse's station to pick up eight prescriptions then drove to Walgreen's to have them filled and also to purchase a book on prescription drugs. Henry had been told he could drink one glass of wine a day and no more. But he wasn't told what size glass he could use. While Patsy was attending to the prescriptions Henry found a 32 ounce glass and purchased it.

At Edgehill Henry walked unaided to their apartment, rolled a joint and poured a whiskey. That night Patsy looked up each prescription in her drug book. Soon she was reading the side effects out loud. A moment later Henry noticed her crying and asked her what he'd done to upset her.

"You didn't do nothing," Patsy answered.

"Then why are you crying?"

Patsy cried harder. "It's all these damn pills. The side effects alone will kill you."

Henry had entered the hospital weighing more than one hundred and eighty pounds. He left the hospital weighing less than a hundred and twenty pounds.

Henry took his pills, drank another whiskey then threw up in the bathroom sink.

The assistant manager of the apartment complex was an elderly lady with a number of health problems. She was forced to quit her job and Nellie offered the assistant manager's position to Patsy. Patsy accepted the offer and gave her notice at Eddy's Diner.

A few weeks later, Nellie, a heavy chain-smoker, was diagnosed with lung cancer. The doctor told her she might live another year or two if she took care of herself, quit smoking and watched her diet. Two weeks later Nellie was dead. The company offered Patsy the manager's position and she accepted.

The tenants loved Patsy. Previous managers had worked the job like an eight-to-five office manager. After five p.m. they disappeared and any trouble or problem a tenant had would have to wait until eight a.m. or so but Patsy couldn't say no to anyone. She always answered the telephone regardless of how late or how early the tenants called. If a tenant got drunk and locked themselves out of his or her apartment all they had to do was go to the house phone and call. Patsy would dress and tell Henry to keep sleeping but he wasn't going to let her go out alone. He would dress and accompany her to and from the tenant's apartment.

Henry got his ass whipped like a tongue-tied step child.

Alvin Roundtree was a short, small-boned, dapper ninety year old black man. Everyone knew and liked his spunk and his attitude. He'd had trouble before in an elevator with a gang member who tried to scare him out of his wallet but the old man didn't scare easily and the thief left empty handed.

Alvin liked to dress in pressed pants, dress shirts, colorful vests and tailored coats. His shoes were always shined and he wore a 'pork pie' hat. He always spoke to Henry and often complimented Henry for a vest or hat that Henry was wearing. Henry always returned the compliments.

Alvin's health was good but his memory was bad and he often forgot what decade he was living in. He left the building every morning, weather permitting, and he didn't return until shortly before dark. On occasion his mind would wander back to the 1940's or 50's and he'd roam the streets looking for his sister's home or a cousin's, forgetting they had passed away years before and the houses were gone. On these occasions Patsy would get a call at the office telling her that a well-dressed, likable gentleman had wandered into their office or onto their porch looking for an address that no longer existed. When questioned all they could get out of him was his name and the name of the apartments. Patsy would thank them for calling then ask Henry to fetch Alvin home. Henry would find Alvin sitting in someone's office or on someone's porch drinking tea or a soft drink provided by the host. People often called him adorable, especially young secretaries or receptionists, and they made every effort to assure Henry that Alvin had been no trouble and he was welcome anytime.

Henry had a call shortly after Patsy left for her office from another tenant who said he was worried about Alvin. The tenant had gone to Alvin's apartment for morning coffee and a young, muscled black man had come to the door. The man told the tenant to come back later, that he had business with Alvin, and then shut the door in the tenant's face. The tenant thought the man might rob or hurt Alvin. Henry thanked the tenant for calling then immediately went to Alvin's fourth floor apartment. A muscled young man answered the door and then shut the door in Henry's face. Henry grabbed the door knob and pushed. The next thing he remembered he was on his knees on the carpet with his right arm out searching for the wall. Both sides of his head was hurting and he could feel both eyes starting to swell. He found the wall and stood up. The young man, Henry would later learn, was Alvin's great nephew and he had come to borrow money. He asked Henry if he wanted to go outside and finish the fight. Henry played deaf. This man could whip Henry's ass any day of the week. He knew the 'macho' thing to do would be to walk outside and get hit a few more times but he wasn't feeling very 'macho'. Patsy was helping him down the hallway when the man asked Henry again if he wanted to continue the fight. Henry still played deaf. All he wanted was a place to lay down and feel sorry for himself. He asked Patsy to help him back to their apartment. She asked if he wanted her to call the police and file a complaint.

"Please don't. It might piss that fellow off and I don't want him hittin' me anymore."

Later Henry staggered to the bathroom and looked in the mirror. Both eyes, from the nose to the eyebrows, were purple and he knew a pair of sunglasses wouldn't hide them. He might as well have a tattoo across his forehead saying 'I got my ass whipped good' but he didn't care. His head was hurting too much.

Henry made up his mind to purchase a gun. He was too old and fragile to have anyone beating on him again. He didn't want to buy a gun from a dealer and have it registered in his name. He wanted one he could throw away if he had to use it without the gun being traced back to him. He didn't know anyone in Tennessee to ask but he knew where he'd go if he was in Oklahoma looking for a Saturday Night Special. He'd go to a bar.

Henry had wandered into the small bar on Eighth Avenue one day while waiting for Patsy to get off work. The sign said 'Blu's Crazy Cowboy—the coldest beer in town'. There were eight men inside the bar, including the bartender, and they all watched Henry enter and take a seat at the bar. They were all smiling so Henry smiled back. Before he could order a beer two men came over and sat down beside him, one on his left and one on his right. The men smelled of strong, sweet-scented cologne and both were trying to introduce themselves to Henry and offer to buy him a beer. The bartender, a short man with thinning hair, smiled and watched Henry and his new friends. A few minutes later he leaned over the bar in front of Henry and asked, "You do know this is a gay bar don't you?"

"I haven't paid that much attention I guess. I just thought everyone was being friendly."

"Well you're welcome here anyway. I need all the customers I can get. What are you drinking?"

"Budweiser."

The bartender sat the beer in front of Henry and announced that he bought new customers their first beer. "They call me Blu and I own this nut house. You're a cute thing. Are you gay?"

"I don't think so."

"Have you ever tried it?" Blu asked. "You won't know whether you'd like it or not if you've never tried it."

"I sucked a pecker in '64," Henry lied. "It took a half gallon of tequila and a weekend in Juarez to get the taste out of my mouth."

"You cute ones are always straight. Leave him alone boys," Blu told Henry's new friends, "he's straight."

Henry spent nearly an hour drinking beer with Blu and his customers. "Do you people mind if I come back later with my wife?"

"You're both welcome here but tell your lady that we have a few 'carpet crunchers' here every evening. I'll tell them that your wife is straight and they won't bother her. My customers are nice people. You're nice too."

"Thank you, Blu."

"Honey if you wasn't straight I'd show you how nice we are."

Henry didn't believe anyone's sexual preference was anybody else's business. Patsy shared his opinion and thought the atmosphere in the bar was perfect for their marriage. She didn't worry about any lady hitting on Henry and Henry could shoot pool and walk out back and smoke a joint when invited without worrying about Patsy. They became weekend regulars at the bar and enjoyed the 'drag' shows Blu held every Saturday night to benefit a charity called Nashville Cares, an organization that helps the gay community.

Henry walked into the Crazy Cowboy a week after his ass whipping. Blu and two guys sat at the bar and Henry told Blu he wanted to buy a gun. Blu made a telephone call and a half hour later Henry was buying a 25 caliber automatic handgun.

Henry would rather take a beating than return to the hospital but he didn't think he really had a choice. His right leg was draining pus from the hole below his knee. The leg had always had some drainage, maybe a teaspoon or so daily but now the pus was running down his leg like a leaky spigot. He could smell the leg and if he could smell it he knew others could too. He believed a prescription for antibiotics was all he needed and he could heal up at home.

Henry had another reason to return to the emergency room at St. Thomas. The past few days he'd suffered from a sharp pain on his left side under his arm pit. He'd had his ribs broken before and he was certain he'd broken at least one or two ribs again but he didn't know where or how or when he could have done it.

Henry sat in the emergency waiting room less than twenty minutes before they called his name. A nurse led him to an unoccupied examination room and took his blood pressure and temperature then told him a doctor would be in soon to see him.

Dr. Watson, the duty doctor, asked Henry what his problem was and Henry told him about the pain in his left side and the drainage from his leg. He asked Henry to remove his boot and pull his pant leg up to the knee. Dr. Watson pulled up a chair and squeezed Henry's leg a few times. He pulled Henry's pant leg back down, scooted backward and told Henry he could put his boot back on. Then he prodded and poked Henry's left side asking every few seconds "does that hurt, does that hurt, does that hurt?" He sent Henry to X-ray where Henry's rib cage and right leg were X-rayed. Henry returned to the examination room and waited for the doctor. An hour later Dr. Watson returned to the room and told Henry they were admitting him to the hospital. "Your ribs are fine Mr. Ridge but you have pneumonia."

A week later Dr. Taylor told Henry he would be released the next morning. That night as Henry was shaving and anticipating the joint he would smoke when he got home he lost his breath. He felt as if someone had flipped a switch on his body and cut his air off. All he remembered later was waking on a stretcher and being pushed down the hallway at a run. He was put to bed in a room full of monitors and wires were attached to his chest and his arms.

Henry had suffered a pulmonary embolism, a blood clot, in his right lung. He was told the blood clot had originated in his right leg. He was given a blood thinner and his leg re-examined by Dr. Taylor, Dr. Watson and a doctor Henry had never met.

"Henry, this is Dr. Handley. He'll be making the morning rounds with me for a few days."

Dr. Handley stood to the side and watched as Dr. Taylor and Dr. Watson examined Henry's leg.

"Mr. Ridge we need to talk about your right leg. We're

concerned that your leg may turn cancerous and we'd like to remove it."

"You folks tell me I've got lung disease and liver disease and kidney disease on top of the bone disease I brought with me and you think I'm gonna worry about some chicken shit cancer? Cancer can get in line and take a number. You ain't gettin' my leg!"

"It'll have to come off sometime."

"You mean if I live long enough? Right now I'm just concerned about living long enough to leave here. When do you plan to unhook me and let me limp on home?"

"In a few days...maybe."

Dr. Taylor asked Henry if he needed anything before they left. "Just leave the door open. It's kinda boring in here. I've been in jails I've enjoyed more."

After Dr. Taylor and Dr. Watson left the room Dr. Handley came in and pulled the door shut. "Mr. Ridge I'm just going to be here long enough to tell you what the other doctors won't. You're not going to be alright Mr. Ridge. There's too much wrong with you. All anyone can do is patch you up and send you home and you might live long enough to see Christmas. I just felt someone should tell you the truth."

Dr. Handley turned to leave and Henry thanked him for coming. "I'll keep this between us Dr. Handley."

"It doesn't matter Mr. Ridge. I'm being transferred soon."

Two weeks later Henry was released and sent home with a handful of new prescriptions. Dr. Taylor had told him that he had a fifty-fifty chance of being on dialysis sometime in the future.

Since leaving the hospital Henry had started walking three miles every day to the Country Music Hall of Fame and back trying to regain some of his health. The Idle Hour bar was the halfway point and Henry would stop and drink a beer on the way and another beer on the way back. The doctor had advised him to quit drinking and smoking but he ignored the advice.

He recognized the girl as soon as he saw her. Amy, a receptionist for Tony Reynolds, a major record producer, sat alone at the bar sipping a rum and coke. She remembered Henry and called him over. He offered to buy her another drink but she refused. "I've had enough," she explained. "I got a three year old boy I need to pick up at the sitter's and I need to be sober."

"Has your boss made any comments about any of my songs?"

"Mr. Ridge...."

"Call me Henry."

"If I talk about this and my boss finds out I could lose my job."

"He won't hear it from me."

"He says you're too country for country music."

"How can anyone be too country for country music?"

"You're not pop enough, Mr. Ridge."

During the years in Nashville Henry had seen Jody several times. When Willie and the band were in the area Jody would call a few days before the band's arrival and tell Henry what motel they were booked in and their estimated time of arrival. Henry would meet the group and visit the band and the road crew either on the band bus or in Jody's motel room.

Henry had lost touch with most of his Texas friends but Jody hadn't. Some of the crowd had scattered to different parts of the country and many of them made an effort to see Jody whenever Willie played their area. They kept Jody informed on the whereabouts and happenings of others. During one visit aboard the band bus, Jody told him about Saul Carter being killed by the Mexican Mafia. A woman Saul took up with had stolen nearly two hundred thousand dollars that Saul owed the Mafia then took off for parts unknown. Someone had to pay for the theft and one night Saul was taken out to a field south of Juarez and made to dig his own grave then shot in the back of his head.

Henry knew several men who called themselves outlaws but Saul was only one of a handful that fit the name. Most had done little more than get a parking ticket but Saul had lived an outlaw's life and wore the name like a medal.

Henry also learned that his old party pal and jail mate, Clay Clayton, had found the Lord and was now a deacon in a Hurst, Texas Baptist church less than four miles from the Hurst, Texas jail. The same jail Henry and Clay had spent a long night in more than thirty years earlier.

Henry couldn't help thinking that life dealt some strange hands.

EPILOGUE

"Will you promise me something Henry?"

"If I can I will."

"If something happens to me you won't let them keep me on life support and I don't want my body embalmed or a bunch of people staring at me. I want you to have me cremated."

"You talk like you'll be going before me. I figure you'll make it to be a hundred, lady, and your picture will be in the local paper with you sittin' in a wheelchair, nearly bald and half asleep, in front of a cake and surrounded by smiling nurses. There will be a caption under the picture saying, 'Patsy, whatever your next husband's name is, celebrates her hundredth birthday' and below that they'll say something like 'everyone at Shady Acres loves Miss Patsy'."

"I don't want to live to be a hundred."

"You may not have a choice."

"What about you Henry? What do you want?"

"You can put me on a spit and barbecue me. I won't care. I'll be dead."

"Why can't you ever be serious? I can't even talk to you about anything serious."

"Okay, have me cremated."

"Where do you want your ashes spread?"

"In a pot-head's garden, over the lettuce and tomatoes. I'd like to think that someday somebody will smoke a joint then sit down at their kitchen table and have a bacon, lettuce, tomato and Henry Ridge sandwich."

"I knew you couldn't be serious. Everything's a joke with you."

"Okay lady, I'll be serious. Where do you want your ashes scattered?" Henry asked.

"If you go first I'm going to keep your ashes till I die and have my ashes mixed with yours." Patsy answered.

"The first time we have an argument in the 'hereafter' you'll probably throw my ashes out."

"That's it," Patsy said. "I knew I couldn't talk about this with you. Just don't say nothing else to me."

"I'll end up in a vacuum cleaner."

"Shut up, Henry," Patsy turned the television up. "Don't say nothing else to me!"

"Probably some old Hoover," Henry mumbled.